Country Matters

TESNI MORGAN

BLACK
lace

To Dorothy, with thanks for your help,
advice and encouragement.

Black Lace novels are sexual fantasies.
In real life, make sure you practise safe sex.

First published in 1997 by
Black Lace
332 Ladbroke Grove
London W10 5AH

Typeset by CentraCet, Cambridge
Printed and bound by Mackays of Chatham PLC

ISBN 0 352 33174 7

Prelude

England

*I*t was the falling hour of the day when the shadows grew long and the slanting light was amber. It struck across the deep emerald lawns, and the old house brooded, golden-grey in the light, purple in the shadows.

The young man was nervous. He stood under the impressive arch of an oak door, staring at it through his glasses, waiting for someone to come. It was chilly, and he shivered, but with anticipation not cold.

Would she be there?

Closing his eyes, he saw her against the darkness of his lids, could feel her soft fingers caressing him, hear the whisper of silk, see the flash of scarlet satin as she moved her foot. He could almost smell the scent rising from her skin, musky and potent.

Tremulously, he had asked that disembodied voice down the phone, 'Will she be present?'

There had been silence, followed by a man's level reply. 'She may. I can't promise. You must come.'

The young man had obeyed. A novice as yet, earning his colours. He felt a stirring in his groin, and swallowed hard. He must not disgrace himself on this, his first visit.

He tried to keep his mind focused, almost wishing he

1

was back at his VDU; safe, coping with the familiar, not tormented by this teasing, exciting sensation of fear that prickled along his nerves and made him harden.

It was impossible. The woman. He had met her once only. Long, silky blonde hair, her body elegantly draped in the richness of velvet. His fingers tingled as he remembered lightly brushing against it. He had longed to trace her curves through it, but had not dared.

Then, beneath the hem of her gown, he had glimpsed her feet. In a moment of blinding revelation every dream, fantasy and yearning that had bedevilled him for years had combined in one single, burning shaft of desire.

And, to his horror and shame, he had known that she knew. Her crimson lips had curved into a little, musing smile and she had lifted her skirt slowly, so agonisingly slowly that his breath had stopped in his throat. The light had caught the dazzle of satin and scintillated on the tiny rhinestone buckles of a pair of court shoes with six-inch heels, thin as daggers.

The young man groaned, caught in the web of memory. He leant a hand against the granite surround of the door. He was rock-hard, in deep distress; shaking with the thrill of anticipation, hovering on the edge.

Suddenly the door opened and he came out of his dream, just in time to prevent the disaster of a premature explosion.

A pale faced, androgynous-looking creature dressed entirely in black stood within the hall. One bony white hand beckoned the young man. He stepped over the threshold, the door shut and a soft, silken scarf was tied about his eyes. Blindfolded, he felt himself being led, his feet encountering tiles, the deep pile of carpet, and the hardness of stone as the acolyte guided him down a staircase.

It wound steeply and the young man felt damp fingers of air touching his face. The way levelled out. Flagstones echoed his footsteps. The smell of incense filled his nostrils. The guide's hand on his arm indicated that he should stop. The scarf was removed.

The underground chamber was long and grey-walled. Smoky flares in cressets pierced the gloom of fan-vaulting. The young man blinked, acclimatising his eyes to the light.

He was being closely observed by a man and a woman, both robed in black from head to foot, their faces concealed by masks. Only their eyes and mouths were visible. They stood a few feet away from him and silence stretched through the vault like a protracted yawn.

Then the robed man stirred. He was tall and powerfully built, his shoulders held back. 'You've done well, my friend,' he said, his voice deep and cultured, with a cool, drawling tone. 'We have decided to reward you.'

'Thank you, master,' the young man whispered, looking up at him with anxious eyes, then immediately glancing toward the woman.

She lifted her black-gloved hands and unfastened the ruby clasp at her throat. The robe slithered from her shoulders, falling slowly to form a velvet puddle at her feet. She stepped away from it, her movements graceful as a ballet dancer's; her slim, angular body and her arrogance suggesting royal ancestry.

Her breasts rose naked from the cups of a tight scarlet satin basque that clinched her slim waist, the nipples red and prominent. The lace edging brushed her pubis, denuded of hair, the dark lips of her sex folded neatly, like the petals of some exotic jungle orchid. Black, gilt-trimmed suspenders stretched across her thighs where they were attached to the tops of stockings of so fine a weave they resembled grey mist.

As she strolled closer to the young man, the scent of her flesh enfolded him, like a pungent drug which made his head spin. His glorious mistress. The Adored One.

Her outrageous attire did not detract from the impression of quality. It added to it. The ice princess was transformed into the whore, but no common streetwalker; a powerful priestess, perhaps: Astarte, Isis, Kali –

3

The young man's eyes were riveted to her feet. She wore black patent leather ankle boots with pointed toes, spurs, and heels so high that her instep was curved in an unnatural, almost perverse manner. He gasped, shuddering with the need for her to raise an imperious foot and drive that spiked barb into his flesh.

Slowly he sank to his knees like a supplicant before an altar. His hands caressed leather and metal as he prostrated himself at the feet of this divinity.

Chapter One

America

'*L*et's toss for it,' Lorna said, as she and Nicole pored over the photographs spread out on the shiny surface of the wide teak desk.

'OK. Heads or tails?' Nicole fished a coin out of her purse and threw it in the air. It flashed in the late afternoon sunshine.

'Heads,' Lorna shouted.

'Don't you have all the luck?' Nicole complained, straightening up, and flicking back her auburn bob. 'He's drop-dead gorgeous, but not our usual type.'

Indeed he isn't, Lorna thought, glancing down at the picture in her hand. A welcome change from the muscle-rippling hunks who queue up at our doors. She turned it over. On the back was his name – Sean Kealy – and a phone number. She and Nicole Paxton and the team at *Image*, had interviewed many applicants for the forthcoming contest, but this one was outstanding.

He was slim yet broad shouldered, attired in the costume of an army officer from the Jane Austen period: not a pretty toy soldier but a scruffy, untidy one, a battle-scarred warrior. He had long dark hair and blue eyes with that sparkle in their depths common to most sons

5

of Erin. His cheekbones were pronounced, his lips firm and humorous, while the lift of his cleft chin suggested stubbornness.

A European, almost one of her own, though from across the water that linked Ireland to England. Nostalgia dragged at her gut, sudden and unexpected.

Nicole shrugged on her jacket. 'Give him a call,' she suggested. 'Maybe he'll come round tonight. You're not doing anything, are you?'

'No. You know Ricky and I have split up.'

'I'm glad you got rid of that creep. I'll ring later and you can report in,' Nicole said, and a smile curved her perfectly outlined lips.

She came over to put an arm round Lorna, giving her a hug. Lorna felt the pressure of a pair of small breasts, and heard the soft rustle of silk against her own more casual cotton T-shirt. Nicole was always immaculately tailored, favouring crisp suits with French labels that emphasised her position.

Lorna owed much to her. They were close friends, too. Now she said, 'I'd rather come to the publishers' shindig with you. I'm lumbered with listening to another aspiring star's pitch.'

Nicole chuckled. 'My heart bleeds for you. It comes with the job, honey. Enjoy. Use the camcorder, then we can both watch the video. Don't forget to lock up.'

'I won't.' Lorna followed her, closing the door when Nicole disappeared into the noisy New York street.

The crime rate was higher in summer, the heat that rose from the pavements trapped among the canyons between sky-high buildings, their turrets disappearing into smoggy mist. Tempers became frayed beyond air-conditioned walls.

Just for a moment, she savoured a memory of soft rain falling on leafy green lanes that wound between hedgerows, thatched cottages with gardens where wild flowers rioted; old, timbered houses that seemed rooted in the soil as if they had grown there. Fields of corn undulating like the sea; waves bashing the rocky Cornish coast;

Stratford-on-Avon, Shakespeare country; even grubby old London. England – her birthplace – and she had not seen it for five years.

New York had become her home, in particular Brooklyn, where the honk of horns mingled with salsa blasting from car speakers, and grey-suited office workers ogled girls in miniskirts bathed in the glow of WALK/DON'T WALK traffic lights.

Lorna had adapted easily, her activities centred on this warehouse that had been converted into the headquarters of *Image,* a successful magazine catering for fans of romantic novels. Nicole was the brains behind it. It was her baby and, year by year, had gained in popularity and helped keep that genre afloat in the erratic, stormy seas of the book trade.

Lorna glanced round the office, which was filled with state-of-the-art hardware. Computers hummed, fax machines clicked and answerphones recorded messages. The next deadline was upon them, coupled with the complicated organisation of the annual convention, a huge trade extravaganza which was to be held in Texas this time round.

The reception area's decor leaned towards Victoriana, except that instead of lithographic prints, the walls were hung with framed and enlarged covers from some of the genre's bestsellers. Slick and smartly executed, these depicted clinching couples wearing period costume, with female bosoms very nearly bare to the nipples and naked manly chests with ruggedly defined pectorals.

Lorna smiled to herself, cynically observing that this was a dream factory, nothing like the real thing.

She walked into her own apartment, which led from the main building, slipping off her shoes and pulling her black T-shirt over her head as she went. She had succeeded in creating an English atmosphere; searching for antiques in the secondhand markets, choosing chintz and old lace, watercolours and delicate china.

One day, she promised herself, when I'm really settled, I'll indulge my love of Gothic architecture, rich velvet drapes, Pre-Raphaelite paintings and art nouveau. I'll give full rein to my obsession with the decadent, *fin de siècle* ambience of the late nineteenth century. Maybe I'll frame copies of Aubrey Beardsley's obscene drawings from the notorious *Lysistrata*.

She caught sight of herself in a gilt-framed mirror. Not too bad considering, she mused. Her figure was trim. She was strong-willed and had steadfastly refused bagels and the sugary confectionery which seemed to be the staple diet in the office. She saw reflected a leggy, twenty-four-year-old brunette with a shaggy mane of curls and green eyes that slanted slightly at the outer corners. Willowy and narrow hipped, she possessed a pair of firm, upward tilting breasts.

Cradled in a black bra, they rose proudly, the nipples still erect from contact with Nicole. Placing a hand under each, Lorna lifted them gently, brooding on Sean Kealy.

The name had an adventurous ring; Errol Flynn, that 1930s heart-throb of the silver screen sprang to mind. It was essential for a male model posing for this market to have an exciting name. Something to conjure up visions of dashing heroes, pirates, highwayman and knights in shining armour. Would he, like that departed demigod of love once voted the sexiest man in the world, leap to iconhood?

No doubt, like the rest of the applicants, Sean was an ambitious actor. She wondered whether he should be selected and entered as a contestant at the Mr Image Cover Model Pageant, the highlight of the convention, the prize an opportunity to be featured on the jackets of the steamy novels the magazine promoted.

Female readers would fall in love with him as they feasted on the purple prose, picturing themselves as the lovely, spirited heroine in his arms. Aching with lust and unrealised dreams, they would bring themselves to orgasm while their insensitive, overweight husbands snored in front of the sports channel on TV.

She had never dreamed she'd wind up promoting romances during her years at university. Once she, too, wanted to write, and imagined producing some meaningful opus that would set the world on fire. Instead, she has arrived here, via several other magazines and a helping hand from an editor who fancied her. The rest was down to her own ability, and she had made it.

Now, she was Nicole Paxton a right-hand man, 'person' to be politically correct. She had plenty of scope for exercising her journalistic skills. And not only those.

She wandered into the kitchen and opened the fridge. Ice-cubes tinkled in orange juice as she carried a tumbler back to the living room. Slipping out of her skirt, she stood in her briefs and bra as she flipped through her CD collection. She was putting off ringing Sean, tired of young men falling over themselves to pleasure her if only she would give them a chance at the contest.

One could have too much of a good thing, she mused. That was half her trouble. There had always been too many men and none of them exactly what she wanted. The problem was she didn't know what she wanted.

She was still bruised by the final row with Ricky Carlyle, an executive who had wanted her to be as much his property as the construction company he owned. She had spent the past six months as his official girlfriend, but had decided to call a halt to the relationship, recognising that her self-worth was on a downward spiral. Nevertheless, Ricky's absence left a yawning gap in her life. As usual when going through a trauma, Lorna turned to music.

Now she selected Maria Callas singing an aria from the opera *Andrea Chenier* by Giordano, used to poignant effect on the soundtrack for the Oscar-winning *Philadelphia*. The music soared, and her tiredness melted away. One good thing that had come out of her involvement with Ricky was the box at the Met he rented to impress clients. He had magnanimously agreed that she continue to enjoy it.

Glorious sounds swept through the apartment, and Lorna listened, completely absorbed, tears rising in her eyes. By the time it was over her faith in human beings was restored and she was ready to take up the gauntlet again, the thought of Sean beginning to appeal. At the very least she would enjoy talking about home with him. They would be able to laugh together, sharing that dry, quirky sense of humour peculiar to the British.

She supposed she would sleep with him and the anticipation of a new sexual partner was always exciting. No two sets of genitals were alike; they varied as much as facial features. Male, female, their uniqueness made them an enthralling study.

Would Sean's penis have a foreskin or would he be cut? Lorna never could make up her mind which she liked best – the circumcised male or the one who was *au naturel*. A coil tightened in her womb and her clitoris pulsed as she thought about this.

Naked now, she stepped into the wet embrace of the shower, leaning against the white tiles with a long sigh. The water cascaded over her breasts, droplets standing out on the bunched nipples before dribbling down across her flat belly to run between her thighs and soak the triangular wedge of fuzz covering her pubis. Lascivious watery fingers dipped between the pink furled wings of her labia, and tickled the passion bud crowning the dark slit. Pleasure coursed through her, her groin heavy with need.

She reached up to push her wet hair from her forehead, face raised to the jets. It felt like warm rain, caressing and cleansing her, washing away the gritty annoyances and petty disasters of the day.

There was always high drama, rising to fever-pitch as publication day drew near. And the date of the convention was fast approaching; the air would quiver with pheromones as the contestants postured at the costume ball.

None of this mattered now. She was free; free to indulge herself, to *be* herself, no longer having to keep up the pretence of being the oh-so-cool and efficient Miss Lorna Erskine. Somehow, because she was English, they expected her to be unemotional and in control. She wore a permanent mask. Sometimes it was fixed so tight she was sure her face was about to crack like plaster. Only Nicole had an inkling of the untamed depths beneath that calm exterior, but even she did not realise the extent of Lorna's need for a change of scene, lifestyle and purpose.

It must be wonderful, Lorna thought, to hand over one's will to someone else. Is this what sadomasochism is all about? It was a field of experimentation in which she had never yet been involved, and certainly would not want to. She was an independent woman, who would never submit, she protested indignantly.

Yet somewhere, locked away in the secret heart of her self, were shameful, unnamable yearnings: things she would not admit, even to herself; wanton actions that manifested only when she was asleep and dreaming.

Lashes lowered and spiky with water, she reached out for the shower-gel. After wiping the back of her hand over her eyes to clear them, she squeezed a puddle into her palm, the sharp, spicy odour of ylang-ylang joining that of her own musky scent. It was a heady brew. Herbs and sea-washed shells, female juices seeping from her vagina, the odour trapped in the tangled curls of her wet bush.

Slowly, luxuriously, she massaged her breasts and belly, shoulders, lower back and thighs. Her nipples rose at her touch, the feel of her own fingers tapping the reserves of desire which were always there.

The perfumed gel was slick and smooth, and she parted her legs, rubbing it into her pubic floss, making twirling patterns. The ache in her belly was more insistent, and she probed between her lower lips, pretending to wash herself there. In reality she was fondling the satiny folds, deep pink now from the heated water and her own friction which sent the blood flowing through them. The twin wings swelled and her clitoris rose from within its tiny hood, raising its eager head, demanding attention.

She delayed the inevitable moment, knowing she was

11

going to bring herself to orgasm. She fondled her breasts, making her clit wait a while. She anointed them, weighed them, jiggled them, rested them in her palms but left her thumbs free to rub across the tingling nipples. They responded instantly, a hotline shooting straight down to her rampant bud. The soapy liquid moved over them with delicious ease, back and forth till they ached. Then she pinched them, rolled them, looked down to watch them rise, tight and hard, their rose hue darkening to reddish brown.

She could not remember when she had last felt so horny. She shivered as she stroked her nipples, longing for a tongue to lick her folds and dip into her furrow. Someone with a feather-light touch. A face sprang to mind; a woman's face with dancing violet-blue eyes and tawny blonde hair.

Cassandra Ashley. She had not consciously thought of the woman in a carnal context for years. Her first female lover, who had taught her so much about her body's needs. If only she was with her now; soft limbs entwined, soft fingers seeking out her erogenous zones, and that darting, knowing tongue. Cassandra, who took her pleasures where she fancied and, with carefree insouciance, had encouraged Lorna to do the same.

Smiling at the recollections pouring in, Lorna yielded to her craving, her fingers idling over her smooth wet skin till they contacted her crisp pubes. As she shifted her feet to part her thighs, her sex-lips opened wider, engorged and slippery and needful.

She inserted her middle finger, working round the stem of her love-bud, then letting the tip gently massage its head. The pleasure was immense, the urgency all-consuming. She knew she would not be able to hold on for long, though sometimes she could play with herself for an hour or more, keeping her climax at bay so that when she finally came it was in a roaring cataclysm of sensation.

Not this time, though, with the jets driving hot against her breasts and those delicious rivulets trickling each side of her clitoris, adding to the delight of her touch on its crown. Moaning with pleasure, she sank down on her haunches, knees wide apart, her pulsating bud protruding like a miniature penis. She held back her labia with her other hand, making her clit strain from its cowl, ever more proud and erect, as she bent her head to watch its performance.

It demanded a harder friction. She obeyed. Faster now, and faster still her finger moved. The waves rose, high and sharper, flooding her very being. With a stifled cry, she abandoned herself to a fierce orgasm that left her gasping and convulsing. She sank down, her head reeling as the last precious spasms died away.

She sat there for a moment, her breathing gradually slowing, then she rose, killed the spray, stepped out of the stall, wrapped herself in a fluffy white towel and reached for the phone.

She was seated in the reception area, reading Sean Kealy's CV and glancing over his portfolio when he came in carrying a sportsbag and a sheathed sabre. The door had swung open at his touch after he had spoken to her through the intercom.

Hello, she thought, looking up and admiring the way he walked, the way he held himself – part natural, part the result of drama school training. He was light on his feet; agile, too. Remembering how he had looked in costume, she could imagine him taking part in duelling scenes and the vision gave her goose-bumps, raising the hair down on her limbs.

Now he was casually dressed in a draped linen suit and pale shirt with a loosely knotted tie. He wore Cesare Paciotti loafers, and his whole outfit breathed class. He hadn't bought that off the peg.

'Good evening,' Lorna said, rising and holding out her hand.

'Miss Erskine?' He took it in his and retained it, a half-smile on his lips, blue eyes twinkling.

His deep voice shivered right down to her epicentre; a

13

lovely masculine voice with the trace of a burr as it penetrated her core as surely as if he had already entered her body. I'll bet he can sing, she thought. An Irish tenor?

'Call me Lorna,' she said, rather unsteadily. 'Won't you sit down?'

'Thank you,' he replied. An electric thrill shot through her at the skin to skin contact as he turned her hand and kissed her wrist where the pulse beat rapidly.

She met his eyes, then freed her fingers and moved over to where a cretonne covered chesterfield stood in the bay. Beyond was the patio and garden, secure and secluded behind high walls. The sweet smell of night-scented stocks and jasmine drifted in at the window. The traffic sounded distant now and, from way overhead, a jet plane purred, its lights twinking faintly in the plumb-blue dark.

She settled herself, her legs tucked up under her, the long diaphanous skirt she wore floating round her. She was achingly aware of her nudity beneath, the way her floss brushed her thighs and the evening air breathed on the scented avenue between. Sean sat beside her, not too close as yet, subjecting her to an amused stare.

He was conspicuously attractive: of medium height and spare build, with what she suspected was an all-over tan. He resembled the designer stubbled, rougher end of the leading man market, except that his hair was glossy clean and his suit by Armani. His style was a cunning blend of streetwise edge and elegance. He scanned the room like a panther on the prowl, almost staking out his territory.

Slow down, lover boy, she thought. This isn't a fore-gone conclusion, charming and full of blarney though you are. A tad too confident, perhaps? Used to women throwing their legs round you and impaling themselves on your prick. Mr *Image*? A champion heart-breaker and bastard no doubt with your brains in your balls.

'I've studied the material you submitted,' she said, ice-cool on the surface but burning within, all too aware of his arm lying across the back of the settee just beyond her shoulder blades.

'You have? Sure and that's fine,' he vouchsafed.

He moved a little nearer and she caught a whiff of *Ricci Club*, blended with the clean scent of his hair and the freshly showered yet pungently male odour of his body. She was glad she had had the foresight to masturbate or this combination might have proved overpowering. She needed a level head to evaluate his suitability.

She opened the file and ran an oval fingernail down a page. 'I see you've had experience on English television and the West End stage,' she said. 'And done some work with the RSC.'

'I took theatre-craft at college, and managed a stint at the Abbey Theatre. That's in Dublin, you know.'

'I know where it is,' she reminded tartly. 'I'm familiar with the plays of O'Casey, Synge and Yeats. Just because I edit a women's magazine doesn't mean I'm a complete moron.'

'I didn't think it did,' he continued, unperturbed. 'Anyway, I went to London, worked as an extra, did anything I could to get a foot in. I was lucky. Happened to be in the right place at the right time when ITV were casting for a series set during the Napoleonic War. Battle of Waterloo, and all that. Didn't get a speaking part, only a walk-on, but it was a start. That led to commercials.'

'Why d'you think appearing on book jackets will help your career?' she asked, and leant a little nearer.

Her top was brief, with a deep scooped neckline. She had not worn it to be alluring but to satisfy her own aesthetic recognition of the contrast between the white stretchy material and her sun-kissed skin.

'Anything that keeps you in the public eye is bound to be OK.' His voice was husky as his eyes fastened on her nipples pressing darkly against the tight top. 'I'd like to get to Hollywood.'

'But don't you think English films and TV are the best in the world?' she asked, trying to be businesslike though

15

she could feel herself growing warmer, looser, a melting feeling starting in her belly and spreading to her vagina.

'Sure I do, but Hollywood's where the money is. This may get me noticed. What do I have to do, Lorna?' he murmured, and she was fascinated by the fineness of his skin and the length of the sooty lashes hedging his eyes. 'Shall I give an audition? D'you want me to read a script?'

'Not now, though I'd like to see you in costume,' she replied breathlessly.

'I've brought the soldier's outfit. You like that?'

'Very much. You wear it well. The Regency period is wonderful for uniforms, and so many romance books are historical. But first, let's have dinner, then later you can change while I get the camcorder running. This is to show Nicole Paxton. She's my boss and has the last word.'

She had laid out a simple meal of salad and pizza sent in from the nearest delicatessen. That was one advantage of living where she did. One could send out for food twenty-four hours a day, any type of food: Chinese, Japanese, Mexican, Thai, Lebanese. The cuisine of the entire world was at her doorstep.

'The only thing it's impossible to get is a properly made cup of English tea,' she said, when they reached the dessert stage. She topped up her glass with red wine. 'No one knows how to make it except the English.'

'Or Irish,' he protested. 'The water's got to be boiling. Come back to my place, Lorna, and I'll brew up for you – sweet and dark and strong – just how you like it. Is that how you like your loving, too?'

Her eyes met his, and she paused in raising the glass to her lips. 'I don't think that's any of your business,' she said frostily.

'No?' One arched brow shot upwards. 'Not now perhaps, but one day, *acushla*.' Then he mitigated the use of this endearment by adding with a grin, 'Once you've tasted my tea, you won't be able to control yourself.'

I can hardly do that now, she thought, feeling the

nectar oozing from her vulva to wet her bare inner thighs. Shower gel and talc, mingled with the tell-tale odour of recently enjoyed orgasm, wafted up across her mons. As she smelt it, she wondered if he could, too.

'Would you like another Guinness?' she asked, clawing her way back to rationality. 'I'm sorry it's only bottled.'

'Don't worry about it,' he assured her, with a wide smile. 'I'll take you to Dublin one day, and we'll go on a pub-crawl down Grafton Street and drink some of the real stuff.'

The wine was strong, and her head was spinning. The prospect he presented to her seemed a delightful one. Maybe he would be something more than a one-night stand, but she baulked at commitment. Hadn't she tried that with Ricky?

'Maybe we will, Sean,' she said, promising nothing.

She had been indulgent with the dessert, ordering ice cream with cherries, fudge and nuts, and tiny bite-sized eclairs bursting with whipped cream and rippling with dark sweet chocolate and mocha chantilly.

Without taking his adventurer's sensual, hungry eyes from her, he scooped up a spoonful of the latter and held it out, nodding as he did so. She hestitated for an instant, then opened her mouth and permitted him to fill it with sweetness.

The confection was cold, bitter-sweet; the warmth of brandy, pastry melting on her tongue. She relished the taste, closing her eyes and murmuring her appreciation. It slipped down her throat and she lifted her lids, met the full blue blaze of his eyes and said, 'Don't you want some?'

He extended a sinewy, sunbrowned hand and wiped away a tiny trace of chocolate from the corner of her lips, transferring it to his own, his fleshy tongue working round his fingers in such a suggestive way that her face flushed and her womb contracted with longing.

'Not from a spoon,' he said. 'I'd like to smooth it over

your breasts and then lick it off. Would you like me to do that, Lorna?'

This was going too far too fast, she decided, and pushed back her chair. He was there to help her as she rose. She could feel him standing behind her, his breath on her neck, his hands coming round to cup her breasts and rub his thumb-pads over the hard tips.

'We've work to do,' she gasped, but could not help pushing back against him, her buttocks contacting the high ridge of his erect penis.

'Can't I have my pudding?' he whispered, his tongue caressing the velvety rim of her ear and setting the pendant earring swinging.

Without waiting for an answer, he came round to face her, hands at her waist, pulling her gently towards him. She opened her lips as he kissed her, tongue tangling with his as he probed and explored the cavity of her mouth, savouring mocha and chantilly and saliva, potent as love-juice.

Without releasing her from his kiss, he reached down, found the edge of her crop top and pushed it up. The air played over her naked skin, the jersey material strained across her chest like a wide white strap. Her nipples stood out, roused by the change of temperature and the excitement roaring through her loins.

Sean eased back and looked at them, his famished, almost gloating expression making her labia swell and her clit ache. It was as if he was already feasting on her, sucking the buds into his mouth, tonguing them with the avidity of a baby.

'You've glorious breasts,' he breathed and, though she knew he had perfected his charm in acting school, she somehow wanted to believe he was sincere.

Before she realised his intention, he reached for his plate and her flesh crept. Her nipples were hard as diamond-capped raspberries as he started to coat them with chocolate and ice-cream. His fingers were amazingly skilful, lingering and smoothing. His head tipped to one side as he considered his masterpiece, the confectionery his paints, her breasts his canvas.

Lorna stood rigid, spine arched towards him, head tipped back, eyes slitted. Sean hunkered down in front of her, bringing his face level with her nipples. His tongue protruded, the tip lightly brushing over the almost painfully sensitive teats.

'Oh ... oh ...' A shuddering moan escaped Lorna, and she buried her hands in his long, thick hair, making certain that he did not move as he knelt there, worshipping at the fount of her breasts.

He took his time, licking diligently till every particle had been devoured. Even then he did not stop, sucking strongly, rolling the nipples between his fingers, brushing them, tormenting them till she was on the point of begging for release.

It seemed that he was concerned with nothing but her pleasure, his own gratification of no importance. Yet, glancing down, she could see the swelling behind his fly, the thick baton of his penis lifting the loose material at an angle. It slanted upward, almost to his waist.

With a final, leisurely massage of her aching breasts, he got to his feet, carefully adjusting her top to cover her. The fabric immediately darkened, stained by the damp residue of his saliva.

'Did you say something about work?' he said huskily, hands hanging loosely at his sides. She marvelled at his control, for his phallus maintained its hardness, an iron-hard weapon needing a sheath in which to plunge.

'Yes ... of course ... work,' she stammered, blinded by the need to take his cock into her mouth and sample its flavour. 'Umm ... you can change in my bedroom.'

'Sounds good to me. Over there?'

She nodded and he moved lithely to the door. While he was gone Lorna set up the camera.

Her heart was beating rapidly. She could feel the jersey cloth chafing her sensitive nipples, and moisture lubricating her secret lips. Concentrate! she told herself

19

sternly. Work first and then pleasure. And pleasure there will be, for I'm determined to have him.

When he returned she did a doubletake. Jesus God! she whispered to herself. Will you look at that? I'm blasé, but even so I'm panting and raring to go. What will he do to less sophisticated readers when he strides across a book jacket? They'll genuflect, half fainting in his presence.

He was indeed magnificent. The bottle-green uniform suited his swashbuckling good looks. He was so beautiful and so frightening, with that suggestion of power in his stance.

His costume was that of a hussar, with a short, frogged and braided jacket and a loose, fur-lined dolman slung over one shoulder. Skin-tight breeches underscored his cock, exaggerating it in an outrageously sensual way. His firmly muscled buttocks and long, lean thighs with the fascinating hollows were a sight to tempt a nun.

A kalpac was set at a jaunty angle on his head, the peak part covering his eyes. Shiny black Hessian boots met his knees and a sabre swung at his left hip.

'What d'you think?' he asked, swaggering across and posing for her, hand resting on the sword hilt, his legs widely planted, giving an uninterrupted view of the impressive package between.

Lorna walked slowly round him, pretending to be interested in camera angles, while in reality possessed of a crying need to handle the goods so temptingly displayed.

At last she ran her fingers over the smooth woollen cloth covering his biceps. She felt him tense, heard his sharp intake of breath. Want curled in her groin and sent the blood rushing to her core.

They stood together, so close that her nipples made contact with his chest. Heat emanated from him, and she was very aware of his shaft almost, but not quite, pressing against her belly. She moved her hips ever so slightly and his arm came out, gripping her waist, hauling her up till she could feel his manhood, hot, damp and urgent through their clothing.

She raised her eyes and stared up at him. His jaw was tense, his mouth a hard line, his eyes a sharp, smarting blue. 'Well?' he said huskily. 'D'you like what you see?'

She had the presence of mind to bring up her hands and wedge them between his chest and her breasts, then she stepped back a pace. 'You look the part. Yes, I think the cover artists will enjoy having you as a model, and we'll pair you up with some gorgeous girls.

'So it's settled then? I can enter the contest?'

She strolled away from him, then stood, hands on her hips, looking him up and down like a prospective buyer viewing a slave on the auction block. 'Very nice, Sean. But have you ever considered taking part in, shall we say, frank and explicit movies?'

'Porn, d'you mean?' He laid the rapier aside, but kept to his role as a victorious soldier.

'Erotica, which is rather different. Nothing crude. We're dealing with female fantasies here, not hard porn for men. There's at least one woman director in Hollywood who specialises in tastefully filmed sex scenes, with a fairly convincing plot. Would you care to try and enact one with me? This will be recorded, you understand.'

Lorna's heart was pounding like a drum. Beneath the flimsy fabric her breasts rose, the nipples puckered, her clit yearning for the touch of his mouth, his teeth, his fingers. She could feel the honeydew pooling at her vaginal entrance.

'I'll give it my best shot,' he said with a slow smile and it was as if some devilish stranger had already taken over, an enemy warrior indeed, ready to plunge into and ravish her.

Lorna's desire cooled a little at the predatory look in his eyes, though this was just fine for her purpose. She fixed the tripod so the camcorder was directed at a divan positioned against one wall. It was draped in tapestries and heaped with bolster-shaped cushions.

21

'OK,' she said. 'Here's the scenario. You're one of the Duke of Wellington's officers and I'm a French lady you've just taken prisoner. It's down to you to rob me of my virtue, in the most seductive way possible.'

'I'll be a pleasure, Lorna,' he replied, his gaze sending prickles down her spine. 'Do I get to act out the whole thing? Or is this a fake screw?'

'Let's see how it goes, shall we?' she murmured, presenting her back to him as she sashyed towards the divan.

He caught her by the shoulders, turning her to face him and she was helpless in that powerful grip. His hands were impatient now, roaming over her entire body, dipping between her thighs. His touch made her shiver, a warm glow suffusing her entire self, culminating in the moist depths of her womanhood.

'Shall we begin?' he asked, close to her ear, his breath a caress in itself.

She nodded and started to struggle. 'Let me go!' she cried, pretending to be a frightened but feisty lady. 'Don't you know who I am? My father is the Comte de Guise. He'll have you flogged for this insult.'

'It's no use fighting me, *mademoiselle*. Your father can do nothing. We've taken the fort,' he answered, and Lorna noted his ease of manner. He was an actor, all right. Probably on his way to becoming an outstanding one. 'I want you. I intend to have you.'

Suddenly his lips captured hers and Lorna forgot her lines. His tongue penetrated her mouth, exploring it, tasting it, his saliva like nectar as it mingled with hers. She sucked it, played with it, lay in his arms as if moulded there. The hard length of him pressed against her, and the heat of his prick burned into her navel. He was too tall to take her standing up, and she was tormented by the delirious idea of having him lift her, raise her open-legged above his penis and then lower her on to it.

The game had gone on long enough. She wanted to see that lively serpent, to handle his balls in their velvety sac, and sample the juice seeping from the narrow slit in his glans.

He swung her up, one arm around her shoulders, the other under her buttocks, though never taking his lips from hers or stopping in his oral delving. Cradling her against his chest, he carried her to the divan. There he laid her down and stood for a second, arms akimbo, raking over her with his eyes. Then he reached out and pushed up her skirt, baring her from waist to dark, wet triangle.

'You're lovely, *mademoiselle*,' he murmured, and his fingers touched her nipples through the cloth, first one, then the other.

Lorna arched her back, her breasts rising high to welcome the pleasure. He teased, pinched, rolled her ardent teats between thumb and forefinger. His other hand fondled her pussy hair, then slid along her wet avenue, opening her labia. He held the lips between his fingers as if he was touching velvet, and moved the middle digit backwards and forwards over the engorged flesh.

She wriggled her hips and moaned her appreciation, moving her legs apart, one foot on the carpet, her pubis thrust invitingly upwards. He dipped into her fragrant pool and slid his finger, slick wet, up and over the head of her clitoris.

Forgetting the script, drugged by his caresses, she lay looking up at him, watchful and excited. He straightened, took her hand and placed it on the mighty bulge surging against the white breeches. She pressed it, worked it, then deftly unfastened his belt and the old-fashioned buttoned flap with a slow, deliberate movement. His penis shot out of the gap, the head rearing from the foreskin at an aggressive angle, seeking an aperture in which to bury itself.

Lorna sat on the edge of the couch with her legs apart, took that impressive tool in her hands and ran her fingers over the glans, using the pearly pre-come as a lubricant.

Sean stood there like a statue, admiring his jerking, inflamed cock.

'Suck it,' he commanded, and buried his hands in her curls, bringing her face down to the hairy realms of his crotch.

She opened her mouth and took the length of it, inch by inch. It felt smooth against her lips, salty on her taste buds. Slowly it penetrated, her lips stretched about it, her jaws aching The cap bumped against her throat and still there was more to go. She knew she could not take it all without gagging, so began to move her head up and down. Sean helped, his grip guiding her into the motion that excited him most.

His penis needed no support, standing up proudly. She eased his breeches lower and slid her hands between his thighs, caressing the spheres that hung there like ripe fruit in a net, bursting with the promise of luscious juice. She squeezed gently and he groaned, his movements quickening. A further trickle of creamy fluid covered her tongue and she eased her head away. He must not come until he had satisfied her.

'No,' she said sternly. 'Not yet. I'm nowhere near ready. You must learn manners, soldier, if you hope to succeed with women. A powerful stud is all very well, but foreplay is of the essence. Let me show you.'

He scowled, and handled his prick himself, stroking it, using a hard, vigorous motion which made it jump in his fist. Lorna covered his hand with hers and shook her head, then lay back on the divan and opened her legs, beckoning him to join her.

She took off her clothes, and undressed him, admiring his body, so slim-hipped and broad in the chest and shoulders, the skin tanned to a deep hue. She admired women, thought them the most beautiful creatures alive, but the sheer power of a masculine body gave her an almost cerebral satisfaction. It was such a perfect machine, the phallus and testicles so cunningly designed by nature for the reproduction of the species. And this superb example was with her now, her plaything to do with as she willed.

She drank at his mouth and fed on his skin, lapping at it and relishing the salty flavour of fresh male sweat. Her tongue flicked over the brown discs of his nipples while her fingers made patterns in his chest hair. She toyed with his penis, played with his balls, had him moaning on the edge of climax then, enjoying her power, withdrew and said, 'Now you can bring me to orgasm.'

She felt him trembling with excitement as he fingered and suckled her nipples, before his tongue moved down to circle her navel and go lower, washing her bush with his saliva. She reached down and parted her love-lips, sighing and sighing as he shifted position till his head was between her thighs.

She had forgotten the camcorder, forgotten that they were supposed to be acting. This was real, a perfect here and now. She became very still, concentrating every part of her being on the feeling of his tongue gently lapping at her clitoris. She nudged her pubis higher, wordlessly urging him on. The waves gathered, glittering against the darkness of her closed eyelids. They receded, gathered again, whipped up into a storm, rising ever higher till she was absorbed in the pleasure gathering in her womb. It exploded in the heartland of her sex, her glorious, pulsating clitoris.

She cried out in her extremity and he held her firm, continuing to lavish sensations on her as her whole body shook with the last ripples of pleasure.

'I want your cock!' she shouted.

He was on her, in her, pressing through the soft-fringed margin of her entrance, plunging and ploughing till a final spasm of his organ told her that he, too, had reached completion.

They lay prone in the afterglow, and Lorna smiled up at the dim ceiling. Coming back to herself, she was once more aware of the camcorder, and savoured in advance the enjoyment Nicole would glean from this show.

* * *

'Wow! Maybe you should change direction and become a porn star,' her friend commented much later.

'I don't think so,' Lorna replied, moving languidly on the couch, reaching for the remote control and pressing the OFF button. Sean had not been gone long and she was possessed of that post-coital need to sleep.

Nicole had insisted on seeing the video, wide awake after a successful meeting with the editor-in-chief of a highly acclaimed publishing house who had promised to help with the conference. Now she wanted to discuss this latest find.

'He's amazing,' she announced. 'What did you tell him?'

'I said if it was all right with you, then he could be a contestant.'

'I agree. He's great in costume. If, along with the others, we give him plenty of exposure in the issues leading up to the event, then I think he stands a chance of winning the readers' votes on his own looks and merit, as well as those of the judges.'

'Good idea.' Lorna yawned, then added, 'As you saw, he's into fellatio. Like most guys he thinks he's in charge. He doesn't know that when it comes to blowjobs, we girls are in the saddle.'

'Dead right,' Nicole enthused. 'It's us who decide how long he has to endure it, when we'll allow him to come and, in fact, if we go down on him at all.'

'Fun, isn't it?'

'It certainly is. Oh, by the way – ' Nicole sat up suddenly and grabbed her purse – this was among the mail today, but Jane must have missed it. I found it in your in-tray.'

'Can't it wait till morning?' Lorna protested.

'It's from England, honey.'

'Another contact with home? First Sean, now this. Maybe someone's trying to tell me something,' Lorna commented, mystified.

She took the long white envelope, puzzled. Who did she know in England apart from Cassandra? And the envelope was typed, not in her friend's untidy, scrawling hand. Filled with curiosity, and with Nicole, equally curious, leaning over her shoulder, she slit the flap and drew out a sheet of headed notepaper.

It was from a law firm called Norcross, Bailey and Grant, and their address was Salisbury, Wiltshire. More and more mystified by the minute, she read:

Dear Miss Erskine,

You will no doubt be surprised to hear from us, but we have been searching for you for some time. The matter in hand concerns the estate of the late Mrs Winifred Erskine, a distant aunt of your father, Mr John Erskine. As far as we can ascertain, you are the only surviving relative of the lady, and stand to inherit her considerable fortune and a house in Wiltshire.

I suggest that you contact me as soon as you receive this and make arrangements to return home without delay.

Yours sincerely,
Dudley Norcross.

Chapter Two

*T*he trilling of the phone intruded into the somnolent peace of the hot afternoon.

'Damn!' exclaimed the naked woman sprawled voluptuously against the frilly lace pillows. She disentangled her legs from those of the man beside her and fumbled for the receiver on the bedside table. 'Who the hell's that?'

He grunted in response, his big, hirsute frame in strange contrast to the femininity of the room and the opulence of the four-poster in which they lay. 'Answer it and find out,' he suggested, yawning widely and stretching till his joints cracked.

'Good thinking, Batman,' she grinned, lifted the phone from its porcelain cradle, pushed back her tousled tawny hair and held it to her ear. 'Hello. Cassandra Ashley speaking.'

'Hi there,' a disembodied voice answered, an instantly recognisable English voice with a trace of American intonation.

'Lorna? How lovely! Where are you?' Cassandra slapped away the hand insinuating itself round her left breast.

'In New York, but listen, I'm flying over tonight. Landing at Heathrow. Can I stay with you while I get things sorted?'

'Of course, darling. Are you really still in the States? You sound as clear as if you were next door. I'll meet you at the airport. What time are you getting in?' The hand refused to be controlled. Now the fingers were teasing her nipple, pinching it into an even harder, rosier peak.

'Around 7.30 a.m.'

'What time is it now over there?' Cassandra's voice was a little breathy, for her companion had left her breasts and was exploring between her thighs, fondling her depilated mons, then worming a finger into the secret mouth of her, buried to the knuckle.

'Seven. I'm at Kennedy. We'll be boarding soon.'

'It's two here.' Love in the afternoon, Cassandra thought, as opposed to the Spanish 'death in the afternoon', when a brave matador meets a brave bull. It wasn't all that different, actually. Both consisted of a passionate, sweaty, power struggle.

'Have I interrupted your work?' Lorna's question brought Cassandra back to present time.

'No. I'm taking it easy. Are you coming over on holiday?'

'I'll tell you tomorrow.'

'Is everything OK?'

'Sure. Couldn't be better. See you in the morning.'

'Fine. I look forward to it. See you.'

Cassandra set down the phone and slid under the floral lawn sheet. Her companion enfolded her in a mighty, odoriferous bear-hug, redolent of semen and sun-oil, asking, 'Who was that?'

'Lorna Erskine. You've heard me mention her. We were at college together. She's been in America for ages, but she's coming to stay.'

He rolled on his back, taking her with him. Cassandra sat astride him, knees either side of his well muscled body, feeling the exciting brush of his chest hair on her wide open cleft. She dipped her pelvis slightly to increase the pressure of her own weight on her inner lips. He might be tough, sometimes rough, but he had proved a more than willing pupil when she had introduced him to the sensual refinements of sex.

A grin lit up his craggily handsome face. 'I remember. Didn't you used to fuck each other blind? Will you do it again? Can I watch?'

'I make no promises, darling,' she said, rubbing her clit against him, leaving a silver trail of moisture. 'I might let you. We're not dedicated lesbians who wouldn't have a man within a mile while they're fucking.' She smiled down into his hazel eyes and stuck out her tongue, its point hovering over his full lips. His own shot out to meet it and for a moment they fenced, tasting each other's saliva.

This was a lunchtime session. Cassandra had been sunbathing by the pool in the garden, listening to the sounds of Wagnerian music thundering from the direction of the studio, accompanied by the thump of chisel and hammer as her lover worked on his latest piece of sculpture. Eventually, she had abandoned her lounger to share a beer, fresh green salad and grilled chops with him in her farmhouse style kitchen.

They had ended up in a slippery wash of mayonnaise, licking the creamy dressing from each other's body with leisurely enjoyment. Cassandra had relished the feel of cool Spanish floor tiles pressing into her back as he knelt between her thighs and slurped juicy slices of melon from her vagina.

There was something distinctly debauched about mixing the pleasure of food with the pleasures of sex. Both experiences were lubricious and messy, satisfying basic instincts, tongues and lips savouring differing textures, enjoying a rich variety of tastes augmented by aromas. Cassandra was uninhibited when it came to her appetites: she revelled in eating, drinking and fornicating.

Now the call from Lorna added to her feeling of well-being. It would be wonderful to spend hours chatting, something which was impossible long distance. They had a lot of catching up to do.

She forgot this as he reached up to cup her breasts in his huge palms, rubbing the prominent, tanned teats till they stood up in peaks. Her sap smeared the tip of his cock as she poised just above it, permitting an inch of entry, no more.

'Teasing bitch,' he muttered, but happily.

'That's right. I'm in control,' she whispered, rising on her knees so his straining phallus was denied contact. To torment him even further, she slid a thigh over his body and dismounted, then lay with her back turned towards him.

He folded himself against her, nuzzling her ear and finding that sensitive spot where the nape of her neck joined her shoulders. Cassandra squirmed and sighed.

It was good to have him around, an unexpectedly gentle giant beneath that irascible exterior. Everyone had their Achilles heel, and hers was Marc Orman, *enfant terrible* of the art world.

People feared and respected him, students and critics alike. His monumentally large sculptures caused controversy wherever they were exhibited. Urban councils wanted them for their parks. Rate payers protested. Editors of local newspapers were besieged by letters. He appeared on argumentative, late-night debates on Channel 4, and answered questions on intellectual programmes on the radio. He was loved, hated, but never ignored.

She had met him when commissioned to do a portrait for the cover of a coffee-table edition of yet another book concerning him. He had roared down to her cottage on a vintage Norton and, though at first infuriating her by his interference and carping, she had been unable to resist his massive build, flaming chestnut hair and the pronounced promise that strained against the fly of his battered leather trousers.

She was from an upper-class background, mad about music, a patron of Covent Garden and Glyndebourne, and had graduated in history, art and drama. His passion was for motor bikes and old cars, the acquiring of which he pursued relentlessly when not engaged in his other obsession – that of transforming blocks of stone into the grotesque, sometimes beautiful but always challenging forms that filled his imagination.

It was an odd combination, but they had art and music in common, besides a rampant interest in sex. She was much in demand for her unusual paintings, and commanded high fees for her vivid illustrations, much influenced by Arthur Rackham, Alphonse Mucha and Kay Neilson but with the addition of her own futuristic stamp.

Now a warm breeze drifted in at the latticed windows, lifting the muslin curtains and cooling the sweat beading Cassandra's spine. She could feel Marc's penis moving against the small indentation at the top of her buttocks, its clubbed cap probing against the tight amber rose of her anus.

She turned into him, supple as a cat, curling up so that her eyes were on a level with his impressive tool to watch what her fingers were doing to it. She loved making it perform for her, that hard shaft her own personal plaything.

Violet eyes slitted with enjoyment, she eased the foreskin back to fully expose the gleaming fiery glans then slid it up again, leaving nothing showing but the slit, repeating this action several times. Her excitement intensified as he tweaked her nipples, diving from one eager crest to the other. As she worked on his prick, so she admired him: those strong, muscular legs; his deep-chested body; the reddish hairy thatch from which his phallus reared, straight as a lance pointing towards the tenting of her bed.

She thought it beautiful, that spear of power, keeping a drawingpad handy and often making sketches of it: in repose or turgid, it was a fascinating thing. She gave it her full attention now, subjecting it to hard friction, then light fondling, reaching down to caress his balls and tickle that ultra-sensitive area dividing them from his arsehole. He grunted with pleasure, and her love-bud tingled. It was intensely satisfying to have this talented, famous man completely at her mercy.

Longing flowered in her depths, that delicious, wanting ache. Her cunt was wet, juices flowing from earlier congress. She gripped his thigh between hers and rubbed her pubis against it, feeling the exquisite pressure on her clitoris, but wanted everything to take place in slow motion, a prolonged, lecherous encounter.

She slithered higher and licked his nipples, her tongue circling them before her lips closed over the taut brown nubs. Marc's chest heaved and his dick hopped against her hip. She moved down with sinuous grace, taking it in hand again, her blonde-tipped curls brushing his underbelly. Holding it firmly, she guided it between her teeth, the point of her tongue dipping into its slit, tasting the tiny, silvery pearl hanging from it like a teardrop.

Languorously she licked him, gradually taking the whole of him in her mouth. She arched her neck to make his entrance easier, moving lightly with barely a pause between the upstroke and the down. Then she withdrew till only the very end of the bulging head rested between her lips.

She kept him waiting for a second, before continuing to lap at and suck it, running her tongue the whole length of the shaft as if it were a particularly luscious ice-cream cone. Feeling the lift of his hips and the extra swelling of his cock that heralded ejaculation, she pressed firmly at the base, delaying the supreme moment of release.

'You do that so well,' he whispered, and his fingers tangled in her hair, holding her to his phallus.

His excitement was echoed in her loins. She started to pull and suck thirstily, milking him, her mouth embracing the throbbing stem, feeling the veins swell and the shaft enlarge and hearing his moans. His pelvis jerked, his cock twitched and a fountain of creamy spunk gushed into her mouth, dribbling from the sides, running over her lips. She held it there, savouring the warm, spicy libation, swallowing before smearing the residue over her body like some exotic massage oil.

'It's the best kind of moisturiser,' she enthused. 'Halts the ageing process. Give me more . . . more!'

He dragged her up against him, kissing her neck, praising her breasts, adoring her pudendum, murmuring lovingly, 'You're a dirty little girl.'

'I know,' she carolled joyously. 'Now it's my turn.'

She straddled his face, felt his lips and teeth gobbling at her, his swirling tongue spiralling round her engorged button of flesh. Holding his head firmly with her thighs, she rode him, the feeling gathering into a powerful force that flooded every inch of her being.

Now she was entirely woman, a votary of the Great Goddess at whose altar she worshipped. Her sex pulsated from clit to uterus, her juices welling. Centre of life. Source of creation. Men feared it, but could not resist the darkness in which they had been conceived, terrified of being sucked back into the womb they so longed to penetrate.

Eyes screwed tight shut, Cassandra concentrated, riding the power surge, screaming as she reached the top of the rollercoaster. She shot off to the stars, then fell down in a fractured shower of rainbow light. The spasms rolled through her core, her vagina clenched on itself, hungry for a cock to satisfy those greedy, pulsating muscles.

Marc's was ready, and she took it deep inside herself, pumping on it furiously to drain the last dregs of sensation from her convulsing cunt, inner muscles slamming together. He flipped her over on her back and she clamped her legs round his waist as he rammed into her hard, butting against her cervix, coming again in a welter of pleasure.

'Phew! That was wonderful,' she said as he collapsed on her. She stroked his face, kissed the saline sweat, then added, 'Get off. You're squashing me.'

His lips brushed her lightly, and she tasted her own essences there. 'D'you want a drink?' he said.

'How did you guess? A long, cool Pimms. Bring it outside. Mustn't waste that lovely sun.'

They spent the afternoon playing in the pool like a couple of carefree dolphins, or lay side by side under the sun's caress. He went as naked as she in the privacy of the old walled garden, though at one time he had been reluctant to part with his old jeans and shabby tweed jacket. Now he was proud of his tan, and they had fun applying coconut oil, fingers skimming over hot flesh, artfully poking into forbidden areas where the sun was too shy to go.

Lorna felt the bite of a strap crossing her breasts as the plane lifted. Her heart thudded and her ears popped at its rocket-like expulsion into the void.

The dead straight lines of yellow runway lights rushed away below, becoming no more than necklaces adorning the throat of some dreaming giantess. The tops of tower blocks, crimsoned by the rays of the dying sun, were jagged, uneven, weird from that angle.

The pulse of powerful engines vibrated through the bowels of the jumbo jet, connecting with her own gut, G-force pinning her to the seat. She felt her sphincter loosen and gripped it tightly, hanging on. At thirty-five thousand feet the pressure relaxed. A light flashed above the gangway entrance. She could unfasten her seat belt, get comfortable and watch the little personal TV screen if she wanted.

The stewards came round, motherly queens fussing over their passengers. Their solicitude was sweet and, yes, she would like a coffee. No, nothing alcoholic just yet, thank you. Was she warm enough? Yes, but an additional blanket would be nice, as she intended to snatch some sleep. Duty-free goods? Perfume, please. Have you Guerlain's *Samsara?* You have? Great. I'll take the *eau de toilette.*.

The coffee arrived, hot, strong and aromatic. Lorna adjusted the clip-on table and felt the tension draining out of her. It seemed incredible that only last week she had been helping organise the convention, and now she was on a plane, flying home to England.

Nicole had been most accommodating, saying, 'Don't you worry. Get over there and take what's yours. Just think, a stately home of your own! Maybe a castle! Could we use it for *Image*? I can visit with fans. It might be the venue for the next big book-fest.'

Lorna had rung Dudley Norcross the same night she received the letter. He had still been in his office, eight o'clock British time. They had talked, his voice dripping public-school charm, confident, persuasive. Of course, she must come over at once. There was much to be settled. She was about to become a very rich women indeed.

'And the house?' she had asked.

There had been a fractional pause, then, 'Ah, well, yes, Miss Erskine ... the house. It's very old, most pictur-esque. The best thing you can do is see it.'

When Lorna finally hung up, she and Nicole had started to make plans. It was remarkably easy, really. A deputy taking over her work on the magazine, probably temporarily. At that point Lorna was thinking of renting out the English property and returning to New York. Nicole had assured her she could manage without her for a while, more excited than Lorna at this sudden stroke of fortune.

Seated on the plane beneath the Heaviside layer, high over the Atlantic Ocean, Lorna thought about the belong-ings she had left in the apartment. 'I'll take care of everything,' Nicole had insisted. 'Just pack what you need. The rest can be sorted later. D'you mind leaving Sean?'

'No,' Lorna had answered truthfully, though maybe with a tiny flicker of regret.

She knew he was about to be launched. For her own part she had not lost her heart to him. No man, or woman for that matter, could penetrate the shield she kept wrapped firmly about her emotions. No commit-ment, no love, no pain.

She rested her head against the backrest, her hands idle in her lap, aware of being tired. Leaving in such a hurry had been hectic. She stared out at the blackness beyond the window.

'You must be thinking about something terribly absorbing,' said a pleasant voice. It belonged to the man occupying the seat on the other side of the aisle. 'Twice I've asked if you're all right, and you've not heard me.'

She looked up, smiling slightly. 'I was taught never to talk to strange men,' she answered levelly, though she had registered him from take-off.

He was a long-limbed Englishman wearing an exquisitely tailored Ralph Lauren suit, a fine cotton shirt, wide silk tie and a matching handkerchief in the breast pocket. Top management, travelling on business? Or maybe even a budding politician.

I've too much on my mind, she thought. I can't be bothered.

'Excuse me.' He pretended to cringe, but his eyes sparkled, crinkling at the outer corners. 'You can't blame me for wanting to chat up the most attractive woman on board.'

'Why don't you try that line on one of the stewardesses, or even a steward?' she suggested sweetly, and went back to her contemplation of the night sky.

The lights in the cabin were lowered. A stewardess came along to ensure Lorna was comfortably settled. It was time to sleep. The seat was lowered into a reclining position, the pillow placed beneath her head, the blanket tucked around her. The Englishman, her fellow-traveller in that secluded first-class compartment, received the same caring treatment.

Lorna took off her sandals, wriggled her bare toes luxuriantly, and unfastened the waistband of her skirt, aware that he was watching her covertly. He had a nice nose, she decided, and a kissable mouth. He looked about thirty, an up and coming high-flyer. The stewardess drew the curtains, enclosing her in a private cubicle.

Her eyelids were heavy, the gentle throb of the fuselage lulling her. When she awoke she would be over England. Her eyes closed and she thought with satisfaction, 'Now I'm asleep,' but there she stayed, unable to fall into oblivion. Half-dreams occurred. She seemed to be back in New York, and suddenly spoke aloud in a natural voice to somebody not present. She woke herself, embarrassed in case the Englishman had heard her.

Eyes firmly shut, she slept again. Or was it sleep? Sean was with her, and she remembered the feel of his cock and the divine smoothness of it on her tongue, each movement of her mouth becoming a caress. She sighed gently and, in her sleep, her hand stole down to the silky triangle that covered her wiry bush. One finger eased round the edge and entered between the damp, ripening lips. She located her bud, and started to caress it. Was it her doing it, or was it Sean? She thought she heard his low, pleasant voice breathing her name.

The voice changed suddenly and, her mind slipping notches like a faulty machine, she fought her way up and out of her dream.

'Hush, it's all right,' the voice said – male, cultured, English.

She could not move, pinioned by the heavy pressure of arms holding her and a body pressed close to hers under the blanket. As she came more awake, she could feel her hand cupping her mound, her finger hard against the sharp, dividing line of her labia. She drew it away, her face flaming. Shy at being caught pleasuring herself, she could not deny that it gave her a strangely excited feeling. His hand closed over hers and he raised it to his nose and sniffed at the lingering fragrance of honeydew, then he started to lick her fingers.

Her blouse was open and she realised he had been fondling her breasts. Now he kissed her, tentatively at first, his breath fresh, his tongue experienced in savouring a woman's mouth. As he kissed, so his hand slipped under her briefs and across her flat belly, stroking the soft fur, sinking deeper between her moist love-lips.

'God, you're so wet,' he whispered. 'You were moaning in your sleep? Were you having a bad dream?'

'I can't remember,' she replied, not yet fully awake. 'How long have you been with me?'

'Just now. You don't object? You aren't going to accuse me of sexual harrassment or anything?'

'It's hardly that, is it? You aren't forcing me.'

'Do you like what I'm doing?'

'I wouldn't let you do it if I didn't.' Curiouser and curiouser, she thought. This is an Alice in Wonderland situation if ever there was. How weird to be having this conversation with a complete stranger.

'What do you think about when you're playing with yourself?' he asked, his voice thickening with excitement.

'I haven't any particular fantasy,' she replied. 'I concentrate on my clitoris, that tiny tyrant who demands that I rub it.'

'Have you been doing it for many years? How old were you when you started? I've always wondered about women and their orgasms. Tell me, please.'

Lorna was astonished at the rapport between them, a bond of intimacy she had shared with no one else, not even her dearest friend, Cassandra.

'I was a teenager,' she said, going back through time to the never-to-be forgotten moment of awakening. 'Mother had always told me nice girls didn't touch themselves down there, but one night I found a little hole in my pyjamas in just the right place ... over my button. I wriggled a finger through and touched it. Such a lovely feeling shot through me. I wanted to rub it some more. I did, and then couldn't stop, rubbing and rubbing.'

'You came?' His eyes shone eagerly, the light from the dim, shaded ceiling bulb slanting across them and running over his lips.

'I did. It was wonderful, but I thought I was going to die, convinced that mother had been right,' she admitted, thinking: good heavens! I've never told anyone this before.

'Go on. Tell me what it felt like,' he begged, and his

39

free hand went to the swelling in his crotch, massaging his cock through the fine cloth.

'Like when you climax, I suppose,' she said, and as she moved her buttocks on the seat the pressure of her wet briefs against her lower lips gave her pleasure. 'I've studied the subject since, and am so glad I've a clitoris instead of a penis. It's a wonderful little thing. A febrile bundle of nerve endings, the only organ in the human body designed exclusively for pleasure.'

'And you fantasise while you're stroking it? What about?'

'I sometimes pretend my doctor's examining me,' she confessed, and longed to touch herself again, clit throbbing. 'Medical men have such beautiful, clean hands. They'd know exactly what to do, and you'd have to obey them.'

'I know what you mean. I feel the same,' he muttered, no longer so controlled. 'Women in uniform turn me on; nurses, policewomen, even traffic wardens. People in power and authority.' He groaned sharply, and his hand movement speeded up. 'Sometimes, when I'm wanking, I remember my nanny and how she used to cane me when I was naughty. Just to say it almost brings me off.'

The light was very dim, shutters across the windows, blocking out the inky darkness of space. Lorna felt secure, liking the warm, masculine smell of him and the smoothness of his cheek held against her own. She stilled, her thoughts suspended, not afraid of him or in the least offended. A good-looking stranger. No ties or expectations, just an acceptance of what might happen. She could say whatever she liked. The chances of their meeting again were slim.

With heat glowing in the pit of her stomach, she watched him rubbing the outside of his trousers. The triangle of silk covering her mound had worked up between her lower lips, tight and wet. She held her breath, then let it slide slowly out as he unzipped and slipped a hand inside his fly, subjecting his hidden penis to stronger attention, his eyes half closed, a rapt expression on his face.

'Would you like to watch me again?' she said faintly, hardly believing she had spoken the words.

He seemed to wake from his trance. 'Yes. I'd love it. Thank you for asking. I'm proud that you'll let me share such a private moment.'

She threw the blanket aside, pushed up her skirt and opened her legs. He moved away a little to give her more room, then knelt in the aisle, positioning himself between her splayed thighs. She lay back and held her panties to one side so that nothing could be seen of them but a narrow, black, lace-edged vertical strip. She paused for a moment, granting him the benefit of this stimulating view, then used her favourite finger, the right middle one, to rub over her nub with light, fast strokes.

Normally, she liked it very wet and slippery, but now she deliberately refrained from dipping down into her juicy vulva, finding something fiercely exciting in the almost dry sensation over the tender head. If not done correctly, it would become irritating, even painful, but she knew the exact amount of play needed to keep the pleasure coming.

The Englishman had stopped fondling himself, resting a hand on either of her knees, holding them apart, leaning forward so that he could witness everything. The hem of her briefs strained up into her groin, displaying the damp, dark hair and red, swollen labia with the hard clit flushed to an even darker hue. It could be glimpsed every time she reached a downward stoke, leaving it exposed for a second. The air was spiced with her strong, female odour.

'Go on, darling. That's right. Do it for me,' he murmured, encouraging her, urging her on.

Suddenly, she closed her legs about her busy finger, trapping it between them, ecstasy bursting like a bubble inside her as she came in a convulsive spasm that took her unawares.

He seized her hand and placed it on the warm python

stirring in his trousers. The material felt like gauze between her fingers and the heat of his erection. She ventured inside and freed his cock from the silk boxer shorts.

He was rather small, but she had never found size mattered as much as men thought it did. She enclosed his manhood with her fist. She felt languid and at ease, as she always did after orgasm, but was curious to experience this man's member. Her knickers were still to one side, and she held one leg open for him to enter her. He thrust straight in and she relaxed under the penetration of a penis no larger than a good-sized finger. She enjoyed the soft, silky motion, and he came quickly, remaining in her vagina for a few moments after, his hands caressing her hair.

Very gently, she moved away from him and slid back the window panel. Behind her was darkness, but they were heading into the red-streaked glory of dawn. The Englishman put his cock away and fastened up, then returned to his own seat. Noises came from beyond their compartment, the smell of coffee wafting through the warm interior.

Lorna made her way to the ladies' room, locking the door behind her. After placing her toilet bag on the tiled shelf, she twirled the tap and water trickled into the basin. She washed the stickiness of come from her fingers, then bathed her female parts fastidiously and dusted herself with talc before putting on a clean pair of panties, popping the used ones into the disposal bin.

She had that headachy feeling induced by a long flight, and her pale face stared back at her from the mirror over the basin. Deciding that she looked drained, and wanting Cassandra's first impression to be a good one, she used cleansing milk and applied make-up, concentrating on her eyes, those wide spaced windows on her soul.

If not classically beautiful, she was undoubtedly attractive, and by the time she had finished, she was not displeased with her appearance. She worked the snarls out of her hair and swept it up, slipping a velvet scrunchie in place. Now she was ready for the fray.

She hoped the Englishman would not prove pushy. She had rogered him on impulse, nothing more. When she returned to her seat, daylight was gaining supremacy and the steward had been busy straightening everything. He then bustled off to fetch breakfast. The Englishman was reading a newspaper. He smiled at her over the edge as she walked in.

Later, when the plane touched down, he slipped a business card into her hand. She did not give him hers and, when she had alighted, dropped his into the nearest waste bin.

The arrival lounge was full and there were the usual irritating delays caused by customs and the trauma of locating luggage on the continually moving carousel. By the time Lorna had rescued her bags and grabbed a trolley, Cassandra was at the barrier, waiting for her.

'Lorna! Darling! There you are,' she exclaimed, her mellifluous accent turning heads. 'Here, let me help.'

'Can I be of assistance?' asked a bystander, a pleasant looking youth in chinos and a baggy shirt. His hair had been clipped close to his head and had elaborate, swirling patterns shaved into it.

'Thank you.' Cassandra beamed and allowed him to wheel the trolley down the ramp and into the car park, where she airily dismissed him.

She was spectacular, with the kind of large, shapely breasts that aroused lustful longings in all who looked upon them. They were barely contained in a skimpy vest, and obviously unfettered by a bra.

Her wide hips and toast-coloured thighs were displayed in a minuscule pair of shorts. These were made of cut-down jeans with the legs hacked off so only a thin strip of material remained, trapped between her nether lips. They were pulled so high into the crotch that when she bent over it was possible to glimpse the twin lobes of her sex, fascinatingly smooth and pink.

'I don't know how you've got the nerve to appear like that in public,' Lorna said, grinning with delight to see her irrepressible friend again. 'That poor guy thought he was going to bonk you in the luggage bay. He could hardly walk when he left us.'

'I've every right to wear what I like,' Cassandra declared. 'If men get stiff looking at me, that's their problem. They can go toss themselves off.'

'Thank you for sharing that with us, Miss Ashley,' Lorna said solemnly, green eyes sparkling.

'You're welcome,' Cassandra responded. 'Don't want you to be deprived of group therapy now you've left the good ole' US of A.'

She stalked round to the driver's side of the Golf in her stilt-heeled sandals, hair gelled high with little wisps corkscrewing against her cheeks. Lorna slowly climbed into the passenger seat, possessed of that light-headed, jet-lagged feeling. Everything seemed to have shrunk since she was last here, dwarfed by outsized, overstated, exuberant America. She did not know whether to laugh or cry, hovering on the edge of both emotions.

'I'm supposed to be meeting a lawyer in Salisbury,' she said, as she adjusted her skirt. It already stuck damply to her legs, the car hot as a Turkish bath, a heat haze shimmering over Heathrow.

'Do you feel up to it?' Cassandra asked, shoes kicked off, eyes on the rear mirror, the car leaping into action.

'I've already arranged it.' As they hammered down the motorway heading west, Lorna recounted everything that had happened.

'That's wonderful,' Cassandra commented. 'It means you'll be back in England, maybe for good. I've missed you. Of course, it's changed. Unemployment and homelessness are rife ... cardboard cities springing up everywhere, beggars sleeping in shop doorways, hospital wards closing for lack of funds. There's a crime wave and the whole country's going to the dogs, but no matter. It's still the best place on earth.'

44

'I've read about the troubles, watched the news on telly,' Lorna said, 'but yes, I'm glad to be home.'

'I'm living with a sculptor,' Cassandra informed her. 'He's a genius and I've turned my barn into a studio. We're fairly reclusive, but there's no shortage of men in the village, if that's what you're into right now.' She shot Lorna a sideways glance, the tip of her tongue coming out to wet her red, cushiony lips.

Lorna smiled and rested her head against the seat back. 'Oh, Cassie, I don't know yet. Let's go with the flow, like we've always done.'

'Whatever you say, darling.' Cassandra laid a golden brown hand on Lorna's bare knee, and pressed her foot down on the accelerator.

The countryside whipped past, and Lorna's spirits rose. Although England sweltered under a heatwave, it still looked lush and fertile, opening out as they travelled towards Wiltshire with its gently sloping hills and mile upon mile of rolling plains.

Cassandra turned off the motorway and they passed between narrow roads where purple foxgloves grew on the tops of banks. Full-uddered cows chewed the cud in fields deep in clover, sheltering under trees, heavy with the fullness of leaf, which swept down to meet them. Horses leant their big, noble heads over hedges and barred gates, and the tall mowing grass was sheened with bronze, the meadows dappled with flowers.

'I'm home!' Lorna shouted suddenly, feeling herself slotting back into this place of thoughts and memories, of moods and happenings and associations. 'I'm really, truly home!'

'The return of the native! Congratulations!' cheered Cassandra as they glimpsed the spire of the cathedral in the distance.

The streets of Salisbury were congested, and Cassandra swore softly as they snaked through the traffic. Ray-Bans pushed up like a blue plastic tiara, she was hunting a space to park.

'Dudley Norcross said his office is at the back of the

45

town Guildhall, where Market Square corners on Fish Row,' Lorna said, bewitched by the sight of beautiful houses of medieval and Georgian architecture, and splendid examples of fifteenth-century black and white timbering.

They found a parking space, and sat for a moment with the windows wound down, replacing the heat inside with that of the melting tarmac without. Cassandra examined herself critically in the driving mirror, adding an extra touch of lipstick. Lorna wiped a tissue over her damp forehead and then stuffed it back in her handbag.

'Are you sure you want me to come with you?' Cassandra asked, the glasses blanking off her eyes, expression unreadable.

'I'd like you to.'

They walked a little way and then found the building that bore the solicitor's brass plate. It was a tall, narrow Regency house, with four wide white steps leading to a front door under a shell-shaped arch. Lorna pushed it open and stepped into an airy hall with a mosaic floor and a delicate ironwork staircase that floated upward to be lost in the light pouring down from a long window.

Lorna picked up a handbell on the hall table and shook it. Almost at once a blonde with a French pleat and a navy two-piece came out, lifted supercilious eyebrows and said, 'Can I help?'

Lorna guessed she and Cassandra were not dressed like the usual clients of Norcross, Bailey and Grant. Indeed, they must seem like advocates for an alternative society, the receptionist's worst possible nightmare – Cassandra in her shocking little shorts and herself in a crumpled gypsyish skirt, revealing, front-laced camisole and thonged sandals.

Up yours, lady, she thought with a lift of her chin. I'm here to do business with your boss.

'I've an appointment with Mr Dudley Norcross,' she said briskly. 'My name's Lorna Erskine.'

The blonde's attitude altered. She became affable,

almost effusive. 'Oh, Miss Erskine. He's expecting you. This way, please.'

Lorna was excited, curious, praying this was not some monumental mistake. Supposing they had got the wrong person? I'll sue them for the air fare, she vowed.

They followed the blonde down a wide passage lined with portraits of town worthies going back a hundred years, interspersed with landscapes in massive frames. She paused, tapped on a door. A voice within called to enter, and Cassandra and Lorna passed beneath an elaborately scrolled lintel into a sun-filled room.

'Ah, Miss Erskine,' drawled the young man who rose from the swivel steno-chair behind an enormous, leather topped desk. He came towards her, hands outstretched. 'I'm Dudley Norcross. Please call me Dudley. And this is my assistant, Ian Carr.' He indicated another young man who got up from behind a computer.

'Hello,' he said, blinking at her through steel-framed spectacles. 'Did you have a good flight?'

'Uneventful,' she replied, smiling to herself as she remembered the Englishman. His ego would have been seriously dented had he heard her saying that.

Ian was unremarkable, a slight, thin-faced man, with straggly hair, wearing creased brown trousers and a somewhat grubby shirt with the sleeves rolled up. Lorna classified him as a computer buff, experiencing life through his modem.

Dudley, however, was something of a surprise. Though his voice down the phone had been intriguing, she had not expected this sleek, agile man wearing a grey silk and cotton mix Kenzo suit over a round-necked white polo shirt. It fitted his lithe body superbly, and complemented his fair good looks. He had a lean face, a narrow mouth and brown eyes, his hair styled rather long, layered to fall to his collar.

'Do sit down, Miss Erskine, and . . .' He cast a glance at Cassandra, his eyes lingering on her prominent breasts where the nipples lifted the thin fabric, hard as pebbles.

Ian was looking at them, too, as he slid back behind his PC.

'Hi, there. I'm Cassandra Ashley. Lorna's friend.' She extended her right hand and took Dudley's, shaking it firmly.

He waved them into chairs, said, 'Coffee, please, Judy,' and dispatched the blonde, who obviously adored him. Lorna thought it more than likely that he slept with her when nothing else more entertaining presented itself.

'Well, Dudley, and what's all this about?' she began, sinking into the soft brown hide seat that received her bottom in a squidgy, sensual embrace.

As she crossed her legs, her button-through skirt opened to mid-thigh. Dudley's eyes switched to her crotch. Her body responded to the way his lower lip softened, imagining him lapping at her secret places. A bright young lawyer, no doubt hiding lecherous secrets beneath that suave exterior.

There was a pause while Judy, obviously resentful of her boss's interest in his two attractive visitors, poured coffee and then retreated huffily.

She definitely fancies the pants off him, Lorna concluded. Poor thing. He's not all that great. I should take pity and introduce her to someone like Sean. That would set her hormones zinging.

'Can we get down to it, Dudley?' she said crisply, used to a hard-edged approach. 'I want to know exactly what all this is about.'

'Of course you do.' Dudley rested his elbows on his desk and steepled his fingers together, observing her over them. 'It's perfectly straightforward. We are the executors of Miss Winifred Erskine's will, and you are the sole beneficiary.'

'How much money is involved?' Lorna met Cassandra's eyes and one of her friend's eyebrows lifted. She, too, was assessing Dudley's attributes.

'A read-out, Ian, if you please,' Dudley snapped and his assistant's fingers skimmed over the keyboard calling up data. 'She died last year, but it's been difficult to trace you.'

'Are you sure it's me? Maybe there is someone else.'

'Oh, no. We've done a meticulous search. I handed it over to Ian. He found you through the Internet. You are definitely the one.' He gave her the benefit of his frank, boyish smile. 'No doubt at all, Lorna . . . if I may?'

'But I've never even heard of her.'

'There was a family quarrel years ago, so I understand. But no matter . . . Her will mentions you, her great-nephew's only child.'

'And the details of the will?' Lorna wondered if she dare permit herself the luxury of believing that perhaps it was true, after all.

'Hinton Priory, its contents and grounds are to pass to you entirely, and there is a large cash legacy at present invested which will bring you in a very comfortable, even lavish, income. I can give you the exact amount later when further details have been clarified.'

'Wow!' Lorna exclaimed, her nerves steadying, a dozen possibilities flashing through her mind. A private income, a house of her own, both appearing out of the blue. The kind of situation most people only came across in their wildest fantasies.

Dudley rose, pacing the room thoughtfully, his hands sunk deep in his trouser pockets. Lorna's eyes were riveted to his slim pelvis, which seemed to exaggerate the shape of his manhood pressing against the left side of his fly. He looked up, met her gaze and seemed to read her thoughts. She felt certain the bulge was growing bigger.

'The Priory is very old,' he continued, coming to rest close to her chair, a hand on the back of it, almost touching her hair. She could smell his aftershave, Calvin Klein's *Obsession*. This was a man with expensive tastes.

'I love old buildings,' she murmured, glancing up at him, seeing the sweat beading his upper lip. There was no cooling system like those in American offices. She

49

was instinctively aware of the almost frightening stillness of the aroused male waiting his chance to strike.

With a brief smile, he went on, 'Apparently it's been in the Erskine family for generations, but now it needs a fortune spending on it by way of restoration. Miss Erskine did not live there; she was abroad most of her life, so it has been neglected, I'm afraid.'

'I don't care,' she averred, staring boldly into his brown eyes. 'I'll have the money to do it.'

'I know, Lorna, but there will be complications,' he warned. 'It's a listed building, you see, and plans will have to be approved by the experts who work for English Heritage. They'll be swarming all over the place on a watching brief to keep the work on line. Do you really want the bother? Why not let someone else cope with all this? Have you considered selling?'

'Selling? No. I've not given it a thought.' Somehow the idea was repugnant to her. A property that had belonged to the Erskines for ages should remain in their possession.

He backtracked. 'It's your decision, of course. But I could find a buyer for you.'

'No,' she said firmly, her chin setting in that mulish way which Cassandra recognised. Once Lorna had made up her mind there was no shifting her.

He shrugged his shoulders under that seasonal light fabric, and smiled as if it was of no consequence. 'It's up to you. I suggest that you stay in the gatehouse while repairs to the Priory are being carried out. I have all the keys here. Would you like me to take you there now?'

Lorna got to her feet. 'No, thank you. Cassandra is driving me and I shall stay with her tonight. She lives in Woodmead.'

'I know the Priory,' Cassandra put in, stretching her legs and rising, too. 'It's not far from my cottage.'

'I'll meet you tomorrow, if you like, and take you over your property,' Dudley offered. 'Meanwhile, what about joining me for a spot of lunch? I usually go to the

Haunch of Venison, an old English chop house, built round thirteen something.'

The women exchanged glances and then, 'If Cassandra agrees,' Lorna said.

Cassandra did agree, intrigued by Dudley and anxious to see how much she could wind him up. Just for the moment, she was happy with Marc, but it was wise to have several strings to one's bow.

Ian watched them go, half hidden by the window frame. It was not until he was sure they had entered Dudley's new Almera, heard the engine rev up and saw the sleek red saloon swing out into the street that he reached for his mobile.

Nothing of what he was about to do must be recorded anywhere in the office. It was a secret.

He was excited, but this was not entirely due to the presence of the two beautiful women whose scent seemed to linger in the warm air, desirable and intimidating though they were. The thrill coursing through him, prickling in his cock and knotting in his scrotum, came from another source.

What he felt was an unaccustomed surge of confidence, even a trace of power, sensations he rarely experienced in his day-to-day existence – timorous and lacking in bodily attraction, he found consolation with his computers who never, ever failed him. They could be trusted to obey his commands, never mocking, putting him down, or making him feel inadequate.

Holding the phone in one hand, he cradled his penis in the other. It was comforting, as was the warm, stinging sensation that invaded his buttocks when he thought about the destination of his call.

Would *she* answer the phone?

It was unlikely, though the call would go through to a private, ex-directory line divorced from the customary connections with the rest of the house.

No, *he* would take it, and the heat spread between the dark furrow of Ian's backside, past the puckered nether hole and into his balls. He was being of service. He was doing something important, helpful, necessary, obeying implicitly. Reporting in, as he had been ordered.

They would be pleased with him and he would be amply rewarded. Still holding the receiver in his perspiring hand, he pulled open a drawer and flicked through its untidy contents, finding what he sought at the very bottom of the heap. It was a cutting from a magazine, showing a rather crude drawing of a pair of women's shoes with incredibly high, thin heels. They were red as blood.

Ian shivered, and dialled the number. The conversation was brief. Pocketing the mobile, he let himself out of the office.

On his return late that afternoon, Dudley made sure he was undisturbed and then pressed a sequence of phone digits connecting him with London. A deep voice answered him, and he could imagine his contact seated at a chrome and glass desk in his penthouse office overlooking Chelsea Harbour.

'Dudley here,' he said, and perched on the corner of his own desk, one leg braced on the floor, the other swinging.

'You've met her?' the voice asked crisply.

'Yes.'

'And?'

'She doesn't want to sell, but I'm working on it.'

'Good. What's she like?'

'Beautiful. Independent. A businesswoman.'

'Don't go soft over her. I'd better come down and handle this personally. We've got to clinch it, Norcross. I've a number of bankers and fat-cat businessmen interested.'

'Don't worry, but come if you wish.' Dudley did not want him interfering. The thought of Lorna caused a stirring in his groin and he fondled his phallus through the pocket lining of his trousers, working a finger round the glans.

52

'I will,' said the voice decisively. 'I'll consult my day planner, give you a bell and you can meet me. Goodbye.'

The phone clicked at the other end and Dudley stared gloomily out at the thinning traffic. His cock ached for relief, rubbing against the material. Having lunch with Lorna and her friend had done nothing to ease him. He had sat at table imagining them on their knees between his spread legs, licking his balls and running their fingers over his prick.

Now his longing was all-engulfing. Had Judy been there he would have called her in to suck him off, but she had gone home. He opened his flies and took out his swollen penis, the tip slippery wet between his fingers. And as he worked it with long, practised strokes, he visualised Lorna, her dusky mane of hair falling over him in a perfumed curtain. It was as if her tongue toyed with his, her breath sweet, that woman smell he loved so much rising from her pussy.

Dudley groaned, the overwhelming pressure of spunk surging in his testicles. He dragged his handkerchief out and came into it with a violence that left him shaking.

Chapter Three

Briar Cottage was reached after turning off by the pub on the village green and traversing a rutted, twisty lane.

'The road's OK in summer, but an absolute fucker in the winter,' Cassandra commented as she and Lorna reached the house.

It was a long, low structure with a thatched roof and thick walls. A substantial and prestigious property approached through double gates, beyond which lay lawns and herbaceous borders. Hollyhocks, their colours drenched in sunlight, stood on guard near the oak front door. Cassandra swung the car into a cobbled courtyard at the rear. Music boomed from a barn attached to the stable block.

'Marc's working. Must be getting close to the end, because he's playing *Götterdammerung*. He's crazy about Wagner,' she said, getting out and waving to a sturdy young man going towards the potting shed, a hoe over one shoulder. 'Give us a hand, will you?' she shouted. 'This is Miss Erskine. She's on holiday from the States. Lorna, meet Gary.'

'How do, miss? Let's get those bags out of there, shall we?' he answered, his accent as thick as clotted cream.

He leant the hoe against a wall and strolled towards

them, his pale blue eyes sparkling with obvious delight as they roved over Cassandra's legs and settled, inevitably, at the shadowy area where her thighs met.

A rustic Adonis, Lorna decided, with that easy geniality and the abundant promise of sexual fulfilment in his crotch which must make him the favourite stud of the district. The look he gave her was not difficult to decipher. Bold, admiring, rising to her breasts now with such concentrated interest that she felt her nipples tingle in response.

She recognised his type instantly. She had encountered the same sort of boy since puberty, starting with the assistant groundsmen at the boarding-school she had attended. This one was flaxen-haired and bronzed, well aware of his endowments, ready to whip out his weapon at the slightest opportunity. She had the sudden feeling that Cassandra knew him in the biblical sense, if not now, at some time in the not too distant past.

His clothes were old, Levis and a denim shirt, the sleeves rolled up to the elbows over brown arms coated with light fur. It was almost as if his body despised clothing, preferring to be naked and ready to service any willing female who presented her rump to him

He reached into the boot of the car and lifted out the luggage effortlessly. Lorna wondered briefly how it would be to feel the touch of those calloused hands. Similar, no doubt, to those of other workmen she had seduced. Her mind did a re-run of early episodes in stables, greenhouses, and gamekeepers huts hidden deep in the woods. Her life in America had been almost saintly by comparison.

After carrying her suitcases to the guestroom as easily as if they were matchboxes, Gary left, but not before giving Lorna a final look and raising a brow at her in an impudent question-mark.

She promptly forgot him, engrossed in the house. Cassandra took her on a tour of inspection. Firstly the kitchen, with a green Aga and oak units having cathedral doors and leaded glass cupboards, then the lounge, complete with inglenook fireplace, deep settees and velveteen upholstered armchairs. There were antiques everywhere, Cassandra being rich enough to spoil herself.

Lorna's own room was lovely; a low-ceilinged attic with black beams and dormer windows. It had sloping floorboards and bulging walls papered in rose print. There was a duvet, pillow cases and valance of the same pattern, echoed by the frilled curtains.

'We'll go down to the pub later. Marc will want a drink,' Cassandra said, reclining on the bed, watching as Lorna unpacked her bags, hung her clothes in the cupboard and stashed underwear in the tallboy.

'Is he here all the time?' Lorna was very aware of her, and kept glancing at the top of those smooth thighs where the tattered hem of the shorts drew the eye to her pussy. Sensuality seemed to ooze through Cassandra's pores.

'Mostly, unless there's a lecture tour in the offing. If it's abroad, then I go, too. Can't bear to be parted from him for long. This might well be love I'm feeling.' Cassandra patted the space beside her. 'Sit down, darling. I can't really believe you're here.'

Lorna came over and put her arms round Cassandra, excited by that pliable, yet strong body under her hands. She caught the aroma of French perfume that wafted from between Cassandra's breasts, mingling with her personal odour – sweet, spicy; the oceanic smell of love-juice wetting the gusset of those exceedingly brief cut-offs.

'Is it *Shalimar*?' she asked, taking an appreciative sniff.

'Of course, darling. The traditional perfume for actresses and whores.' Cassandra's hands coasted over Lorna's spine, fingers tracing every knobble, right down to the dimple at the base. 'What do you think of Gary?'

'Yummy,' Lorna answered with a smile, their eyes locking in that intimate understanding generated by years of close friendship. 'Does he come up to expectations?'

'Oh, yes, if one's in the mood for a simple shag. I expect a full recital, in detail, of the men you've screwed since we last met. I'll bet there've been dozens. And I want to know about Nicole. But now, what about a swim?' Cassandra suggested, her eyes exerting their customary magnetic pull. 'Let's go skinny-dipping, like we used to at uni. Do you remember?'

'Could I ever forget?' Lorna whispered.

Golden boys and girls, novices at sex but avid to learn. Older people, too, dons and professors, some satisfactory, others not. Cassandra and herself, experimenting, trying this one and that but always finding the greatest delight with each other, sure there would be no disappointment.

They undressed quickly and compared notes. Neither had put on weight, but, 'You've shaved!' Lorna exclaimed.

She was struck by that brazen display. Cassandra's pubis stood out prominently, denuded of hair. This revealed the cleft, high and sharply defined, offering itself to Lorna's gaze almost defiantly.

'I don't use a razor, darling ... much too harsh. I wax it,' she declared, arching her spine and thrusting her sex forward invitingly. 'Would you like me to do yours?'

'No, thank you,' Lorna answered, smiling as she admired her friend, the exposed slit so attractive that she yearned to finger it.

She herself was lithe and agile, her dark hair glinting with flashes of gold, matching the thicket that hid her female secrets. Cassandra possessed an enviable, seamless tan, her breasts larger and more rounded, waist slightly wider and hips fuller.

She went to the armoire and took out two brightly patterned Indian skirts, winding one round herself, sarong-fashion, and handing the other to Lorna. Then barefoot, they padded down to the oblong pool.

The air was balmy, the sunset-edged clouds of evening casting their indigo veil over the sky. The submerged

57

lights rendered the water deep azure, reflecting off the ceramic lining.

The pool was bordered with terracotta pots from which brilliantly coloured geraniums cascaded, the whole area made private by an old stone wall draped in ivy and toad-flax. Cushioned loungers, deckchairs, small rattan tables and huge striped umbrellas were positioned on the ochre paving slabs ringing the poolside.

Cassandra peeled off the single garment and walked down the half-moon series of steps at the shallow end, her calves, knees and finally the juncture of her thighs covered by the gently rippling water.

'It's delicious,' she cried, sitting on the lowest step, the wavelets creeping into her secret places and stimulating her coppery nipples. 'Warmed by the sun all day ... Couldn't be better. I adore the summer!'

'This certainly beats steamy old New York,' Lorna said, dropping her sarong and joining her, adding, 'We look like a couple of ladies from one of Alma-Tadema's paintings, very Victorian and lush.'

'I know what you mean. *The Tepidarium*, perhaps. I love my house, and this dreamy garden,' Cassandra went on, resting back on her elbows. Her gleaming brown legs moved under the water, darker still in the twilight glow, tangling with Lorna's paler ones, a foot sliding sensuously over the arch of Laura's own.

'It's lovely,' she agreed, aroused by the touch,

'I feel so close to the Mother Goddess. Do you remember how we belonged to Wicca? I'm still an advocate. Have you continued, or dropped out?'

'There hasn't been much time to think about it,' Lorna confessed. 'But I've not forgotten what you taught me.'

Cassandra had sparked off her interest in folklore and legend, opening her eyes to the possibility of truth behind the earlier religions, when a female deity ruled supreme. How much of it had been a sincere belief and how much Cassandra's fervent feminism at the time, Lorna had never been quite sure.

'Did you know there's a spring on your land?' Cassandra asked suddenly, a wet hand fondling Lorna's bare shoulder. 'Legend has it that it's a holy well.'

'Oh? That's interesting,' Lorna said, sensations tingling through her body, every nerve attuned to the clear, unmistakable message in Cassandra's fingers.

'Not many people know where it is, but I do.' Those slender digits tightened and Cassandra's eyes shone as she continued. 'It's under a ruined temple in the grounds. At a glance you might think it's no older than the eighteenth century, a folly or somesuch, but I think it's Roman and this makes sense. The Romans usually built their places of worship over earlier sites with mystic connotations – Druidic groves or Stone Age megaliths.'

'So, I've a magic spring as well as a house and a fortune? Nicole will be over the moon.' Lorna freed her hand, then lay down, her head supported by the step, relishing that cool embrace.

From somewhere behind them, the notes of a flute stole through the evening air, a lingering, plaintive tune and spine-chilling chordophonic harmonies. Lorna could feel her core tightening, a prickle starting under her skin, running up her vertebrae to her cortex. Her thighs shivered and her nipples clenched, and it was nothing to do with cold. The sheer poetry of the music was turning her on almost unbearably.

'Debussy's *Syrinx*,' Cassandra murmured in her husky, smoky voice, leaning on one elbow and watching her intently as she parted her own legs a little. 'I never thought I'd find a man who'd like my type of music, but Marc does.'

Lorna's hands sank slowly through the water, skimming over the curves of her own breasts, the nipples rousing. Eyes closed, lost in the sounds, she remembered with perfect clarity the heat that had flowed through her body when the Englishman's fingers walked down her belly to connect with her clitoris, and the exciting scene that had followed.

'Just to think of Marc makes me incredibly horny,'

Cassandra purred. 'It's hours since I had him. He doesn't like me interrupting him when he's working.'

Lorna backed against the steps, arms and legs widespread, and Cassandra leant over her and kissed her deeply in a well-remembered way. No one had ever kissed her quite like Cassandra, whose tongue now traced over her lips, then explored all the caverns and hollows of her mouth, gums and teeth. It was a thorough kiss, a lascivious, exciting kiss – a kiss for which she had unconsciously been thirsting.

She could feel those taut nipples rubbing against her own, a twin dance of delight, and that gorgeous, hairless mons lightly touching her hip. The water sloshed round them, little trickling fingers creeping into their vaginas, mingling with their own essences, even as their limbs twined round each other.

Lorna caressed Cassandra a shoulders and arms, the line of her throat, the swell of her chest, and those dark areolae spreading like sunbursts around the puckered nipples. Cassandra's active pubis ground against her, but her fingers were as skilled as her lips. Reaching down through the shining water, they burrowed through Lorna's maidenhair and homed in on the hidden treasure between the velvety petals.

Lorna's clitoris swelled beneath that tender stroke, its erection like a bud about to burst into flower. Cassandra's lips gently moved over her face, and her eyes glowed like amethysts in the gathering dusk.

'You want it so much?' she whispered, her breath a warm zephyr spiced with cinnamon.

'Yes. Please give it to me,' Lorna moaned, enthralled by her own response to this friend, this sister and lover.

There was no need for further speech. Cassandra knew exactly how to pleasure her, as if she was doing it to herself. Even the water between them became a caress. Cassandra took one of Lorna's nipples in her lips and provoked it with the tip of her tongue till it was double its size.

Then Lorna felt Cassandra's fingers nudging her

entrance, sliding inside, while her thumb rubbed persistently at the engorged nub crowning her avenue. She ground herself on those knowing digits, pleasure burgeoning to an intense peak, orgasm roaring through her like a furnace.

'You're late. Where've you been? Sniffing round some woman, I suppose,' shouted the petite, redheaded girl, hands on her rounded hips, legs apart in her denim mini-skirt and small feet in espadrilles planted firmly on the mat. Her fleshy thighs were bare almost to the apex, displaying a V-shaped flash of white panties.

'Working,' answered the young man who was the subject of this tirade. 'You always think I'm off with a woman somewhere.'

'Well? Aren't you? Don't try to kid me you don't shag everything with a pulse, Gary Curtis.'

The early evening sunshine poured through the windows of Alison Cooper's little tied house which was part of the deal for her work at the vicarage.

He sidled up to her, and insinuated an arm round her tiny waist that contrasted so excitingly with those top-heavy breasts. 'You've got it all wrong,' he protested, his large hand reaching round to pat her bottom, attempting to wedge a finger in the crease covered by the lycra gusset.

Her knickers had slid up between the cheeks of her behind, gathering in the crack and stretching over her mons. Wisps of pubic hair protruded from the sides. These were brown, giving the lie to the hennaed locks crowning her head.

'Get away!' Alison snapped, though her nipples were already stiffening at his touch, needing to feel his wet lips fastening on them and sucking strongly in that wonderful way he had.

She had sampled other men, but no one pleased her as much as Gary. He was a virile young animal at the peak of his prowess; a farmer's son, uncomplicated and earthy, his nut-brown skin tanned by wind and weather.

Stocky, broad-shouldered, wearing tight stone-washed jeans faded to white over his muscular thighs, only he could assuage the love-hunger that flowed like a turgid river through her own ripe and healthy body.

'Aw, Allie love. You don't mean that,' he pleaded, taking no notice of her and simply hauling her close to his chest again. His shirt was open, a pale gold pelt glinting between the gap. 'I'm sorry I kept you waiting, but Miss Ashley got back with that friend of hers from America and wanted me to help with the luggage.'

'Why you? Where was Mr Orman?' Gary was not being quite truthful and she knew it.

'Dunno. Busy hacking at stone, I expect. He's given me a couple of tickets for a gig at the Salisbury Arts Centre. Want to come?'

She ignored this sop, rigid again, instantly suspicious. 'What's she like, this American tart?' she demanded.

Cassandra Ashley was a thorn in her side; too glamorous by far, and rich as well. Alison had been relieved when the sculptor hoved on the scene, eclipsing Gary, who worked at Briar Cottage as gardener and handyman: far too handy with Cassandra, in Alison's opinion.

'All right, I suppose.' Gary was non-commital, so engrossed in persuading her to open her legs that he could not be bothered about anything else.

'Pretty?' She was still guarded, jealousy gnawing at her gut.

'So-so.' He drew her towards the old settee that stood in front of the television in her living-room, scene of many a lubricious mating. 'She talks a bit like a Yank, but I think she's really English, from what they were saying, anyway.'

'Tell me about her.' Alison put her hand over his, stopping any further invasion of privacy, though her sex ached and her other hand edged almost involuntarily towards that plump swelling concealed by the denim at his crotch.

That particular spot was more faded than the rest, worn by the continual pressure of the thick rod behind it and Gary's constant use of the fly. The buttons had indented the fabric. She visualised his fingers undoing them – dressing, undressing – for urination and copulation.

He eased closer to her, one arm across her shoulders, the other palm acting as a support for one of her large, soft breasts. 'Nothing to tell,' he said, his face a picture of innocence. 'Didn't take all that much notice of her.'

'Liar,' she protested, but could feel herself melting, ripening like a peach. She wanted only to be devoured, her vagina yearning to have him licking at it, plunging into it, then stretching and filling her with his generous shaft.

He undid her blouse and lifted her breast up and out of the white bra she wore beneath, the nipple rising like a delectable strawberry above the lacy edge. He lowered his head and his lips fastened round it, tongue and teeth teasing and tormenting. He sucked feverishly for a second and she shivered with need.

Her thighs fell open and Gary lifted his head and smiled into her eyes, tweaking that sensitive tip with his work-roughened fingers. The power-pack in his jeans was ready, nudging against the buttons, seeking release from confinement.

'Why should I notice what other girls are like when I've got you?' he whispered with practised flattery.

'Oh, Gary, you're such a bugger,' she sighed, already relenting, never able to resist the promise of his mighty member, and those artful fingers that knew exactly how to wring the last iota of pleasure from her clitoris.

'But you love me, don't you?' He pressed home his advantage, rubbing a finger across the wet briefs still tucked up between her secret lips. They swelled each side of it, moisture glistening on the hairy fringe.

'Do I? Suppose I must do to put up with you,' she sparked, though her breath was shortening.

As he ran his fingers across the contours of her mons and settled on the hard bud rearing from its folds, Alison felt her trickle of nectar become a flood. She submitted, to his desire and hers, lying back and accepting.

Watching as he unbuckled his leather belt, she anticipated the magical moment when he would lift out his weapon, that generous member, thick and long. Upward-curved and smooth-skinned, it was the only part of him which was not sun-tanned. Even his firm, high, muscular buttocks were exposed when he swam in the river, and lazed on the bank afterwards.

He delayed deliberately, till at last she said impatiently, 'Get it out. Go on. Show me.'

'Ask nicely,' he commanded, slipping down her panties, his fingers finding the cowl of her clitoris and sliding it backwards and forwards till she arched her pubis higher, unable to resist rubbing against that tantalising friction.

'Please, Gary,' she cried as his finger moved faster and she knew she was approaching orgasm, needing him to fill her as soon as she came, giving her something to grind against.

He reached into his fly and produced it for her inspection, working his fingers over its bulbous end, already sticky with pre-come. Reaching out and touching it, her hand moved alongside his to make it even larger and more powerful. His jeans slipped down below his hips, and he lowered himself between her thighs, his stiff penis touching her pubic bone, before working between to hover at the entrance to her vagina.

The settee creaked protestingly beneath their combined weights and he suddenly rolled off and urged her to the carpet, placing a cushion under her head and wedging another beneath her buttocks. Her skirt was up round her waist, her panties a crumpled scrap by the sofa leg. Her mons arched high, thighs splayed on either side, salmon pink labia wide open and greedy clitoris a swollen pearl, vulnerable and needy.

Gary positioned himself between her legs, his arms reaching upwards. A hand settled on each of her breasts, fingers pinching and rolling, rubbing and tickling her nipples. Her head dropped back, eyes closed, her breath coming in thick, short gasps. The sensation in her nipples was firing straight down to her clit. The scent from her parted love-lips was so strong it seemed to hang over them like a mist.

Gary's tongue descended on her bud, circling round its stalk to trace its root right back to where it conjoined her pubic bone, every movement causing her shock-waves of pleasure. Then he flicked the head, made it ache, retreated, advanced, took it between his lips and tongued it vigorously. Alison felt great bubbles of air rising in her throat as she screamed out her climax, a firework display lighting up her entire being.

Then he was inside her, and she wrapped her legs round his waist and crossed them at the ankles. His frantic thrusts pierced her profoundly. She felt herself skewered on him like a butterfly pinned to a display-board. Ecstasy pounded through her as his rough strokes built in a crescendo. She beat on his back with her fists, hardly able to breathe, as he convulsed in the final throes of orgasm, falling on to her and sighing her name into her hair.

Later, they lay and shared a cigarette, while the Star of Eve peeped in at the window, bats skittered and swooped between the trees and an owl hooted some-where deep in the woods.

'How come you don't mind what happens up at the vicarage? You're not jealous, then?' Gary enquired, shift-ing her over so that her head was pillowed on his shoulder.

'Ah, well, that's different,' she answered, her hand still holding his prick as if it was a talisman against evil. 'That's work, isn't it? Part and parcel of the job, and I goes there more than you.'

Gary digested this and made no further comment. Alison decided to leave it at that; the goings-on at the vicarage, a manse no longer but an exclusive hotel, were divorced from normal life, so strange as to appear dreamlike. What she did there, and sometimes Gary, too, had no relevance to their daily routine.

A shiver ran through her from her toes to her core, breasts and brain as she remembered, and wondered and desired.

The White Hart was a popular watering-hole, noted for the excellence of its ale. It had stood, solid as an English oak, on the foundations laid in the Middle-Ages. It was then that an enterprising and hard-up housewife with the bailiff on her back had hung her besom outside the door to denote it was now a hostelry, open to all comers, provided they could pay.

It had changed down the centuries, but retained many of its original features. When Lorna first walked in she pictured Nicole's face if she were ever to come over and they visited there. She would declare it to be 'so old', unable to credit it had been an inn for six hundred years.

'I'll get the drinks,' Marc offered.

He moved towards the bar, loose-hipped and bulky. His aura was a powerful one. Now in his middle years he had travelled far and seen the underside of life, projecting a world-weary, cynical ambience. He was also extremely sexy, a bull of a man.

His progress was followed by a dozen pairs of lusting female eyes. His presence in the village had set hearts fluttering and supplied a wealth of masturbation fantasies.

'You're lady of the manor now,' he said to Lorna when he returned, setting down his pint and two glasses of wine. 'Will you take us on a tour of the stately home?'

A girl came over to clear the empty table next to theirs. She was a generously bosomed redhead, and Cassandra said, 'Hello, Alison. Are you on duty tonight?'

'Yes, Miss Ashley,' she answered, looking daggers at her.

'This is my friend from New York, Lorna Erskine,'

'Hello, miss,' Alison responded with a curt nod.

The animosity in her eyes was puzzling, for they had

66

not met before and Lorna wondered why she was so brusque. Alison picked up the loaded tray and went back to her post behind the bar.

Cassandra grimaced. 'I think she's pissed off with me because of Gary,' she said. 'All right, so I did have a thing with him once, but that was a long time ago.'

'She's got a good body. Maybe she'd pose for me,' Marc countered, rubbing his chin thoughtfully.

'I'm sure she would. Gary says she'll take off her clothes for anyone,' Cassandra retorted a touch acidly.

He gave a rumble of laughter and hugged her to his chest. 'Don't worry. I'm only interested in her as a model.'

The flash of jealousy Cassandra displayed was unusual, and Lorna could see that she was extremely fond of Marc. She found him interesting herself, but he was Cassandra's and, as such, sacrosanct. Lorna had no intention of breaking the eleventh commandment: Thou Shalt Not Hurt Another Woman.

'Good God! Look what the cat's brought in!' Cassandra said, her expression tight, even hostile, her eyes fixed on the door.

A man had just entered and as Lorna glanced across her jaw dropped, aware of tension in the air, hot, heavy and thick. She caught a distinct whiff of danger, prickles running all down her spine.

He was distinguished and aristocratic-looking. In his late thirties, tall and spare with a deep tan, he had good shoulders and lean hips. His jeans were tight, looking as though they were sprayed on, and his soft cotton shirt had come from an expensive fashion house. His dark hair was winged with silver at the temples, and swept back into a queue confined with a black leather thong.

His grey eyes pierced hers, transmitting a wave of louche sensuality that invaded her, body and soul, and flashed like an arrow from her G-spot to her mind. A chill rustled over her skin. She was gripped by over-whelming, gut-wrenching lust.

He came across the bar towards her, and she was

thankful that she had dressed up for the occasion in a pale floral chiffon slip dress, moss-green silk jacket and high-heeled mules. She was bare-legged, bare-armed, bare of jewels, briefs or bra, the night too hot for underpinning.

His chiselled lips parted over even white teeth as he smiled round the table. 'Hello, Cassie ... Marc. May I join you?' His eyes returned to Lorna.

'Sit down,' Cassandra replied ungraciously, adding, 'this is my friend, Lorna Erskine, just arrived from America. Lorna, let me introduce Ryder Tyrell.'

'I'm very pleased to meet you,' he said, subjecting her to his deep, hypnotic smile. 'Are you staying long?'

'I've not yet made up my mind.' God, but he's handsome, she was thinking. He'd blow Nicole's mind.

'She now owns Hinton Priory,' Cassandra informed him sharply, and Lorna was surprised by the metallic tone in her usually honeyed voice.

'Really? Then we shall be neighbours. My partner and I bought the vicarage two years ago and turned it into a hotel. It was rebuilt by a rich squire in the time of George III, though some of it is much older, dating from Tudor times.'

He leant closer, and Lorna felt uncomfortably warm, the sweat trickling down her ribs from under her breasts. She could feel a single drop lengthening and advancing into her navel, across her lower belly, joining the dampness in her pubic hair.

'I've inherited the Priory from a great-aunt. Miss Winifred Erskine. Might you have known her? The lawyer says she wasn't in this country much, but you may have caught a glimpse.' She was fighting to remain logical and controlled but was finding it increasingly difficult under the assault of his powerful attraction.

'I'm afraid not.' He shook his head and lifted his glass, the local brew dark and frothy within. Its peaty smell lingered on his breath.

'That's a pity. I want to know more about the house,

too. Perhaps I'll be able to consult the county records office; that's bound to contain documents.'

'The Salisbury Diocesan archives may hold more,' he added helpfully.

'That's right. Thank you for suggesting it.' She was impatient to view the Priory and learn more about the Erskines, feeling the pull of an ancestry she had never before considered important.

Now, suddenly, she was a part of Woodmead and its history. Within her ovaries she carried the genes of people long dead, who had been born, loved and lived around here. It was as if she could reach out and grasp that cord of continuity, suddenly beguiled by the strange pattern of destiny that seemed to be emerging before her. If she had children, they, too, would be a part of it. No matter what Dudley Norcross said, nothing would induce her to sell the property.

'I'll see what I can find in my library,' Ryder said, the hard muscles of his thigh burning hot as he pressed it against hers on the bench they shared. 'History fascinates me and I've many books.'

Lorna glanced towards his lap. His penis was resting between his legs under the denim. Her fingers itched to pull down the zip and take the stalk of it in her hand. She could feel wetness soaking the matted curls of her bush, her internal tides flowing.

'I suppose, being a local, you've heard of the holy well?' Cassandra broke in, her eyes never leaving him. They shone purple in the artificial light, holding an unaccustomed belligerence.

He shrugged and gave her a steely look in return. 'Hardly a local. One has to be here at least a hundred years to be accepted, doesn't one? As far as I can see the whole area is full of such skories. Ley-lines, UFO sightings, crop circles, the henges. Wiltshire is riddled with myths.'

'Don't forget devil worship and covens,' Cassandra added, and she was serious.

'I'm always cautious and cover my back,' Ryder

rejoined, giving Lorna a sideways smile as if taking her into his confidence and making her party to a deep, enigmatic secret.

'Sounds far-fetched,' said Marc, with a grimace directed at Lorna. 'But I've always been a sucker for horror movies.'

'The well is best viewed at dawn or by moonlight.' Cassandra cast Marc a worried glance, winding her fingers in his hair as a child will when uncertain, leaning against his chest as if needing the protection of his strong arms.

For some inexplicable reason, Lorna did not want a crowd around her on her first visit to the spring. 'Not tonight,' she said. 'I'm tired. Jet-lagged. I need to sleep.'

'Very wise. I'll say goodbye now,' Ryder murmured, rising and lifting her hand to his lips. His mouth hovered just above her palm, his breath stippling her skin. 'Would you care to come to dinner with Sybil and me one evening soon?'

'Sybil?' Was he married? Lorna wondered. He didn't look the marrying type.

'My business partner. The vicarage is our home as well as our livelihood. She'll enjoy meeting you. I could show you my books. Perhaps you might find a reference to Hinton Priory.'

'Thank you. I'd very much like to come,' she answered.

'I'll phone and fix a time.'

'That will be fine.'

What am I letting myself in for? she wondered. Even as she accepted, Lorna was considering the possibilities. Yet the lure of books was irresistible. Not only that. It was as if he was challenging her, and she never had been able to resist a challenge.

Alison sped along the path through the woods. The inky gloom was punctuated by patches of moonlight lying like silver discs on the forest floor.

Many girls would have been scared, but she had lived

70

in the country all her life and would have found darkened city streets more alarming. It was past midnight, and her stint at the pub was over. Now she could shed the rôle of barmaid and become somebody else – who, she was not quite sure. She only knew that at times like this she could give full rein to a part of her far removed from Alison Cooper, a being that only the master had recognised lurking in her depths – recognised and brought to the surface.

He was expecting her, had summoned her as he left the White Hart. She had watched him talking to the American woman, resentment burning like a brand in her breast. Lorna. That was what Cassandra had called her. Alison envied their dress-sense, sophistication and confidence, though the mistress possessed the same poise and she was not jealous of her.

And that big, handsome man, Marc Orman. Alison had seen him on the television. It had not seemed fair that she should be pulling pints, rinsing glasses and putting up with crude cracks from the punters while those two women sat in the lounge bar with a celebrity like him.

Gary had not been straightforward about them. She knew for a fact he had slept with Cassandra, and had recognised the look in his eyes when he mentioned Lorna, panting like a dog after a bitch on heat. But the crowning insult had come when *he* walked in, making straight for Lorna. Even he wanted her, it seemed. Ryder Tyrell, Alison's employer, teacher and master.

Yet he had left alone, driving off in the direction of the vicarage. Alison had finished up after the landlord had called time, emptied ashtrays, wiped over table-tops, stacked clean glasses, and then shouted a cheery goodnight, before following him on foot.

It was not far if you took the shortcut through the woods, and soon she came to the high wall skirting the vicarage grounds. The tops glittered like diamonds, the moon's rays reflected off jagged broken glass cemented on the copings.

The drive was bordered by elms, beeches and walnut that hid the outer world with a shivering, rustling barrier. The lawn beyond shone under the stark blue-white light, the monkey puzzle tree casting weird shadows. The upper windows of the huge old manse glowed orange. Alison had a key, and let herself in at the back door.

The house was sunk in sleep and silence. There was no sign of life in the kitchen or hall as she slipped through. Two Herculean figures acted as newel posts for the great staircase which, instead of banisters, had long gilded beasts who slunk up to the first-floor landing. Her feet made no sound on the thick burgundy carpet.

The air was perfumed with incense which thickened when Alison reached the private apartment. She paused before the double mahogany doors, so high and ornate they might have been the portals of a tomb. Excitement knotted her stomach and sent a spasm shooting through her vaginal walls. Her buttocks started to sting, her blushing skin remembering other visits.

She was aroused, wet, engorged nipples jagging deliciously against the fibres of her dress. Sound swelled from the room behind the closed door – a sombre composition by Messiaen, a toccata for church organ. The chords vibrated under Alison's feet, juddered up her legs and into her core. She did not appreciate classical music, but was stirred nonetheless, associating these powerful sounds with the master.

She opened the door a crack and eased round it. The dimness was alleviated by the star-spears of candles, dozens of them, standing on the overmantel, on chests, tables and shelves. The room was vast, draped in sump-tuous velvets.

It reminded her of the interior of a church, with carvings, paintings and statues, the blue clouds of scented smoke swirling up to the panelled ceiling, the colour and emotional potency of the music adding to the impression of solemnity.

And the sombrely curtained, towering bed was the master's altar.

Everything was larger than life: gargantuan furniture, tapestries of hunting scenes, and figures of naked nymphs fleeing from goat-legged, horned satyrs sporting enormous phalluses. Peculiar foreign idols and strange Egyptian grave-ornaments mingled with artefacts from India, Greece and Turkey. On an easel stood a painting of a woman making love to a snake.

Alison recalled being frightened the first time she was invited there. Now the trappings served to whip up a frenzy of excitement, desire sending tongues of flame shooting through her loins.

He was there, standing spread-legged before the great fireplace, regal and beautiful to look at in his silk robe embroidered all over with Eastern designs. She could see the line of his penis pressing against the brocade, and feasted her eyes on him adoringly, mesmerised by the implement he held between his narrow hands.

He did not move, keeping her waiting till the music ended in a crescendo that rocked the room, then, 'Make obeisance, slave. What is your excuse for being late?' he said sternly, looking at her with a strange intensity. The crisp articulation of his voice made her gasp with longing.

She immediately fell to the floor, the carpet chafing her bare knees, her trembling hands clasped to her breasts. Her eyes were cast down, studying the floral pattern. She never dared to raise them to his face, much as she longed to gloat over those wide cheekbones and sensual mouth. Dampness oozed from between her love-lips, soaking the gusset of her panties.

'Forgive me. I couldn't get away from the pub,' she whimpered.

A minute passed, and her nerves were taut as bowstrings. Would he lavish a blow or a caress on her? The uncertainty kept her on a hook which seemed to pass through her entrails. Then she heard him move as he said, 'Come closer.'

She went down on hands and knees, bottom raised high, her skirt riding up to display her tiny knickers, no more than a strip of material trapped between her nether lips. She crawled across the carpet to his feet and, without waiting to be told, placed her lips on his bare instep, kissing it abjectly.

The hem of his robe brushed her face, and his legs rose above her like pillars. She ached to stare up at the solid mass of his balls and cock hanging over her. Unable to resist, she sat back on her heels, then slid her hands towards his thighs. A sharp rebuke froze her. A shiver of anticipation ran through her cunt and buttocks.

'No touching till you're told,' he said softly, more in sorrow than anger, as if lecturing a recalcitrant child. The cane he held tapped her across the shoulders. 'Take your clothes off. Head down, now. Don't look at me.'

It was a matter of seconds for Alison to peel off dress and bra and drop her knickers. Then she stood before him, face turned aside as she raised her arms and placed her locked hands on her head, gazing at the carpet. Her breasts pointed towards him as if inviting his touch. She felt him come nearer, smelled his hair and cologne and sweat, and the smoky undertone of ale.

He paced round her with measured tread, his robe rustling. Then he paused, saying thoughtfully, 'Have you been good today?'

'Yes,' she whispered, her throat constricting.

'Yes what?' he cracked, changing from gentleness to anger. The cane flicked over her quivering thigh.

'Yes, master.' She had learnt not to yelp.

'That's better.' She felt his hand running over the mark, soothing it, a cool hand after the heat engendered by the cane.

'But you've been having sex, haven't you?' He seized her wrists suddenly, wrenching them down from their position on her head. 'Having carnal knowledge of Gary. Isn't that so?'

'Yes, master.' She shook in his grasp, but her body

leant into him, pressed against the solid bar of flesh in his groin.

'Did he bring you to orgasm? Did you enjoy it?'

'Yes, master. I did.'

'I shall have to punish you,' he said, and took up a length of thick twisted cord. He fastened her wrists securely, then bent her over and tethered her tightly to the bed-post, naked backside lifted towards him. 'Tell me you want to be punished.'

'I do,' she moaned, pressing her forehead against the smoothness of the polished wood.

'Say it louder.'

'I want you to punish me, master.'

Intense desire flowed through her as she felt his hands moving over her buttocks. She strained and lifted her hips against him, opening her legs, searching for that finger she needed so desperately to probe into her forbidden hole, or plunge into her love-nest.

'Say it,' he said evenly.

'I want you,' she implored. 'Please, master. I'll do anything.'

'Anything?'

'Yes.'

His knuckles brushed the mound of her sex, dividing the two plump wings, and he pinched her clit-head between thumb and forefinger. She moaned her pleasure, almost climaxing with the intensity of feeling. His sudden abandonment of her bud left her in mid-air.

The cane hissed, cutting through the stillness. He brought it down on her tender skin, the pain a searing brand. She bit down on her lip, stifling a cry. Again his fingers found her clitoris with laser-beam precision, bringing her to the edge without relief, his other hand massaging the undersides of her breasts.

He lashed her again, a white-hot sting that left a scarlet welt in its wake. His arm rose and fell thrice more, and now the sensations were blurred as he caressed her aching nub. She could not tell where pain stopped and pleasure began.

'I want you to do something for me.' His voice reached her as if from a great distance. 'Will you do anything I ask?'

'Yes,' she whimpered, every sense concentrating on the burning sensations on her behind and the heat gathering between her legs, her mind in an agonised fret lest he leave her unsatisfied.

'Spy on Lorna Erskine,' he commanded, and implemented his order with another stroke of the switch. 'Report back to me.'

'Yes, master,' she said on a strangled sob, and could feel his breath cooling her welts, and the smoothness of balm being worked into the smarting flesh.

He released her and she fell into his arms. He carried her to the side of the bed and laid her, face down. He continued his ministrations, massaging her waist, her back and under her armpits to her breasts, the nipples rising to welcome those agile fingers. She dared to glance over her shoulder.

His mouth was tense, his grey eyes glinting, and she saw him drop his hand to his girdle and open the robe. He was naked beneath, penis at full surge. With his hands under her hips, he shifted her to the edge of the mattress. Her legs dangled, the backs of her thighs and reddened bottom raised high. She felt the brush of his chest hair against her back, and his hands cupping her breasts from underneath, kneading the full orbs and fondling the distended teats.

Growling, low in his throat, he eased himself against her and rubbed his phallus up and down, then reached between her legs and smeared her nectar across the dark crease between her bottom. A slippery finger eased its way into the tight, puckered moue of her anus.

Alison wriggled her pubis against the sheet, seeking friction for her rampant kernel, fearful that he would forbid her to climax. In her anxiety, she reached down and found her pleasure point, her finger sliding rapidly into her cleft and spreading the wetness over the pulsating, wanting clitoris.

76

Rubbing herself frantically, she came in a quick, incandescent spasm, and his cock plunged into her rectum with a force she was not prepared for, exploding in rapid-fire action. He quickly slid his fingers into her other opening, and Alison received them gratefully, the painful weals on her rump augmenting the feverish pleasure rolling through her innermost depths.

'Don't forget,' he whispered, his teeth nibbling at the back of her neck. 'I want to know everything Lorna Erskine does. Where she goes, who she fucks ... everything. Do you hear me?'

'Yes, master,' she sighed, bottom pressing against the black wire coating his underbelly, hoping for a repeat performance, never able to get enough of him.

He pushed her away and stood up. 'Go now,' he said.

She scrambled to her feet, grabbed up her clothes and made for the door. As it closed behind her, music burst forth within the room, the emotions it expressed ecstatic, violent and strange.

Alison did not begin to understand – any more than she did the obsessive passion that possessed her and made her the master's slave.

Chapter Four

*I*t stood neglected but still elegant within its ring of high stone walls and tangled undergrowth. Hinton Priory rested on foundations laid by monks in the thirteenth century, yet was older still by far, its tentacles rooted firmly on the site of an even more ancient cult.

The stone that forged its walls came from a nearby quarry, the beams of its roof fashioned from oak. It kept its secrets and bided its time. Owners might come and go; there could be wars, feuds, conflict, bloodshed, yet the Priory remained inviolate, as it always had and always would.

Lorna stood before its solid front door, stared up at the massive façade and was instantly aware of a presence so old and wise and immovable that her scalp prickled.

It was a hot summer morning. Birds carolled a hymn to the sun, pollen-dusted bees caressed the stamens of wild flowers, and butterflies flirted wantonly, intoxicated by the odour of buddleia. Yet Lorna was chilled to the marrow. Not with fear, but with race memories, recognition and acceptance. The house welcomed her like a lover of long standing: tolerant; uncritical; taking her for what she was, warts and all.

It's my ancestral home, she thought. Every stick and

stone, every blade of grass, every acre of land belongs to me. Or rather, *I* belong to it.

She was puzzled as to why her father had never mentioned the manor, but her parents had divorced when she was five. It had not been one of those trendy separations where both parties behave in a friendly manner, but an acrimonious upheaval during which the child Lorna had lost contact with him. Later he had died in a climbing accident, and her mother had finally succumbed to a fatal illness brought about by alcohol abuse.

Lorna wondered about that long-ago quarrel among the Erskines, the effects of which had been so far-reaching. Now by some curious quirk of fate the estate had come to her, the only remaining claimant.

'Impressive, what?' drawled a voice at her side. 'Of course, it's going to cost a mint to put it right, besides all the hassle with the authorities. I'm surprised you want the bother of it, Lorna.'

'No problem. I'll have the money, and will be proud to liaise with the English Heritage experts,' she answered crisply, and started to mount the shallow, crumbling steps. Clumps of cushiony green moss sprouted in the cracks, and two weatherbeaten stone lions with licheny heads stood on guard.

Dudley shrugged his shoulders under the poplin shirt and silver-grey Pierre Cardin jacket. 'It's your choice,' he conceded, his mouth taking on a petulant slant. 'Far be it for me to stand in your way.'

She found it hard to focus on his words, though she was aware of a subtext beneath them. The Priory demanded her attention, a powerful force despite the widespread destruction. The graceful tracery intersecting the lofty mullioned windows was broken, and the fantastic stone pinnacles and carved coping to the gable ends were falling to pieces. Even the gargoyles leering from gutterings had a drunken, disreputable look. It was a solitary place of creeper-covered walls and breast-high weeds, vast, mazelike and enchanting.

The front door was securely fastened and Dudley produced a bunch of rusty keys from his briefcase.

'You've been in already?' She knew he had before he answered. It was as if the house whispered to her of an intruder.

'As Miss Winifred Erskine's executor, it was my job to make sure the place was still standing.'

'May I unlock it?' It was a demand more than a request.

He handed over the largest key reluctantly, saying, 'If you must, but it's heavy and hard to turn.'

Not for me, she thought, passing under the portico and slipping the key into the elaborately chased escutcheon. She heard the tumblers fall, turned it once more and the mechanism rolled into place. The door creaked on iron hinges, and the smell of the Priory infiltrated her nostrils. It was a highly individual potpourri, comprised of age, dust and seasoned wood.

Dudley was at her heels. She had been tinglingly conscious that he wanted to touch her ever since he had called for her at Briar Cottage. Cassandra and Marc were still in bed after a late session during which Lorna had sunk two bottles of Chardonnay with them. When her head finally hit the pillow she had fallen into a dreamless sleep.

Awaking refreshed, her energies at full tilt, she had made Dudley instant coffee and sat with him on the patio in the glory of a morning that had dawned blue and cloudless. It was the sort of day only found in England, where the ghost of a sickle moon would ride high throughout, and the warm breeze was aromatic with new-mown grass.

Now, in her highly-strung state, she could feel her blood running hot and looked over her shoulder at Dudley speculatively. Should she have sex with him, or would it lead him to imagine he had some hold over her? This was a keen young man. Keen on *her*, or was there a hidden agenda? Probably. It was best to wait and see what happened.

The hall was shrouded in an even deeper silence, almost a vacuum. The dusky darkness was broken by a single ray of light falling through a jagged hole high up in the hammer-beamed ceiling. Suits of armour lurked in corners, their eyeless helmets turned towards the strangers. Rusted weapons hung on the panelled walls between ragged flags and crossed pikes. Lorna felt herself coming under the cold scrutiny of deceased Erskines staring down from painted canvasses in elaborate gilt frames.

'You see what I mean?' Dudley said smugly as they passed beneath an arch into a lofty reception room. Much of the plaster lay in chunks on the filthy carpet and a section of the floor had collapsed to form a crater that had to be negotiated with care.

'Nothing that can't be put right,' she replied airily, resenting his patronising manner.

'It's entirely up to you, Lorna,' he said smoothly, flicking dust from his immaculate trousers. 'This is undoubtedly a Grade One listed building and, as I've said, there will be a barrage of time-consuming permissions to negotiate. It could take months to get started. You don't know what snags you'll come up against. Dry rot, woodworm.'

'Deathwatch beetle, skeletons in the cupboard and something nasty in the woodshed,' she cut in with a laugh, then looked up into his eyes, her own narrowing shrewdly. 'It can't be that bad if Miss Winifred resided in it sometimes. Why the concern, Dudley? You'll have done your job in finding me, and can now hand over and take your percentage. Isn't that what it's all about, or is there something you haven't told me?'

He met her gaze, his own eyes wide and guileless. 'Like what?'

'I don't know. You tell me.'

'There's nothing to tell.' He was closer now, the sunlight which streamed in touching his hair and giving him an undeserved halo. 'I say, Lorna, I do find you most terribly attractive. Shall I show you the bedrooms? They're worth a look . . . Wonderful four-posters.'

Her smile deepened and her eyes took on a feline slant as she subjected him to her frank, searching stare. 'Really, Dudley? Did good Queen Bess sleep in one of them?'

His hands were sunk deep in the pockets of his stylishly baggy trousers and she could see the prominence of his penis behind the button fly fastening. She ran a hand down her own bare thigh. Her shorts were brief, but nothing like as revealing as those worn by Cassandra. Even so, they fitted snugly round her mound, pressing between the petals of her labia, the seam slightly stained with the honeydew moistening her panties. Her body cried out for sexual release, but was more aroused by the house than Dudley.

She was constantly aware of the chafing of material against her clitoris or breasts, nipples and bud leaping into response at the slightest friction.

Men lay such great store by their cocks, the length, the staying power, yet women's secret parts are so much more sensitive, she thought. I'm glad I'm not a man, and here's one of them trying to lure me into his trap. Do I want to be lured? she wondered. It might be amusing.

She smiled at Dudley and permitted him to lead her up the staircase with its wide treads and turned newel-posts, along echoing corridors and into a chamber at one side of a T-shaped intersection.

'The master bedroom,' he announced, standing back so she might precede him.

'You sound like an estate agent,' she giggled. 'Is there a bathroom en suite?'

'No. It's too old and hasn't been modernised,' he answered pompously. 'The master of the house always used it as his own.'

'In that case, it's now mine,' she said, calmly strolling across the oak floorboards bestrewn with jewel-hued Persian rugs resembling islands in a brown sea.

The main feature was the ornate bed. It was impossible

to ignore it, no matter that the chamber was the size of a ballroom.

'I still think you'd do better to stay in the gatehouse, at least until the main services are connected,' he countered, his brown eyes watchful and a light sheen of sweat on his good-looking, boyish face.

'OK. That's fine. Just till then, no later,' she agreed and, climbing the narrow wooden steps running round it on three sides, pressed her hand into the mattress of the king-sized bed. A little puff of dust rose from the embroidered coverlet.

Its tester towered towards the ceiling where splotches of damp marred Italianate scenes depicting the gods on Mount Olympus. The posts were crowned with carved ostrich plumes, the heavy velvet drapes faded in purple stripes and held back with gold cords ending in tassels a foot long. It was ostentatious, a flamboyant monster of a bed, and Lorna revelled in it.

'I'll need an army of cleaners,' she commented, enthusiasm rising as she visualised the house restored. 'Is the phone working in the lodge?'

'I've had it reconnected for you.'

'Thanks, Dudley. You think of everything.'

'I try,' he said earnestly, and rested a foot on the lower step, leaning towards her, an elbow on his knee. 'Just call me any time you hit a snag.'

A pulse started to throb in her core, spreading up to her breasts, which peaked in anticipation. It was an almost irresistible scenario: an old house with no one but themselves in it, a hot summer morning, the excitement of discovery, the sense of adventure. She could feel his breath fanning her cheek as his fingers lightly grazed her stiff nipples, their contours swelling like cob nuts under the skimpy top.

Dudley was charming and personable so why did she hear this tiny voice telling her to stop? It was not like her to turn down such an opportunity. She shivered under his caress, filled with carnal heat, yet at the same time aware of danger.

Confident of success, Dudley moved in for the kill. One arm slid round her waist and pulled her towards him while, with an urgency that had seduced more than one member of his office staff, his lips swooped and captured hers. She felt the press of his fleshy tongue as it darted between her lips and possessed the wet cavern of her mouth.

She was conscious of several things at once: the slippery surface of his tongue delving and probing; the pressure of his arm crushing her breasts against the blue and white stripes of his shirt; his penis like an iron rod pushing into her belly. He was intent on nothing but releasing the spunk from his balls.

It occurred to her to wonder if he was quite the Don Juan he imagined himself to be. Did he, in fact, know what the clitoris was or where it could be found? Something about his brash approach convinced her that he did not.

She tore her mouth free, brought up her hands and wedged them between her breasts and his chest. 'Take it easy,' she chided softly.

Dudley was not to be put off. He seized one of her hands and pushed it in the direction of his fly. 'Oh, come on, Lorna. Don't try to tell me you're not begging for it. I'm ready. Have a feel.'

It was humid down there between her shorts and his groin. Her palm came to rest on his upward pointing cock trapped by his trousers. He fumbled with the buttons. They opened and he thrust her hand into the gap. Her fingers encountered his shirt but no under-pants. Had he come prepared for this? Then all other thought was wiped out as she felt the rounded head of his penis nudging at her hand like a hopeful pet. Instinctively, her fist closed over it and Dudley emitted a long, shuddering groan.

'That's right,' he muttered, grinding his pelvis against her. 'Good girl. Make it work. Give it a hard rub, and while you're about it, suck my tits.'

With his free hand he jerked his tie loose and opened

his collar, spreading his shirt wide. His chest was covered in a mist of fine brown fuzz. This thinned as it intersected his navel, then darkened and thickened into a bush when it reached the lower portion of his belly. He grabbed her by the hair and pushed her face against him. She could taste his sweat, and smell it, too; the sharp body odour of a sexually active, excited young man, overlaid by the pungency of *Joop!*

Oh, dear, Lorna thought, the inferno in her loins cooling rapidly. This isn't the way to a girl's heart, or even her sex. Someone should give him lessons in sexual etiquette, but it won't be me. I can't be bothered.

His prick was jerking, her fingers already sticky with pre-come juice. He obviously thought he was doing well, his eyes slitted in ecstasy, and mouth half-open, with a dribble of saliva dewing his lips. One hand gripped her right breast as if he was hanging on for dear life, his thumb and forefinger pulling at the nipple with a force that was painful, not pleasurable.

Lorna had had enough. 'Your technique is lousy,' she hissed suddenly, giving his cock a brutal squeeze. 'What are you used to? A quick grope behind the filing cabinet? A fumble on the back seat of a car?'

His eyes snapped open and he glared at her in astonishment. 'What do you mean?'

Lorna removed herself from his reach. 'This caveman stuff may impress your secretary, but it leaves me cold. I may enjoy a bit of rough trade sometimes, but I expect rather more from someone like you.'

'I don't know what you're talking about,' he muttered, a sulky expression spoiling his face. 'Don't you want me to fuck you?'

'No.' Lorna moved further away, ruffling a hand through her curls and brushing them up at the nape to cool her neck.

'What's wrong? Are you a lesbian?' He threw her a hostile glance, and she thought how ridiculous he looked, standing there with his trousers open, penis deflating as quickly as his ego.

'That has nothing to do with it,' she said, and to avoid this embarrassing situation, prowled the room, coming to rest before the stone fireplace where the overmantel was upheld by statues of muscular, handsome Titans with genitals that put Dudley's to shame.

'Then why don't you want it?' He caressed his sagging member lovingly and it started to perk up again. Watching her slyly, he continued to fondle it, stroking the swollen stem and wetting the glans with the clear juice seeping from its single eye.

'I'm not in the mood,' Lorna said, knowing she lied. She was in the mood all right, but not for him. Sean Kealy sprang to mind and her clitoris pulsed. Sean, who knew more about lovemaking than Dudley had ever experienced in his wettest of wet dreams.

She could sense his lust, made even more rampant by her refusal. He wanted to shock her, to continue to exert power over her, even from a distance, masturbating within her sight. To her annoyance, his action stirred her – a dark, perverted warmth aching in her womb. She could not keep her eyes from that inflamed, bulbous head peeping from between his fingers as he rubbed the stem briskly, the skin sliding backwards and forwards.

'Look at me,' he whispered, a catch in his voice. 'I'm nearly there. Kneel in front of me. Catch my come in your mouth.'

'Get lost,' she snapped, but was mesmerised, nonetheless.

She inched closer. Dudley grunted as the blissful moment approached. His hands flew over his manhood, the cock-tip slippery wet between his fingers. He convulsed, cried out, his expression that of a tortured saint as semen shot from him in long, milky jets.

He sighed deeply and sagged against the bed-post, then his eyes met Lorna's. 'Teasing bitch!' he growled.

She laughed without mirth, annoyed now. 'Don't tell me you didn't get a kick out of it, exposing yourself like a dirty old man, having me watch?'

Still glowering, he pulled himself together, fished a

tissue from his pocket and wiped his penis before tucking it away and buttoning up. 'Shall we look over the rest of the house?' he asked coldly.

'Right,' Lorna said, but she had a sudden, bad feeling. Oh, damn, she thought, I've made an enemy, and that wasn't my intention.

The dark panelling reflected the candlelight like polished glass. Outside, the sunset spread a glow of fire over the land, but within the chamber the sumptuously patterned Genoese velvet portières were drawn tightly across the windows.

All the furniture was florid and heavy. It owed much to the artists of the Victorian period, the chests painted with fanciful scenes harking back to the days of chivalry, the chairs upholstered in bottle green plush or stamped Spanish leather with gold fringing and brass-headed nails.

Sybil Esmond stood before a Venetian mirror positioned over the mantelpiece, staring intently at her reflection. She was naked, her white-blonde hair streaming over her shoulders to meet the transparency of a alabaster skin. Her body was flawless, and so fair complexioned that the vertical crack slicing her Mount of Venus came as a shocking contrast. It was hairless and of a deep pink, at once arresting, fascinating and faintly obscene.

She was tall and stately, her head held at a regal angle, rounded chin lifted proudly. She turned and viewed herself from another angle, her image flung back by a cheval-glass on a mahogany stand. She sucked in her ribs and lifted her breasts, beautiful, tip-tilted globes with rosy nipples standing out from brown areolae. Her waist was very thin, her hips slender and her thighs long and slim, ending in exquisite feet with arched insteps.

A gaunt woman, dark hair strained back into an unbecoming bun, stood by the bed watching Sybil with smouldering black eyes. She was strongly built and entirely lacking in beauty, her mouth large and thin-lipped, flanked by broad cheekbones. Her uniform was plain, high-necked and ankle-length. Around her waist she wore a silver belt from which hung a chatelaine with keys attached by narrow chains.

'The carmine, madame?' she asked in a guttural voice with a foreign intonation.

'Yes, Marta,' Sybil replied, and held out her hand.

Marta moved to the intricately carved dressing-table and selected several lipsticks from among those lying on a cut glass tray amidst a jumble of perfume flasks and jars of costly unguents.

Sybil considered for a moment then chose one and, bending towards the mirror, took off the top, screwed it up and applied it to her nipples; first one, then the other. The proud flesh crimped under the creamy, smooth touch of the scented cosmetic. Now the tips glowed crimson, inviting the fondling of mouths and tongues, or the nip of razor-edged incisors.

'Perfect, madame,' Marta breathed, hands folded at her waist, lips curled back in a vulpine smile, eyes feeding on those glorious breasts.

Sybil posed, hands on her hips, admiring herself, but critical, too. 'Yes,' she agreed. 'A vibrant colour. I like it. Continue, Marta.'

The maidservant picked up a garment from a chair and advanced across the deep-pile carpet. Sybil lifted her arms with sinuous grace and her waist was immediately encased in a black corset, the leather as supple as satin. The whaleboning forced her breasts unnaturally high, cupping the undersides and raising the bare upper edges so the nipples rested, shining like ripe raspberries, on the narrow edge.

'Tighter, Marta,' she insisted and her breath came out in a rush as the woman heaved on the back laces. Sybil's waist became smaller and ever more constricted, the swell of her hips, her backside and bosom exaggerated and provocative.

Marta fastened the laces firmly and tucked the ends inside. Now the skin of Sybil's lower belly had taken on a faint blush, the restriction causing a congestion in her inner self that was exciting in the extreme, pushing her to the brink of orgasm but never allowing her to tip over into blessed relief.

'Are you comfortable, madame?' Marta asked, and slid a hand under each of Sybil's buttocks, smoothing the flesh and working it gently, before wriggling a finger into the deep slot between.

'Comfort is not the objective, Marta,' Sybil reminded, a catch in her voice as she eased her hips over that searching digit till its tip toyed with the puckered anal mouth. 'You should know that. Wasn't it you who taught me, under the direction of the master, to learn the painful pleasure of restraint? And isn't it now my task to pass on this knowledge to others?'

'Yes, madame.'

Marta removed her finger and Sybil sat on a padded stool. The maid sank on her haunches and rolled a stocking up one of those long, elegant legs. Once the gossamer fine silk encased the slim feet, narrow ankles and thin calves, it turned from black to slate, insubstantial as smoke.

Marta's hands touched the inner thigh, paused, hovered. Her bony knuckles brushed the two little gold rings that pierced the hairless labia enfolding the mystery of Sybil's sex. And Sybil was reminded yet again of he to whom she belonged and the memorable day on which the rings had been inserted: that agonising, ecstatic day when she had also been branded on her bottom cheeks, his initials seared into her flesh for all time.

Marta remembered, too. She looked up and her eyes met those of her mistress. Leaving the stocking in situ, she repeated the action on the other leg.

The basque ended just below Sybil's hip-bones, curving downwards at back and front and attached to black suspenders. These were now clipped to the stockings, forming a pleasing surround for her naked pubis and rump. Marta went to the wardrobe and took a pair of shoes from among the dozens of others neatly arrayed on racks.

She handled them as if they were new-born babes, her fingers soft and caring, caressing the leopardskin uppers, the shiny black patent leather trim, glittering gold studs and stiletto heels.

Sybil extended one stockinged leg and waited while Marta, on her knees again, slipped on the shoe and fastened the front lacing that extended to the ankle. Its tightness echoed the mounting pressure Sybil was experiencing in her loins; her sex on fire, salty liquid escaping from her vulva. She rotated her ankle, further excited by the effect of pewter silk against leather and fur.

Above all materials, be they lace, satin, silk or velvet, she loved wearing fur. She relished its texture on her naked skin, and the feral smell that clung to it even after being drenched in the most expensive perfume from the flower fields of Grasse. It made her feel extravagant and libidinous and wickedly decadent, sensations of which she could never get enough.

She knew men liked to see her in it, too; one young man in particular. Ian Carr, who pleaded to be allowed to debase himself before her. She had other slaves, of course, but there was something about Ian's vulnerability and cringing adoration that roused her and brought to the fore all the innate barbarity of her flawed personality.

After covering her hands and arms in elbow-length gloves, she banded her wrists with wide bracelets and Marta locked them with a tiny key taken from her chatelaine. They resembled handcuffs, though they were made of gold and embossed with semi-precious stones.

'The cloak,' Sybil ordered, then narrowed her eyes, considering her reflection again as the servant draped a flowing black cape over her shoulders. Its wide collar was lined with ocelot and cunningly wired to form a frame for her face.

'I look like the Wicked Queen in *Snow White*. She wore

collars like this,' she said, her lips curved in a musing, vermilion smile.

'You're more beautiful,' Marta breathed, her hands on the hard-crested swell of her own breasts concealed under the grey fabric of her uniform.

Sybil knew the rules and that she must abide by them, but always felt this electrifying excitement while dressing for the rôle Ryder demanded that she play. He encouraged this tension, of course, and she was aware of being watched by unseen eyes – *his* eyes – observing her from the other side of a trick mirror near the bed. It was a window into the next room, especially constructed to give an uninterrupted view of everything that took place in her bedchamber.

She rested a hand on either side of the glass, bracing herself on stiff arms and leaning forward, placing a kiss on her own reflected lips. Opening her mouth she gave the voyeur a glimpse of her curling pink tongue and sharp white teeth.

'Enjoy, darling,' she whispered, and touched the tips of her breasts, tweaking the rouged nipples into even harder points. 'Bring yourself off while you watch Marta frigging me. Don't worry. It won't harm my performance. I'm in the mood for meting out punishment tonight.'

She stepped back but remained within sight of the mirror, snapping her gloved fingers at Marta. The blood was singing in her veins, nerves like hot wires under the surface of her skin. She felt powerful, omnipotent and in need of instant satisfaction.

Marta crouched before her while Sybil parted her legs and held back her labia. Her body thrilled as the maid touched her, and the slippery little sliver of flesh swelled from its tiny foreskin. Her salmon pink avenue was fully exposed, secret lips glistening with silvery moisture, the gold keepers shining. Marta took the lipstick in her fingers and drew the tip over Sybil's aching bud gently and enticingly, colouring it glowing scarlet to match her nipples.

Sybil writhed and moaned, holding her breasts in her hands and playing with the teats, the leather-covered tips of her fingers tantalising the sensitive nubs. Nectar flowed from her throbbing vagina, and Marta lapped at it, her agile tongue entering every fold and crevice.

Sybil was swamped by vivid and explicit lascivious thoughts. Total wantonness possessed her as she visualised mens' cocks of all shapes and sizes pushing into her orifices. She wanted to taste their juices, milk them of their elixirs, feel them plunging into her female heartland or ravishing the forbidden nether hole that led into her darkness.

Her hands dug into Marta's scalp, disarranging the bun as she held the woman's head to her. 'Go on,' she whispered hoarsely. 'Suck me harder. Drag on my clit. I want it now!'

'No, darling,' Ryder said, appearing from behind an arras. 'You must wait.'

'Oh, Ryder! Please!' she begged frantically as Marta obeyed him. 'Don't be so cruel!'

'I'm cruel to be kind,' he said gently, and drew her into a tender embrace. 'You'll thank me in the end. Think how strong the climax will be when I finally allow it to sweep over you.'

She leant against him, her face upturned to his, staring into his cold grey eyes with her luminous sea-green ones. 'I know. You're right. You always are.'

His hand moved to her hip and found a suspender. He traced it down to the stocking top, then reached between her legs and fingered her vaginal crease, murmuring, 'You're extremely wet, and I love the effect of red lipstick. Thank you for displaying it to me, my sweet.'

He lifted his fingers and inhaled the musky scent of her secret parts.

'Did you masturbate?' Her hand strayed to his groin. His erection was very much in evidence.

'Not to completion,' he answered seriously. 'We have important business afoot tonight and need to be so full of sexual force it will seem we have been abstinent for days.'

He bowed and held out his arm. She laid her fingertips lightly in the crook of his elbow. As formal as if about to enter a banqueting hall, they walked towards a glass-fronted bookcase built into one of the walls. There they stopped. Ryder pressed a catch disguised as a carved rose, a portion of the panelling slid back, and he escorted her through the aperture. Marta followed, and the door closed behind them.

'Well, if you're quite sure, but you know you're more than welcome to go on staying with me,' Cassandra said, eyeing the lodge kitchen dubiously. 'This place hasn't been lived in for a year, ever since the yuppies left. They rented it as a weekend home, but didn't last long. They missed their apartment in Camden Lock, the quiet of the country was too much for them.'

'It's OK, honestly,' Lorna declared, dumping her suit-case on the quarry tiled floor. 'Just needs a clean. If you think this is bad, wait till you see the Priory.'

'Don't!' Cassandra repressed a shudder and perched herself on the corner of the pine table, a foot braced on a Windsor chair. 'Anything that faintly resembles house-work appals me. I'm allergic. Furniture polish brings me out in a rash.'

'You're bone idle,' Lorna answered with a grin, remembering the state of her room in the flat they had shared at university.

'I'm an artist, darling, and it's traditional for artists to live in pigsty squalor.'

'You could hardly call Briar Cottage a slum.'

'Ah, but I can afford to pay someone else to tidy up after me.'

'As I said ... a filthy dirty, lazy slut,' Lorna said lovingly. As she talked, she took stock of the lodge, her property as much as Hinton Priory. 'D'you realise I'm now a woman of substance?'

'And as such have to be protected,' Cassandra replied,

and Lorna was arrested by the thread of gravity running through the remark.

'Ho-hum, you make me sound like a Brontë heroine.'

'Maybe that's just what you are.'

The kitchen was quaint, but had been tastefully updated. The alcove that had once housed a range was now occupied by an electric cooker. There were pine shelves and a Belfast sink, plenty of cupboard space, a washing machine and fridge-freezer; in fact everything she would require. The latticed windows had been double-glazed and gave a pleasant view of a garden and small orchard, out of control now but easily restored by a few hours of enthusiastic digging and weeding.

'We'll soon have that sorted,' she said, leaning her head against the thick stone frame. 'A bit of exercise will do us good.'

'Speak for yourself,' Cassandra demurred, coming to stand beside her and looking disapprovingly at the wilderness. 'I might break a nail.' She spread out her tanned hands where the manicured fingertips shone like diamonds in a mine. 'No, my darling, you need help. Gary can do the garden. Remember him? That well-hung specimen who greeted us on your first day here? I thought you might. And we'll call in the services of TTF.'

'And what, in the name of all that's holy, is TTF?'

'Tara's Task Force,' Cassandra answered, hands coming to rest on her shapely hips. Her cheesecloth shirt was knotted under her breasts, exposing her narrow waist and the dimple of her navel.

Her wraparound skirt was short and low slung. It swung open when she moved, showing her bare legs and, sometimes, the flash of the narrow strip of silk that cut between her labia majora.

'I'm not with you.' Lorna shrugged, puzzled. Cassandra had a habit of talking in riddles.

'Cleaners, dear. Tara Linklater is an enterprising lass who, after leaving her husband, decided to go it alone and start her own company. She has a van, and half a dozen stalwarts who work with her. She's a tower of strength, organised and efficient, and takes on anything from an attic to cellar spring-clean, to laundry, ironing, dog-walking, baby-sitting . . . You must meet her.'

'Can she be trusted?'

'Absolutely. A veritable treasure.' Cassandra fumbled in her tote bag. 'Here's her number. Give her a bell, though you'll only get the answerphone at this time of day.'

'I'll do it later,' Lorna promised. After a fruitless search, she added, 'there's nothing to drink. No tea, coffee or squash. I didn't really think there would be. The electric's on, and the phone and water, but the cupboard's bare.'

'We'll take a sortie to the shops, or should I say "shop"? There's only one grocery store here, but it'll be quicker than trailing into Salisbury.'

'I want to see the other rooms first,' Lorna said, and opened the door leading into the sitting-room.

It was full of old-world charm, with a rustic fireplace, woven rugs and a sofa covered by a coarse linen throw-over. The lodge had been let furnished, and the upwardly mobile couple had looked after it during their lease. Horse brasses hung on leather straps from beams. Tongs, poker and a wicker log basket stood near the hearth.

'Tara will make short work of the tarnish, and have a field day with the ornaments,' Cassandra observed.

The parlour led into a minute hall, with a hatstand made of antlers. A narrow staircase wound to an upper landing, two small bedrooms and a bathroom.

Lorna was looking forward to her own company. She had much to think about, decisions to make, and several long-distance calls to put through. Nicole would want to know the score, and one of the last things Sean had said to her was, 'Don't forget to ring me.'

'I'll stay here tonight,' she said decisively, heaved her case on to the bed and flung back the lid.

Cassandra cast her a worried look. 'There's no need.'

'I want to. Can we get the rest of my things after we've been shopping?'

'OK, if you insist, but I do wish you'd get used to Woodmead first.' Cassandra sat on the edge of the mattress, bouncing to test the springs.

'What is there to find out? It's just a small, peaceful community, isn't it? I won't interfere with them, and I don't suppose they'll bother with me.'

Cassandra bit her full lower lip, her eyes troubled. 'I've a feeling there's one person who will.'

'Oh, and who is that?'

'Ryder Tyrell.' A hard note crept into Cassandra's voice.

'The spectacular, film star-looking guy in the pub last night?'

'Yes. He's definitely interested, Lorna.'

'So? What's the matter with that? Is he the local perv or something?' Lorna had a quick flash of a patrician nose and penetrating eyes, a lean, though powerful body and aristocratic mien.

More than that. The fire smouldering in her epicentre suddenly shot up in flames. He was infinitely desirable, giving off a sizzling sensuality which was impossible to resist.

Cassandra had become very still, seated cross-legged on the bed, her hands loosely linked in her lap. 'Do you remember what we learnt from Wicca?' she asked seriously.

'Some. I've not done anything with it in ages.'

'That doesn't matter. You'll use it subconsciously. Surely you get impressions when you meet people?'

'Doesn't everyone? A kind of gut feeling of liking or aversion. It's useful in the magazine business. Nicole works on hunches. So do I. There's nothing mystical about that. Call it good, old-fashioned intuition, if you like.'

'Then what did you pick up from him?'

Lorna could feel her mental shutters closing. Cassandra was her dearest friend, and yet she found herself

96

deliberately blocking anything disparaging she might be about to say regarding Ryder.

'He seemed all right as a person. Helpful, too. I'd like to get to know him better,' she said stubbornly.

'He's asked you to dinner.'

'He said he'd ring.'

'He will. There's no doubt about that. You'll accept?'

'Yes.' This interrogation was proving irksome. I don't need a nursemaid, Lorna thought crossly, and added, 'I'd like to see his house and meet his partner.'

'The glamorous Sybil Esmond. Now there's a strange lady, if ever I met one.' Cassandra stretched and got to her feet. 'Be careful. All is not as it seems. Don't take things at their face value.'

'I wish you'd explain. You're being annoying,' Lorna said.

Cassandra reached out and brushed the hair away from Lorna's forehead tenderly. 'Would you listen to me, if I did? You've always been Miss Independent, as stubborn as a mule.'

Lorna grinned ruefully. 'I guess you're right. Don't worry about me. I've met the likes of Ryder Tyrell before, eaten their balls for breakfast and spat out the skin.'

'Not anyone quite like him, I think.' Then Cassandra's mood changed and her eyes sparkled as she said, 'Let's go shopping and give the village something to talk about. I provide them with free entertainment, and the news of your arrival will have got them going.'

The store was situated in the market place, along with several other shops, three public houses, a dental surgery and a Queen Anne property belonging to a covey of doctors who were in partnership.

'Dishy they are, too, but it's no good thinking you might bonk one of them. Woodmead's so small, inbred and close-knit that you can't even fart without everyone knowing about it,' Cassandra commented, as she parked in a side-street.

There was a Methodist chapel made of red brick and a mellow Norman church with a squat square tower.

Dusty yews of great antiquity stood sentinel over the graveyard, and Lorna particularly liked the Celtic cross just inside the lychgate.

'It's a fine example,' Cassandra agreed. 'I must take you to see the holy well. We'll go by ourselves tomorrow.'

The store had been transformed into a supermarket, and Lorna was able to fill her trolley with necessities. 'You moving into the Priory?' asked the young assistant at the check-out. She was a wide-hipped girl with an open, friendly face. A tag bearing her name, Tracy, was pinned to the overall covering her full breasts.

'How did you know?' Lorna asked, switching her mind from dollars to English currency.

'Word gets around,' Tracy answered. 'American, aren't you?'

'No, but I've lived there a long time.' Somehow this prying was not offensive. It seemed like genuine interest and concern.

'Spooky old place, that Priory,' Tracy said with a shiver. 'Don't know as I'd like to live there on my own, but maybe you're married?'

'No.' Lorna avoided the I-told-you-so look in Cassandra's eyes.

'Got a boyfriend, then?'

'No.'

'Oh, that'll please the local lads. They likes fresh blood. You want to come down to the disco some time.'

'And where is that?' Lorna packed her goods in plastic bags and replaced them in the trolley.

'It's out near the Green Man, a pub that's opened up the skittle alley for dancing. We get a proper DJ there, and sometimes live bands.'

'How does that grab you?' Cassandra said sarcastically, leaning over and helping Lorna. 'Do you fancy a couple of sweaty farmhands?'

'Shut up,' Lorna hissed from the side of her mouth.

'Then there's the gymkhana and cheese show soon,' her informant continued. 'The fair will be coming for that.'

'An endless round of entertainment,' Cassandra commented as they wheeled the trolley to the car. 'How have you managed to survive so long without it?'

'I don't know, but there's one thing I can't manage without and that's music,' Lorna said as they closed the boot. 'I've brought all my tapes and CDs with me, but I haven't got anything to play them on.'

'Come this way,' Cassandra insisted, and took her into a small shop that sold electrical goods.

Lorna came out the proud possessor of a top quality portable sound system, a Nicam television set and video player. She had also purchased a bottle green cordless kettle, a matching toaster, and the latest in microwave ovens.

They called in at Briar Cottage on the way back, collected most of her belongings and hijacked Marc to set up her new equipment.

Contentment settled round Lorna like a snug blanket as she listened to Luciano Pavarotti singing Neapolitan love-songs while she sat with her friends in her own kitchen, eating baguettes and Camembert washed down by a reasonably passable Beaujolais.

'Are you going to take me home and fuck me?' Cassandra asked Marc when, replete with food and wine, she sat on his lap and wound her fingers in his curling mane.

He had his hand under her skirt, fingers buried in the soft dampness of her smooth pussy. 'That's my sinful intention,' he murmured, scraping his chestnut-bearded cheek across the rising swell of her partly exposed breasts and burying his long nose in her cleavage.

'Come on then,' she said, getting to her feet unsteadily. 'We'll see you in the morning, Lorna. Give a ring if you want anything, or find it too lonely. Marc can come and get you. He'll have to drive. I've had too much to drink.'

Lorna walked with them down the uneven path to the gate, then said, 'I must get a car – '

'Now that you know you're staying,' Cassandra finished the sentence for her, face a pale blur in the twilight. 'You are going to stay, aren't you?'

'Seems like I am.' Lorna was surprised to find she had already decided. It was insanity, maybe, throwing up a promising career and burying herself in the country, but it felt right. 'And thanks, both of you, for helping me.'

'What are friends for, lovey?' Cassandra said, kissing her fingers and blowing the kisses towards her.

When Lorna re-entered the kitchen and shut the door behind her, that sense of homecoming intensified. If I feel like this in the gatehouse, she thought, then how will it be when I take up residence in Hinton Priory itself?

She stacked the dishes in the sink. Should she watch television, catching up on BBC programmes, the best there was? Or should she indulge herself to the full and play the whole of Puccini's cowboy opera, *Le Fancuilla del West*, on her brilliant new stereo? Or maybe simply have a bath and go to bed, there to masturbate in celebration of her arrival?

Duty called first. It was too late to phone a builder or TTF; she would do that first thing in the morning, but now she must get in touch with Nicole and possibly Sean.

Five p.m. in New York and Nicole would still be in the office. Sean? She wasn't sure if she would catch him at home yet.

The trilling of the phone startled her. Who could be calling at this time, and with her only just moved in?

'Hello, Lorna. Ryder Tyrell here. Hope I haven't rung at an awkward moment. You weren't in bed with a lover, were you?'

Bloody cheek, she thought, but the rich timbre of his voice made her knees weak.

'No. I'm settling in. How did you know my number?'

'I was friendly with the Grantleys, the couple who lived there before. The number's the same.' He sounded so reasonable that Cassandra's warnings flew right out of the window.

'I see,' Lorna said, then paused, unsure what to say next.

'I was wondering if you'd come to dinner one evening this week. How about the day after tomorrow?' he continued blandly. 'Sybil is so looking forward to meeting you.'

'Well, yes. I'm free then. That would be great.'

'I'll pick you up at seven, shall I?'

'Yes. Fine.'

'Till then, Lorna. Good night. Sleep well. Dream of me.'

'Good night,' she said calmly. The conceit of the man, she thought as she replaced the receiver on its ivory cradle. Dream of him, indeed!

But she was thoroughly unsettled by his call, wandering the rooms, switching on the TV and putting it off again, even her beloved music offering no solace.

With a supreme effort she dialled the States. Nicole was out. Jane, her secretary, expressed delight at hearing from her, took her number and promised to let Nicole know. She drew a blank with Sean, too.

Her heart sank and disappointment was keen. She suddenly needed to speak to him. At least they could have had a lovely conversation, full of sexual innuendoes. Every inch of her body seemed to have its own particular itch. She wanted a man with a fierce passion who made her breasts ache and the tiny bead of her clitoris stir.

Ryder Tyrell. She thought of his dark face and strong hands, and the promise of the snake that had slumbered between his thighs as he sat beside her in the White Hart. She yearned to have it in her, its head butting against her cervix, its width opening her to capacity. She was sure he'd be well endowed. He just had to be.

In the end she gave up the fight to be sensible, poured herself a gin and tonic and fell into the supremely comfortable couch in the parlour. Her hand slid down the zip of her jeans and held aside the hem of her panties, seeking the plump leaves of her labia and the slippery

101

ridge of flesh crowning them. Heat pooled in her loins and sweat broke out in her armpits. She felt full and warm and randy. She fixed her mind on her caller, imagining it was his mouth sucking her nipples, his thumb revolving on her quivering bud.

Her finger moved faster, the warmth infusing her entire body and, as she reached the acme of her bliss, so she cried out a name.

'Ryder!'

Chapter Five

'*E*nterprise Builders?' Lorna asked, cradling the phone against her cheek and holding a bath sheet round her with the other hand.

'Yes. How can I help you?' answered a pleasant female voice from the firm's Salisbury headquarters.

'My name's Lorna Erskine and I've recently inherited Hinton Priory near Woodmead. I need someone to come out, survey the property and give me a quote for renovations.' Lorna reached for a pen and her organiser. 'I gather that I'll need planning permission from the powers that be, as it's an historic building.'

'That's true . . . Mrs . . .'

'Miss Erskine.'

'Right. Let me see . . . yes, we can send one of our people over and he'll make the arrangements for you. It won't be till tomorrow. Shall we say in the afternoon, about 2.30?'

Lorna made a note of the time and hung up. Next she dialled TTF. 'You've just caught me. I was on my way out,' said a bright, breathy young voice.

'Is that Tara's Task Force?'

'It certainly is. Tara speaking.'

'I'm a friend of Cassandra Ashley. She's recommended you.'

'That's decent of her. Fire away.'

Lorna hurriedly explained her position and the conversation ended with Tara promising to add her to her list of customers, get to the lodge by the end of the week, give it a going-over and put her down for an extensive cleaning operation when the builders had finished with the Priory.

'Looking forward to meeting you, Miss Erskine,' Tara concluded briskly. 'See you on Friday. 'Bye.'

That's that done, Lorna thought happily, and realised she was already matching her pace to the slowness of the country, far removed from frenetic New York. I like it, she decided, as she refilled her coffee cup and returned to her bedroom to dress.

It was barely nine o'clock and the sun was already blazing, though cotton-wool cumulus hovered on the horizon. She intended to go over to the Priory and have a look round on her own, but a car horn parped from outside and she saw Cassandra waving at her from the rolled down driver's window.

'I thought we'd take a trip to the well,' she cried. 'Are you ready?'

'Give me a minute.'

Lorna shook out her damp hair, which twisted into corkscrew curls halfway down her back, slipped on her sandals and snatched up her shoulder-bag. Heavy with the responsibility of ownership, she went round the cottage on a security check, then closed the front door carefully behind her. Honeysuckle and climbing roses made a perfumed arch over her head, picturesque but unkempt.

I really must get in touch with Gary about gardening, she thought as she ran between the cockleshells bordering the weedy path. I never realised there was so much to do when one has a house: nay, two houses.

'Did you have a good night?' Cassandra asked, slanting her a lively violet-blue glance and purring with contentment like a she-cat who has been out on the tiles. 'I certainly did. That man goes from strength to strength.

104

Insatiable, my dear. He keeps asking me to marry him. I might just take him up on it.'

'Ryder phoned,' Lorna said, squirming as the heat from the leather seat scalded her bottom through the floaty dirndl skirt.

'I thought he might,' Cassandra answered, as she turned the car out through lodge gates and into the lane beyond.

'And he's asked to me dinner tomorrow tonight.'

'I knew it! You accepted, of course?'

'Yes,' Lorna looked down at her fingers laced in her lap, feeling embarrassed and annoyed with herself for this reaction. It was nobody's business but hers.

'Take care. That's all,' Cassandra advised crisply, and put her foot down.

'I thought you said the spring was in the Priory grounds,' Lorna said, for they seemed to be driving away from it.

'It is, but we'll be less conspicuous if we approach it from another direction.'

'How can we be conspicuous out here? It's completely deserted. And what does it matter if we are?'

'It's wiser not to be seen taking too much interest,' Cassandra replied, her eyes blanked by mirror sunglasses. 'Trust me in this, Lorna.'

The lane divided and there was the beginning of a track on the right. A sign was nailed to a gnarled elm. It read, 'Keep Out. Trespassers will be Prosecuted.'

Cassandra took the turning, driving slowly as they bumped over the rutted surface. The trees and undergrowth were thick, and branches met over their heads. It was like entering a dark green tunnel in caverns beneath the sea.

Lorna clung to the seat, safety belt crossing and separating her breasts, a throb of apprehension and excitement augmenting the hunger that had not abated since Ryder's voice caressed her ear like a lecherous tongue-tip.

Why was Cassandra being so evasive, not only about him but the spring, too?

There was light ahead and the car left the gloom, emerging into the glory of a buttercup and daisy-starred meadow. Hinton Priory could be seen, framed by over-hanging boughs. There it lay in a dip of the parkland, a quarter of a mile from the road. And close by stood what Lorna at first took for a mock-ruin, one of those pretty conceits erected on a rich man's whim.

'A folly,' she exclaimed, as the car rolled to a halt on the grass. The engine died and nothing disturbed the silence, not even bird-song. 'What a great place for picnic parties.'

'It's not a folly,' Cassandra corrected, climbing out and stretching her bare legs. 'That's the real thing A genuine Roman temple.'

'You're kidding.'

'Not at all. I'm surprised the archaeologists haven't pounced, though we're pretty remote down here and no one seems to have taken any notice of it. Maybe the Goddess has kept it hidden from exposure, for the spring lies directly beneath.'

The stillness, the smell of humid loam and wild garlic, the very remoteness affected Lorna strangely. Despite the illusion of openness, she had the sense of being more enclosed, more inescapably confined than in the midst of the woods.

Cassandra's eyes shone with excitement, her breathing uneven, and Lorna was very aware of the rise and fall of her friend's generous breasts under the sun-top that barely concealed them.

The sun beat down, blazingly hot, and insects buzzed. Falteringly, she followed Cassandra up the worn marble steps and into a circular area. Leaves drifted over what remained of the tiled floor, exposing a tiny area of blue and white stones laid by a master craftsman in the civilised days of Roman occupation before the Dark Ages shrouded Britain.

Cassandra took her hand, her fingers hot, the long,

filbert-shaped nails digging into Lorna's palm. They stood in the centre of the temple, their heads caressed by fingers of sunlight creeping through the vines garlanding the jagged columns that had once supported the roof.

'It's right that we're here together,' Cassandra murmured, and pressed her body close to Lorna's, seizing one of her thighs between her own hard polished knees and rubbing the moist, pink flesh of her pubis against her. 'We don't really need men, you and I – only to use for our own purposes.'

'Our own enjoyment,' Lorna added, her head swimming, bright light falling around her feet in a haze of golden dust.

'Remember this, and don't allow anyone to put you down,' Cassandra went on, peeling off her top and freeing her magnificent bronzed breasts. 'It's time we entered the sanctuary.'

'It's not your first visit?'

Cassandra shook her tawny curls. 'Once I worshipped there frequently, but not lately. The atmosphere has changed. Perhaps we can work towards restoring its tranquility.'

She knelt and tugged aside a thick mat of earth and leaves, exposing a grating, fastened with a padlock. Lorna leant over her shoulder, staring down into the darkness glimpsed between the iron bars. The air breathing up from it carried the musty smell of rotting vegetation.

'It's locked to keep intruders out,' Cassandra explained and searched in her bag, producing a key and a torch.

'How come you have a key?' Lorna asked, finding it harder than ever to keep a grip on reality. The temple, the secret entrance, the mystery, all took on the ramifications of a weird dream.

'It was Marc and I who discovered it. He fixed the grating and I kept the key until the day when its rightful owner returned. That time has come. Unlock it, Lorna.'

'I wonder if Dudley Norcross knows about this.' Lorna

hesitated, unsure if she really wanted to go down there. Part of her longed to, yet the other, more sensible part, was afraid.

'I'm sure he doesn't. There have been legends and rumours, but it's only within the last few months that anyone has been remotely interested in Hinton Priory. It's lain deserted ever since I've lived in Woodmead, and that's got to be five years or more.'

Lorna bent over and inserted the key, saying, 'This seems to be my job of late, undoing the gates to enchanted regions.'

The padlock sprang open. She yanked at the bars but nothing happened. Cassandra joined her and they heaved, shoulder to shoulder. With a nerve-jarring squeal, the grating started to lift, inch by tortuous inch.

'I'd forgotten how heavy it is,' Cassandra panted, passing the back of her hand over her sweat-beaded brow. 'I got Marc to do it before. Come on.'

She went first, and Lorna followed cautiously. Stone steps, worn in the middle twisted down into darkness lit only by the fitful uncertainty of Cassandra's torch. Cold, dank air gave them goose-flesh. Water trickled some-where below. Then candles speared the gloom when Cassandra flicked her lighter and ignited the wicks. Lorna's fumbling feet reached the last of the steps and encountered solid ground.

She was in a big chamber, possibly an enlarged natural cave. The candles stood on ledges carved out of the damp, greyish walls. Water sparkled, cascading from a fissure into a basin from which it flowed down a gulley to enter the earth again between a jumble of rocks.

'It's beautiful,' she breathed, overcome with awe. 'Are you sure it's not a man-made grotto?'

'Look at the wall over there, on your left,' Cassandra said impatiently. 'Surely that will convince you? Do you see them? The three spiral circles, the Goddess trinity ... Birth, death, rebirth. The eternal cycle ... fertility and the life force.'

'I see them,' Lorna answered, mouth dry, sex wet as

she gazed at the whirling patterns imprinted there by some ancient hand. 'The Goddess as Maiden, Mother and Grandmother.'

'Crone. Hag. Divine ruler of Earth, Moon and Waters,' Cassandra added.

'Not eighteenth century then, nor even Roman?' Lorna whispered, drawn to stand by the pool. She was shivering with cold, burning up inside with lust.

'Much earlier, though I expect the Romans used it, too, and later on Regency bucks held orgies here. I guess it was no secret to your ancestors,' Cassandra answered in a hushed tone. 'There are probably coins and trinkets at the bottom, thrown in as offerings. It would be interesting to get them out, but sacrilege to disturb it.'

Further circles were carved into the wall to the right of the waterfall. Lorna gripped Cassandra's arm, exclaiming, 'More spirals, but going the other way.'

'They symbolise the Goddess's consort. The Sky and Sun God, master of storms and weather.' Cassandra sank on the rim of the pool, head bowed, her hands cupping her bare breasts.

Lorna was staring in wonder at the wall, images flashing across her inner vision. She told herself firmly that these impressions were caused by the flickering candles, but for a split second thought she saw the sky spreading over the stone and a mighty god with feathered wings flying swiftly towards her.

It vanished, but there was something in the air, a pressure that weighed on her skull cavities, a tingling feeling rising from the earth through the soles of her feet to penetrate her core. Her knees weakened and her womb contracted. She could feel her secretions dewing her thighs, and needed a touch, any touch, to ease this raw, sexual ache.

'Oh, great Goddess,' Cassandra chanted, her voice echoing through the chamber. 'Mother of the universe from whom flows sleep and life, all memory and forgetfulness, bless and keep us, your faithful daughters.'

Her breasts were taut, nipples standing out as she

dipped her fingers in the spring and dribbled the ice-cold water over them. Her eyes were half-closed, her back arched, breath hissed from between her clenched teeth as she inserted a finger along one side of the tightly stretched crotch of her shorts.

As Lorna watched her masturbating, so every fibre of her being seemed to vibrate. She was yearning to be felt, longing to be stroked. Without realising what she was doing, she held her skirt up about her waist and slipped her hand into her briefs, rubbing the soft fur and parting her labia. Her thumb found her bud, the seat of sensual pleasure, and began to massage it.

A glow seemed to emanate from the cave walls, and it was as if fingers other than her own touched her lips, and heated her nipples, vagina and anus. Her head rolled from side to side, her legs were shaking. She reeled, dumbstruck, consumed by an endless blur of orgasmic sensations.

'I told you this was a powerful place, didn't I?' Cassandra murmured, dragging herself to her feet. Her face was peaceful and childlike, washed clean by the extreme pleasure she had experienced. 'It's important that it doesn't fall into the wrong hands. Keep schtum about it if the Heritage people start poking about. Let them have the temple if they must, but don't tell them about the spring.'

Lorna had recovered her equilibrium and felt once more in control. 'I can't fathom what happened just now, but you're right. It should be treated with the greatest respect.'

'I don't know about you, but I feel as if I've just been fucked by a rhinoceros,' Cassandra remarked with a chuckle. 'This hasn't happened to me with such intensity when I've been down here alone. It must be the old team working together.'

'I'll not mention it to anyone, least of all Dudley,' Lorna said resolutely as they mounted the steps.

'He's a minor problem,' Cassandra affirmed. 'Why do you think I advised you to be careful of Ryder?'

110

They stepped out into the meadow. The sun shone brightly, but clouds were rolling up from the west, tipped with gold. Sun God? Earth Goddess? Was there anything in it, or just superstition? Lorna wondered.

A breeze rustled the trees and cold fingers walked down her spine. She felt as if something from beyond her comprehension had embraced her in the cave.

'Right. What's the scam?' Hugo Pendleton cast Dudley a pulverising stare, exuding male arrogance and sheer animal magnetism.

Hugo always succeeded in reducing his associates to jelly. A big, ruggedly handsome man, he worked out regularly and relished the pitch and toss of the business world above all things. Brooding on this – and he rarely thought of anything else – he had come to the conclusion that he enjoyed it even more than the feel of women, so vibrant yet so soft, with their fascinating, piquant smell. He viewed them simply as creatures to be bent to his will. Annoyingly, he had just come up against one who was refusing to do so.

Dudley fidgeted, hooked a finger under his collar and eased his old school tie. He then looked despairingly at the ceiling as if beseeching help from the angels on the painted frieze of the Farrier's Arms, a five-star, fiercely expensive hotel situated on a choice site between Salisbury and Woodmead.

They had reached the brandy and cigars stage, having just partaken of a gourmet meal; the hotel featured in every prestigious Good Food Guide on the market.

'Well, it's like this.' Dudley prevaricated, drawing on one of Havana's finest and wishing himself miles away. 'I took her over to the house.'

'This American . . . Lorna Erskine?'

'She's English actually, but yes.'

'And?' A pair of hard sapphire eyes bored into him.

'And she doesn't want to sell,' Dudley ended feebly, wits deserting him in the presence of this clever, confident, ambitious man.

'You told her about the difficulties of permission and such?'

'I did, and it hasn't put her off.'

'That's a bloody nuisance.'

Hugo lay back in his chair, muscular legs in Savile Row tailored trousers stretched out under the table. He surveyed the room with considerable satisfaction. The hotel was a Queen Anne mansion that had been bought and updated by a consortium operating under his expert guidance.

He had his finger in innumerable pies, each successful business venture giving him an adrenalin rush second to none and rousing his considerable sexual appetite, in the satisfaction of which he was as ruthless as he was in the field of competition. He took pride in his appalling reputation with women.

Women. He needed them, with their nipples and breasts and warm, wet cunts. And now here was another of the troublesome, fascinating bitches who thought to challenge him. Miss Lorna Erskine. He had no doubt he could crush her like a ripe peach and sup off the sweetness of her juices.

But he would be fair, even generous. She would be offered a sum she could hardly refuse. He spoke his thoughts aloud to Dudley.

'I'll talk to her. By the time I've done she'll probably be glad to get shot of the place and bugger off back to the States,' he said, his voice rolling and deep, with the public school accent he had cultivated so assiduously.

He had attended the right establishments for the education of boys, but in reality he came from New Money, not Old, his father and grandfather North Country industrialists who had made a fortune from supplying armaments throughout the whole of the war-torn twentieth century. The Great War, the Second World War, the Falklands War, the trouble in Ireland and the Middle East and Bosnia: they had sold munitions to all, never fussy about the source as long as the money came rolling in.

Dudley wished he had Hugo's confidence in his ability to shift Lorna. In his experience she was a feisty, stubborn, intimidating girl who would bow the knee to no one.

He shook his head gloomily and said, 'Wait till you meet her and you'll see what I mean. She doesn't need money. Her inheritance is huge. And she's taken a fancy to the old house, wants to put down roots there or something equally daft.'

'You haven't used the right tactics, my boy,' said Hugo, eyeing his accomplice and wondering if he knew which end his arse hung. These lads, fresh from university, were too precious by half. 'Did you get her into bed?'

'No, I didn't,' Dudley confessed, blushing to the roots of his hair. 'She's a difficult female.'

'What?' Hugo shot him a disparaging glance. 'You mean to tell me you were with her in a deserted house and didn't get her up against the wall and give her a good seeing to?'

'I tried, but she wasn't having any. She was horny as hell – '

'But didn't fancy you, eh?' Hugo could feel his penis stirring under those beautifully-cut trousers, the thought of Dudley and this unknown girl together arousing him. He lowered his voice and leant closer to his companion. 'I'd make her take me in her mouth, then I'd go down between her legs and suck her quim till she begged for mercy.'

Dudley's own cock was twitching at Hugo's words. 'I wanked in front of her,' he confessed, and his hand went down under the cover of the table cloth, sliding between his legs and fondling the bulge that craved caresses.

'That's more like it,' Hugo said, sitting back with a leer. 'Is she pretty?'

'Oh yes ... Long legs, lots of hair, big tits. She's beddable, all right.'

Hugo narrowed his eyes and regarded Dudley

through a blue haze of cigar smoke. 'I'll stay here for a couple of days and we'll cook up some sort of meeting.'

'Very well, sir,' Dudley agreed.

Hugo sat forward, his eyes like gimlets. 'We've got to pull this off. I've people interested, important, influential people. We'll build a leisure centre second to none, even more luxurious than those already operating. Holiday camps for the rich, with everything they could possibly want, and things they didn't even know they wanted. A huge glass dome over a heated swimming area. Shops, restaurants, a concert hall, a lake, massage parlours, exercise rooms. I'll have the authorities eating out of my hand, for we'll keep the Priory in perfect order as our headquarters. We'll clean up, my boy, and you'll get your cut.'

'I don't doubt it, if you can get Lorna to sell,' Dudley said, the prize Hugo dangled before him so dazzling that he was prepared to agree to any skulduggery.

'She'll sell,' Hugo replied positively. 'Just set up a meeting and I'll do the rest. Meanwhile, send for your secretary, the bosomy Judy, and tell her to bring the plans of the Priory to my room so I can look at them. She's obliging, isn't she?'

'Very,' Dudley replied, hot memories of sessions with her making his prick thicken.

'Does she give good head?'

'The best.'

'Fine. That's all then, Dudley. I'll speak to you again tomorrow,' Hugo said, waving a hand dismissively.

He snapped his fingers at a waiter, who jumped to attention, coming over with another brandy, then sat back savouring the Armagnac and the anticipation of fellatio. Soon Judy shimmied across the room on her high heels, wearing a black skirt and white lace bodysuit.

She came towards him slowly, her breasts stirring as she moved. The pink tips were just distinguishable through their filigree covering. Hugo's cock took an upward bend that pressed the tip against his boxer shorts. His balls ached for release.

Lorna Erskine beware, he thought as he gave Judy the full benefit of his tigerish smile. Perfectly mannered and impeccably attired, he rose to greet her, the drape of his suit jacket successfully concealing the huge erection that rubbed against his belly.

Lorna sighed with satisfaction. Hinton Priory was hers, all hers, her breath the only thing that stirred the great echoing hall and silent rooms.

She had asked Cassandra to drop her off after their visit to the spring, crossing the hay-field of a lawn and entering by the back door. This was reached via a cobbled stable yard, where stalls and grooms' quarters stood empty, and only doves declaimed their plaintive love-songs as they paraded along the gutterings on turned-in toes.

The yard was quiet and hot, a sun-trap where once there had been the bustle of coaches arriving and departing, and horses being exercised in readiness for the master. There would have been other servants, too; at least thirty for the house and many more outside. Almost obscene, really, that a family of perhaps no more than half a dozen should have been in the position to enslave so many.

Ah, well, it kept the unemployment figures down, I suppose, Lorna ruminated as she let herself into the kitchen. Of barnlike proportions, it needed a complete overhaul. But I won't have it altered too much, she thought. Everything must be tastefully carried out, even if it costs me deep in the purse.

Her sandals made no sound on the stone floor and, after passing through the green, baize-covered door that had once separated the elite from the lower orders, she eventually found herself in the great hall. From there she explored further, discovering a library with wall-to-ceiling bookcases behind whose glass-fronted doors dozed a multitude of leatherbound volumes. Next she found the solar where once ladies had retired to work on their *petit point*, and a smoking-room hung with sporting trophies, including the mounted heads of lions, tigers, deer and wild boar

So many treasures in that rabbit-warren of a house to please her eye and satisfy her hunger for antiques, a hodge-podge of styles mixed together to form a harmonious whole: medieval, Jacobean, Georgian, Victorian and Edwardian. All were neglected, thick with dust and festooned with cobwebs.

The music salon was at the end of a corridor and filled with sunlight from western windows overlooking the garden. The air quivered with the smell old, unoccupied rooms acquire. It was as if the past was trapped there: memories of days and nights filled with dancing and laughter, intrigue and illicit love affairs.

That walnut daybed over there, for example.

Lorna could imagine a fornicating couple on it, locked in the throes of passion, the lady with her hooped skirts hitched high. No knickers, of course. It was considered immodest to wear them as they were thought to be masculine garments, resembling breeches. And her gallant on his knees before her, satin breeches agape, displaying a fine, fat prick poking forth from beneath a frilly lawn shirt. His sword, tricorne hat and triple-capped cloak had been cast aside. This was a hurried mating while the lady's husband was otherwise engaged, at the gaming table, perhaps.

Her legs were spread in total abandonment, bare white thighs gleaming above the edge of pink silk stockings fastened just below her dimpled knees by diamanté-studded garters. Her hands caressed the beau's lightly powdered hair as his jutting tongue delved into her luscious delta. She moaned as she lured him to continue his assault on her virtue, pressing his head more tightly to her sex.

Oh, naughty, immoral pair, like characters from *Dangerous Liaisons*. Lorna could almost hear the tinkling sound of a minuet, and her fingers gravitated towards her own swelling clitoris. She permitted herself this indulgence for a moment, raising her skirt and rubbing the crotch of her panties where it pressed against her demanding nub. It was not enough to bring her to orgasm, but produced a pleasant, warm tingling sensation.

The black Steinway concert grand attracted her. Once, she had reached Grade Eight on the piano, but had not practised for years. Did one lose the skill or was it always there, like riding a bicycle? I'll have it tuned, she thought. Take it up again. There's bound to be a piano teacher around.

She lifted the dust-grained lid, put out her finger and touched an ivory key, then ventured a chord. Rings of sound pulsed through the room like ripples from a pebble dropped into a pond. Piano music, more than any other, seems to go on after the player has stopped, and Lorna felt both exposed and alone, as if she had betrayed her presence foolishly.

She stood there listening. Silence, then her bottom clenched as a loud thud reverberated from over her head.

Fear jangled through her. She wanted to turn and flee, her heart thudding so loudly it seemed to fill the room.

'Oh, my God,' she whispered. 'Not a ghost, surely?' Her rational mind was overturned by her body's instinct for self-preservation.

She turned for the door but was arrested by the clatter of footsteps on the bare staircase. If it was a ghost, then it was an exceedingly noisy one. Other fears crowded in: a burglar, a rapist, an escaped lunatic. If she opened the window and dropped over the sill she might escape that way. There was still time.

There wasn't time. A man appeared in the doorway, and a crisp voice said, 'What's this? A welcoming committee?'

He was standing in the shadows where the sun did not reach and she could not see him properly, but got the impression that he was very big and very tough. Her newly-acquired sense of ownership rose up in indignation and annoyance.

117

'Who are you, and what are you doing here?' she demanded, clenching her fists.

Whatever happened, she would not give in without a fight. He'd be sorry he tangled with her. He wouldn't be the first pushy guy she had kneed in the bollocks.

'I could ask you the same thing,' he said with a low-pitched laugh, and strolled towards her. Now he was only a few feet away.

She didn't like his laugh, or the cocky way he was looking her up and down. Didn't like *him*. No, to be honest, it was possible she might like him too much. Her mind rejected him but her body did not.

Here I go again, she sighed inwardly. I'm a sucker for this kind of man.

He was certainly handsome, athletic of build, with wide shoulders straining against a checked cotton shirt, and scruffy jeans so tight that it looked as if he had been poured into them. Too tight; blue fading to white over the thighs, round the button-holes of the fly and at the fullness of the extremely interesting package encased within it.

'I'm Lorna Erskine, the owner of this property,' she said, the words dropping, freshly chilled, from her lips. 'I suggest you come up with a convincing explanation of why you're here, or I'll call the police.' She hoped he did not realise the phone had been cut off.

'Ah, so it belongs to *you*.' He looked at her intently, pushing an unruly lock of dark hair back from his forehead with a strong, sinewy hand.

Lorna could feel herself flushing under the smouldering fire of his brown eyes. She despised herself for this weakness, yet was consumed by a burning, craving need to kiss his mouth, feel his fingers teasing her nipples, and his penis penetrating her like a hot steel bar.

This was ridiculous! Where was her dignity? How could she be possessed with this overwhelming desire to fall down with a stranger and make raw love to him on the dusty floor?

But the air hummed and the old house watched, and

118

she was teetering on the brink of disaster. Something told her, deep in her soul, that it would be a grave mistake to get involved with him.

This would be no barnyard mating, quickly over and as quickly forgotten. If she yielded to the force of her own desire, then she could kiss her independence goodbye. She might even become one of those pathetic females who hung around waiting for the phone call that rarely came, the sad plaything of some unreliable, ego-centric macho man.

She tried again, purposefully ignoring her rapidly dampening pubic area and the breasts that seemed suddenly too big for her bra. 'Now you know who I am, you'd better tell me your name and business.'

His smile was lupine, matching his slanting golden-brown eyes, and she was intrigued by the paradox of a mouth with a hard upper lip and a full, pleasure-loving lower one.

'Who do you think I am?'

'I don't know.' She wished he would stop playing this silly mind game.

He raised an eyebrow. 'Do you take me for a squatter, or a New Age traveller? Is that it?'

'Are you?' She turned defence into attack.

He threw back his head and laughed, the cords standing out on his suntanned throat as if sculpted. 'No, Miss Erskine, though I'm often taken for a gypsy. There's possibly a trace of Romany blood way back, but it can't be proved. They'd not squat in your house anyway. Don't like living "in brick".'

'Come to the point. You've not answered my question.' Her temper was rising rapidly and she was finding it hard not to slap him across his mocking face.

He came closer, towering over her, his olive skin complementing the sepia curls that coiled, snakelike, around his neck. She trembled as his fingers skimmed over her cheek, thumb pushing down the full pout of her red bottom lip. His touch had an arresting quality. She found it impossible to move away.

119

'I'm Christopher Devlin,' he murmured, and his hands came to rest on her shoulders, his fingers gently kneading the soft flesh beneath her T-shirt. 'I'm a freelance architect, and specialise in restoration. Enterprise Builders gave me your address. I thought I'd get the feel of the place before I officially started. This is a magnificent house, Miss Erskine. I promise you I'll tend it with loving care.'

We'll be working close together. I can't stand it, she thought, then clung frantically to the old adage that familiarity breeds contempt. 'I'll expect a complete survey and estimate,' she quavered, wondering why the hard-bitten New York resident had suddenly decamped.

'OK. And you can leave the Heritage authorities to me. I've worked with them before and I know the ropes.' He did not move, still holding her by the shoulders and looking down into her face with a quizzical smile. He was so tall that the top of her head did not reach the pit of his throat. She could see the pulse beating there, her own pumping in response.

She could smell that intoxicating scent of man; a combination of woodsmoke with a musky marine base. Crisp dark chest hair curled at the gap where his shirt was unbuttoned. She nearly placed her lips there, but stopped herself just in time.

This shocked her so much that she almost scooted off to the other side of the room. 'You'll tell me what's to be done?' she said, her voice sounding unnatural and shrill in her ears.

He stood back, leant an elbow on the carved chimney breast and regarded her solemnly. 'Very well, Miss Erskine. Now, if you don't mind, I'll get on with it. The sooner we can do a costing, pending the usual permissions, the quicker I can get started.'

'You'll need a key,' she said, happier now she could plunge into practicalities and forget the lustful thoughts he provoked. 'How did you get in?'

'The French windows of the drawing room are dodgy.

You ll need a complete security system. But yes, it would be more convenient to have a key.'

'I'll get a spare cut.'

'Fine.' He nodded, smiled and turned to go. 'Are you staying?'

'No. I've things to do.'

'Can I give you a lift?'

'No, thanks. I'll walk. I'm living in the gatehouse. It's not far away. I didn't see your car.' She was still suspicious.

'It's parked round the side. I guess I'd better show you my ID to put your mind at rest.' He pulled a card out of the back pocket of his jeans. Everything was in order. He was indeed Christopher Devlin, with a string of letters after his name.

More disturbed than she cared to admit, Lorna left the house. His intrusion had completely thrown her. She had intended to have an afternoon of peaceful rummaging among her new possessions, helping them come to terms with the fact that she was now their owner.

All this had been scattered to the four winds by a large, forceful individual who had, it seemed, the power to shatter her peace of mind, agitate her hormones and make her as randy as a bitch on heat.

She was sitting in the rush-seated carver at the kitchen table sipping a glass of orange juice, when a shadow blocked the open back door and knuckles beat a light tattoo on the panel.

'Hello, there,' said Gary Curtis, grinning broadly. 'Miss Armitage said you wanted to see me.'

'Oh, yes. It's about the garden. Come in. Would you like a cold drink?' She was flustered, her mind still floating with sexy images of Christopher. These had followed her all the way home and she could not shake them off. A shower had cooled her skin, but not the furnace inside.

'Thank you, miss. I would that. Still hot, isn't it? Though I like the hot weather, don't you?' He did not need a second bidding, his solid bulk seeming to fill the room. 'The girls walking about in their little skirts and tops, it's enough to put a bloke off his ale.'

Lorna smiled, lightening up. This man was so uncomplicated, like labourers she had known in the past. He appealed to her in a coarse, earthy way. He had a big frame which in time would probably run to fat, and a beer belly develop, but just for now he was firm and muscular. His buttocks were small enough to be cupped in the palm of a woman's hand, his chest deep, his thighs well developed through playing in defence for the football team. And his cock?

Lorna didn't know yet, but she intended to find out.

Christopher had roused untamed passions in her, complex passions which she did not welcome. Yet she needed satisfying by something more than a vibrator, her own fingers or even Cassandra's. She wanted a great, throbbing, living phallus to ride up and down on, making it slip in and out of her yearning cunny till she came, clenching her inner muscles round its bulk. It had been some time since she had known this pleasure.

'Aren't you going out with the redhead who works in the pub?' she asked, seated opposite Gary at the table. She could see how the rays of the sinking sun played over his short blond hair and glittered on his furred lower arms.

He shrugged offhandedly. 'Happen I am. But there's nothing settled. We aren't engaged.' He glanced down at his broad hands with the thick, spatulate fingers. They were deeply ingrained with oil. 'Sorry 'bout the state of me. I should have had a wash before coming, but I help out at my brother's garage.'

'I thought you were a gardener,' she said, still smiling. Such bashfulness was charming, yet she sensed it to be an act. He was a slyboots who knew very well that ladies often liked their meat raw, relishing dirty, sweaty men mounting them like rutting rams in the breeding season.

His blue eyes came to rest on her breasts, admiring their shape under her thin shirt. Her nipples prickled and she wondered how long it would be before he touched them.

'That's true, miss. I do gardening, but anything else that turns up, too. A Jack-of-all-trades, you might say. And my brother'll make me a partner one day. I'm good with cars.'

Lorna leant across the table and refilled his glass from the pottery jug, aware that her action brought her cleavage in line with his eyes. 'I'm sorry it's not beer,' she said.

'That's OK, miss. I'm driving, and the pigs are always on the prowl. I don't want to lose my licence.' He looked from her breasts to her face, his expression one of naked lust.

She sank back in the carver and crossed her legs. Of necessity, this brought her jeans into closer contact with her labia. If she wriggled ever so slightly, the pressure increased.

He had not moved from his chair, yet she felt as if he had come closer. Such a muscular, virile young stud. Would those calloused fingers be harsh in their handling of her flesh, or would he know how to explore, sliding and circling? Would he stroke her clitoris with the care of a woman touching a piece of silk?

'I need a car,' she said at last. 'Can you help me find one?'

'Sure thing. How much do you want to pay? I expect I can fix you up with something. Bob's got a tidy little Fiat Punto down the garage. Suit you a treat.'

Lorna was not worried about money. She had plenty of her own in the bank, but even so she hoped Dudley would not delay too long in settling her affairs and releasing her inheritance. Part of it would remain invested, but the cash and interest would keep her in luxury. Just for the moment, however, it might be wise to buy a modest vehicle. Besides, it would give her an excuse to dally with Gary.

'Could I see it?' she asked, watching avidly as he savoured the last drops of orange juice, his fleshy tongue coming out to lick over his lips in a most suggestive way.

'You can see it any time you like, miss.' He heaved to his feet, grinning mischievously.

'The Fiat, Gary,' she reminded him.

'What else, miss?' Country bred he might be, but Gary was very much aware of the rules of the game, fencing verbally. 'There's no time like the present, I always say. Grab life by the throat before it grabs you.'

'Let's go,' she murmured, his coarseness and need acting like a powerful aphrodisiac on her already over-heated passions, nipples rising and stiffening, her secret lips thickening and juice escaping from her lower mouth.

The garage and petrol station were locked for the night but Gary had a key. He swung up the metal doors and switched on the light. Harsh fluorescent tubes glared down on the stark interior.

Disembowelled cars, once someone's pride and joy, drooped sadly like lost pets: metal, twisted and spiky, glinted menacingly; wheels and cogs, winches and oily chains cluttered every available surface and the air was redolent of gasoline and grease and cellulose.

The workshop covered a substantial area, with a deep, dark oubliette of an inspection chamber. There was a small, glass windowed office. 'We make tea in there,' Gary explained. He was proud of Bob's business acumen and his own part in this family concern.

'Where's the Fiat?' she asked, picking her way across the blackened floor, wondering if it was possible to remove oil if it got on her jeans.

'Over here, miss.' Gary whipped off a dustsheet, revealing a neat and shiny runabout, just the thing for her at that present time.

'Nice,' she murmured. 'Will it come with a warranty?'

'A year, as it's so new.' He leant a forearm on the roof and looked down at her as she tested the driver's seat. 'We can see about insurance and it's got six months' road tax. Just the ticket, isn't it?'

They discussed the price before Lorna said, 'I'll get

Marc to look it over.' She had no clue if Cassandra's man knew anything about cars, but it sounded sensible. Gary mustn't think she was a pushover, in any direction.

She got out and they stood together under the overhead lights. 'You're all right, you,' he whispered. 'And you've got that accent that makes me go all funny inside. I've always wanted to go to America.'

'Don't believe all you see in the movies,' she warned, but relaxed against him.

He pushed her back against the bonnet of the car next to the Fiat, a large midnight blue Mercedes. Her hips were forced forward by the angle, pelvis lifted to meet his. His face came down, mouth opening as he met hers, his tongue sliding between her teeth. Lorna closed her eyes and gave herself up to the sensation of hot lust trembling through every particle of her body.

He hurried. *They* hurried, neither prepared to wait. He dragged her shirt open, found the front fastening of her bra and clicked it apart with experienced fingers. The cream lace cups fell apart, and her breasts rose to meet his fingers. She gasped and lay back. Gary bent over her, staring down at her nipples and flicking them into sharper peaks, while fiery sensations ignited her clitoris.

She tugged at her jeans and wriggled them down about her hips. Gary's were already undone and she raised her head to get a glimpse of his cock.

She was not disappointed, awarded the sight of his great pink serpent uncoiling and lifting its smooth head towards the garage roof. Uncut, it was a specimen to be proud of, the shaft thick and richly veined, the glans throbbing and red, already wet and slippery.

Her furry pubis was still hidden by her briefs. Gary gave vent to a low growl as he worked his fingers around the hem. He tangled with her floss, tugging at it gently, then probed lower with his middle digit, burying it in her crack and letting it slide between the pouting lips and past the entrance to her innermost haven.

Lorna gripped his weapon, her thumb and forefinger just about meeting round its girth. 'Take your trousers off, Gary,' she hissed fiercely. 'I want to see all of it and your balls.'

'Can't do that, love,' he protested. 'Someone might come in. Just you shift down a bit so I can get your knickers out the way, and we'll manage fine.'

He rolled her over on her stomach and bared her bottom to the evening air. She could feel his prick pressing into the deep crease between her buttocks, bypassing her anus and driving home into her vagina. The surface of the Merc was slippery, and she clung to its chromium trappings, a hand on either side, bracing herself against the force of Gary's possession.

'I can't come this way,' she cried, butting up against him in frustration.

'Want your little button rubbed? Is that it?' he panted into her ear. 'I'll do it for you.'

She felt his hand slip under her, cupping her mound in his palm. Then his finger massaged her pleasure spot with rough, arousing strokes that sent tremors though her limbs and set her juices flowing.

'More,' she sobbed, beating on the bonnet with her fists. 'Do it harder. Make me come!'

'Jesus!' Gary muttered, pumping at her furiously, his finger matching the speed of his movement.

Now she could feel it, that imperative thrusting every other consideration aside, a heavy, insidious pleasure building up in her loins. The feeling was gathering force, pouring over her, wave upon wave carrying her higher to a climax so intense that she yelled as it peaked.

Someone other than Gary heard Lorna cry out, a silent watcher who had crept in through the partly opened door and kept herself hidden.

At first Alison had been furious, wanting to fling herself on her faithless lover and scratch his eyes out, before turning her wrath on Lorna Erskine. Then she remembered Ryder's instructions. He had told her to spy on the American woman.

Her heart throbbed with the pain of betrayal, but her

hungry nub pulsed with another sensation. She had come there with the intention of finding Gary and playing with his cock, needing a daily injection of its vital fluid. He was otherwise engaged, but a curious, perverted heat warmed Alison's insides and tingled through her clit as she watched that coveted serpent burying itself in another woman's wet and welcoming nest.

She thrust a hand under her skirt and fingered herself. Her sex-lips unfurled and she moistened the hard kernel of flesh that crowned them. She was so near the edge that it took but a few strokes to have her writhing and jerking in orgasm.

She came down from the heights to see Gary withdrawing from Lorna's cleft, drops of pearly spunk dripping from the condom as he pulled it off, knotted it and dropped it into the wastebin. She was accorded the uninterrupted view of his paramour wiping her pussy before pulling up her jeans.

Bitch! Alison thought, envying her slim waist and flat belly. Just you wait till Ryder Tyrell and Sybil Esmond get to work on you.

Chapter Six

'You'd flip if you could see my house,' Lorna said to Nicole, catching up with her later that night. She was wide awake, still aglow from Gary's lovemaking. 'It needs a lot of repair, but it's going to be magnificent when it's finished. It'll be worth a fortune, though I'll never sell it.'

'I must come over, but it won't be till after the convention,' Nicole answered, sounding no further away than Briar Cottage, instead of the *Image* office on the other side of the Atlantic. 'Sean misses you. We all miss you, honey.'

'How's it going?'

'Don't ask, but we'll make it.'

'You always do, and it'll be another huge success.' For a moment Lorna regretted not being back there in the thick of it. 'I don't know what's going to happen in the future,' she continued. 'I love this place, and I feel at home here, but I don't want to give up work entirely.'

'Don't worry, hon. We'll figure something out,' Nicole soothed, sensitive to the problem. 'There's no way I want to lose you, but just for now take a sabbatical. Tell me about those dishy English guys.'

'Have you got a week?'

'So many, huh? Wow, I'll get the next flight!'

'If only,' Lorna sighed, and told her about Dudley and Christopher and Gary, mentioning Cassandra's liaison with Marc, and that she was going to dinner with a suave neighbour who had opened up an exclusive hotel in the former vicarage.

Tears pricked her eyes when she hung up, the lodge seeming lonely and desperately quiet after the eternal hum of a huge city. I'm not complaining, she told herself and immediately phoned Sean.

His soft Irish voice trickled into her ear like honey. He was funny and understanding, teasing and curious.

'Who've you been sleeping with, sweetheart? Giving the local studs a going over? I've been so lonely for you I've had to do the five-knuckle shuffle.'

'You? Lonely? I can't believe that,' she said, pleased but sceptical, memories of their brief but torrid encounter making her nipples crimp.

'I kid you not,' he avowed, then his voice darkened, dropping to an intimate murmur. 'Tell me who you've been screwing. I want to hear every last, dirty detail.'

'Where are you?' she asked, needing to visualise him.

'On the couch in my apartment. You dragged me from the shower.'

'Are you naked?'

'I'm wearing a white towelling robe. It's a cute little number, sort of thigh-length. It's undone and my cock's up just through hearing your voice. I've got my hand round it.'

The picture his words conjured was so vivid that Lorna's body rippled with excitement. She was aware of the scent of recent coition and the flood of fresh juice oozing from her vulva. It seeped round the briefs drawn so tightly between her sex-lips as she sat, open-legged, on the arm of the wing chair in the parlour. By rotating her pelvis ever so slightly, she could bring pressure to bear on her bud.

'Go on. Tell me what you've been doing,' Sean urged, and she imagined him sprawled at ease, muscular thighs apart, the robe fallen open over the thatch of wiry hair coating his belly and his cock rising between his fingers, glistening and purple-headed.

'Well, there was this Englishman on the plane,' she began. 'It was night and very quiet. I was asleep and woke to find him caressing me between my legs. We had sex, then and there, on a seat in the first-class cabin.'

'Was it wild?'

'His cock was the smallest I've seen, but yes, it was wild, I guess.'

'And?' he prompted, his breathing ragged, and her mind whirled with thoughts of what he was doing to himself.

'And then I made love with my friend, Cassandra, in her pool.'

'I didn't know you were bisexual.' He sounded surprised, intrigued and exceptionally excited.

'There's a lot you don't know about me.'

'Darling, how could I? You won't let anyone near you. I wish I'd been there to watch you with your lesbian pal. Go on.'

Lorna refrained from trying to explain that Cassandra was not strictly gay, merely open-minded and experimental. Instead she said, 'Tonight I went to look at a car with Gary, the handyman. I'm thinking of buying one. He's young, hunky, sexy and crude, and he's shafting the barmaid of the pub and anything else that breathes. He pulled down my jeans and put his big fat dick in me.'

'Keep talking, *acushla*, I'm going to shoot my load any minute. God, you make me so hot!'

'I hope there isn't an operator listening in on this call,' she said, suddenly overcome with prim reserve. Guilt mingled with the pleasure stabbing into her loins.

'Don't worry about that. I want to hear what you did with Gary.'

Lorna closed her eyes and relived the scene in the garage, her own heat matching Sean's. 'I was lying on my back across the bonnet of a Merc. It was so slippery, and the garage was dingy, harshly lit, and his hands were ingrained with oil ... Strong hands, the jagged nails flicking over my tits. I could smell his sweat, an earthy, petrol-tinged, musky smell. He was rubbing himself against me, making me take hold of his length, then stroking me till I came. It was wonderful and I screamed with pleasure, and he pushed into me, thrusting and pumping.'

Sean gave a long drawn groan as he achieved the quintessence of bliss. 'Oh ... oh ... yes! Yes! Yee – es!'

'You're coming?'

'I certainly am,' he said in a strangled voice. 'Phew! That was some turn-on. Have you brought yourself off? Are you going to?'

'I've got my hand down my knickers,' she replied, jeans upzipped as she stroked the rim of her labia. Her heart was thumping, but more through sharing his enjoyment than with the need for completion. 'I don't know if I'll come. I wish you were here, Sean.'

'There's a chance I may be over to work on a film for British TV. My agent's getting it together,' he replied, his tone back to normal now.

Lorna never failed to be amazed by how quickly men recovered once their balls were milked dry; she could imagine his smile, his long brown hair, and those impish azure eyes tilted at the outer corners like a leprechaun's, hedged by incredibly thick lashes.

'That's great news,' she murmured, and hugged the phone closer.

'It won't happen yet. I've got stuff to finish here, and then there's the Cover Model contest, but I promise to come. How does that grab you?'

What could she say but 'Yes, that's wonderful. Let me know. Come and stay here.' And all this without appearing to be too eager.

When she finally replaced the receiver on its console, she immediately fretted in case she had appeared too cool. Even though she had pleasured him long distance, maybe he had expected a stronger reaction. But this is all I can give him at present, she thought. I can't let him get into my blood, any more than I can permit myself to dwell on Christopher Devlin. That type of man is anathema to me.

She made herself a coffee and sat on the window seat, staring out. The darkness seemed on the verge of revelations. It was one of those nights whose magic lies like a cloak on the spirit. There was a bank of streaky clouds on the horizon, moon-washed and silver-tipped. The garden, so friendly by daylight, seemed to hold a secret in its depths.

She was still worried about her response to Sean. Had she seemed too cold? Lacking in the enthusiasm he obviously expected? Would she have given him the impression she was not really interested in him?

It was hard to get it just right; not appearing too keen, not appearing too cool.

Relax, she told herself. Unwind from the hurly-burly of New York. Think of nothing but the present. Put Sean and *Image* on hold. Don't even dwell on the meeting with Ryder and Sybil. Just be.

Beyond the boundaries of the Priory grounds lay open countryside. The area lived up to its name, being composed of woods and meadows, with wide expanses of arable and grazing land, sheep dotting the landscape like fluffy toys, and beige cows with swinging udders nudging their dark muzzles contentedly into the lush grass.

The latter looked up to stare as Lorna passed, their eyes limpid and long-lashed, strings of saliva hanging from rubbery black lips. The ground was covered by a carpet of clover and she bent to pick a flower, pulling out a petal and sucking on it as she had done when a child, the nectar flowing sweet over her tongue and taste-buds.

There were poppies and cornflowers, scabious and thistles, and she stood in the clover patch, her skin warming to the sun's caress while the breeze lifted strands of loosened hair that tumbled across her shoulders. She contemplated making a daisy-chain

132

wreath and wearing it on her head, then laughed at herself for being childish.

She had awakened with the need to walk, leaving early before Cassandra called, or Dudley or anyone who would remind her of her responsibilities. She needed to be alone, free to think and make sense of the things that were happening to her almost too quickly.

England is so beautiful, she thought, and wandered towards a dark smudge of woodland. It was cool among the trees, the sunlight dappling the forest floor with a lacy pattern of leaf shadows. The broad avenue with its grassy glades and giant oaks reminded her of a church nave. Her mind grew still as she breathed in the fragrance of rich earth and damp undergrowth disturbed by her sandalled feet.

The trees thinned and she came out into the open. The clouds had begun to pile up, light and shade sweeping across the fields. At one moment the grass was vivid green; in the next it had sobered to drab olive. She climbed a rise and saw a house below her, sunk in a hollow surrounded by trees.

It seemed to drowse, a column of smoke drifting lazily upwards from one of its many ornamental chimneypots. Was that the old vicarage, Ryder Tyrell's lair?

Wanting to take a closer look, she plunged into the woods again, following a path which she thought would lead her to the house She would not call on Ryder, of course, but at least she could peep over the walls and see how the land lay.

But when the track ended, she found herself standing in a glade, deep shadowed and isolated. The silence was absolute. No bird, no insect disturbed the heavy, brooding stillness. It was a deathly silence, yet in some strange, tacit, insidious way alive – waiting – but for what?

And then she saw it.

An upright stone some five feet high, grey and pitted with age, reared proudly from the earth. Its shape resembled the Celtic cross near the church, but there any similarity ended. Lorna stared, fascinated. It was nothing more nor less than an outsized phallus, the rounded glans carved to represent a face peering out from a rolled-back foreskin, the base of its shaft rooted in a pair of giant testicles.

She paced round it. The back of the monolith was even stranger, decorated with a snake standing on its tail, the whole thing symbolising a powerful potency.

Filaments of excitement electrified the air. Obeying some primitive instinct, she faced the phallic stone, spread out her arms and clasped it, grinding her breasts into the lichenous surface. It felt warm under her hands – an uncanny living warmth. A secret heat pervaded her honey-slick core, a build-up of tension tingling through her sex tissues.

She stood there daydreaming, her mind filling up with pictures of ceremonies in this place. Perhaps an Iron Age tribe had erected the stone as their totem. Maybe they had danced round it at the year's first solstice, tethering a virgin with garlands of flowers, a gift for the god chosen from among the most beautiful maidens, the ritual performed to promote the fertility of the earth.

The discordant, savage strains of Stravinsky's *Sacre du Printemps* rang in her head. By an odd coincidence she had been playing the CD while she breakfasted, its weird cadenzas stirring atavistic memories within her. The Rite of Spring, evoking powerful forces. The mind might rationalise these feelings, but the blood, flesh and sex recognised and accepted something so much stronger than human intervention.

The urge to strip was too overwhelming to resist. Slowly, she started to unbutton her cotton dress. This quiet, remote spot offered a perfect place to worship through the body, and for this she must be skyclad.

The air played over her bare skin as her dress opened all the way down and she slipped her arms out of it. Her bra felt tight, and she released her breasts from bondage. The nipples sprang up, stiff as cones, responding to the light breeze feathering over them and sending tiny sparks along her nerves from the pink-brown crests.

Only her panties remained and she stepped out of them. The air lapped at her bush like a silky smooth tongue, flicking playfully at her secret lips as she parted her legs, feet planted firmly in the soil.

'Is this what you want, Forest God?' she whispered, addressing the phallic head which seemed to watch her, a faintly lustful, cryptic smile on its stone lips. 'Will it please you if I climax?'

The dell was hot, the golden bowl of the sun held between the tall trees. Lorna's senses swam, drenched in the shimmering glow and mystic, pervading green. She relaxed, hip thrust forward, her weight on one leg, the other slack, and her hands drifted down over her naked body, smoothing the flesh as delicately as if she was caressing a lover.

Heavy eyelids closed, she admired the sleekness of her waist and belly through the agency of her fingertips, revelling in the softness of the tanned skin, the crispness of her downy floss. Her deep pink sex folds thickened, and sultry essences escaped from her inner chamber, wafting up to join the scent of crushed verdure.

Blood warmed the erectile membrane of her bud. It swelled between her labia, a pleasure point at the apex of the furry pubic wedge. It throbbed to the rhythm of her pulse and she ached to touch it, but held herself in check. Every moment of this communion with the Forest God must be savoured; a time of long, leisurely caresses that would summon up a passion surge from the wellspring of her desire till, at last, unable to control it, she would reach the peak of tumultuous ecstasy.

She placed a hand beneath each breast, lifting the firm, bare globes and teasing the nipples with her thumbs. The most exquisite sensations radiated from the puckered tips, darting to her groin and inflaming her clitoris.

Oh, how she needed to rub it! It was easy to imagine the feeling of her fingers slipping between her thighs, parting the dewy lips and dipping into the pool of her vulva, then up, across her sex-valley to the ardent fulcrum of her pleasure.

'I must do it. I must!' she whispered, but maintained hard-won control, still playing with the succulently swollen nipples. She shivered with want; her bud felt fit to burst, very nearly brought to climax by the friction on those coral tips, but not quite. The torment was not over – not yet. She had further to go before she spent herself.

She concentrated on her physical being, going deeper into herself till she reached a trancelike state, aware of nothing but the feel of her fingers on those dual points of joy. It was as if she could see the nerves, like silver threads, linking them with her pulsating bud. The blood drummed in her ears and the velvety walls of her vagina spasmed.

'I can't wait any longer. I can't,' she moaned, and slid one hand past her navel and down, down, to pass over her bush.

'You can, Lorna. And you will,' said a voice behind her.

She started as if stung, dropped her hands to her sides and spun round. Her feelings rushed into one enormous, panicky wave of terror.

The sun was shining directly into her eyes, and someone stood in silhouette at the edge of the woods: a tall, black figure haloed in crimson against the denser blackness of the trees. Just for a blinding moment she thought, the Forest God incarnate!

Then he moved closer and, 'Mr Tyrell,' she quavered, her face as flushed as her sex.

This flesh and blood man seemed oddly godlike as he stared at her with eyes burning like a sheet of ice under a wintery sun, his face autocratic. His features were finely drawn, his dark smile full of promise, a caress in itself.

'Mr Tyrell? How charmingly formal, under the circumstances. Are you always so correct when a man disturbs you when you're masturbating?' He reached out and grazed one of her breasts with the palm of his hand.

'I ... ah ... that is ...' she stammered, thoroughly disconcerted. Then she gave up trying to find excuses, wanting only to feel his slim, sinewy fingers fluttering over her nipples.

'There's no need to explain,' he said softly, and she had never desired a man with such raw, unbridled lust as that which rampaged through her limbs and made her knees shake. 'I hoped to find you here, and in this state, too. It fulfils my wildest dreams, and I have been dreaming of you, Lorna, ever since I met you the other night.'

He was an impressive figure in tight black jodhpurs that fitted without a wrinkle, smoothly form-hugging from waist to below the knee where they met the tops of highly-polished riding boots. Even these restricting, superbly tailored breeches could not disguise the thick, sap-filled bough of his penis, lying solidly along his left thigh. It thrust against the material, a prisoner intent on release, and there was nothing Lorna wanted more than to help it escape confinement.

He dropped the reins of his great, glossy Arab stallion, and it lowered its head and cropped the short, springy turf, the sunlight making stars sparkle on its inky coat. Like its master, its strength and beauty took Lorna's breath away.

She was laved in waves of heat, the combination of leather and horse-sweat emanating from his clothing, coupled with his own personal odour, making her feel faint. She was gravid with need, wanting him with a desire that was pure agony.

His arm came out, snaked round her waist and pulled her slowly towards him till the hard points of her nipples touched the linen of his shirt. She tried to hang back, to hold on to her reserve, but the feel of his hard body pressing against her made the longing for him intolerable.

With a sigh of pure defeat, she reached up to caress his smooth-shaven cheeks and the hair that sprang back in silver spangled wings from his temples. He looked down into her face with a sardonic smile, his swelling cock nudging at her belly even though his flies were still securely closed.

'So, Miss Erskine. What is it you want, eh?' he asked, a thread of mockery weaving through his deep voice. 'To please the Old Ones? To propitiate the gods? Did you know that Celtic head-hunters put up these phallic stones? They decapitated their enemies and stuck the heads on stakes, believing them to be a potent source of virility. The head, the phallus; the two objects were one in their minds. They worshipped the serpent, too, and its significance is glaringly obvious.'

She shifted impatiently. 'That's all very interesting, but you can tell me about it tonight.'

'You want action, I take it?' He sounded cool, yet the upraised tribute of his penis betrayed his inner fire. 'Tell me what you need, Lorna.'

This made her angry and afraid. His tone was simply too persuasive. He would tear the deepest secrets from her soul if she let him. She struggled to get free, forming her hands into fists and pushing against his chest as she muttered, 'I need nothing from you.'

He hardly registered her protest, his sombre smile deepening.

'Speak of your desires, my child. You can say anything to me. You're a pagan, Lorna, a wild thing from the wild woods.'

'What d'you want of me?' she cried, exasperated by her own reaction, and his.

'Everything, Lorna, but pleasures must be taken slowly, savoured and anticipated. Haven't you learnt this lesson yet?'

His hand slid from breast to waist, circled her navel and caressed her belly. Then he cupped her mons veneris and taunted the outer lips of her labia with adept fingers, making her gasp with the sheer pleasure of it.

She squirmed, bearing down, wanting more. His long middle finger parted the swollen wings, exposing the pink pearl within. With a feather-light touch, he stroked over the tender head, whispering, 'This is the seat of your arousal. Without proper fondling of this perfect gem, you'd find it impossible to reach the zenith. I know, Lorna. I appreciate every inch of a woman's body and can play on it like a finely tuned instrument.'

Is he serious? she wondered, stars dancing under her closed eyes as she rotated her pelvis against that skilful finger, frantic to come before he stopped pleasuring her.

'Be still,' he drawled and, as she feared, left the anguished clit-head, rubbing each side of it and fondling her slippery wet delta. 'I know you need orgasm desperately, but you have so much to learn. To start with, we must offer libation to the god.'

He released her abruptly. She staggered back, frustrated and furious. Watching her with those piercing eyes, he unzipped his breeches and took out his penis. Even in its semi-erect state it was larger than average, a weapon any man would be proud to flaunt.

He faced her, opening his jodhpurs wide so her eyes could feed on it. She stared greedily, aching to slake her thirst. Her mouth parted as she longed to take the bulging knob between her lips, to tease the slit with her tongue-tip, taste his salty juices and gently squeeze the ripeness of his testicles. They hung there in their velvety purse, like prime fruit overloaded with delicious liquid.

She made an involuntary movement towards him, but he merely smiled and faced the stone. Then, legs astraddle, he aimed his cock and released a jet of steamy, amber urine that frothed as it hit the ground. The earth around the monolith's base hissed as it soaked up his offering. Then, after shaking off the last remaining drops, he looked at Lorna, his handsome penis still exposed.

'Now you shall do the same,' he said.

'I can't ... not in front of you,' she gasped, but her bladder was full and she needed to relieve it. Why the hell did I drink that last cup of coffee? she berated herself. Coffee's a diuretic. It's impossible to hang on for long.

'I order you to do it,' he said, and the sternness of his

tone made a bolt of fear, and something as yet unnamed, shoot down her spine.

'Order me? You've got to be joking,' she shouted. 'Who the hell d'you think you are, ordering me to do anything, let alone pee?' But she could not stop looking at his penis.

It arched arrogantly from his fly, the helm fiery red, bare of foreskin, thrusting out from the black hair of his under-belly, a mighty bar of flesh. He stood, legs apart, and his hands were at his testicles, cradling their weight, fondling them. They were so obviously the balls of an experienced, mature man who had taken his pleasure at many an orifice.

She wanted to hold them, to enjoy the feel of that spongy mass, and spread the fluid of his arousal over the clubbed, circumcised head. Her sex organs throbbed, her bladder ached, and she was in turmoil, a victim of her own inhibitions.

Ryder stepped towards his horse, saying, 'Give yourself up to me, Lorna. Accept me as your master. You'll do it, you know, willingly or not. It makes no odds to me. You're too full of yourself. America hasn't done you any favours. It's time you learnt to submit.'

His hands moved over the pommel of his saddle and he returned to her carrying a slim, silver-headed crop, its subtle leather sinuous as a serpent. He caressed her nipples with its tip, and she shuddered at the sharp joy it engendered. It flicked across her stomach and he drew the thong between her thighs, her juices staining the leather to a darker hue.

'Ryder!' she whimpered, as it contacted her quivering bud, giving it a flick that seared like fire, an equal measure of pain and arousal.

'Master,' he rasped, all gentleness banished. 'You must call me master.'

Her wanton desire shamed her, yet she gloried in that humiliation. 'Master,' she repeated.

'Again,' he ordered, dragging the strip of leather tightly into her tender crack. 'Say it louder.'

'Master!'

'That's better. I expect obedience from my slaves.' He held her chin in one hand, yanking her up to him.

She tried to resist but he refused to be denied her mouth. His tongue forced itself between her lips, a hot arrow hellbent on penetrating the depths. He chewed at her lips, bit at her tongue, forced her to yield to his will. His ruthless, vicious kiss left her dizzy with desire.

His hands covered her breasts, the whip digging into the soft flesh, then he bent and closed his teeth over one nipple, gnawing at it. She yelped with fright. and he turned the bite into a nibble. His tongue lapped across the sore and crimsoned bud, caressing her fleetingly before he stepped round behind her.

She felt his hands between her buttocks, probing the dark pink furrow, and then the silver top of the whip at the entrance to her fundament, seeking to open and possess it. She clenched tightly to keep this invader out and her water in, the pressure on her bladder increasingly urgent.

Ryder's breathing was rapid as he ran his lips over her shoulders, the midnight shadow of his stubble stimulating that sensitive spot where her neck joined her spine and lingering beyond the point where pleasure bordered on irritation. His finger entered her vagina to the first knuckle, then the second, and finally the whole of it was buried in her wet warmth. He ventured another finger, then three, opening her wide, spreading the ridged walls, poking against her cervix, and her bladder.

She cried out in distress, trying to free herself, but remained impaled on his fingers. He held her relentlessly, the heel of his hand pressed against her belly, the palm cupping her mound, the fingers buried inside. Then he shifted his grip and began to insert the whip handle into the prepared depths of her sex.

It felt hard and foreign, and very cold, but her vagina drew it in, bathing it in fluid so that it warmed as he moved it backwards and forwards. The sensation was strange and sharp, and she moaned as he twisted this unusual dildo mercilessly against her inner walls.

She was bathed in sweat, the pleasure acute. So was her discomfort. I shall either come or wet myself or both, she thought in desperation.

Still holding her speared on the whip, he guided her to the stone till she stood above the spot where he had urinated. Now he removed the intruding crop and the blunt snout of his cock took its place, not penetrating but rubbing over her cleft from behind. It passed the tight rosy mouth of her anus, caressed the engorged labia, and nudged against her clitoris, activating it.

Pulling her back against him tightly, he slipped both hands down to her pubis, forcing her legs open and holding her lips wide apart. She could feel his regular thrusts, and her sex spasmed yearningly, but he refused to enter. He tweaked her bud, his fingers circling and tormenting it, rousing but not satisfying the turgid button of flesh protruding blatantly from its cowl.

'Do it, Lorna,' he urged, as his buttocks powered his cock, the thickness of it rubbing against the outside of her genitalia and making her open her thighs wider. 'Give the god your water that he may drink.'

She gritted her teeth, determined not to obey, but now he placed his hand flat on her abdomen and squeezed. Lorna shuddered as her bladder let go, a stream of golden rain cascading down to mingle with his, soaking the ground in front of the god.

She burned with unspeakable shame, and it seemed that she peed for a long time like a mare in a field, experiencing a floating sense of relief and appreciating the simple pleasure of being an animal.

Her water washed over Ryder's fingers and as she finally released the last spurt, he removed his hand, raised it to his nose and sniffed the strong fragrance.

Her emotions were on a seesaw. Never before had a man treated her in so cavalier a fashion. She did not know what to expect from him, and the uncertainty kept her on the rack. Would he fuck her now? Would she feel the force and power of his mighty prick?

With her head down, her face half hidden by her ringletted mane of hair, she was helpless in his hands as his fingers bit into her shoulders. He turned her, gripped her chin and forced her to look up at him. He eyes glittered with icy triumph, and he was smiling, that mocking, cruel smile she detested so much yet could not resist.

'You were slow to obey my order, slave,' he said in a low, restrained voice. 'I'll be lenient, as this is your first time, but I expect a better performance in the future.'

Before she knew what was happening, he swung her round like a rag-doll and pushed her face-down against the stone. She thrashed and writhed, tingling with an intoxicating mixture of fear and excitement.

'Be still!' he commanded. 'You must be punished!'

Every nerve in her body jangled as his hand slashed across her bottom. She yelped with shock and pain. A second blow fell before she had time to move.

'Spread your legs,' he shouted.

'But . . . but . . .'

She obeyed.

This time the blow was lower, close to her anus and vulva which seemed to be gaping with a strange kind of hunger. She could not control this or endure the fiery smacks, her anger and pride at breaking point.

Her buttocks stung, her sex, too, and her unsatisfied clit quivered at every blow. 'Oh, please, please,' she cried, tears scalding her eyes, but was not sure if she was begging him to stop or go on.

The sixth agonising slap from that hard palm came in a jumble of sensations. Her rump was on fire, the glow spreading between her legs, everything deep within her core seeming to melt. The seventh blow followed without pause and a fierce, rending convulsion flooded her with violent pleasure.

Ryder stopped spanking her, and sank his fingers into her spasming sex while she clung weakly to the stone.

He nodded, satisfied to find lubricious evidence of her excitement, betraying juices trickling across the insides of her thighs.

She rolled round slowly, careful to hold her smarting rear away from the harsh surface, her green eyes tear-washed, yet defiant. 'What the hell was that about?' she whispered.

'A lesson in good behaviour,' he answered coolly, and adjusted his clothing, then hitched a foot in his stirrup and swung himself on to the stallion's back.

Lorna couldn't believe her own eyes. 'You've leaving? Just like that?'

He sat his saddle like an emperor, tall, straight and indifferent. 'I'll pick you up at the lodge around seven.'

He clicked his tongue, bobbed his heels against his mount's sides and wheeled towards the pathway that wound through the trees.

'You've got a bloody nerve!' she shouted, standing with arms akimbo, glaring at his retreating back. 'What makes you think I'll come after the way you've treated me?'

He glanced across his shoulder at her, eyes heavy with disdainful superiority, and her heart contracted and her pussy clenched at the sight of his dark, smooth face with the aquiline nose and sensual lips.

'We've unfinished business, Lorna. Oh, and by the way, I don't want you playing with yourself. Do you hear me? You must be keyed up and ready for this evening. Listen to arousing music, look at pornographic photographs, do anything to stir your senses to fever pitch, but don't allow yourself release.'

With that, he touched the crop to his lips in a brief salute and rode away.

Chapter Seven

*H*uge grey clouds moved ponderously yet swiftly towards Woodmead as Lorna reached Briar Cottage. The air was oppressive and thunder rumbled in the distance. Her head ached, her reddened bottom smarted and her pride had taken a severe nose-dive.

She was completely confused. Ryder was the first man to have had intimate contact with her without seeking his own gratification. The first man to slap her backside. The first man to deny her his penis.

Damn him, she thought, I won't go to dinner with him tonight. He can rot in hell!

The front door stood open, and Lorna entered the hall noiselessly. She paused. The cottage was silent save for the tick of the long-case clock, but she was certain Cassandra would be about somewhere, possibly with Marc in the studio.

She was not quite sure if she wanted to see her friend just yet. It was too soon after the episode in the woods. Shrewd Cassandra would worm details out of her and it was not the kind of thing she wanted to talk about. It was probably better to simply pop upstairs and collect the dress she had left hanging in the closet. She needed it for the dinner party.

What dinner party? I thought you weren't going, she reminded herself cynically.

Oh, might as well, I suppose, her other self argued, see what else he has on offer.

It was decided, but she had to take care: who sups with the devil needs a long spoon, Lorna reproved her alter ego sternly. It's not a bit of good you wriggling your arse to feel the marks of his hand, and wondering if you'd have got a bigger buzz had he used the riding whip.

She ran lightly up the stairs to the guest room, opened the wardrobe door, lifted the dress from the hanger and laid it over her arm. She was about to leave when a slight noise captured her attention: a small, melodious moan coming from the direction of Cassandra's bedroom. This was at once followed by a throaty male chuckle and the creaking of bedsprings.

Lorna stood rooted to the spot, a dark skein of excitement weaving through her blood. It connected with the vivid imprints of Ryder's palm emblazoned on her rump and made her clit thrum. The recent adventure had done nothing to reduce her sexual heat; if anything it had exacerbated it.

I'm obsessed, she thought. Turning into a nymphomaniac. It's this village, the holy well, the phallic stone. But she could not resist creeping into the passage. The partially opened bedroom door was magnetic. What was going on in there? She could no more stop herself from taking a look than she could stop herself breathing. With a pounding heart and the dew of arousal moist between her legs, she peeped through the crack.

The room was dusky, the curtains dragged across the windows carelessly, as if pulled in a hurry, rays of light striking through gaps in the rose velvet drapes. The bed was bathed in the opalescent glow of a Tiffany lamp.

Cassandra lay within, her wheat-brown skin contrasting with the pristine sheets. Her body was slack, her legs parted, her sex exposed like a fullblown damask rose, the subdued lighting throwing the nooks and crannies of her pudendum into sharp relief. Lorna could feel her excitement mounting at the provocative sight of the cloven inlet extending into the depths of the anal recess.

Marc rested between Cassandra's thighs, his hands toying with the long pink stalks of her nipples. He lowered his leonine head and supped at her honeydew, and her hands caressed his bearded face, a soft, adoring expression transforming her features.

Lorna had never seen her so radiant and feminine. Cassandra had always been notorious for her one-liners and sheer high-octane bitchiness. Not any more, by the look of things.

Could it be that she was in love? Would wedding bells be ringing? Heaven forbid! thought Lorna.

Feeling ashamed, as if she was intruding on some hallowed and very private ceremony, she tiptoed away.

The storm that had built up during the afternoon broke overhead as Lorna let herself into the lodge and went upstairs to change. A clap of thunder rent the air. Vicious forked lightning split the black clouds, releasing a solid wall of rain.

Lorna swore as she ran for the bedroom window, slamming it shut. It was so dark she switched on the lights. They dimmed, then sprang up again.

' "Lovely night for a murder," ' she quoted, talking out loud to herself. 'Just the thing for visiting Tyrell and his mysterious partner.'

She threw off her crumpled cotton dress and stained panties and twisted round to squint at her back view in the mirror. The marks on her posterior had faded to a faint, strawberry blotch. Even so, it was enough to bring the memory of Ryder sharply to mind, making her skin smart.

Hair skewered to the top of her head, she stalked naked into the bathroom, spun the taps and added a generous measure of oil to the tub. The hot water gushed out and the distinctive fragrance of sandalwood rose on the steam.

It was a novelty to loll in a bath. She had become

accustomed to showers, so quick and efficient, but here she had time to lie and soak and reflect, popping the foamy bubbles and squeezing water over her pleasure-hungry breasts with a fat, yellow sponge.

'All I need is a rubber duck and life would be complete,' she mused. 'Though a vibrator would be more fun, if only Ryder hadn't forbidden masturbation. And why am I obeying him, for Christ's sake? I must be losing my marbles.'

The thunder rampaged outside, but here she was cocooned in warmth, drowsily contemplative. She raised one knee, watching the water slide away to leave her skin glistening with diamond drops. The contrast between the snowy suds and her tanned flesh was visually pleasing, but when her fingers strayed to her nipples they crimped with want. Seeing Cassandra and Marc in bed together had stimulated her even more. Her hand began to descend towards her clitoris.

Then as clearly if he had suddenly materialised, she heard Ryder saying, 'Don't play with yourself.'

She sat up and washed herself briskly. Even the application of body lotion did not persuade her to relieve the tension that had been mounting for hours, pre-empting the storm. But she noticed that her hand shook as she sat in front of the dressing-table mirror and lifted her mascara wand.

'Get a life, woman!' she scolded herself. 'He's only a man, with a cock and balls like any other, not some damn prophet!'

She wanted to look her sophisticated best, however, and knew she could do it. The dress she had chosen was black, a slinky tube that touched her ankles, but had a thigh-high slit at one side which parted when she walked, showing a flash of leg. Daring, the shop assistant in the evening gown department of Bloomingdales had dubbed it. Lorna thought this was going too far, but there was no doubt it suited her reed-slim figure.

But before she put it on there was the vexed question of underwear. Should she or should she not wear any?

Did she cradle her breasts in the satin luxury of a bra, clinch her waist with a suspender belt, conceal her pussy under a triangle of black silk?

No, she decided. I'll amuse myself by knowing I'm bare beneath the gown. Let him spend time guessing. Is she? Isn't she? Can I see a knicker-line or is it my imagination?

She had not worn the dress before and it lived up to its expectations. It fitted her body closely, sleeveless, backless, the bodice supported by two shoe-string ties to create a deep valley between her breasts. Her nipples stood out, sharp crests under the clingy crêpe. To confuse Ryder even more, she rolled black stockings up her legs, craftily designed to stay put without a suspender belt.

She slipped her feet into high-heeled shoes, and shook out her layered, gypsyish curls. She wore more make-up than usual, her lashes blackened, her lids shaded moss-green, her brows winging up at the outer corners. Blusher accentuated her cheekbones and she outlined her lips, then filled in the bow with poppy red.

Jewellery? She tried out several pieces and opted for a pair of swinging ethnic earrings and a thick, 24-carat gold rope. Nails? Poppy to match the lipstick, she decided, and painted them last of all, applying two coats and blowing on her fingertips to dry the lacquer.

And all the time her stomach was full of butterflies and her heart was racing.

You're like a teenager on her first date! she admonished herself, adding another, quite unnecessary, spray of her most exotic perfume.

She picked up a multi-hued shawl and black clutch bag and went downstairs, lit a cigarette, took two puffs and crushed it out in the ashtray. Stood up, sat down, stood again to pace the carpet. How she hated waiting for men. Nothing annoyed her more.

Ryder was definitely getting to her. Her thighs quivered, her womb ached and love-juice escaped from her vulva to wet her crisp fleece. And still he kept her strung out on the rack, at least fifteen minutes late.

She went into orbit when the bell rang, leaping towards the little hall, then deliberately slowing, playing it cool. He stood there, an umbrella held over his head, the rain lashing down.

'What time d'you call this?' she started in angrily.

'Ready?' he snapped, ignoring her question.

'Yes.' She flicked off the lights and closed the door, then ran down the path with his arm round her and the umbrella bobbing and showering them with droplets.

They reached the Range Rover and, refusing his hand, she grasped the door frame and swung up and in. She was still seething. He offered no explanation, and she came to the conclusion that he probably never apologised for his actions, a law unto himself.

The leather upholstery was chilly, penetrating her bottom through the thin dress but doing nothing to cool the volcano raging within. Ryder slipped the engine into gear and the vehicle moved off. Lorna peered out between the frenzied activity of the windscreen wipers. The torrential rain continued, the wind thrashing the trees and whipping the tattered clouds across the sky.

The lane twisted and turned alarmingly and Ryder kept up speed. She sneaked a sideways glance at him. The tip of his cigarette glowed, a point of fire in the dimness. In the brief glare of a passing headlamp she saw his hawklike profile, his narrowed eyes fixed on the road.

Although he drove fast and the conditions were treacherous, she felt safe, as if he could master the elements. He was silent, making no comment about their last meeting, giving no indication he was in the smallest degree interested in her. He was the most baffling of people and she could not get his measure.

'What a storm!' she ventured at last, all too conscious of his hands on the wheel, his body in that faultless evening jacket and trousers, and the coiled snake drowsing in his crotch.

He did not deign to reply, and she sank back in her seat, thinking, be like that, then. See if I care.

The car turned into a tree-lined avenue. A particularly fierce flash of lightning illuminated the house momentarily. She glimpsed a large, solid building with a steeply pitched roof and arched windows, then all was lost in darkness again. Ryder drove the car round to the back and slowed down.

The double doors responded to sensors and they passed under the arch. He turned the ignition key, and his eyes gleamed in the interior light as his arm came to rest along the back of her seat.

'We had part of the stable block turned into a garage,' he said, conversationally. 'Do you ride, Lorna?'

'I used to, years ago.'

'We do a lot of riding here, one way or another.' His glance encompassed her face, then went lower, scrutinising her breasts, partly exposed by the flimsy bodice. 'I intend to introduce you to my friends. You're an asset to our little community, Lorna.'

'Thank you,' she replied, blushing. There was something about him that reduced her to a tongue-tied mess.

He bent his head and, without touching her, breathed on the black fabric covering one nipple. Lorna gasped with pleasure under that warm exhalation. He looked up at her, brow raised in a quizzical arch, then reached across and opened the passenger door.

She remained absolutely still, bound by the seat belt. There was a sensation at the tips of her fingers as though they were brushing through his pubic hair, her nostrils responding to the scent of aftershave and masculinity and sex.

He came round to help her out, her hand resting on his forearm, while he stood there courteously. But before she could pass him he thrust into the side opening of her skirt, his fingers walking up her thigh, circling the stocking top, and stroking across her bush.

'As I thought,' he murmured, sinking a finger between her lower lips. 'No panties. Admirable. You're learning, my dear.'

He dropped his hand and her skirt fell back into place.

Lorna had imagined she was prepared for anything, but his breath on her nipple and his sudden examination of her private parts, following hard on his silence and disinterest, shook her to the roots of her being.

She wished Cassandra was there, or Nicole, two confident ladies who would not have stood any nonsense. And yet she had a sneaking suspicion that even they might have fallen under his spell if put to the test. He might prove to be a monster of depravity, but he was still the most charismatic man she had ever met. No one, surely, would be proof against his extraordinary sexuality.

A corridor connected the outbuildings to the rear of the house. They entered through the servants' quarters where once there had been boot rooms for polishing footwear, and oil rooms for the tending of lamps, a butlers' pantry, larders, wine cellars, sculleries and the kitchen.

Some of these were now used for storage, but the kitchen was still in working order. Although equipped with every labour-saving device, it had retained many features from the era when it had catered for the appetites of a succession of vicars and their large families.

It was filled with warmth and mouth-watering smells. An angular, strong-featured woman looked up from taking a pan from the oven of a gleaming red Aga, and a long, lean man wearing a turban, a white tunic and narrow trousers, stood by the well scrubbed table, a wine bottle in his dark-skinned hand.

The woman's eyes were like shards of flint as they went over Lorna from head to toe, and there was something lewd in the way her tongue emerged to lick over her lips.

'Marta, Rashid ... this is our guest for the evening, Miss Lorna Erskine. I trust you'll see she has everything she desires.'

The woman bobbed. The man bowed from the waist.

Lorna thought it odd that Ryder had bothered to introduce her to his staff. Marta gave her a very uncomfortable feeling in the pit of the stomach. As for Rashid? He was as handsome as a fairy tale prince of Persia, upright and stately. Were there other servants? This was indeed a peculiar household, everything out of kilter, not quite normal. But then, she reminded herself, what was normal?

Ryder led her through another door, along a passage and into a hall where a monumental staircase, upheld by carved dragons, disappeared into the dimness of a galleried landing. It was not as large as the great hall at Hinton Priory, but contrived to be awe-inspiring.

The ambience was oppressive, all dark panelling, dark paintings, sombre hangings. There were chiffoniers and chairs of uncompromising hardness. Each door was crowned with foliate heads, their grinning faces peering through a smother of vines.

'It's hardly changed since the last parson lived here,' Ryder said. 'I had central heating installed and the wiring and plumbing updated. It must have been like a morgue in winter.'

'Is it a popular hotel?' she asked as they strolled across the black and white chequered tiles towards a high cedarwood door.

'It's not exactly a hotel.'

'A conference centre?'

His lips curled in a smile. 'You could call it that, I suppose. We cater for a select club, mostly at the weekends, so it's quiet for much of the time. Sybil and I like it that way.'

'Are Marta and Rashid your only helpers?'

'Oh, no. There's Alison Cooper – I think you've met her already – and Gary Curtis sees to the grounds. We employ a chef and waiters, chambermaids and cleaning staff when required. Sometimes we're busier than others. You'll get to know our routine, in time.'

'Shall I?'

She stopped when he did, and his eyes burnt with a cold fire as he stared at her, a muscle twitching at the side of his mouth. She remembered the feel of his fingers on her sex, and was aware that her limbs were lax, the mouth of her vulva opening, even her bladder recalling his mastery over it.

'Of course you will. You're a very sensual woman, Lorna, a beautiful, desirable woman. I'll never let you go.'

She wondered if she had imagined these words, which were so out of character. As soon as he had uttered them he was his cool self again, standing back so that she might precede him.

The walls of the drawing room were hung with silk, the carpets and drapes of ecclesiastical hues. Chandeliers with crystal drops brought out the full brilliance of the gilded woodwork, the exquisite statues, and the lush upholstery of the furniture. Cloying perfume drifted from the waxen trumpets of white lilies arranged in Chinese vases.

A woman rose from the scroll-backed sofa set in the bay. The curtains had not been drawn and the storm hurled itself against the window panes. A blue-white flash formed a penumbra round her for a second.

She extended both hands as she came across the Aubusson carpet. Her walk was graceful, sensuously languid yet vital, her body swaying rhythmically from the hips as if she was fully aware of its glory and power.

'Miss Erskine, I'm so pleased you're here,' she said in a low, musical voice. 'Ryder's told me so much about you.'

What has he told her? Lorna thought guiltily, as her hands were captured and held.

Sybil moved in a shimmer of pailettes, a sea-green sparkle that matched her eyes, her hair an unbroken sweep of white-gold, reaching to her waist. The gown flowed over her like a mermaid's scales, and she wore nothing beneath it, red pointed nipples pressing against the chiffon backing, a shadowy haze between her thighs.

She reached up and lifted Lorna's left breast in her palm, crimson lips parting, aquamarine eyes staring straight into hers. Lorna was unable to restrain a quiver, longing to touch the pale marble smoothness of her skin, and feast on that delectable mouth.

'He said you were beautiful, Lorna,' Sybil continued, releasing the breast reluctantly. 'And he was right.'

'I'm sure he exaggerated,' Lorna stammered, struggling to retain her composure in the face of this outlandish behaviour.

'I didn't,' he put in, and rested an arm round the waist of each woman. 'This is how I wanted to see you both – Light and dark; Sybil as fair as an angel and Lorna as dark as a demon. "Strange harmony of contrasts."'

'Cavaradossi's aria from *Tosca*,' Lorna exclaimed, losing some of her uneasiness.

'Exactly,' he said, smiling in the most charming and ingratiating way. 'And isn't this true? I'm a lucky man, surrounded by beauty tonight.'

We're all surrounded by beauty, Lorna thought later as she sat at dinner in a room that matched the other in opulence. I feel like I'm on the set of some extravagant costume drama.

She glanced down the oval table. The damask cloth was white as freshly fallen snow, the three place settings symmetrically arranged, each with a golden bread roll. Beeswax tapers in sterling candelabra struck scintillating facets from the cut-glass goblets, providing an infinity of intersecting lights.

Music by Pergolesi drifted from hidden speakers, and the food was served by Rashid. Lulled into a false sense of security, Lorna snapped to attention when this handsome, impassive Arab leant over Sybil's shoulder to place a dish in front of her.

As he did so, her hand closed round his penis and stroked it through the thin white linen of his trousers. He straightened up and stood immobile, only the increasing size of his bulge betraying him.

Ryder ignored them, even when Sybil took Rashid's hands in hers and placed them on her breasts.

He continued to caress her nipples while she went on eating, and Ryder, seemingly unaffected by this lustful play, said to Marta as she wheeled in further serving-dishes, 'Well done. You've surpassed yourself tonight. Try some of this, Lorna, my dear.'

She was highly embarrassed, pink-faced and aroused. No longer hungry for food, she felt a slow burn starting in the slippery folds of her cleft. These were most unconventional table companions. She tried to avert her eyes but could not help watching as Rashid pushed his hands inside Sybil's bodice. Remaining deadpan, he rolled the nipples between his fingers, and his mistress continued to eat, giving no indication of excitement.

Ryder smiled, and urged Lorna to sample tiny parcels of quail wrapped in filo pastry, accompanied by buttery new potatoes garnished with mint and nestling among asparagus tips. It was the finest cuisine, but she merely toyed with the food on her plate, hypnotised by the scene on Sybil's side of the table.

Rashid had pushed down her shoulder-straps, baring her breasts to full view, and Marta had disappeared under the cloth. Driven by irresistible curiosity, Lorna deliberately dropped her napkin. Whilst retrieving it, she caught a glimpse of the maid crouched between Sybil's parted legs.

It was too dark to distinguish what was happening but Marta had pushed up the sequinned skirt. There was a flash of lily-white flesh, and her head moving up and down as she feasted between Sybil's legs.

'The shrimp bisque is excellent,' Ryder said, and Lorna flushed scarlet as she surfaced, napkin in hand. 'And these vegetables melt on the tongue. Try some.' He lifted a forkful to her lips. She parted them obediently as he fed her like an infant.

'I recommend the *fruits de mer*,' Sybil commented with never a quiver. Lorna wondered if she had imagined Marta's preoccupation beneath the cloth, but there was no doubting the fact that Rashid was still tweaking her hostess's prominent nipples.

'A splendid choice,' Ryder agreed, and shot Lorna an oblique glance.

She dragged in a breath, wanting his touch most desperately. She eased her bottom on the chair seat, her juices flowing so abundantly they dampened the back of her skirt. Ryder took her hand and rested it on his groin. Her fingers closed round a penis that was swollen, hot and moist, emerging from his unzipped fly.

She was tormented with the desire to experience this weapon deep inside her body, knowing the tension of unsatisfied passion. She fondled his cock while her nerves tingled unbearably and her bud throbbed. He sat there calmly, sipping his wine and accepting her homage, as Sybil accepted Rashid's and Marta's.

The music had changed, baroque replaced by the Impressionistic tone poems of Debussy; ethereal, sensual and dreamlike, they were a perfect foil for this eccentric meal.

'You may serve the dessert now, Marta,' Sybil said in a level voice and the woman emerged from under the table, her lips smeared with silvery liquid.

Rashid retired to stand with his back to the wall, arms folded across his chest and Marta carried in the pudding. Sybil rearranged her bodice and Ryder gave Lorna back her hand. It was time to pay full attention to gastronomic rather than sexual delights.

The dessert was perfection: a sponge-cake base, its hollowed centre filled with poached apricots, coated with meringue and browned in the oven. It was served with a jug of hot apricot sauce laced with brandy, and lashings of whipped cream.

Licking traces of this perfect confection from her lips, Lorna prayed she would be able to find a cook like Marta. The question of staff would arise as soon as the Priory was completed. But would she find a Marta so skilled at cunnilingus? Or a Rashid who would pleasure her to order? It was debatable.

'This wine was laid down ten years ago,' Ryder said, holding his glass of Bonnes-Mares to the light and admiring the colour. 'It's just about ready to drink.'

'You're an expert? I admit I've not made a study of fine wines,' Lorna responded, matching his calm.

'You should start,' he advised. 'I'm sure there are large wine-cellars below Hinton Priory. If it once belonged to monks, then there's bound to be.'

'I don't know. I've not explored that far yet.'

'Have you not?' He exchanged a glance with Sybil and slipped a hand into Lorna's lap, finding the hollow where the skirt was caught between her thighs.

She tried to be as cool as he, but it was nigh impossible. 'No, indeed. But the renovations are in hand. A man came to see me from Enterprise Builders. An architect, name of Christopher Devlin.'

'Has he started?' Ryder's eyes darkened and his seeking finger wormed its way under her skirt, caressed the flesh at the top of her stockings and began a gentle motion on the super-sensitive crest of her clit.

'Not yet. I'm waiting to see his plans and estimate. He's also dealing with the Heritage people for me.' She felt dizzy, light-headed. There had been too much wine and far too much excitement.

'I hope he knows what he's doing. There are a lot of cowboys about, but then the conservation crowd won't let anything untoward happen.' Stroking, rubbing, Ryder's finger was coated with her secretions.

'I'm sure he's very competent. He has impressive credentials. An Associate of the Royal Institute of British Architects. But it's kind of you to take an interest. I'm sure you're very busy and I don't want to impose on your time.' Her voice shook, and she knew he wanted her to be controlled, able to carry on talking while on the brink of annihilation.

'It will be a pleasure to help. Won't it, Sybil?' His eyes cut to his partner, who nodded and smiled back.

'Absolutely,' she murmured.

Flick, flick, went his finger and, as Lorna stiffened in delirious anticipation of orgasm, so he abandoned the tortured clitoris and rubbed the labia instead, denying her the climax she craved. Then he removed his finger altogether, leaving her with an ache in her loins and anger in her heart.

'I'm particularly interested in fine buildings,' he continued, while Rashid poured coffee into fragile gilt-edged cups. 'Especially ones that have a history, like the Priory. You're not considering selling, I hope?'

'Oh, no.' She shook her head and sipped at the sweet, strong brew, her fires dying back to smouldering embers. It appeared the game was over for the time being, and they were to pretend to be an ordinary host and guest.

'I'm glad to hear it. But, if you ever find your circumstances have changed and you do want to sell, I'd be grateful if you'd give me first refusal,' he continued, a spark in the depths of his grey eyes, approval on his aquiline face.

He was pleased with her apparently. She was learning the rules. 'But you have this fantastic place,' she answered calmly. 'You can't want another?'

'I would hate to see the Priory fall into the hands of someone who wouldn't appreciate it, Lorna.'

'I don't see that happening, but yes, I'll remember what you've said,' she agreed, willing to grant him almost anything if only he would make love to her, properly, thoroughly and to completion. 'You told me you had some books which might mention the Priory.'

'That's right. They are upstairs. Shall we go?'

The first thing that caught the attention when entering Ryder's chamber was the viceregal bed, fully seven foot long and six wide. Though he conducted Lorna to the bookcase and started to pull out this volume and that, her eyes kept returning to the bed.

She wanted to lie down on it with him, and have Sybil there, too, that sultry witch with her flaxen hair and shimmering body. The luxury of the house and density of the atmosphere stole into Lorna's system like a narcotic. Memories of the glade were still with her, mixed up with that Mad Hatter's dinner party, her thought patterns confused by the wine she had been drinking and the sexual deprivation Ryder had forced on her.

The phallic stone appeared under her hands, but it was only a photograph in a book Ryder placed on the buhl table. 'It's like the one I saw today,' she whispered, and her finger traced over the smiling face carved into the glans, the thick stem and bulging testes.

'Ryder said you'd been there,' Sybil whispered, arm looped over Lorna's shoulders, her sweet body scent rising up between her breasts from the depths of her perfumed garden. 'You paid homage to the god, I understand. Now you have been chosen for inclusion in our group.'

'A self-help group, is that it? It's the thing nowadays, closest to having your own personal shrink,' Lorna replied lightly, but sensed there was much more to it.

'Actually, it's not like that at all,' Ryder put in, the grooves each side of his mouth deepening in an ironic smile. 'We call it the Club Dionysus. But, yes, like psychoanalysis, it offers the relief of tensions and inhibitions.'

'How?'

'You'll find out soon, but for now take your fill of these,' he replied and spread his arms wide, encompassing the room.

It was dimly lit, even sinister in aspect. Tapers in branching candlesticks glowed on a collection of statues and paintings, every one of which had a sexual connotation.

Bronzes stood on plinths and shelves, painstakingly detailed figures of curly-headed satyrs with horns sprouting from their foreheads and huge penises jutting out from between their shaggy goats' legs. Some had pan-pipes raised to their leering lips, while others held naked nymphs firmly while thrusting those massive tools into accurately carved vulvas or anal rings.

The subjects of the paintings were in a similar vein. Centaurs sodomised fauns; soldiers ravished Sabine women; Jupiter lay with Leda, transformed into a swan but with the fully developed genitals of a man; a bejewelled, naked Salome made obsessional love to John the Baptist's bloody, severed head.

One picture shone out from the rest. Framed with exquisite taste, it stood on an ornate ebony easel.

'Isn't she wonderful?' Ryder breathed close to Lorna's ear. 'A woman to drive you insane. The Madonna, or is it Eve? This *mater amata* has a less than holy function. "Call me mother, call me whore, call me Abraxas".'

The portrait possessed a triumphant femininity, brazen and beautiful. The nipples were scarlet, rising from brown areolae, the breasts white spheres overflowing with nourishment. The naked body was enfolded in flowing hair and the coils of a large serpent. It wound up between her legs, its green scales rubbing across the glossy black plumes, the swollen labia, the dark-red inner bud.

Lorna shivered. The painting roused her sexuality even more than those showing every conceivable variation of coitus.

'You like them?' he breathed in her ear. 'You enjoy seeing couples straining in ecstasy? It's exciting to be a voyeur, isn't it? Even better when the protagonists are real. Didn't you experience that thrill at dinner?'

'I don't know. I've never ... well, hardly ever, and then only porn movies,' she stammered, heat rushing up from her loins, across her belly, breasts and face, her forehead bedewed with sweat.

'You're an innocent, despite your important position with *Image*,' he said, and reached for a handbell on the table. Marta and Rashid stepped into the room.

They were both wearing dark brown hooded habits, and stood passively awaiting orders. When Ryder snapped his fingers they cast the robes aside.

Marta had shrugged off her servant's persona. A black leather bodysuit covered her thin frame. Spike-heeled boots made her even taller, and she flaunted a nine-inch rubber dildo strapped between her legs. She carried a tawse, lovingly running the pliable thongs through her fingers.

Rashid's blue-black hair fell about his shoulders, muscles rippling beneath his mahogany skin. His neck was circled by a studded leather collar. Chains stretched down across his chest to link with a wide belt. Supple trews encased his legs, but were designed to leave his buttocks bare and his penis and testicles exposed.

Sybil made noises of approval, seated cross-legged on the bed, her hands parting her depilated lower lips. The gold rings inserted through her labia caught the light, and her clitoris protruded between them, crowning the rose-pink slit.

Ryder pulled Lorna over to her. 'You see? She reaps the benefit of body-piercing. It makes her constantly aware of her need for orgasm. One day you too will enjoy this feeling.'

'I can't imagine that,' she said breathlessly, waves of excitement stabbing through her groin.

Sybil rose from the bed and approached Rashid, rubbing her body against him lasciviously. She lifted one slim thigh and hitched it round his waist, her crease exposed, clear glistening juice wetting his skin as she gyrated her hips.

Her head was thrown back, her hair pouring down in a golden stream as she clasped her hands behind his neck. He lifted her, his hands under her taut buttocks, then with slow deliberation, lowered her on to his rigid upright shaft.

He took her weight without effort, moving backwards until his legs contacted the seat of a wing chair. He eased into it, and Sybil remained speared on his cock, her thighs splayed, one knee hooked over each chair arm. She arched her spine with agile grace, moving up and down on his slippery length.

'Time for another lesson, Lorna,' Ryder ordered and signalled to Marta.

Half afraid, yet riven with desire, Lorna allowed Marta to lay her back on the bed and flip her over on her stomach. Her hot face was buried in the cool linen of a lace-edged pillow and she felt the soft sensation of silk banding her wrists as scarves were tied to each one and looped to the headposts.

Her skirt was lifted up to her waist, and she instinctively went to scissor her legs in order to prevent the exposure of her twin openings and labia. But hands were on her ankles, prising them apart and using further bonds to tether them to the solid oak columns supporting the tester at the foot. She was helpless and her heart pounded, adrenalin pumping, sex lubricious with wanting.

Never had she felt more alive.

Head to one side, she could see Sybil writhing on Rashid's engorged cock, hearing the woman's sharp cries as she approached pleasure's crisis point. He was pumping up to meet her thrusts, his hands holding her bottom, brown fingers sunk between the rounded cheeks.

Lorna moaned in desperate need and squirmed against the satin quilt, feverishly seeking friction for her needful clit. The mattress sagged slightly as Ryder knelt between her spread thighs. She could smell his expensive cologne and hear the sound as he unzipped his trousers. Hope flared, pouring over her. At any moment he would find her creamy wetness, divide the pouting lips and massage the gnawing ache pervading her clitoris. Then she would feel the bliss of his mighty member penetrating her yearning love-channel.

Instead he shifted to one side, hands beneath her hips to lift her higher, the bonds just slack enough for her to rise to her knees. He bent his mouth to the inviting opening of her body, tonguing the inside of her thighs, licking her mound, then withdrawing. His fingers slipped between the sex-lips and found her clitoris hard and erect. He pressed it firmly, then subjected it to rapid strokes. She felt her womb contract and the first, pre-orgasmic waves ripple through her lower back, her womb, her aching vagina.

He immediately changed tactics, gently exploring the

swollen flesh surrounding her epicentre, denying her the final massage that would bring her to paradise. Her clitoris throbbed as he avoided its head, circling the protective hood, then rubbing the lips on either side of it. Even as her juices began to flow to this artful stimulation, accepting the rosy warmth that replaced the burning heat, he changed his movements again and tapped the very tip of her bud, his touch too hard, dry and almost painful.

'Make it wet,' she begged, writhing her hips, irritated by this brutal stoke and needing him to bring her to a merciful conclusion.

'Impatient,' he scolded, his voice tense, and continued to rub it from stem to tip, increasing the harsh sensation.

Can I get there? The thought wiped out any other, the urge beyond all reason. I must. I can't stand it. It hurts. It's wonderful. Can I come with a hard rub? Have I ever? I need his finger wet, slippery as silk, gliding over my poor, tortured nub.

Just when she was about to give up, having reached that perilous plateau where the slightest move can halt the impending flow, he dipped into her vulva and slid the marvellous cooling moisture all the way up her cleft to coat the button of flesh.

'Yes!' she cried. 'Do it like that, please!'

He laughed low in his throat and withdrew his finger. With expert cruelty he repeatedly brought her to the edge of orgasm and then denied her the final explosion, until the langourous pleasure changed to a deep ache, and the heat became an agonised need.

It was then, when she would have welcomed anything to send her spinning off into climax, that Marta brought the whip down across her upraised haunches.

Lorna yelled sharply at the fiery bite of pain. Her body jerked against her bonds, white heat combining with the terrible longing in her loins. The whip came down again and, as it did so, Ryder subjected her clitoris to the most tender stimulation.

'Punishment and reward,' he murmured close to her

head. 'Yin and yang. Pain and pleasure. Are you beginning to understand?'

She nodded, tears running across her temple to drip on the pillow as she experienced the contrast between a smarting bottom and an achingly sensitive core.

Marta positioned herself between Lorna's thighs. The *godemiche* stabbed at her perineum. She felt the brush of leather and a hand pulling at her maidenhair, then the press of the huge rubber dildo as Marta moistened the tip with the vital fluid seeping from Lorna's vagina and eased it into her eager opening.

It was foreign, alien, cold but warming rapidly under the caress of her juices and welcoming muscles. She pushed back hard, needing it to penetrate her to the full, too long denied the ultimate caress. Once it was drawn deeply into Lorna's body, Marta reached forward to push aside her bodice and hold her breasts, pulling at the aroused nipples.

Ryder lay on the bed close by, stroking the swollen shaft of his penis, cock-tip slippery wet between his fingers as he watched Marta increase the swiftness of her movements.

The dildo seemed to take on a life of its own, becoming a great, stiff pleasure engine that stretched Lorna's inner walls and butted against her cervix, invincible and inexhaustible. Ryder worked his cock with long, firm strokes, and his eyes met and held Lorna's.

She pressed back, riding the dildo, and felt Marta's fingers leaving her nipples and finding her clitoris, falling into a rhythm that matched her plunging hips and the woman's manipulation of the phallic extension strapped over her pubis.

Lorna's eyes focused on Ryder's, then her lids rolled shut. At last she was climbing to the heights, breaking out into the sunshine at the mountain top. She cried as the climax claimed her, tossing her and sending her spinning over the edge of the precipice. Racked with spasms, she sank down on the bed.

The dildo was withdrawn. She felt cold air on her body. Lying there with eyes closed, she was suddenly aware of wetness spattering her back as Ryder ejaculated in warm milky spurts.

Chapter Eight

*D*riving on the left again took some getting used to. The Fiat was a nippy machine and Lorna practised in the side roads before venturing into Salisbury. Gary had carried out his promise. The vehicle had all its necessary documents and Lorna was now a legal driver.

She had an appointment with Dudley. He wanted her to sign more papers. Banks, lawyers – there was an awful lot of red tape involved in inheritance, but the time was fast approaching when the Priory and the fortune it entailed would be hers to dispose of as she wished.

'It's OK to give Chris the go-ahead,' she said, carrying on a conversation with herself. 'He seems to know what he's doing. The estimates he's worked out look cost-effective, and the plans for restyling the kitchen and bathrooms are OK. He's a tad more expensive than others I consulted, but what the hell?'

She tried to ignore the frisson that heated her blood as she thought of sparring with him again. Christopher Devlin did not interest her in the least.

She cruised past Stonehenge. The car park was full of chartered buses and cars. Gaggles of tourists stood at the fences surrounding this circle of prehistoric standing stones, gazing at it wistfully, no longer permitted hands-on contact. A group of neatly suited, bespectacled Japanese gentlemen aimed expensive cameras. A guide went through his spiel.

Lorna thought of the holy well and the wall carvings and wondered if she should open that place to the public. Not for the money, but to share this find. The idea was oddly repugnant. It was a very private place, hers alone.

Salisbury traffic proved a challenge, but she reached Dudley's office eventually. Judy sat at the reception desk, speaking to someone on the phone and buffing her nails. She looked up, said to her caller, 'Hang on a minute, Monica. Don't go away,' and addressed Lorna with an almost imperceptible sneer. 'Mr Norcross is expecting you.'

She pressed a button on her receiver. 'Miss Erskine is here, Mr Norcross. Right-ho. I'll tell her.' She stared at Lorna again. 'He'll be out in a couple of minutes. Take a seat.' Then she flicked a switch and resumed her conversation.

Lorna sank into a deep armchair, and crossed one knee over the other, swinging her foot in its toe-post sandal. She glanced across. Judy's legs were open under the desk, shapely legs with rounded calves and slender ankles. Her short tight skirt revealed suspenders and the small red triangle that barely covered her intimacies.

Had her boss pulled out his cock in front of her? Had she fallen to her dimpled knees and worshipped at that strange shrine, taking him between those red painted lips and sucking him to glory? Lorna wondered idly, feeling a creeping warmth in her own moist centre.

She brought her thighs together surreptitiously, her tightly closed labia pressing on the little button of flesh at their apex. To mask her inner disturbance, she picked up a copy of *Homes and Gardens*, but had scarcely turned a page when Dudley came out of his sanctum. Judy put down the phone, a blush spreading up her neck to her cheeks. He walked by her as if she was invisible.

'Sorry to keep you, Lorna,' he said, once more the urbane young man she had first met. 'Come in, there's someone I'd like you to meet.'

She had temporarily forgotten how attractive he was, dropping her guard as she accompanied him, her wayward desires at full spate. Then she remembered his bedroom behaviour and cooled. They had exchanged a few brisk and businesslike phone calls since that incident at the Priory, but had not met face to face.

Ryder, too, had gone to ground. There had been no sign of him since Rashid had driven her home from the vicarage in the small hours. Exhausted by her ordeal, she had crawled into bed and slept. It was not until next day that she had mulled over the peculiar dinner party and subsequent events.

It would be best, she knew, to ignore any calls he made, filtering them through the answerphone, but all reason and common sense fled at memories of his cunning arousal. Just to recall the kiss of Marta's tawse gave her a deep, visceral feeling and made her itch to repeat that sensual cocktail of pain and ecstasy.

As she entered Dudley's office, she noticed Ian Carr working at the computer. He stood up awkwardly, mumbled, 'Hello,' and sat down again.

Then another man rose to greet her, ruggedly handsome and perfectly groomed. Lorna forgot Dudley and Ian. Even Chris and Ryder faded into insignificance under the power wave surging towards her. He was not only large in stature, but in sheer presence, too.

'Lorna, may I introduce Hugo Pendleton,' Dudley was saying, his voice coming from a great distance as she fell into the glacial lake of the bluest, most piercing eyes she had ever encountered. 'Hugo, this is Miss Lorna Erskine.'

'How do you do?' he said, enfolding her hand in his. It was the strong hand of a labourer, yet the nails were carefully manicured.

'Mr Pendleton is a property developer,' Dudley continued, as she took a chair and both men seated themselves.

'Among other things, Miss Erskine,' Hugo said, with a disarming smile that encompassed her face, her breasts, her thighs. 'But I prefer to be known as an entrepreneur.'

'Mr Pendleton has been looking over the plans of Hinton Priory,' Dudley informed her stiffly, playing with his gold pen, tipping it end to end as if needing something to occupy his fingers.

'Oh, yes?' Lorna said, brows lifted enquiringly, while her nipples peaked, hard as cherries in the underwired cups of her bra.

'I know it's no business of mine,' Hugo went on, leaning forward. His body seemed to be touching hers, though he was three feet away. 'But when Dudley told me that you were tackling the refurbishing alone, well, I just had to take a look. I hope you don't mind.'

'Feel free,' she answered, staring at this man with the wide shoulders and barrel chest under the superlatively tailored navy blue pinstripe suit. He took up more space than the others, his aura and force of will filling every corner of the room.

Yet he looked reassuringly normal, an archetypal tycoon; astute, practical, a touch ruthless. She was used to dealing with his sort in the publishing world. His smile was sincere, yet carried a hint of steel. His forehead was wide, his jawline strong, while his firm mouth hinted at restrained sensuality. She wanted to rest her hand on his knee, then slide it higher, flirting with the solid bulge of the mature equipment resting between his immaculatingly trousered thighs.

She felt suddenly enriched and refreshed, glad that she had elected to appear in town wearing a tobacco brown dress, rather than the jeans or shorts she had been slopping around in lately. It was sprinkled all over with tiny white flowers, the skirt swirling out from the hips and reaching her ankles. It flowed softly, reminiscent of garments worn by maidens at the turn of the century. She guessed that Hugo would respond to its temptingly feminine, almost virginal design.

He edged a little closer and she smelt aftershave spiced with pine, the warmth of cigars and a whiff of brandy. In an instant she was whirled back to long-ago

Christmases when she was small and Daddy was around and her world had not yet toppled into the abyss.

'May I see your house?' he asked, in a low voice, smooth as dark chocolate.

'Of course, Mr Pendleton,' she replied unsteadily.

'Will you call me Hugo?' he murmured, his eyes never leaving hers.

'I'd be delighted. I don't go much on formality, Hugo.'

He chuckled and looked at Dudley. 'You didn't tell me to expect someone so lovely,' he said, with mock reproof, then turned back to her. 'I happened to call in to go over some deeds, and Dudley said he was expecting you. Then he told me a little about your circumstances and how you have only just come from the States. You've taken on a great deal, young lady. I wonder if you know quite how much.'

'I'm beginning to get an inkling,' she said with a rueful grimace. 'It's going to be some task.'

'Let's talk about it over lunch,' he suggested briskly, glancing at the Rolex on his darkly furred wrist. 'What do you say, Dudley?'

'Sorry. I'm already booked,' Dudley replied on cue.

'Oh, too bad. Will you trust yourself to me, Lorna? I feel we're already friends, and hope you regard me as such.'

She could feel her cheeks growing pink under his intense gaze and looked at Dudley, saying, 'Weren't there papers you wanted me to sign?'

'Don't let me interrupt. I'll be waiting in reception,' Hugo said decisively, patting her shoulder on his way the door.

When everyone had left for lunch, Ian sat on in front of the black screen where the green cursor flashed expectantly. He exited the system but left the machine running, unearthed a packet of clingfilm-wrapped sandwiches from a supermarket carrier bag and laid them near the keyboard.

Then he went into the cloakroom and locked the door.

He took his mobile from the inner pocket of his jacket and paged Ryder Tyrell.

'Hello. Ian here. Is that you, master?' he asked nervously.

'Yes,' Ryder answered brusquely.

'I've something to report,' Ian mumbled, his tongue suddenly too big for his mouth.

'Be here on Saturday.'

'Will the mistress see me?'

'Yes.'

'Will she let me serve her?'

'Yes.'

Ian gulped, his spectacles steaming up, even the smallest reference to Sybil making his normally flaccid penis stand, rock-hard. He could feel a wet patch spreading along the Y front of his pale blue underpants.

'Oh, thank you ... thank you, master ...' he began, but Ryder had already hung up.

Ian slipped the mobile back in his pocket and went into the cubicle. There he rubbed his cock till it released a jet of semen into his hand, wiped his fingers on a wad of toilet-paper, threw it into the white toilet bowl and flushed it away.

He returned to his operator's chair, undid his sandwiches carefully and scoffed the sliced brown bread filled with egg and mayonnaise. When Judy returned, he was already working.

Lorna and Hugo lunched at a fashionable eating-house in the centre of Salisbury and then he took her round the cathedral, pointing out the newly restored spire and telling her of the concert that had been held there in celebration, a grand affair graced by a performance by Placido Domingo. Afterwards they explored the numerous antique markets, and bookshops filled with a bewildering display of literature.

She realised she could learn a lot from this knowledgeable older man. He was courteous and humorous and kind, though with the underlying, flattering suggestion that the emotions she engendered in him were far from avuncular. He made her feel protected and feminine and happy with herself.

It seemed the most natural thing for her to agree to have dinner with him, and she followed his Bentley to the Farrier's Arms.

They occupied a reserved table in a secluded corner. The maître d' was deferential, the food superlative, the wine heady. Hugo called for a Sauternes to accompany the lemon mousse he ordered for dessert.

He talked, impressing her with his grasp of architecture and décor and the convolutions of business deals, listening to her attentively when she told him about New York. He had lived there, and it was enjoyable to converse with someone who knew the restaurants and theatres, Manhattan, Broadway and Greenwich Village.

Then, still talking while the lights of the dining room came on, other diners chatted and background music played, he slid a hand under the cloth and caressed her legs, finding the button opening at the front of her skirt. He paused when he reached the tender flesh at the inside of her thigh, but by then she was panting for him to continue, the soft wet heart of her hot as a furnace.

He simply sat there, looking at her intently, then murmured, 'Will you stay with me tonight?'

'Yes,' she answered, trying not to sound too eager.

His apartment was the finest there, kept for his own use. Drinks were served in the sitting-room, where twin chamois-upholstered sofas faced each other across silk Chinese rugs, and the four tall windows were draped in burgundy velvet.

'You like my hotel?' he asked, while she sipped a Margarita, appreciating the taste of salt rimming the glass. 'It's one of a chain in which I own shares.'

'It's magnificent.'

'The interiors were designed to my specification. We kept as many of the original features as possible.'

'I wish I had your experience,' she answered, yet could

hardly continue the conversation, her body vibrating to the controlled lust emanating from his.

'I've offered to advise you. Leave it to me, Lorna,' he said, devouring her with his eyes.

He switched off all but one of the lamps. This remained on a side-table, suffusing the room with a pale apricot glow. He slid across the few inches between them on the settee. Gathering some of her hair in his hands, he lifted it to his lips, inhaling its fragrance and kissing it. Then he rose, pulling her to her feet.

The gentleness vanished. He held her tightly, her breasts crushed against his chest, the nipples rising harder, firmer, rejoicing in the chafing. He reached for her hand, kissed it, sucked the fingers into his mouth. A tremor of ice and fire shocked through them, down her wrist, into her arm, eventually connecting with her sex. She arched her pelvis, bringing her belly in line with the tumescence behind his fly.

He abandoned her fingers and found her mouth, tantalising her with his kisses. His tongue slipped between her teeth, a velvet explorer fired with desire. Her own met it with equal fervour, sucking, licking, tasting, an aperitif for the moment when she would savour his phallus while he found all her hidden pleasure zones. The anticipation was delirious; it stirred the lining of her vagina, making her folds moist, and overloading her clitoris with need.

He unfastened her dress and slipped it off her shoulders. It fell in a brown, daisy-strewn heap on the carpet. 'Let me look at you,' he murmured.

She experienced a moment of shyness under his scrutiny, naked save for her satin and lace bra and panties. This was quite absurd. She had nothing to be ashamed of; her body was sleek, honed by dieting and weekly aerobic classes, though she had to admit she had paid less attention to keeping it in shape since being in England.

She lifted her chin, straightened her spine and posed, one hand resting lightly on her hip.

Hugo moved, swift as a hunting cheetah. He seized her by the wrist, propelled her into the sybaritic luxury of the bedroom and thrust her down on the oversized divan, covered with matched jaguar pelts. Ecologically unsound, a hedonistic statement of Hugo's disregard for a threatened species, the luxurious feel of this rare, forbidden fur transmitted itself to Lorna's bare skin and increased the flow of her arousal.

Standing where she could view him, he stripped rapidly, his body glowing red as a demon's in the subdued rosy light. It was an extraordinary body for a man in his middle years, muscular and dynamic, it held the promise of masterful lovemaking.

His penis reared up imperiously from the dark pelt coating his underbelly. Lorna's breath rushed out with a hiss. He came towards her, his mighty appendage swaying but never losing an iota of stiffness.

'Open your mouth, Lorna,' he grated harshly, then knelt over her face and impaled her on his outrageous erection.

She gasped as the purple clubbed head pushed between her lips. It was big, filling the cavity and making her gag as it nudged the back of her throat. He withdrew half an inch, moving it slowly in and out, and she could taste the rich brew of his juices as she slid up and around, working her tongue along the pulsing, vein-knotted shaft.

His fingers touched the wet crotch of her briefs, teasing her sex-valley, the blood racing through her stiff little organ as he pinched it. She was so tense and aroused that she came in a welter of ecstasy, bucking on his cock with her mouth as if he penetrated the very entrance to her womb.

Then she relinquished him in a slow, leisurely withdrawl, teasing him as he had teased her. He smiled into her eyes and, squeezing her breasts in both hands, inserted his prick into the deep fissure formed between them, smearing the honey-tanned flesh with the clear pre-come fluid of his desire.

She lay there languidly, the hot spasms of orgasm fading to be replaced by an ache in her vagina. She needed to be filled and stretched by something huge and demanding. He crouched over her, and she stared into the eye of his penis as it appeared and retreated in the cleft of her tightly squashed breasts.

He grunted, but removed it before he reached his own apogee. He rolled her over in his arms and stretched her on her stomach. Panting with excitement, he slipped off her panties, caressed her buttocks with his hands and raised her to her knees.

Ah, the traditional position, she thought, relaxing her vulval muscles to make his possession slippery smooth.

But he did not enter her, holding his phallus and rubbing the head against her vaginal orifice, wetting it thoroughly with her secretions. Lorna was beside herself with impatience, lifting her hips higher and opening her legs wide that he might thrust his weapon into her and give her the ploughing she wanted. Instead, she felt the tip slide past her fevered tunnel and press against the eyelet of her arse, dilating it as he started to deflower the place where she was still a virgin.

His other hand was beneath her, craftily fingering her unfurled labia, the love-bud vulnerable and exposed. He tweaked and played with it, finding its very root, and as the pleasure rolled through her again, so he ground the head of his enormous fleshy tool into her innermost recess.

The pain was something she could not escape, yet as she struggled she became aware that her body was expanding, opening to take all of him, her anus like a ring sliding along an enormous rod. His fingers on her clitoris brought on her climax and she came with a wild cry, submerged in a frenzied convulsion as he, too, reached completion in the darkest cavern of her body.

Pale grey-pink dawn smudged the sky beyond the window curtains as Lorna slipped quietly from the bed, wrapped Hugo's dressing-gown round her and went to the bathroom.

She was sore, wincing as she recalled Cassandra's comment in the cave concerning a rhinoceros. Every tender membrane in her loins was on fire. If that was sodomy, she thought, I'm not sure I want a repeat performance.

She let the wrap drop and stepped into the shower stall. Warm water cascaded over her weary body, and she directed the jet between her legs, soothing the bruised outer tissues of her genitals. The soreness receded and warmth took its place. She could feel the hard imprint of Hugo's penis within her, and remembered the enigma of wanting to expel the object lodged in her arsehole, while at the same time clamping round it to prolong that exciting and unnatural sensation.

Powerful men had always appealed to her. It was as if she believed some of their magic would rub off on her during intercourse. Ricky Carlyle came to mind for the first time in ages, her former lover who had wanted to own her.

But you don't like to be owned, she argued inwardly as she soaped herself with chestnut scented gel. So why not give Hugo the elbow?

Musing on the ambiguity of her emotions, she swaddled herself in a bath sheet and walked back into the bedroom, another towel wound turbanwise round her head. She glanced over at the bed. Hugo was sleeping, looking younger, almost innocent, the harsh lines smoothed away.

Why had he come into her life and what did fate intend?

As she passed the armchair, she saw a briefcase propped against the leg. The temptation to pry refused to be denied. Very carefully, so the clasps did not snap back, she opened it, knelt on the carpet and hurriedly ransacked the contents.

There she found the answer to her question.

Lodged among other papers that did not concern her,

she came across a letter from Dudley, addressed to Hugo and marked Private and Confidential. As she read, so their scheme became crystal clear. Hugo wanted to buy Hinton Priory and its land and erect some monstrous, money-making pleasure centre.

After further rifling she found a plan of her property and a carefully detailed drawing of how the site would look once it was completed. She flipped through Hugo's day-planner and found a memo underlined in red biro: 'Saw Dudley Norcross today. Apparently the American doesn't want to sell. We'll see about that. I'm sure I can persuade her. There are more ways than one of skinning a cat.'

Lorna sat back on her heels and her eyes narrowed. Bastard! she hissed through her teeth. Conniving bastard! He can go fuck himself. I'd not sell to him if I'd lost every penny. I'd rather sell my body.

Yet even though she blazed, heaping maledictions on his head, so an odour swept up from her cleft. She had washed herself thoroughly, yet it remained, a pungent, persistent aroma: ozone based but with a resinous undertone; the smell of Hugo's sperm. Damn him! She should never have screwed him. Now she would never be entirely free.

Borne on a wave of furious indignation, she gathered up her scattered clothing and shook out her damp hair. Just before she left the room, she laid the incriminating documents on the bed where Hugo was bound to see them the moment he opened his eyes.

OK, so she had acted dishonourably in reading his personal papers, but nothing could compare to his own diabolical betrayal.

'Wow! That's what I call a challenge,' said Tara, when Lorna opened the baronial main door set within its own crenellated porch.

'Can you do it? Is it possible to get it straight once the workmen have decamped?' Lorna stood in the Priory's hall, thumbs hooked in her jeans pockets, looking around her with something akin to despair.

'Leave it to the Task Force,' Tara replied positively, tiny but determined, with her boyish figure and plum-coloured, feathery hairstyle. She had swept into Lorna's life like a miniature tornado, and Lorna now found it impossible to imagine coping without her.

'Could you get to work on the bedroom right away, and make the kitchen useable? I want to move in today.'

'You do?' Tara's eyes widened. 'But the place is a mess. There's no electricity or hot water.'

'I can manage,' Lorna said, stubbornly. 'If I want a bath or a washing machine or the phone, there's always the lodge. And Chris Devlin says the team from Heritage have already been round to inspect it, and taken his plans away for approval. He has good contacts with them, apparently. Once they've given the go-ahead it won't take long to get the wiring done and heating installed and the plastering and major decorating finished.'

'You're barmy!' Tara declared, but hauled in her cleaning paraphernalia anyway, grumbling, 'Oh, sod it, I shan't be able to plug in the vac. What's the matter with staying put till it's all done?'

'I just need to get in here,' Lorna answered with a shrug.

She could not explain to Tara or even Cassandra the compulsion driving her to move to these less than salubrious surroundings. Finding those papers in Hugo's apartment had put her in a blind panic. She had the awful feeling that somehow, in some underhanded way, he would rob her of her home. It would be no holds barred with him.

She now understood the enormity of the responsibility she had taken on. Not only for the Priory but for Woodmead, too. At one time her ancestors had been the liege lords of the district for miles around. Even now, she held the future of the village in her hands. Could she really allow its character to be destroyed by Hugo's exploitation?

The first step to ensuring this never happened was for her to take up residence in the heart of it: Hinton Priory itself.

'What's going on?' Chris demanded when he strode in to find her and Tara dragging suitcases upstairs.

'I'm moving in,' she replied, wiping her hand over her sweating face and leaving a smear of dirt behind.

'Are you mad?' He scowled at her, eyes peat-dark and hard, his abundant hair swept back. He carried a crash-helmet under one arm, seeming formidable and alien in scuffed black leather trousers and a fringed, metal-studded biker's jacket over a sleeveless vest.

'Mr Devlin, I can assure you I'm perfectly sane,' she retorted, looking down on him from her position half way up the broad, noble sweep of the staircase. 'This is my house, you know.'

'And I'm responsible for your safety while it's under reconstruction,' he snarled, glaring at her. 'It's much easier to get things done if the place is empty.'

'Oh, pardon me! I'm sorry to cause you any inconvenience, but that's the way it is. Let's get at it, Tara,' she countered and proceeded up the stairs. Getting no response, she glanced back down.

Tara was goggling at Chris, and Lorna reluctantly conceded that he was well worth a second look. They had only conversed by phone since their initial stormy meeting, yet that rude, arrogant, self-opinionated man had often impinged on her thoughts.

The light fell directly on his head from the stained glass window filling the half-landing. His upturned features were exaggerated from that angle: high cheek-bones; dark bar of brow, and those smouldering eyes.

He gripped the banister rail and mounted the stairs, two treads at a time. 'You'd better let me help, if you insist on this stupid move. I need to take a look at the master bedroom, make sure it's safe,' he said, and came to rest beside her.

She melted inside, loose and moist, unable to resist glancing at the bare chest displayed by the rounded neck of his vest and the trousers that clung like paste to his sleek hips, the firm outline of his cock emphasised by constricting leather.

'If you insist,' she said off-handedly.

'I do,' he replied with a low laugh that mocked her and her pretence at indifference.

'Come on, Tara,' she said, and rushed ahead. Her whole being was on fire, the very thought of the beast hidden in his crotch making her feel dizzy, even unhinged.

After inspecting the master chamber, he nodded and went away. Lorna was left with damp knickers, an itch in her clitoris, and a disgust with herself that she took out on Tara, running her ragged.

She could hear him below, conversing with workmen, and then the clump of heavy boots marching all over her house. The sounds of hammering, sawing and the West Country drawl of the labourers rang through the once deserted rooms. It seemed that Christopher entertained no doubts about cooperation from the authorities.

When she reached the hall on her way out to fetch further luggage from the car, Chris introduced her to the foreman. 'Miss Erskine, this is Fred Meadon. He's in charge. Fred, say hello to the boss-lady.'

'Pleased to meet you, miss.' Fred, a short, porcine man with sagging jowls, dragged off his flat cap, bald head gleaming as he shook Lorna's hand. 'You've given us a fine old job here, ain't you? Never seen nothing like it,' he vouchsafed, twinkling at her.

'Is it impossible?' she asked, taking an instant liking to this salt-of-the earth craftsman.

'Nothing's impossible, miss, not if you sets your mind to it,' he returned. 'And you've got a good 'un, here. Chris Devlin's one of the best in the business.'

'He's looking for a bonus,' Chris joked.

'Not at all. You know your trade inside out, Mr Devlin.'

Lorna felt eyes boring into her back and realised she and Tara were coming under the libidinous gaze of a couple of jeans-clad apprentices. One had a shaven head tattooed with a spider, the other wore a red bandana tied round greasy, rat-tailed locks.

'You going to the Cheese Show?' they asked, grinning impudently. 'We are. Maybe we'll see you at the disco. Save us a dance, eh?'

'Oi! Just you get on with your work,' shouted Fred. 'Sorry, miss,' he apologised. 'Don't know what's wrong with lads these days. They've got no idea. But don't you fret. I'll see they pull their weight.'

'I've every confidence in you, Fred,' she replied, amused to see Tara smiling at the youths, her bird-bright eyes encouraging.

What was going on here? Tara acting the flirt, that briskly organised female, who rattled round in her van, giving her employees lifts, working late and starting early? Lorna knew she had survived marriage to a man who had been too handy with his fists, but had thought no further than that. Now she saw her in a fresh light, a feisty lady who commanded male attention.

Leaving her to it, Lorna went to the car alone. Chris caught up with her. 'D'you need a hand?' he offered.

'No, thank you. Tara will be out in a minute.'

It was quiet in the sunny stable yard. Chris watched her with a bland expression, his legs crossed in front of him with his backside on the seat of a gleaming red and chrome motorcycle propped up on its stand. A bare-breasted harpy sat astride a snarling wolf, which loped over the alien landscape sprayed on the petrol tank.

'Do you want to fuck?' he said, and gave a slight arch of his pelvis.

Lorna's clit jumped and her vagina clenched. 'What d'you take me for?' she shouted as soon as she found her voice.

'A lady who likes fucking,' he answered calmly, his face poker straight.

'Mind your own business, Mr Devlin,' she replied frostily. 'Or you'll find yourself out of a job.'

He smiled then, a wide smile to which she could barely resist responding. 'Never mind the Neanderthals in there. How about coming to the Cheese Show with me? I'll pick you up on the bike around noon next Saturday.'

Was there no end to the surprises this quixotic individual had up his sleeve? she thought, then curbed the glow that had started to radiate in the region of her heart.

'I don't rate that as a good idea. I prefer to keep strictly to business,' she replied haughtily.

'I can use the car, if you want. Maybe you're scared of riding pillion,' he challenged, the sun shining across his eyes, turning them to sherry gold.

'No problem. I've done it before.' Even as she answered, she cursed herself for falling into the trap.

'That's settled then.' His strong thighs straddled the seat as if he was mounting a beloved mistress. He lifted the helmet and set it on his head. Full-visored, it transformed him into a Teutonic knight.

Knocking up the stand with one booted foot, he steered the bike's sleek bulk till it faced the gate, then kick-started the engine. It roared like a mighty dragon, startling the doves who circled the cote in a white cloud. Raising a hand in salute, he screeched out of the yard.

'I haven't said I'll come!' she shouted, running after him, but it was too late. He was already nothing more than a black blob on a shiny red streak careering off down the drive.

Lorna pushed open the lodge door and just avoided the white envelope lying on the coconut mat. She picked it up, ran her thumbnail under the flap and drew out a deckle-edged card. It was printed with gilt lettering that read: You are cordially invited to attend a meeting of the Club Dionysus. Saturday next at 8.pm.

It was signed Ryder Tyrell and Sybil Esmond.

Resisting the temptation to toss it into the wastepaper

bin, she tucked it into her pocket, then busied herself collecting up the last few items she needed for her first night in the Priory.

Dusk was settling when she returned. No Tara or Cassandra. Just herself and her family seat. The shadows thickened as she entered by the back door, but dispersed a little when she lit an oil lamp and several candles in beautiful silver holders she had discovered in a cupboard. Marc had supplied her with a camping stove and her music centre could be operated by batteries. She would just have to do without television for a while.

She could not be bothered to cook and drove down to the White Hart for pub grub. Cassandra and Marc were there. 'Don't do it,' her friend begged. 'Or let us come and camp out with you. You can't possibly stay there alone. It'll give you the willies. It would me and I'm made of stern stuff when it comes to spooks.'

'I'm not in the least afraid,' Lorna answered truthfully. 'The Priory has a warm, welcoming air. I feel I belong there, and it's as if it knows I'm going to restore it to its former glory. We get on well, the house and me.'

'Call us tomorrow from the lodge. Promise,' Cassandra insisted.

'OK, or you can drive over if you want. Meet the workmen. Tara's already got two of them after her.'

The warmth seemed to have increased when she returned through the moonlight, parked the Fiat and opened the back door. She had provided herself with a torch, and already felt perfectly at home, busy making plans.

She would have Nicole and the staff of the magazine to stay. Maybe Nicole would organise an *Image Literary Tour of England's West Country*. She could see it in her mind's eye, emblazoned across the glossy pages. No one got into advanced publicity quite like clever Nicole.

Still thinking along these lines, she took the back stairs to her bedroom, lighted oil lamp in hand, a new box of candles in her bag. The stairs were dark, the passages long, but everywhere she looked there was some new marvel. It really was an enormous house, full of rooms and as yet unexplored crannies, and she was under its spell.

Summer was a fine time for a project like this, she decided. Long hot days and short nights. It would have been an impossible undertaking in the winter. Tara had swept and dusted the room, and a duvet and pillows had been brought across from the lodge.

Lorna undressed by candlelight, smiling to herself as she imagined the scenes that must have been inacted there down the centuries. Wedding nights when the feudal lord took a bride. Secret assignations when he was off fighting in some crusade; maybe she'd have had a string of pretty young pages or a roving minstrel or two.

The adjoining bathroom was antiquated, the water cold, but she was filled with the pioneering spirit. It was a challenge to rough it, away from mod cons and soft living. She did, however, take the precaution of locking the bedroom door. No need to court disaster, though every window in the house was fitted inside with heavy wooden shutters and the outer doors possessed substantial iron bolts.

Slipping on her silk kimono, Lorna knelt on the padded seat in the window embrasure. The indigo sky still retained a faint flush of orange on the horizon, and the moon splashed its pale silver light over the garden. She reflected on the vagaries of fate. Had someone told her, six months ago, that she would be sitting in her own manor house in England, she would have said they were crazy.

She was too excited to sleep at once. My very own four-poster, she chortled, climbing into it. Our readers would go wild. Better get some shots to send to Nicole. The caption would run, 'Our roving editor, Lorna, in her romantic bed in Hinton Priory. If any aspiring author is thinking of researching in this historic part of England, she'd just love to have you visit her.'

She slept and dreamt, but thought herself awake. She

was in the woods and it was hot. Her skin was on fire and she tore off her clothes. Dried twigs pricked her feet, and invisible hands were touching her intimately – between the legs, pressing into her vulva and anus. The honey flowed from her as fingers circled her clitoris, flicking the head, fluttering, tormenting.

She lay on the pine carpet covering the forest floor. Chris's hair mingled with the foliage from which his eyes mocked her. She wanted to speak to him, but her tongue cleaved to the roof of her mouth. Her hands ran over his chest and shoulders, thighs and phallus. She palmed his member, ascertaining its length and width. He was caressing her, his mouth probing the flower of her labia, his hands toying with her nipples.

She moaned in her sleep, writhing under the duvet. Now she was running through the dream landscape. Brambles tore at her skin, branches lashes her naked buttocks – or was it Marta's whip? She rejoiced in the pain. She could hear Ryder's taunting laughter, and rejoiced in that too. He caught her, threw her down among tall, spiky bracken. She imagined that it was his hand slipping across her mound, finding her diamond-hard kernel, but caressed herself in her sleep.

She woke as climax flared through her. She was drenched in sweat, the quilt twisted between her thighs. For an instant she could not remember where she was. The room was pitch black and instinct told her she was no longer alone. She sat bolt upright, staring into the darkness. Someone was breathing close by.

She gasped as her arms were seized and a heavy body bore her back on the mattress. This was no dream. There was a presence in her bed, solid, very strong, giving her no quarter. The shaft of his erection was forcing its way insistently into her sex.

She fought, beat at him in the dark. Her hands encountered a hard carapace, fingers registering the texture of leather. The creature, demon, angel or man, was completely encased, apart from the bulging naked phallus.

186

His breath brushed her cheek, but he did not utter a word. His face, even his hair was encased in hide. No human feature she could identify, no voice to give a clue. Even his smell was masked by a feral, animal stench that was as arousing as it was alien. She struggled, but every movement drove him deeper into her.

'Who are you?' she managed to say.

A gloved hand was clapped over her mouth and, though she still kicked and thrashed, her fury changed to desire, and the frenzied motion of her hips against his driving loins became those of passion, matching his thrusts.

It was a harsh, jungle mating, basic in the extreme, a silent struggle for dominance which he won. He spread her legs and rode her, his mammoth organ stabbing into her. She was ravaged by a transport of pleasure, giving vent to a long wail stifled by the hardness of his hand over her face. His body shuddered and gave a final convulsive heave, the pounding of his heart slowing.

Then, abruptly, she was released from his crushing weight, his cock slipping from her body. The mattress creaked and sprang back. Lorna sat up and fumbled for the torch. It fell from the table and she wasted precious time groping for it on the floor. At last its beam punctured the darkness. The room was empty.

Chapter Nine

'*D*on't lie. I know you've been fucking that American. I saw you in the garage the other night,' Alison stated flatly, her eyes shooting sparks at Gary.

'I was only selling her a car,' he protested.

'Oh? Is that the new sales pitch, bonking lady customers?' Alison tossed her hennaed curls and flounced past him towards the kitchen door.

Gary caught her by the hem of her skirt, slid a hand between her legs and grabbed her plump mound. 'So what if I did screw her? It's you I love, Allie.'

'Get your hands off me,' she yelled, but he simply gripped her pussy more tightly, almost lifting her from her feet, dragging her panties between her vaginal groove.

'You don't really mean that, do you? I think you want me to pull down your knickers and stuff my cock up you,' he replied with a confident grin.

'If you think I'm going to let you put that thing in me after what you've been doing with *her*, then you've got another think coming,' she exclaimed viciously, but her voice shook, her anger no match for the knee-trembling excitement he aroused in her.

She and Gary often fought and it turned her on, their reconciliations as violently passionate as their quarrels.

At the end of the day she would probably wind up marrying him, a white wedding in the village church with all the trimmings. Happy ever after? He found it impossible not to play away, and she sometimes took other lovers out of revenge.

'You shouldn't have been spying on me, should you?' he teased.

'And you shouldn't have been fucking her.'

She lashed out at him, a she-devil with wide spread claws ready to rend and tear. Gary laughed, blood heated by the sport, holding her flaying hands immobile with one huge fist. He opened the buttons of her blouse, fingers skimming over the ripe breasts cradled in white nylon lace. Then he hitched the heavy globes up over her bra where they swelled, forced high, the nipples berry-red and succulent.

His mouth came down, clamping on one of those generous teats, sucking strongly, and Alison shivered with reluctant want, resistance weakening. He looked good enough to eat in a clean blue plaid shirt, a new pair of jeans and Reebok trainers, all spruced up for their trip to the fête.

The fair had been set up in a field next to the show ground, and he would be with her for the whole of the long, hot afternoon. Her lusty man, acknowledged swain and escort. She could be sure of him for a few hours, cocking a snook at any other woman who might fancy lying down with him.

His crisp, sun-bleached hair smelled of shampoo, and the fresh sweat engendered by their struggle rose like incense, bewitching her. She yearned to surrender, to have him toy with her clitoris till she screamed for release, but was determined to punish him for his infidelity with Lorna Erskine.

She pushed him away, shouting, 'Leave me be. I want to go to the show – now – and you said you'd take me.'

'Prick tease,' he grumbled, putting down a hand to adjust the cock pressed painfully against the front of his denims. 'Can't we have a quick one before we go?'

'No, we can't,' she said, assuming a demure pose.

'Then can I stay the night?'

'There's a do at the vicarage, remember? But you can come back here when we knock off, if you behave yourself.'

'Will she accept the invitation?' Sybil asked, running her hands down her thighs as she admired herself in the pier-glass. Riding gear might have been specially invented to show off her elegant figure.

'Of course,' Ryder answered, standing behind her, his hands cupping her trim buttocks, the jodhpurs so figure-hugging he could trace his initials where they were branded into her flesh.

Sybil leant back, watching him in the mirror through hooded eyes, glossy crimson lips parted over small white teeth. He always looked spectacular, whatever he wore a perfect choice for the occasion. Like her, he was dressed in riding breeches, boots and hacking jacket. He too was divinely sexy, lean and masculine, his sleek flanks and taut arse displayed to full advantage, the thick branch of his penis drawing her eye like steel to magnet.

They were alike in aims and ambitions, two amoral people greedy to drain life's heady sensations to the dregs. From similar backgrounds, aristocratic but penniless, they had met years before, discovered a mutual interest in the more bizarre aspects of sex, then parted when Sybil married for money. Ryder had continued to live off his wits and pursue any number of pie-in-the-sky ventures.

When Sybil's husband died, leaving her comfortably off, he had approached her with a scheme that would provide them with a lucrative and satisfying existence. The vicarage had just come on the market and she had used a portion of her legacy in order to buy it. Thus the Club Dionysus was born, an exclusive brotherhood which offered the fulfilment of physical desires in return for a substantial membership fee.

And I take pride in my work, Sybil thought, gyrating

her bottom against his hands. Her husband had done nothing but rake at her fires without dousing them. She had not shed a tear at his demise. A multitude of other lovers had failed to quench her lust. Spoilt and indulged, she had met her match in Ryder and become his willing slave. Perhaps she even loved him, if love could find a place in her cold heart.

'She seems very keen to keep the Priory,' she reminded him as he released her with a stinging flick of his riding crop.

'We need it more,' he answered, his saturnine face setting into even harsher lines. 'The sacred spring is necessary to the club. Our members love drinking the waters. They like to think they are taking part in pagan rites which will increase their sexual prowess.'

'And aren't they?' she asked, sitting before the dressing-table and coiling her hair into a knot at her nape. She fixed it with pins and attached a snood.

He gave a cynical smile. 'We're illusionists, you and I. We take the chosen to the limits of voluptuous pleasure, as if the whole business of copulation is a dream fashioned by their fevered imaginations.'

He came across and placed his lips at the side of her throat, teeth bared as he nipped at the soft skin. It was as if a spark of electricity crackled at his touch. She could feel it coursing through her veins and erupting in an exquisite pain. She pressed her sex against the padded stool so the tiny rings tugged at her labia.

'Then it's essential we retain the shrine,' she whispered, reaching round to caress the swollen, upward-curving phallus.

'We shall, darling, have no doubt about that,' he promised, his eyes as grey and cold as the Arctic sea. 'Even if I have to marry her to do it.'

Chris called for Lorna as promised, though she had doubted he would. 'Tuck your skirt out of the way,' he said briskly. 'You should have worn jeans.'

'It's too hot.'

'Shorts then, like mine,' he said, gesturing towards them.

They were old denims, cut off way up above the knee. Lorna was mesmerised by the large bulge nestling at the crotch. He wore a black waistcoat on his upper torso, no shirt or jacket. There wasn't an ounce of fat anywhere. Beautiful chest muscles were crowned with erect nipples, arms, shoulders and firm thighs were tanned a rich brown.

His bare feet were encased in a pair of sport sandals, designed for protection and comfort; no smelly biking boots for him on this glorious sunny day.

She sat pillion, put on the spare helmet and clung to his waist as the machine gunned along the open road. The speedy power charge was unbearably arousing. Her skirt was hitched high and only a fragile bit of silk lay between her rose-pink lower lips and the leather saddle.

She could smell tarmac, Chris's body and her own honeydew. Her legs opened wider, the velocity forcing the bead-shaped head of her clitoris against the seat. It almost exploded at the sudden rush of pleasure. She longed to reach down and massage it, but dared not let go of Chris as he leant forward, gripping the handlebars with utmost concentration.

Lorna surrendered to the sensations ricocheting through her loins. Each bump rocked her to and fro on the back of her fiery mechanical steed, the friction causing turmoil in her pulsating clit. She ground her breasts into Chris's back, the motion chafing the sensitive tips and sending a hotline down to her nub. It thrummed, the frottage of the gusset producing a burning feeling that gathered momentum.

Lorna moaned, her voice muffled by the helmet, a wave of sweet, suffocating anguish carrying her higher. Nothing mattered except attaining the peak. She moved her hips, pulling the sliver of fabric tighter, gasping as her climax broke in a burst of light and heat.

Chris seemed unaware, his control of the bike unfaltering. They reached the show ground and he paused to buy tickets at the gate, one leg taking the weight as the engine ticked over. Weaving in and out among the pedestrians, he followed the signs to the field designated as a car park. An attendant wearing an important air waved them to a suitable spot. Chris killed the engine and free-wheeled to a stop.

He took off his helmet, damp curls coiling round his neck, then swung a leg over the saddle and stood up. Lorna also freed her head, shaking out her hair. She dismounted slowly, wind-blown and satiated.

'You OK?' he asked, raising one eyebrow in a sharply quizzical arch as he saw the dark streaks her juices had left on the red leather seat.

'Sure,' she replied brightly. There was no way she was going to let him know she had just enjoyed a unique orgasm.

'Let's go,' he said. 'I want to try my luck at the rifle range.'

'And I intend to watch the gymkhana. Ryder Tyrell's taking part.'

'You know him?' Though Chris did not shorten his stride or look at her, his voice changed, hard and wary.

'He's my neighbour.'

'I'm aware of that.'

'You've met him?'

'He wanted me to do some work for him when he took over at the vicarage.'

'Then you know Sybil Esmond?'

'Oh, yes.'

The smell of hot dogs was attracting a queue and they joined it. Lorna fidgeted beside him, her bare arm brushing against his, filling her with the carnal desire to have his cock moving inside her. Jealousy gnawed at her gut as she wondered if he had screwed Sybil.

'How well d'you know her?' she asked, as he handed her a paper napkin folded round a beefburger-filled bap with fried onion.

'Mrs Esmond? Not as well as she would have liked,' was his ironic rejoiner. He licked a smear of tomato ketchup from his lips and cast her a sharp glance, adding, 'If you want my advice, which I don't suppose you do, you'll stay away from them. Like any deadly drug, they're too beguiling.'

The Woodmead Show was an annual event that had taken place since time immemorial. Once it had been a venue for selling sheep and fleeces, with a deal of trade in horseflesh. But it had gradually altered, though still an important event in the social calendar.

The ladies of the WI entered home-made preserves and cakes; members of the fuchsia society vied with one another to produce prize-winning blooms; gardeners spent months coaxing vegetables into enormous size and splendour. There was even a baby contest judged by the local MP.

Marquees had sprung up overnight like mushrooms, and an area had been fenced off for the gymkhana. Participants came trooping in early, their mounts in horseboxes behind four wheeled drive vehicles. A large proportion of supporters wore green wellington boots, Hermès headscarves or tweed caps, while Barbour jackets were *de rigueur*.

Lorna was on the look-out for Ryder. She had a question to put to him. Had he anything to do with the visitation in the master chamber?

It had only happened once, and she had been more intrigued than frightened, though she had spent the remainder of the night with the oil lamp burning. A thorough examination of the room next morning had shown nothing. The door was still locked and though virginia creeper gave the outside of the house a look of cosy bagginess, it was unlikely an intruder would have sneaked into the bedroom that way.

She had told no one. Tara would have freaked and Cassandra insisted on informing the police. Admittedly she had gone to bed the following night with some trepidation, but also in a ferment of excitement, anticipating the return of her demon lover.

He had not appeared, leaving her to cope with her frustration and rack her brains as to his identity.

Chris proved to be a crack shot, even with the dodgy rifle supplied by the showman. He won a teddy bear which he presented to Lorna. She was impressed with the way he haggled with the harridan flogging bric-à-brac at the Flea Market, acquiring a risqué gilded bronze Art Deco figurine of a dancing couple. He eventually knocked her down to a hundred and fifty pounds. Signed by Claire Colinet, it was worth far more, but he insisted Lorna have it.

These incidents displayed a different aspect of his complex personality. He was the sort of man who carried out any undertaking with precision and a huge concentration of energy. There were no half measures with him.

Ryder was magnificent in the ring, and so was Sybil, cleaning up the cups between them. 'Pot-hunters,' Chris remarked scathingly.

'Why are you so nasty about them?' Lorna asked crossly. 'You're the only one here who is. If you look around, you'll see the women drooling over him and the men getting a hard-on for her.'

'That's what I mean,' he said, and stopped short in the middle of the field, grabbed her tightly to him and stared down into her eyes. 'Don't get mixed up in their games, Lorna. A friend of mine has come to grief financially because of them.'

'I don't know what you're talking about,' she shouted. 'As a matter of fact, I'm going to the vicarage tonight. You'd better take me home.'

'I'm not ready to leave yet,' he growled, releasing her so abruptly that she tripped.

'OK. That's fine. I'll find my own way.'

She stalked off across the grass to where Tara's van was parked beneath a tree. The afternoon sun blazed down. Music swelled from carousels and pipe-organs. A voice, tinny and distorted, was making announcements over the PA, and sirens blasted as a dozen steam-driven traction engines chugged to the starting point for their race.

Lorna peered in at the rear window of the van. She stopped dead, trying to make sense of the tangle of limbs inside. Yes, it was Tara all right, and she wasn't alone.

Naked, she lay on her side in the sixty-nine position, her mouth clamped round the crop-headed apprentice's shaft, milking him of every last drop of semen while he, face buried between her legs, feasted on the manna oozing silkily over her tops of her thighs.

The other youth, jeans rolled down about his ankles, was pistoning away at her, his long thin cock sliding in and out. All were oblivious to the shadow Lorna cast across the window. She hadn't the heart to interrupt them.

'Ahoy there!' Cassandra carolled from the open-topped Range Rover as Lorna made her way towards the gate, facing a long trudge home. 'Do you want a lift? We've had enough of these rustic revels, and the adulation Ryder's receiving from the frustrated females of the parish. It makes me want to puke.'

Lorna swung up into the back, hefting her bear and the precious statuette. She had been tempted to hand them back to Chris, but this seemed a childish gesture, and here was Cassandra giving Ryder a lambasting, too. He certainly had the power to arouse extreme emotions; loved, hated but never ignored.

'Good evening, madam,' Marta said, as Lorna walked through the main door and into the hall.

She was a late arrival, having been in a dither about what to wear, eventually settling for a pure white sheath that bared her arms and her back and the top half of her breasts. It clung to her sensuously, a perfect foil for smooth sun-kissed flesh, and had a tiny matching beaded jacket.

A manservant had guided her to the side of the sweeping gravelled area at the front of the vicarage. It was already full of gleaming Jaguars, Bentleys, and a

Ferrari or two. She concluded that the members of Ryder's club were a well-heeled bunch.

So far, it was a sedate gathering, but Lorna found her nerves tightening with anticipation. The brilliant, prismatic light of the chandeliers sparkled on people in faultless evening attire, the women like gorgeous butterflies in top-of-the-range designer gowns, their escorts wearing formal black tuxedoes and white shirts. Voices rose and fell amidst the brittle tinkle of female laughter and the beat of jazz-rock. Stately flunkies passed among them bearing trays of champagne flutes.

The servants wore white wigs, and were liveried in blue velvet knee breeches and coats with flashing gold epaulettes. Rashid was in charge, resplendent in the robes of a Bedouin chieftain, a striped *Kaffiyeh* covering his hair, a braided *agal* round his forehead.

'They are selected for their height, good looks and large cocks,' Marta murmured in Lorna's ear. 'Mrs Esmond interviews them personally, and Rashid and I are allowed to assist her. We examine the maids, too,' and she pointed to where four girls stood, hands folded neatly in front of their aprons.

Each was pretty; two blondes, a brunette and one with flaming red hair. Their tightly boned basques reduced their waists to doll size and forced their breasts to rise over the lace edging. Their skirts consisted of full chiffon layers, and their legs gleamed through the material, curves exaggerated by the high heels of black court shoes.

'Turn round, slave,' Marta commanded the redhead, aiming a blow with the switch she carried. 'I think you'll recognise her, Miss Erskine. Her name is Alison.'

Oh, damn, Lorna thought in dismay. Gary's girlfriend. What's she doing here?

Alison displayed no emotion as she turned to face the wall. Her shirt, rucked up at the back, showed her rounded, naked buttocks and deep anal avenue. Her dimpled flesh was skimmed by narrow suspenders, and the smoky black tops of her stockings. Red welts contrasted vividly with her ivory skin.

Marta pushed two fingers inside her, opening her sex wide. Alison neither moved or complained, staring straight ahead at the linen-fold panelling. 'Try her,' Marta urged in a soft, coaxing voice, smiling slyly at Lorna as if she could read her deepest secrets. 'She's sweet and wet. Or give her a few strokes with the cane if you prefer.'

Lorna shook her head, but was conscious of a heavy, pulsing ache between her thighs. Something deep and dark responded to Marta's invitation. 'I can't beat her,' she exclaimed. 'I've never whipped anyone in my life.'

'How selfish of you,' Marta commented, inserting the tip of the switch between Alison's labia and twisting it.

Lorna remembered how Ryder had done this to her and the hot feeling it had produced. A shiver ran through her, an electric thrill that arched from her groin to her nipples.

'She wants you to enjoy her,' Marta continued. 'But suit yourself. That's what everyone does at the Club Dionysus ... suits themselves. They give free rein to their appetites, but nothing is ever done against a person's wishes. Protest though they may, it's only pretence. All are consenting adults. That's the rule.'

Lorna could not understand Alison's passivity. On the one occasion they had met at the White Hart it had seemed she hated and resented her. The whole scene made her apprehensive, yet her heart was pounding, her precious love-liquid pooling in her vulva.

She drew Marta to one side, saying, 'I don't think you quite understand. Alison's jealous of me. She's going out with Gary, my gardener, and to tell the truth, I've encouraged him.'

'We know about this, madam. Alison won't object. She has learnt to be submissive. So has Gary. Don't you recognise him?' And she pointed to where a broad-shouldered footman crossed the hall, bearing a salver of canapés.

It was Gary dressed in full regalia: a powdered wig and eighteenth-century costume, pink silk hose, buckled shoes, the lot.

'Perhaps you'd rather have him? Shall I call him over?' Marta offered, lips quirked into a thin smile.

'Thanks, but no thanks,' Lorna said. 'I'll go mingle a little.'

She was accustomed to circulating at functions, able to drop into conversations with ease, but these people withheld themselves from her, though the atmosphere was thick and expectant. The footmen filled Baccarat glasses from jeroboams of champagne standing in antique, ice-filled wine-coolers. Lorna accepted one.

It was a first-class vintage, deliciously cool, slipping over her tongue in an effervescent tide, bubbles tickling the back of her nose. She drained her glass and a waiter appeared with another. She was not drunk, simply elated. It had cleared her mind leaving her thoughts razor sharp.

While sipping a third she moved through the crowd, searching for familiar faces and finding none. The maids and footman hovered, offering *hors d'oeuvres*: fingers of toast coated with caviar arranged like starfish on Royal Doulton; wafer-thin ham curled within crisp lettuce parcels; mackerel paté spiced with lemon; Mediterranean olives stuffed with anchovies and served with a sauce of sun-dried tomatoes; black grapes resting on beds of vine leaves; the scents of summer captured within dishes of strawberries.

Delicious aromas titillated the nostrils, mingling with the unmistakable smell of success, and the expensive perfumes and hormonal essences rising from hot, aroused bodies. The voices were louder now, formality giving way to basic needs as the champagne hit home.

Then Rashid picked up a felt-headed hammer and struck the huge brass gong hanging in its carved ebony stand. The noise reverberated to the rafters.

When it died away, he declaimed, 'The master awaits!'

The hall darkened. Two footmen opened the double doors at the end of the hall, and the guests moved slowly towards the opening. The air vibrated with organ music swelling from powerful speakers.

The adjoining salon was long and lofty, dimly lit by a huge central dome of coloured glass high up in the ceiling. Chevron parqueted flooring, walls draped in silk and paintings of Arcadian scenes of hermaphrodites locked in passion; all were patterned with vivid rainbow shards falling from that dazzling cupola.

At the very end was a dais beneath a velvet canopy fringed with scintillating gold tassels, and on this platform stood two thrones attained by broad, shallow, carpeted steps.

Lorna was so engrossed by the sombre magnificence of her surroundings and the sweeping resonance of the music that she did not notice she was completely alone. She stood in the centre of the floor, unable to move. Her limbs felt weighted, as in some nightmare when one wants to run but finds oneself tangled in a sticky web.

Then, gradually, she became aware of people. The guests had returned, now wearing cowled robes. They formed into a semi-circle, facing the dais. The music faded, and the lights dimmed to nothing.

When they rose again, Ryder stood on the platform, his hair unbound and streaming around his shoulders. He looked like a god, immensely tall in a purple silk caftan with gems flashing at the neck and round the hanging sleeves that reached the floor. It was open all down the front, displaying his beautiful erection, a wand of power jutting from his lower belly.

'Welcome, acolytes of Dionysus,' he said in a loud, clear voice.

'Hail, master,' they intoned.

'I wish to propose a new candidate. Come forward, Lorna,' he said, his voice husky and compelling.

It took great effort to place one foot before the other. Yet she had not the will to refuse him; his mesmeric voice, the champagne she had drunk and the lust he inspired, prevented her from doing other than obey.

She reached the bottom step and looked up at him.

His head seemed to touch the cupola, his eyes glittering like stars. Now hands were on her, removing her gown. She felt herself submerged in a sea of sinuous limbs, curtains of perfumed hair, of breasts and arms and phalli, the soft wetness of vulvas, and fingers stroking her clitoris and making dancing circles round her anus.

These disappeared and still she stood before the dais, the cool air playing over her bare skin. Ryder fixed her eyes with his, and she started up towards him. He lifted a shining shot-silk cloak from one of the thrones and placed it round her shoulders, the sides of his hands lightly caressing the tight points of her nipples. Then he turned her to face the crowd.

Feeling tingling elation mixed with shame, she stood with legs parted to balance her weight on her high-heeled, gilt-strapped sandals. The cloak spilled down around her feet, but Ryder arranged the front folds so that her breasts, belly and abundant curling pubic hair were visible to the onlookers.

The crowd remained silent, staring at her, then they dropped their robes. Some of the men had changed into wasp-waisted corsets, garter belts and stockings, their dicks poking through split-crotch panties, their masculine footwear abandoned in favour of stilettos. Others had parts of their bodies covered in leather, with metal studded armbands, and jockstraps cradling their cocks.

A few of the women wore Parisienne maid's outfits, with aprons and caps, their shaven pussies showing every time the tiny skirts swirled high. A couple of the men also favoured this French farce look.

Several hoydens strutted in PVC catsuits, their breasts projecting through cut-outs, their fleshy bottoms bare. Large dildoes bobbed in front of them, fastened over their pudenda. There was a number in rubber shorts, with braces that drew the crotch up into their cracks, hairy labia swelling on either side. Some wore stilt-heeled shoes, some thigh-length boots. All, men or women, displayed provocative portions of their genitalia.

The glass doors leading to a conservatory were suddenly flung wide and, with the rumble of iron-bound wooden wheels, a vehicle came bowling through. It was a smaller version of something from *Ben Hur*, a carved and gilded Roman chariot, the only difference being the human steed pulling it along.

The light bounced off glittering straps and buckles and leather, and the charioteer, who stood with the reins bunched in one mailed fist. In the other she flourished a bull-whip, applying it mercilessly to her slave's quivering, naked rump.

'Ooh ... ooh ... Thank you, thank you, mistress,' Ian moaned through the bit held between his teeth.

'Whoa! Stop, you miserable wretch!' Sybil shouted, hauling on the reins, her command augmented by another resounding crack of the whip.

The chariot slewed to a halt at the bottom of the steps.

The throng cheered, and she raised an imperious hand, bizarre and beautiful in a chain-link corset covering her from upper pubis to just below her breasts. These rose naked and full, the nipples stone-hard and rouged a deep crimson.

A thick gold torque encircled her neck, with a heavy, spade-shaped pendant dangling between her breasts. Her arms were banded by massive bracelets, her legs covered in metal grieves from ankle to knee. Great hooped earrings swung against her loosened hair. Brushed into wild disarray, this was topped by a head-dress with a set of horizontal horns and a pair of ostrich plumes that added three feet to her height.

She was a goddess indeed: a witch, a whore-priestess. Every man's dream of a cruel, dominating mistress.

Lorna was shocked into sobriety by the sight of Ian Carr chained between the shafts. She was sure it was him, though the dull little computer operator had turned into a two-legged horse. He was naked, apart from leather strappings and a dog collar round his neck with chains linked to the rings piercing his nipples. A spiked belt spanned his waist, attached to the harness that bound him to the chariot.

Behind him, a crupper passed through the crack of his skinny backside and circumnavigated his balls, hoisting them up and forward, and lifting his cock high. It needed little help, being ramrod stiff. A ring passed through the foreskin, with a further chain connecting it to the one in his navel.

He was blinkered, his head covered by a close-fitting cap ornamented with discs. A fine chestnut mane poked through a hole at the crown. It matched the long, flowing tail rooted in his fundament. His bonds were tight but, at a whim, Sybil could make them even tighter. Yet, far from looking distressed, he wore an expression of sublime happiness.

She gestured and two hulking specimens of manhood stepped forward. 'Grooms, unbuckle this pathetic specimen,' she cried, alighting from the chariot and pacing round to the front, the metal tips of her red leather boots giving a sharp clack at every step.

Ian trembled, juice escaping from his cock-tip.

'Disgusting individual!' Sybil declared, trailing the knotted end of her whip up his stem, then flicking at it. Ian howled with joy and pain.

'Mistress! Beloved mistress!' he cried, his penis jerking ludicrously against the whiteness of his belly.

'Be quiet, dog! You've no control.' She spun round and addressed the crowd. 'What shall we do with him?'

'Punish him!' they chorused. 'Whip him! Paddle him!'

She walked up the steps, head held high, and took her place on one of the thrones. Ian, released, crawled behind her on all fours, then made obeisance, his forehead pressed on her foot.

Sybil lounged in the carved chair with a Sphinx-like smile. Her thighs were parted, moisture glistening on her rouged and bejewelled lower lips, her clitoris as red as her mouth. Ian moaned.

'Touch me,' she ordered.

He rose to his knees and, wetting his fingers with

spittle, stroked them over the pouting bud. Sybil's smile did not alter. She raised one leg in its glittering grieve and poked his tormented penis with the thin, spiky heel of her boot, then ran it over the balls bunched taut in their hairy net.

'Oh, mistress . . . Oh . . .' he whimpered.

'Say thank you.'

'Thank you, thank you . . .'

'Down!' she snapped.

At once he crouched lower, his genitals resting on the carpeted step. Sybil stretched her leg, driving her heel into his testicles and cock. He cried out and spurted a fountain of spunk over her scarlet boots.

She withdrew in disgust, shouting, 'Horrible little insect. Now look what you've done! Lick it off, every last drop. Do you hear me?'

Ian's tongue came out and, grovelling, he slurped up his own secretions to the sound of the grooms flogging his back with their many-thonged whips.

He was like a saint relishing martyrdom, his face contorted in ecstasy. The cult members, inspired by the charade, were rubbing their own genitals or one another's. The footmen, though retaining their sumptuous velvet jackets, now flaunted their bare buttocks, wearing nothing but a flap at the front, which could be lifted at will, should anyone desire to examine their equipage. The maids, skirts hooked high, were available to whoever fancied penetrating their quims or arses.

They carried baskets of dildoes, and Ryder beckoned Alison over as he murmured to Lorna, 'Try any of these you wish. You're familiar with the pleasure of such things, I suppose, an enjoyable adjunct to masturbation which is in itself sublimely erotic. An exclusive love, in which one is both the lover and the beloved.'

She felt his cock harden and press against her bottom. She was in a waking dream, her eyes on Marta's basket of treasures. She reached out and her fingertips moved over the forest of phalluses contained in the basket. They were arranged upright in a variety of colours, some like toadstools, some pointed, while others did not in any way resemble a male organ, being more like mop-heads.

They were made of latex, warm and silky, or ivory, cold as charity. There were oriental wooden lingams, carved and painted or ones of polished ebony with lifelike knots, veins and retracted foreskins. Short or long, thick or slender, curved or straight, Lorna was spoilt for choice.

Ryder selected one for her, a gilded horn that had been modelled closely on nature.

'Caress yourself,' he breathed, putting it into her hand.

It was large but her juices were in full flow. She opened her legs and inserted the tip into her vulva, holding it there and feeling it grow warm in her tunnel. She lay back against Ryder, his penis between her buttocks, and slowly slid the dildo further in.

Alison was watching her, her hand at her own pubis, a finger buried in the deep cleft between the damp hair. All around, people were laughing, moaning, exclaiming as they reached their peaks; men with men, women with women, some with both sexes – a wild tangle of limbs difficult to define.

Sybil relaxed on her throne between two men. She was holding the erect prick of one in her right hand, and her mouth was fastened round the engorged member of the other while she ran her whip between his legs, from scrotum to anus. Ian's face was buried in her pussy as he licked her clitoris, his hands reaching up blindly to fasten round her nipples.

The huge golden horn was not as hot as Lorna's vaginal lining. It moved in and out of her, driven by her own hand. Her womb ached and her clit was unsatisfied. She lifted the dildo out of her and applied the tip to her centre of pleasure. She could feel Ryder's breath on her neck and his thumbs circling her nipples. She closed her eyes, abandoning herself, nothing more than a voluptuous body immersed in sensations.

Her release was upon her and she cried, 'I'm coming! I'm coming!'

As it rolled over her, she rode the imitation prick, plunging it inside her and taking its every inch, her muscles contracting round the iron length.

Before she had time to recover from the onslaught of lust, Ryder snatched the dildo from her and wrapped her in the cloak. Alison brought a silken scarf and bound it round Lorna's eyes. Plunged into darkness, she felt herself lifted over his broad shoulder, one of his arms under her rump, the other across her back as she dangled, head down.

It was colder now, Ryder's footsteps echoing on stone. She could hear the whisper of voices, the patter of feet, the crepitus of clothing, and could smell different odours, no longer perfumed but musty.

They were descending, deeper and deeper, Ryder twisting and turning as if the stairs spiralled. She hammered on his back with her fists, shouting, 'Where are you taking me?'

He did not pause, or answer.

Little sparks of fear shot along her nerves, and excitement clenched in her belly. What was going on? It was obvious they were now deep underground. She could not get over the astonishing spectacle of Ian Carr coming over Sybil's shoes, after being stabbed in the balls with her heel. And the beatific look on his face as he was whipped.

Was Ryder intending to whip *her*?

She shuddered with terror and anticipation. Warmth flooded her entire being, the harshness of Ryder's handling making her ache to have his cock possessing her. He had encouraged her to pleasure herself, then flung her over his shoulder like a sack of potatoes. It was monstrous behaviour from someone she had seen win trophies that afternoon, a model country gentleman.

No echoing flagstones now, but a dull sound, like earth flooring. No chink of light penetrated the scarf, and the smells were definitely of dank soil, like those she had encountered beneath the temple. It brought memories back, of Cassandra and the circles and a juddering, powerful climax.

Ryder stopped and put her down. Her feet met an uneven surface. She could feel the press of warm bodies, smell sweat and semen and perfume. The acolytes were silent, and over and above that silence came the gentle trickle of water.

The scarf was whipped away. Lorna blinked as her eyes became accustomed to the candlelight. She stood at the side of the natural basin into which tumbled the holy water. The circles carved into the walls greeted her, Earth Mother, Sun King.

'This is my cave,' she cried, rounding on Ryder. 'You have no right to be here.'

'On the contrary,' he replied, his saturnine face even darker, his mouth more sensual. 'The spring belongs to the Club Dionysus. We used it long before you came, and so did those who owned the vicarage before us. There's a connecting passage. You will not deny us access. I, your master, command you.'

'Oh? We'll see about that,' she retorted.

She was seized roughly and spreadeagled on a wooden frame, her arms outspread and manacled, her ankles also. Ryder paced round her, crop in hand, tapping it against his palm.

'Rebellion?' he said in a low, smooth voice. 'I can't have slaves being headstrong and impudent. You must learn obedience, Lorna. Bind her eyes again.'

Sybil was smiling, a thin crimson smile and Ian looked up from his dog-like position, his collar fastened to a leash she held in her hand. He slavered as he eyed the whip, eyes alight with longing.

'Stop this silly game, Ryder,' Lorna shouted, though she felt she would die if he did.

'I didn't hear you address me correctly,' he said, and she yelped sharply at the first blow.

'That's your name, isn't it?' she snarled through gritted teeth.

'You must call me master. Say it!'

'I won't.' Damn him, she muttered to herself while her buttocks stung and lust boiled like molten lava in her loins.

The second white-hot lash took her off guard. She screamed as her body bucked, the cuffs biting into her wrists.

'Say it.'

'Master . . .'

'Louder.' The third blow was lower, meeting the tops of her thighs.

'Master!' Even as the word was forced out of her, she knew it was what she wanted to say. An intense wave of pleasure coursing through her, a dark hunger which only he could assuage.

'You want me to take you?'

'Yes . . . oh, yes . . .' She was shamed by her body's betrayal, yet exalted by the thought of feeling his weapon thrusting into her, making her his slave indeed.

She felt his withdrawal with a pang that seemed to drag at her bowels. Then other hands were creeping over her, and a tongue was at her clitoris, licking and stroking at it. Gloved hands came across to tweak her nipples. Mouths were on her lips, feasting on her saliva. Other hands slid along her thighs and oiled fingers penetrated her anus.

Suddenly she lost the last of her inhibitions, rejoicing to be the object of their worship. She became the spirit of the grotto, the Earth Mother to be venerated. As that unknown tongue sucked and licked her to ecstasy, so she felt a hard, bulky penis penetrating her vagina. It plunged fast and deep, the furious strokes increasing until it swelled ever larger and twitched in orgasm.

Her body writhed sensuously. She was wetter than she had ever been, and other cocks took possession of her, other hands enjoyed her breasts and anus and the deep avenue of her sex.

Alison watched Lorna's initiation, and satisfaction warmed her belly. She had witnessed her rival blind-folded, chained and whipped; had listened while the master commanded her and she obeyed. Now Lorna, too, had experienced humiliation, shame and pleasure.

Next time Gary looked at Lorna's bottom, he would see scarlet weals. Alison's triumph was complete.

Her hand stole down to her clitoris and she pleasured herself as she saw Lorna being used by the members of the club. But there was one man who stood aside, his arms folded across his chest as he observed how his latest odalisque reacted. He was the only man who made no attempt to couple with her. The man Alison had known carnally but Lorna had not. Their master.

Chapter Ten

'You beat me to it this morning,' Chris said, strolling into the Priory kitchen. 'I didn't expect you to be here.'

'And where did you think I'd be?' Lorna answered coolly, getting out another mug, spooning in coffee granules and adding boiling water.

'You tell me. The Tyrell bashes usually go on for days, or so I'm told,' he countered, shooting her one of his mocking glances. 'Wasn't it any good?'

'On the contrary. It was out of this world,' she said truthfully, and handed him the mug. She tried to avoid looking at him. He was too attractive in jeans and T-shirt, and her body clamoured for closer contact. 'But I came home in the early hours of yesterday morning and spent a quiet day recuperating.'

'That good, huh? Glad you enjoyed it. Maybe the stories I've heard aren't true,' he opined, regarding her thoughtfully, his rangy, loose-limbed frame propped against the stone sink. 'Some think the vicarage is a kind of Bluebeard's Castle.'

'There's a saying that goes, don't believe anything you hear and only half of what you see. You might start considering that,' she replied reprovingly, stamping heavily on the almost uncontrollable urge to fondle the curving bulge at his crotch, pushed into prominence by his stance.

'I'll bear it in mind,' his said dryly. 'Do you usually get up so early? I'm surprised you didn't sleep on.'

'With Fred and the gang arriving at seven-thirty? You've got to be joking. They're like a herd of elephants.'

'I'd better go and consult with the inestimable Fred. Thanks for the coffee.' He twirled the ancient brass tap and rinsed his cup. 'Sorry about Saturday. My fault. It was a misunderstanding. Obviously you know Ryder and Sybil better than I do. I assume you got home OK?'

'Yes, thanks. Courtesy of Cassandra. Marc's interested in your bike. He's a collector.'

How odd humans are, she was thinking. We both know we want to fuck each other senseless, yet there's this pretence, this polite chit-chat, hedging, pretending, a very strange courting ritual indeed.

'Perhaps you could introduce us, next time I bring it along,' he suggested, carrying on the game. Then, face sobering, he came to the crux of the conversation. 'I've got tickets for a show in Bath on Thursday evening. Japanese Taiko drums. How about coming with me?'

'On the back of the bike?' she answered, smiling despite herself.

He had the grace to look uncomfortable. 'I'll pick you up in the car. We could have supper afterwards. What do you say?'

His eyes were smiling, complicit, letting her know he had not been taken in by her bluff about the party. She had spent Sunday alone, wandering through her house, wrestling with her emotions, still on an adrenelin high from her encounter with Ryder. His slave? Demanding that she give him licence to use the spring? Ha, dream on, Sunshine! she thought contemptuously. Away from him she could be defiant.

'I'd like to come,' she said.

It was on the edge of her tongue to mention she had seen Dudley's aide at the orgy, but thought better of it. This was another problem with which she must grapple

211

alone. Did Dudley know Ian had peculiar tendencies, and was enamoured of Sybil's footwear? Had he leaked her business affairs to Ryder?

'Lorna? It's Hugo. Please don't hang up. We need to talk.'

He had caught her when she was at the lodge, having just bathed after a sweaty day sorting through the Priory's attics with Tara. These had proved to be an Aladdin's Cave of wonders, her inheritance getting better and better.

She had taken the call on the receiver in the bedroom, standing naked, water dripping from her hair to trickle across her breasts. Drops hung on her pricked nipples, before falling to course down her belly and soak into her maidenhair.

'I don't want to talk to you. Not after finding out you wanted to trick me,' she said angrily.

'Trick you? My dear girl, you've got it all wrong,' he protested. 'It's not like that at all.'

'Are you trying to tell me you don't want to buy the Priory?'

'I do want it, but I'd like to discuss it with you.'

'There's nothing to discuss.'

'All right. I won't pressurise you. You have every right to take that attitude. But I need to see you again, Lorna. Nothing to do with the house. I had no idea you'd affect me so much. Can't we meet?' His voice was softly persuasive.

'I don't think so.' Why are you wavering? she asked herself. It would be simple to hang up.

'You can name the time and place. There are absolutely no strings, I promise you,' he continued, and she could tell by his tone that he assumed he was winning.

She remembered a useful tip taught her by Nicole. She allowed a second of silence, then said, 'I'd like to think about it, Hugo. I'll call you back. Are you at the Farrier's Arms?'

'Right now I'm speaking on my car phone. Here's the

number.' He reeled off a string of digits which she did not take down, cutting him off.

Hugo smiled to himself, and pulled over in a lay-by. It was a secluded stretch of road bordered by hedges and with a gate leading into a field. Traffic passed at a distance, and the sun warmed the luxurious, leather-upholstered interior of the Rover.

He had not returned to London after his first abortive effort to soften Lorna up so that she might part with Hinton Priory. When he realised she had the measure of him, he had decided to leave it for a day or two then try once more to win her over. If this failed, he would put Phase Two into operation, calling in a favour from an important person in the Woodmead and District Council Office.

'Judy, my dear,' he said as she leant across and placed her hand on the prick hardening beneath his trousers. 'Have you ever had a mobile phone rubbed against your pussy?'

'No, Mr Pendleton. Goodness, the things you say!' she answered admiringly, giving a breathy little giggle.

'Then it's high time you did.' His hand slid to one of her breasts and tweaked the nipple through her silky blouse.

Her skirt rode up. Glancing down he could see the brown fuzz crowning her mound, many shades darker than her sleek coiffure. He slipped a finger into the moist wetness, appreciating the ripe female aroma rising from it.

'Good girl,' he said in that deep voice which he knew could transform the most chaste woman into a harlot pandering to his lust. 'I'm so pleased you've done what I asked and left off your panties. You know by now I'm a very busy man and have to take my pleasures quickly.'

Judy spread her legs further. The sun sparkled on the honeydew clinging to the hairy fringe bordering her cleft. Hugo leant closer, running a finger over the flushed, swollen area. Judy moaned. He touched her with the slim side of the mobile, stroking the smooth black plastic over the ridge of her labia.

'Ow! It's cold,' she complained, but wriggled against it.

'A new sex toy, my dear,' he answered, excited to see that status symbol resting between his latest conquest's lips. The next time he used it for business, he would remember the sight and be tougher, harder, even more ruthless.

It gave him an intoxicating sense of power. He moved it, wetted the top with the juices seeping from her vulva, drew it slowly, tantalisingly, over her clitoris. Judy bore down on it. Hugo moved it away. He needed to feel her slippery smooth flesh, to steep his fingers in her nectar and make her come. Another proof of his invincibility.

He placed his hand on her pubic bone and drew the skin up towards her navel. This put stress on her clitoris, pulling its tissues high. The nub protruded from its cowl, and Hugo pinched it between his finger and thumb, then leant forward and flicked it with his tongue-tip.

Judy's head fell back, her eyes rolled and her body jerked. 'Oh, sir . . . sir!' she gasped. 'I love you!'

This was a little more than he had bargained for but, in his opinion, no more than he deserved. Judy's dramatic coming assured him of her undying devotion. Besides giving him a raging hard-on calling for immediate relief, it boded well for his future plans. Lorna might refuse to bend but there was no doubt about Judy obeying him to the letter.

Hugo lay back and received her attentions like a sultan in his seraglio. Just for the moment, she was his favourite houri. Still breathing fast, she opened his fly and dived inside to curl her fingers round the stiff length of him.

He permitted this caress, then grabbed her by the back of the neck and pushed her down till her mouth hovered over the fiery, throbbing cap topping his shaft. Judy gasped as her mouth encompassed him and he thrust his hips upwards to meet her first downward slide. His nails dug into her scalp as he rocked her back and forth.

It was gathering in him. He could feel it. He was riding the serpent fire roaring along his spine, its tongue a mighty spear transfixing his loins with an agonising ecstasy that wrung a cry from his lips. He ejaculated with such force that Judy could not swallow all the creamy flow which filled her mouth.

'It's an architectural gem,' Chris said as they crested a rise above Bath. 'I've been all over the world, including Italy, but there a nowhere like it. Not only does it have these truly wonderful eighteenth-century buildings, but superb Roman remains, too.'

The city sparkled, spread out in its deep hollow. It was indeed unique, the splendid design of crescents and squares laid out two hundred years before when it was a fashionable spa, a Mecca for gamblers and profligates. The sun was low, striking across parks and greens and the silver snakelike thread of the River Avon.

Such beauty was not lost on Lorna, but she seized on his mention of travel. She knew next to nothing about him, and snatched at every crumb of information. A constant source of surprise, he had arrived at the Priory in a red Porsche. No longer the biker, he was wearing a superbly tailored birdseye check suit which she could have sworn was by Gianfranco Ferre. With this went a grey silk shantung V-neck shirt and slip-on shoes of fine leather, no doubt also by an Italian craftsman. Romeo Gigli, perhaps?

He looked supremely, though casually, elegant and to her further astonishment, was welcomed like a long-lost son by the manager of the Theatre Royal, and ushered to his own private box.

Lorna made no comment, waiting for him to explain. When he didn't, she looked up from the programme and said, 'D'you live here?'

'I have done, but spent a lot of my time abroad.' He changed the subject, admiring the crimson plush and gilt adorning the old theatre. 'It's perfect, and it's hardly been altered since it was built.'

His cynical expression had gone, replaced by an endearing enthusiasm. Lorna put her suspicions on hold. She was going to enjoy herself, out for the evening with a most desirable man.

The show was fantastic: an enthralling tour de force of powerful, traditional Japanese drumming and percussion. Banners and festival costumes interacted with atmospheric subtlety and demon masks. The players were agile and sexy, the fierce beat matching the throbbing in her blood as, heated and excited, Lorna leant towards Chris, his shoulder pressing against her, his thigh brushing hers now and again.

During the interval, they sat in the foyer, drank coffee and discussed the performance. She was sweating beneath her simple black slip-dress. More inner than external heat. She wanted him to drag her into the corridor, force her against the wall, ruck up her skirt, lift her on to his cock and take her without further ado.

'Supper?' he said when the last pounding encore shook the chandeliers and the rapturous ovation finally died away.

They ate in a steak house off Beaufort Square; another place where Chris was well known. It seemed exactly right to be seated on a plush-covered bench with him, consulting the menu. Now he was more open, his eyes and the glancing touch of his hands letting her know that he wanted her. They drank wine with the starters, but there he stopped. He was driving. She continued to imbibe, a Beaujolais with the medium rare fillet steak, a light, dry Chardonnay with the fresh fruit salad.

Salsa was playing and a few couples swayed on the pocket-handkerchief-sized floor. Lorna slipped into Chris's arms as if made for them, moving to the rhythm, following his lead. He was light on his feet for so large a man, and her body rubbed against his in the closeness of the sensual South American dance. Her nipples crimped into tight points as they contacted his shirt front. Her pubis lifted of its own volition as his leg moved between hers.

She loved the smell of him, the feel of him, his cheek pressed to hers momentarily. She turned her head swiftly and her lips were on his; just a swift touch, but it fired her more than the most intimate probing of tongues.

His arms tightened and he held her to him. 'Let's go,' he said.

They walked through the streets to the multi-storey car park. It was still light and everywhere were tourists, students, holiday makers and locals, the air fragrant with the scents from innumerable flower-filled hanging baskets.

'Will you come to where I live?' he said, his sherry-brown eyes burning into hers as they stood by the Porsche.

'If you'll take me home afterwards.'

'I promise. If you still want to go.'

The car enclosed them in a dusky private world. He kissed her as she sat beside him, no light kiss this but a questing, plunging meeting of tongues with a hint of teeth, their mouths tasting, learning, getting to know one another.

He let her go and drove her to his home.

It was called Tinker's Mill, and still possessed the original mechanism which he set turning for her, the clatter of the great wheel in the path of the stream and the rush of water making her exclaim in wonder.

Inside everything was plain and old, dating from the time it was built. All on one floor, it consisted of a long, low studio divided by a carved wooden screen, a kitchen and bathroom added at the back.

It was a very masculine, functional place, though there was evidence of his eclectic taste; a few pieces of Jacobean furniture, African masks and hand-dyed Peruvian rugs pinned to the stone walls. Though the night was warm, Chris took a match to the kindling in the rough-stone fireplace. The logs caught and fire roared up the great chimney.

'Is this yours? D'you own it?' she asked, oddly nervous. This was part of Chris' attraction: she never quite knew what he would do next.

He nodded, kicking off his shoes, now barefooted. 'It was in a state when I bought it, but I'm getting there.'

'Architecture pays?'

He gave a quirky grin. 'I'm not complaining.'

'So I must expect a substantial bill?'

He laughed then, saying, 'Nothing is for nothing, Lorna, but you'll be delighted with the result. It's coming together. The electricity will be connected this week, the phone will be on, and the heating fixed up very soon.'

She half expected him to stop talking and go for the kill, but instead he said, 'Do you like flamenco? You move so well to salsa I feel sure you must appreciate the gypsy music of Spain.'

'I'm not all that familiar with it.' Surprised by his control, she sat on the large couch drawn close to the fire and fluffed her hands through her hair, watching him, her nerves taut with waiting.

He switched on the video recorder and selected a tape from many ranged like books along a shelf. 'I learnt to love it when I was in Andalucia,' he continued. 'This is an easy recording to start with. It's a programme about Joaquin Cortés, Spain's new star. He's taken Europe by storm with his show *Gypsy Passion*. It's not entirely traditional, for he's also studied ballet and incorporates it.'

He settled beside her and slung an arm round her shoulders, drawing her close so her head rested on his chest. The fire crackled, and the scent of sizzling resin pervaded the room like joss-sticks. The music was fiery, too; sensual, passionate, with the lead dancer a dark, haughty young savage, possessing great strength and controlled grace.

'He's a gypsy,' Chris said, his chest pressing lightly against the side of her breast. 'I've lived with the *gitanes*. Spain is my second home.'

Her body tingled at his closeness, and her blood beat

to the rhythm of the music, the harsh, grating voice of the singer rising like a call to prayer.

'It contains every element of human passion; love, betrayal, joy and sorrow,' Chris murmured, running his fingers through her hair as they settled deeper into the luxurious comfort of the couch. 'They sing of death, too. They're a religious, superstitious people, who believe in God and the devil, in demons and magic and ghosts. Death is close to them, and they celebrate it at their fiestas. The bull-fight is symbolic of this, and the matadors are gypsies, as agile as flamenco dancers.'

He's seducing me with words and music, Lorna thought, dizzy with wine and expectation. We're making love in slow motion. He's not going to rush it like other men I've known, and this is wonderful – long, sensual foreplay.

His back felt warm beneath the silk shirt and she smoothed it lingeringly as he removed her earring and whispered, 'I've wanted you all evening, Lorna. No, I'm lying. I've wanted you ever since you thought I was a squatter. You're too beautiful to be had by any one but me.'

He kissed her eyelashes, nibbled her lips and traced over them with his tongue; moved down her chin, touched her throat and then sucked her nipples through her thin dress. She sighed, ached for him to go faster, yet was glad when he did not.

Chris proceeded at his own pace, kneeling and taking off her sandals, then lifting one foot to his mouth, tonguing each toe as if it was a clitoris. He worked between them, over them, going higher to lick her ankle, the sensitive area inside her knee and the tender flesh of her thigh, stopping short when he reached the place where she wanted to feel it most.

She opened her arms and he sank into them, on to her mouth, into that, too; drawn inside by her ardent tongue, which was determined to possess all of him. They kissed for a long time, learning to know the contours of each other's mouth, the feel of teeth, the taste of saliva, wringing every last exquisite sensation from the congress of lips.

His hands were skimming delicately over her, wooing her. She was drowning in a sea of desire, high on the sweet drug of his mouth. She could almost breathe the perfume of his blood.

He was rock-hard, his loose trousers pushed out of shape by the mass inside them. Lorna was now experiencing actual discomfort, her breasts and clitoris ready to explode with the need to have him investigate them thoroughly. She released her lips and sat up, freeing her dress from beneath her and pulling it up and over her head. All she wore beneath was a pair of tiny tanga briefs.

He leant forward and fastened his mouth on one nipple, sucking strongly. Then he left it to concentrate on the other. The engorged tips took on a deeper tone. Lorna closed her eyes, a rushing feeling beginning at the base of her spine coursing into her thighs and gathering in intensity between them. Her whole being was swallowed up in the heavenly feeling.

Unable to wait, her hand slid down into her lap, her finger pushing aside the tiny black triangle of material and stroking her enlarged clit. He watched her, his eyes narrowed, and then he loosened his belt, drew off this shirt and, standing, dropped his trousers to the floor.

He was as swarthy from the waist down as he was above, except for the area covered by the inky curls at his crotch. His penis did not disappoint her, as long and thick as she had expected, fully erect. He came to her then and she touched the rim of his foreskin, rolled back by the rise of the powerful, twin-lobed glans. He lay beside her, his body locked to hers as if he would never let her go. His cock quivered against her belly, hard as a bough of wood. Lust surged up in her, and she pulled free to kneel on the floor by the couch, taking hold of him and drawing the shining cap of his splendid weapon to her wet lips.

'Oh, Christ,' he groaned as she flicked over the taut

dome and licked it clean of the transparent liquid dewing the slit.

The anguish in his voice excited her, his submission magical. He had been in charge at every encounter, till now. She gripped his tight buttocks, and slid a finger in the anal crack between. Exploring further, she toyed with the tender skin covering his balls, weighed them, gently squeezed them. Her red, wet mouth sucked them in; ripe plums for her delectation, soft, fleshy orbs surging with semen. Holding them in her hand, she slid her lips lasciviously up and down his throbbing shaft, her tongue circling the cone as if it was a luscious ice cream ready for her consumption.

'Lorna,' he murmured, and his strong brown fingers suddenly grabbed at her tousled hair. He pulled her up and back, drawing her into his arms. 'I'll come if you go on. I don't want to do that yet. I want to share it with you, darling.'

She wanted it, too, untying the ribbons at her hipbones so the tanga fell away. But she had not yet had her fill of his wonderful penis. She straddled him and slithered down his body, licking him as she went, sucking the tiny discs of his nipples, his rib cage, his navel, and following the dark trail of hair leading down to his pubis. She rubbed her cheek in it, inhaling the strong, male fragrance. Starting where his penis emerged from the fur, she slowly drew her tongue up its length, kissing and licking it.

She moved round, her back to him. Her knees were spread wide, the rounded mounds of her buttocks fully opened, her plump, moist labia and rosy anus exposed to his gaze. The thought of him staring at her very private treasures was exhilarating. With a deep-throated moan she sank on to the head of his cock, her vagina spasming as she felt him shudder with pleasure. Then his hands were on her hips, pulling her down towards his mouth, and her eyes closed in ecstatic slits as she waited in breathless anticipation, aching to feel his lips kissing her bud.

The touch of his tongue was a fluttering breeze at first, then it hardened driving against her power point, sure and strong. She fell to one side, his cock still embedded in her mouth, and his tongue followed, showing no mercy. One hand supported her thigh, a finger of the other slipping into her love-tunnel, opening it, stroking it, while his tongue never let up on the pulsating, aching clit-head.

The sweeping strokes became harder and faster, driving her to an intense orgasm. While she hung there in blissful ecstasy, he turned her on her back, opened her legs and lifted them high to rest on his shoulders. Then, kneeling between them, he guided the head of his heavily swollen penis into her haven.

He paused, bracing himself on his arms and looking down into her eyes. 'Are you ready for this?'

'Yes, Chris, yes. Do it now,' she gasped, her cheeks wet with the tears of release.

He thrust into her with measured pace and depth, and her body was a sheath, enfolding his powerful weapon. It stabbed deeply, touching the mouth of her womb, filling her every crevice, her muscles clenching round it gratefully. Slowly, deeply, he moved, drawing powerful sensations from her inner walls, and she watched his eyes, seeing them narrow, watched his face and saw how his lips curled back as if in pain.

She lifted her hands as he hung above her, and gently rubbed his nipples, saying teasingly, 'Stay still. You musn't move your cock. See how long you can stand it.'

She pulled the small points, flicked and fondled them. She felt his penis twitch deep inside her, but showed no mercy.

'God, Lorna,' he groaned and arched his hips.

'No. Not yet,' she commanded, gripping his tightly clenched buttocks. Then, taking pity on his distress, she whispered, 'All right. Go for it.'

By now the pleasure was too much for both of them. He plunged and bucked, and she closed her eyes, delighting in his savage possession and rocking on the strong waves of a primordial ocean. The sap of life flowed hot, carrying them to an unbelievable peak of excitement, and her hands were curving cat's claws drawing blood from his back.

He cried out and slumped on her, and tears burnt behind her lids. She could see them shining like crystals spilling out of a fountain, and woke from her trance to smile into his eyes.

'Well now, here's a turn-up for the books,' said Hugo. 'Let me tell her. It'll give me enormous satisfaction.'

'She's been spending a lot of time with him,' Dudley replied doubtfully, with a nervous shuffling of papers on his desk.

'Hasn't she just! This'll take the wind out of her sails. Christopher Devlin, eh? Crafty bugger. Do you think he knew? Is that why he's been so keen to get in her panties?'

'Could be,' Dudley said, steepling his fingers together in an attempt to look profound. 'Though I have my doubts. He may be nothing more than a genuine architect, or an opportunist. Hers is the greater claim.'

'But he's a man, and males usually win out when it comes to property. You should know that. The law's an ass, isn't it?'

'It wouldn't be easy in this case. What shall we do?' Dudley said, glancing apprehensively at the older man.

Hugo's smile did not reach his eyes. They were like chips of blue ice. His balls stirred and his penis, though hanging slack, felt swollen. Fate was playing into his hands. He was a great believer in fate, though he was prepared to help it along with a little manipulation on his part.

'I shall see her and tell her about your discovery in the family archives,' he said decisively. 'Though there's no need to add that Christopher would have been an Erskine, not a Devlin, if his great-great grandfather hadn't been born on the wrong side of the blanket.'

'This would go against him if it went to court,' Dudley reminded.

'I know that.' Hugo rose, pacing the carpet restlessly. 'But she doesn't have to. Keep your trap shut about that part of it, Dudley, and we're home and dry. No Chris Devlin influencing her.'

'But supposing she's too cock-struck to care?'

'Then, my boy, there's always the good old district council compulsory purchase order.'

'So that could put a stop to Chris Devlin's game,' Ryder said when Ian brought him the latest news from the office of Norcross, Grant and Bailey. 'The mistress will be pleased with you, slave. She'll want to reward you.'

'I can't stay, master,' Ian muttered regretfully, his eyes darting round Ryder's bedroom, hoping to catch a glimpse of her.

'I'm sure you can. Ring the office and tell them you're ill. You don't want to upset the mistress, do you?'

'No, master.' Ian was in torment. His job would be on the line if Dudley found out what he had been doing, but his blood boiled and his cock itched as if he had been stung by an army of mosquitos at the mention of Sybil. He had to see her.

Within minutes he was entering her chamber, that dusky, scented apartment where she sat like a bejewelled spider, weaving the deepest mischiefs into her silken web. She saw him come in, and picked up her whip, teasing the thongs through her fingers.

A bell clanged in the servants' quarters, and Lorna looked up to see which one it was among the several hanging in a row on the whitewashed wall.

There were little faded labels stuck under each, and the one still quivering was connected to the front door. 'Damn,' she said, irritated at being interrupted in preparing her supper. 'Who can that be?'

She mounted the back stairs and walked along a passage into the Great Hall. In the distance she could hear the bell clanging again. 'All right! Hold your horses. I'm coming,' she grumbled, crossing the floor on bare feet.

She was not ready to receive visitors, grubby from another day of work with Tara and wearing a sweaty vest and dirty jeans. Her temper did not improve when, on opening the heavy door, she found Dudley and Hugo standing there.

'Sorry to disturb you,' Dudley said insincerely. 'I phoned the gatehouse but there was no answer.'

'There wouldn't be. I'm living here, mostly,' she said ungraciously.

The shadows were long and low, night drawing its indigo veil across the sunset-edged clouds. She resented anyone disrupting her peace, communication with the old house precious to her.

'Can we come in?' Dudley said, venturing a foot over the threshold.

'If you must. What is it? And why are you here, Hugo? I said I'd call you.' She felt as if she was being taken over by them, a distinctly annoying feeling when it was her house they were entering, forcing their unwelcomed presence on her.

'Something has come to light that we feel you should know about,' Hugo answered smoothly, not in the least perturbed by her coldness.

'You'd better come to the kitchen. It's the only habitable place at the moment,' she replied, and led the way.

'Devlin getting on with it, is he?' Hugo remarked, looking around, scanning the great hall and connecting passage as if he was assessing the cost of putting it to rights.

'He's very competent, and so are his workmen. It will soon be finished,' she answered, disliking him more with every passing moment. Despite his well groomed appearance, she caught the distinct whiff of dark alleys and deceitful dealings.

She was glad this was her territory. No one could harm her there. And she was certain he meant her harm, wondering how she could have been such a fool as to trust him. The thought that she had been to bed with him made her writhe with shame. 'O villain, villain, smiling damned villain,' she quoted to herself.

In the kitchen, she stood with her back to the window and faced them, thumbs hitched in her jeans' pockets. 'Well, what's so important as to drag you all the way from Salisbury?'

Hugo glanced at Dudley, and the young lawyer, looking exceedingly uncomfortable, explained, ending lamely, 'We thought you ought to know that Devlin is related to the Erskines way back. He could stake a claim on the property.'

'What!' Lorna stared at him, open-mouthed, unable to take in the full import of his words.

'He's not to be trusted,' Hugo said forcefully. 'How do you know this isn't a ploy on his part, blinding you to his real motives? At any time you may get a letter from his solicitor. I did warn you to be careful.'

'I don't believe a word of it,' she snapped, while her mind raced, tormented thoughts buzzing in her head like demented bees.

Chris a traitor? It wasn't possible, was it? She desperately needed him there to face these accusations, but he had gone to London for the night on business; *her* business, as it happened. He was trying to match the old hand-painted paper that covered the drawing room walls.

Her former doubts returned with a vengeance. Was it still true then? Were men definitely not to be trusted, not even one like Chris who she had been daring to let herself love?

Hugo raised his shoulders in a shrug under the silk and wool mix of his jacket. 'Why should I lie? Or Dudley, for that matter. We have your welfare at heart, my dear.'

'How very noble,' she said acerbically. 'Nothing in it for the boys, I suppose?'

Hugo sighed, and sat down on a kitchen chair without being asked.

'Lorna, why are you so aggressive? I'm here to make you an honest offer for the property. A large offer. We're talking telephone numbers here ... three million pounds to be exact. That can't be bad, can it?'

'You've got a nerve!' She stood her ground, hands on her hips.

'Not enough? OK, let's get down to business.'

'No. Please go.'

'You can't mean that? No harm will come to the Priory. It will be the hub and heart of the enterprise. The complex will be built around it, very tasteful and discreet. It will bring employment to Woodmead, a great deal of employment. You must admit this would be an enormous advantage. Won't you reconsider?'

'No. Go away now.'

'Lorna ...'

'Just leave!'

When they had gone, she walked slowly through the drawing room and library and into the music room, remembering how she had first chanced upon Chris.

Was Dudley telling the truth?

It was painful to think he might be. Lorna prided herself on being a good judge of character. Maybe you were right first time, she thought. You were suspicious of Chris, remember? It seems your gut feeling was accurate after all.

And yet the past few days had been so sweet. She could not forget that night after the drumming, when desire had whipped through her veins, the interplay of hands and limbs moving her to ecstasy. She had slept with him, lying in his lap with him folded, spoon-fashion, against her back, his penis resting between her legs, the head nudging against her clitoris.

Since Ricky, she had become unaccustomed to spending all night with a man. And Chris had held her throughout the dark hours. It had made her feel warm and secure. Waking in his arms and in his bed had seemed so right, the best decision she had ever made. He had made love to her again before driving her back to the Priory, and since then they had met every day, not only while working but during their free time as well.

Now Lorna paced the room, driving her fist into her palm. 'Fool!' she said aloud. 'You let your defences down, and you'd promised yourself you wouldn't do that again. Serves you right if you find you've been taken for a ride.'

The house, big as it was, seemed suddenly claustrophobic. She raced out and drove like a maniac to Briar Cottage. Cassandra listened and advised and poured numerous cups of tea. 'Stay with me for the night,' she suggested. 'Marc's away. Let's have a bitching session. Men aren't worth the hassle.'

'I thought you wanted to marry Marc,' Lorna said gloomily.

'I do, but that doesn't mean I'm besotted. I know what he's like, what all of the buggers are like. Big though he is and old as he is, he throws a tantrum if thwarted.'

'Everyone seems to want the Priory. Ryder, Hugo and now Chris, if they're telling the truth.'

'Don't jump to conclusions. Ask him, next time you see him.'

Lorna drove home through the bright glow of a full moon, and stomped upstairs, still fuming. She was more annoyed with herself and her own gullibility than with Chris.

What was the use of asking him if he knew he had Erskine blood and was after the house? She tore off her clothes and jumped, naked, into bed. He was bound to lie. She cursed to herself.

The four-poster was vast, seeming far too big for one person. Bigger than ever now, for Chris had been with her lately when she had not been staying with him at Tinker's Mill.

The electricity was connected and she could switch on the table lamp. She plumped the pillows up behind her and sat in the middle of the bed like a queen, but the throne was lonely and she felt as if she would never be able to trust anyone to share it with her. Not after this.

What was it Queen Elizabeth was reputed to have said during a disagreement with her ministers? 'If I was crested instead of cloven, gentlemen, you would not have spoken to me thus.'

How true, Lorna decided, clicking off the light and sliding down under the duvet. Men treat us women like dirt!

She had been driving herself hard physically, and sleep claimed her quickly in spite of her topsy-turvy emotions. Once more she was in the forest, standing by the phallic stone, and Ian was there caparisoned as a horse. Members of the Club Dionysus pranced round the glade, and Sybil was rubbing her pubis with a whip handle, while Ian ejaculated over her red leather boots.

Lorna shifted and stirred, dragging the pillow close to her between her thighs, her consciousness drifting. Then it seemed that he came to her, the mysterious night-visitor who had appeared only once. He held her fast and she came up out of sleep to find he was real.

Silent, powerful, leather-clad, he entered her as she fought with the reality of the situation. His huge phallus passed into her body with brutal force, and her body took him, moistened into arousal by her dreams. He was a part of them, satisfying that hot, primitive need which wiped out rational thought. Her inner muscles responded to his pounding thrusts, and his gloved fingers curled into the damp whorls of her secret flesh, finding her clitoris and subjecting it to hard friction.

He was a dark thing made up of the darkness around him, his breath like spice on her skin, and her crisis came like a bolt of lightning, plunging her almost into uncon-sciousness. His teeth fastened in her neck as he shuddered in release, and then his heat was abruptly withdrawn.

Lorna did not reach for the light. She knew it was useless. Whoever it was would have already departed. Too exhausted to cope with more, she sighed and bur-rowed into the pillows, falling into a dreamless sleep.

Chapter Eleven

Costume-clad extras stood around waiting orders, some shy and awkward, others old hands at the game. Cameramen gave vent to picturesque invective as they supplemented the dullish day with arc-lights.

Harassed-looking figures bearing clipboards rushed about making busy noises; make-up persons nabbed actors for further attention; a fleet of mobile canteens stood beneath the trees, dispensing endless cups of tea and coffee, pre-wrapped sandwiches and wilting salad. Half a dozen Portaloos were ranged against a stone wall, well out of the way.

The stars kept to themselves, using their own private caravans where they retired when they could escape the tyrannical director, a renowned Oscar-winner who knew precisely what he wanted and was merciless in the getting of it.

Leaving her car, and clearing herself with security at the gate, Lorna walked across the lush green sward fronting the stately home which its titled owner had hired out to the film company. She had driven there that morning after finding a message on the answerphone.

It was from Sean, saying, 'I'm in England. Got offered a part in an adaptation of a classic novel for TV. It happened all in a rush. We're on location at Rushford

Manor, Amersham. I couldn't phone you before as we've been rehearsing non-stop. It's being directed by Raoul Lamont, a brilliant guy but a bloody slave-driver.'

He had given her his hotel number but she had decided to surprise him by turning up on set. His invitation came at just the right moment. She had been avoiding Chris and Ryder, trying to get her head together. What with Hugo, Gary, Dudley and her mystery lover she was in need of a break. At one time she had imagined rural surroundings to be peaceful, only to find herself caught up in a hot bed of intrigue.

Anticipation charged the air. The extras were herded into place and given their instructions. Cameras focused on the entrance to a copse. Silence prevailed.

Then someone shouted 'Action!' and Lorna saw Sean ride through the trees, handling his mount effortlessly. She was possessed of the sudden overwhelming urge to be the animal between his muscular, buckskin-covered thighs.

By his side rode an actress whose face was familiar. Both of them wore period costume. She was lovely, but it was Sean who stole the show; a compelling presence, handsome and dashing with those slightly oblique, fuck-me eyes. A coil tightened in Lorna's womb and her pussy moistened. Perfectly aware that he was the young man she had interviewed in New York, she was yet bewitched by the fictional character he now portrayed.

As he swung gracefully from the saddle and helped the lady dismount, he was transformed into a raffish beau with a ruthless slant to his lips. He wore a bottle green cut-away tail coat, a high white stock fastened under his cleft chin, top boots, and breeches so tight they outlined the ridge of his foreskin.

Lorna was working from memory, feasting her eyes on the plump curves of his cock and balls. The dark, wanting heat within her increased by the second, rising in her belly and tingling towards her clit.

They repeated the scene over and over then, 'Cut!' bellowed Lamont for the last time, and everyone relaxed.

Sean took off his low-crowned topper and wiped over his forehead with the back of his hand. 'Don't smear your base, ducky,' twittered a butch being with a cosmetic tray, shaven head, leather jeans and a pierced left eyebrow.

Lorna went to Sean through the press of people, and touched his shoulder. He spun round and his face broke into a delighted grin.

'Let's get out of this. My dressing-room's in that caravan over there.'

His hand was under her elbow, guiding her, and her bare flesh tingled at the contact with his firm, dry fingers. He looked even more striking made up, his skin darkened to a deeper hue, his bright blue eyes lined with khol, the lashes blackened. Even his lips were redder, more full and sensual.

'You're so bloody sexy I need to fuck you right now!' he announced, and she knew at once it was the same outspoken Sean underneath the glitz and glamour.

He kicked the door shut behind them, tore off his jacket, cravat and waistcoat, then hauled her into his arms, his strong lean body irresistible. There was no foreplay. She was ready for him, her vulva sticky with desire. His erection was massive and demanding, lying like a baton against his belly. He opened those revealing breeches and it sprang from its confinement, rampant as ever.

'No jockstrap?' she asked breathily, her hand closing round its pulsating length, fingertips smoothing the veins, the satin skin, the glinting helm.

He chuckled, low in his throat. 'The costume department won't allow one. They're sticklers for accuracy. Besides, the female audience go wild over pronounced bulges. Why do you think Regency movies are so popular?'

'So it's all down to sex?' she whispered against his open mouth.

'Hasn't it always been?' he said, then shot his tongue between her lips, stopping further talk.

She dropped her cotton palazzo pants and lay down for him on the floor. He eased his breeches out of the way and knelt over her, his cock ramrod stiff, the glans fiery and moist. His hands felt beneath her sweatshirt, homing in on her hard nipples, then he caressed her hair and face as he lowered himself on her.

'Ah, Lorna, I've missed you,' he murmured, and his sincerity was like a fresh breeze blowing across the Irish Sea. 'Talking smut to you over the phone wasn't enough.'

'Sean, Sean, you're so good for me,' she sighed, and with one sharp thrust he buried himself in her fragrant, lubricious sheath.

She hugged him to her, tracing his shoulders under the thin lawn of his loose shirt, feeling the muscles honed by exercise, hard riding and rigorous fencing classes. His body was his livelihood, and he needed to keep it at its peak. Her whole body seemed fused with his, her inner core clenching round that mighty weapon moving swiftly in and out of her silken opening.

She writhed under him, threshing her head from side to side and pumping upwards, impaling herself on him. She felt him penetrate deeper as she moaned with the fierce pleasure of it. He grunted, seized her hips and anchored her to his cock as he rolled over so she sat astride him.

She gasped and lay back, shored up by the thickness of him. She supported the small of her back with her fists, thrusting her breasts forward. Then, impatient of their covering, she raised her arms and pulled off her sweat-shirt. Now her breasts swelled, crowned by two hungry peaks needing his mouth. They swung loosely as she leant over him and he reached up to grab at a nipple, sucking it between his lips. Lorna spread her legs wide each side of his hips, her pubis bearing down on his cock-root.

This way she could bring the most blissful friction to her clitoris, needing a harsh mating, a quick fusion of flesh to flesh. She was igniting a blaze that might well consume them for all time. Waves of pleasure shot through her as she rocked to and fro, feeling the pressure on her pleasure centre, rejoicing at the powerful surge of his penis plunging ever deeper into her body.

He speared her, martyred her, violated her sanctuary, brought her to ecstasy. Amidst the crucifying bliss of orgasm, she felt his ultimate convulsion and heard him cry out his satisfaction. She was his for that precious moment, his alone.

Yet, as his sweating body slumped and she awakened from the madness of completion, so another face impinged on her mind, another voice whispered in her ear. Props littered the dressing-room, and she chanced upon a riding whip. Her buttocks stung in response.

Ryder Tyrell, that devilish magician, had infiltrated her, mind, body and soul. It was as if through sorcery he had grafted a part of him to her, making them one.

Someone tried the door. It opened and a blond-headed young man with a Byronic haircut looked in. He started, and his eyes widened. 'Sorry, Sean!'

'That's all right, Johnny. Do you want something?'

Sean did not move, merely turning his head towards his fellow actor, cheek still pressed against Lorna's neck. He covered her almost completely, but she was embarrassed by this sudden interruption. It was one thing to appear naked at the Club Dionysus, but quite another to be caught in the act by one of the cast.

'No, no. Nothing that can't wait,' said Johnny, unable to drag his eyes away. His face flushed and the prick confined within his trousers grew longer and fuller, stretching up to brush his navel.

'Give me half an hour and I'll be with you,' Sean promised, smiling and kissing Lorna's slack wet mouth.

When Johnny had backed out, shutting the door carefully, Sean moved to one side, his legs still locked with Lorna's, his penis slipping from her to lie wetly against his thigh. They smiled into each other's eyes; the contented, loving smile of friendship lit by passion.

'You're doing well,' she said, while he eased down so he could pillow her head on his shoulder.

'Seems so,' he agreed. 'My agent's working a miracle.'

'Will you still enter for the *Image* contest?'

'Sure. I'll be back in the States by October. Can you come with me?'

'I don't know,' she answered slowly. 'Maybe for a visit, but it's the house, you see. I'm kind of involved with it.'

'Are you sure it's the house? Not a man, by any chance?' He played idly with her bush, rubbing his fingers through the fur, and her clitoris stirred at this tantalising caress.

'No man. Well, nothing permanent,' she assured him.

'Plenty of one-night stands, eh?' His eyes crinkled as he smiled, and she knew he was not in the least jealous.

'One or two,' she conceded, then, wishing that he felt the slightest hint of commitment she added, 'Why don't you visit? It's only a couple of hours' drive away.'

He put her from him and sat up, breeches gaping, his semi-erect phallus dark against the white puffs of shirt. 'I can't, darling. I'm too tied up here, and there are several interviews on chat shows lined up. This is my chance, and I'd be a fool not to make the most of it.'

'I know,' she said regretfully, and reached over to take his hand and lay it on her breast. 'You're so sweet, and I'd not do anything to hinder you.'

'I'll come down later,' he promised, palming the heavy swell of her breasts and tweaking the nipples. With an agile movement he pinioned her under him again, braced on his arms as he stared down into her face, all laughter banished. 'You mean a lot to me, Lorna. Maybe when things are more settled there will be time for us. Meanwhile, let's enjoy the here and now.'

She spent the night with him, after entering that mad world of cinema when they went out to dinner with Raoul Lamont and the leading actors. Sean was hot property, soon to be hotter. She knew it. They all knew it. But just for a while she was his lady.

Driving home next day, she realised he was sincere when he told her he loved her. But she wasn't sure of her own feelings. Was it his star quality she wanted or was it him? It was as well he was working so hard and she had so much on her mind. Time would prove if they were right for each other in the long term.

Seeing him again had made her homesick for the showbiz razzmatazz of *Image*. She was tempted to return to New York, and let those who wanted Hinton Priory have it. Yet, when she entered the beech avenue leading to her house and saw it framed between the trees, as foursquare and solid as if it had grown from the soil instead of being built by man, she knew this could not be.

Unwilling to tackle Chris just yet, she parked up and lost herself in the woods, her feet taking her to that ancient penis-shaped stone. The day was overcast, and the dell no longer warm, or even friendly, and yet her heart lightened as she stood before the carved monument, allowing its influence to wash through her.

Sean and she had made love up to the last possible minute, till they were exhausted and sore. They had drunk wine together and very nearly cried because their paths led in different directions. She felt physically and mentally dislocated, without form or definition, and could smell him in the juices seeping from her inner self, even though she had showered before she left.

The forest offered a haven, though she had the feeling of intruding at her peril into some private domain. She had the absurd compulsion to make an offering to appease that sense of imminent danger exhaling from the silent, impenetrable thickets.

'Don't be afraid,' said Ryder, stepping from the shadows. 'You are accepted. You watered the earth and became one with it.'

'How did you know I was here?' she said, her voice dreamy, her movements slow as if she walked under water.

'I know everything about you,' he answered gravely,

and placed an arm around her shoulders. 'You've been away, trying to escape your destiny. It won't work. This is your place and I am your master. Marry me, Lorna. Become blood of my blood, flesh of my flesh.'

'I've never considered marriage.'

'Neither have I. Till now.'

'But is it me you want or Hinton Priory?'

'Is there a difference? Darling, you *are* Hinton Priory.'

He smoothed the strands of hair from her brow and stood behind her, cupping her breasts and rubbing his thumbs over the puckered nipples. His tumescent cock pressed into her buttocks. She reached backwards to clasp him closer, then ran her hands over his taut arse.

She widened her legs and watched his hands creeping down, stretching the elasticated waist of her pants, disappearing inside and moving relentlessly towards the slit of her mons. His peeled her outer labia apart, and laid a finger along the length of her wet furrow.

Pleasure swamped her as he stimulated her clitoris.

When he lifted his hand to her lips, she sucked away her own salty taste. Her knees felt weak. She was all sex, every nerve and fibre liquid and insubstantial. He wetted a finger with her arousal and bored into her anus. She moaned as he slipped from one orifice to another. She was at breaking point, about to spill over, but he did not take her. Neither did he bring her to climax. Once again, she experienced the slow burn of frustration.

The sky darkened and a brisk breeze rustled the leaves. A few heavy spots of rain fell on the glade.

'Sybil is waiting,' he murmured. And with his arm holding her close, she allowed him to take her to the vicarage.

'What's up?' Marc asked, his hairy chest and wide shoulders emerging from a frothy white sea of bubbles. He stretched out one leg under the water, and his big toe connected with Cassandra's pussy-lips.

'Oh, so you've noticed?' she asked, slim brows arching sharply. 'I'm worried about Lorna.'

'How so?' He wriggled his toe and grinned at her down the length of the sunken tub, prodding at her clitoris, gauging her reaction.

Cassandra spread her legs, opened her arms wide and gripped the turquoise blue tiles surrounding the rim. 'She's not been around for a few days. Tara hasn't seen her, and neither have the workmen.'

Marc slid across the porcelain on his rear, making waves in the honeysuckle-scented water. He laid his hands on her inside thighs and pushed back, opening her wider. The water passed the portal of her vagina, warm and tickly. He lifted her on to his lap, his curving cock rubbing against her cunt-lips, his broad, sculptor's thumb massaging her nub.

'What about Chris Devlin?' he asked, but disinterestedly, more concerned with advancing his mouth towards her shiny bronze nipples.

'She doesn't want to see him. Not after what Dudley told her.' Cassandra lifted her hands and placed one either side of his bearded face, bringing her lips to his, tongue-tip flicking over his bushy moustache.

'She'll be all right. She's a big girl now. Stop mothering her,' he advised, his fingers slippery with soap and love-juice, circling her clit, rolling a nipple into an even harder point to double her pleasure.

She lifted her hips and settled back again, up and down, water sloshing and penetrating as he moved his shaft inside her tunnel. It felt wonderfully tight. Thoughts of Lorna faded as she lost herself in the rhythm. Her breasts jiggled and she arched back, trying to witness the joining of their bodies through the screen of churning water.

He was solid inside her, his biggest cock she had ever had. 'Don't let anyone kid you size doesn't matter,' she muttered, increasing her speed, thrusting harder and harder, waves sloshing over the edge of the tub and pooling on the marble tiles.

Marc gripped her hips and increased the tempo, pistoning hard and deep, connecting with her cervix. His lids were closed and he was smiling, then he opened his eyes and fixed hers. Gazing at each other, they synchronised thrusts, the speed increasing in a crescendo.

Cassandra's fingers were at her clitoris, giving it a final rub that tipped it over into rapture. She came in a wild blur of sensation, and felt him climax at the same moment, spilling over and pulsating in ecstasy deep inside her.

'Come in, Lorna. Where have you been?' Sybil said, stretching her svelte limbs voluptuously among cushions heaped on the four-poster.

She was seductively dressed in a black satin bra, her rouged nipples peeping through the opened tips. Her matching, wide-legged French knickers were pushed to one side, showing her smooth pussy.

Sinking her talons in his hair, she shook the head of the man engaged in bathing her toes in his saliva, sucking at each one as if it was a tiny penis. 'Don't stop, slave,' she commanded.

Ian. He's a spy, Lorna thought, but somehow it no longer mattered.

'Has she been disobedient, master?' asked Marta, her mouth set in a grim line, arms folded over her thin chest.

'She has,' he replied, and pushed Lorna forward, one hand clamped round the back of her neck.

'What has she been doing?' Sybil said, rising from the bed and coming closer. Ian crawled along behind her, dragged by the lead clipped to his collar.

He wore an animalskin suit, a large pair of ears attached to his head. His chest and belly were bare, his penis and testicles braced by a leather ligature. He was in a permanent state of arousal, pre-come dribbling from his cock-eye, his knob a dark, angry-looking purple.

'She's been shagging, like the dirty slut she is,' Ryder answered, and turned his steely grey eyes to Lorna, adding, 'I'm displeased because you let another man lick and suck you and drive his cock into your cunt ... one that I didn't select. You musn't do that, my dear. I shall

239

choose your partners and take pleasure in seeing them possess you.'

The bedroom was candle-lit, the drapes drawn across the windows. Shadows flickered over the panelled walls, the figures on the tapestries in constant movement. The air was redolent with the heady aroma of joss-sticks.

Ryder snapped his fingers and Rashid came forward, acting the valet and helping him undress. It was done slowly and provocatively. First his loafers, then the black shirt parting to leave his broad-shouldered torso naked, followed by the casual unbuttoning of his chinos.

Lorna's tongue crept out over her lower lip. She ached to lick his smooth, tanned chest, the nipples like brown pennies. He freed his hair and shook his head, the ebony mane tumbling halfway down his back. Flicking it away, he turned to face her, legs astraddle, the top buttons of his trousers undone. His stance was haughty, a thin strip of plaited leather braced between his hands.

His masculinity was fierce, aggressive and totally dominating, and Lorna adored it. She cringed inside and became a wimp, longing to obey and serve him. Deliberately, she fostered and revelled in submissive fantasies.

Sybil observed them, a knowing smile lifting her red lips. Ian crouched before her, holding back the lace-trimmed leg of her knickers and pressing his tongue into the groove between her shaven, bejewelled lower lips, subjecting her clitoris to little catlike laps.

Ryder jerked his head. Marta and Rashid seized Lorna and bent her over a stool. Her arms were pulled forward, and fur-lined manacles slipped over her wrists, locking them together. Next a gag with a three inch rubber penis was pushed into her mouth and a blindfold fastened over her eyes. She twisted her head, but there was no escape.

Her senses focused into smell, touch and hearing. Her pants were stripped off, the cool air playing over her naked bottom and thighs. Hands splayed her legs. A bar was wedged between them, her ankles chained to it.

Someone planted a light kiss on the split almond of her cleft from behind. A finger poked into her nether hole and excitement stabbed through her loins, the hot blood rising to flood her neck and face.

'Let me,' said Sybil and Lorna smelled a sweet and nutty perfume as a fleshy female rump was lowered over her.

The gag was removed and her blind face was enveloped in satin and love-juice and essences. Her tongue explored exotic territory, working into the cracks and soft folds of Sybil's pudendum. The skin texture was delicious, the taste musky, the smell oceanic. Lorna's tongue masturbated her wetly, and the heat swamping Sybil's genitals found an echo in her own secret place, brazenly exposed to view.

The enveloping flesh was abruptly removed, and Lorna licked Sybil's honey from her lips. Almost at once her place was taken by a large phallus. Lorna opened her mouth willingly, took in its great length and sucked it.

Was it Ryder's? She didn't think so, certain she would remember the shape and size. It tasted of cinnamon, smelled of it, too. Spices from a foreign skin. Rashid's love-organ, without doubt.

At the same time, another object was thrust into her innermost recess, too warm to be a dildo, sleek and firm. Her helplessness exaggerated her sensations. To be trussed and used was an experience she had longed to repeat, though hiding the shameful truth. Here she could indulge it, submit to it, glory in it.

She was apprehensive, her nerves tingling, ears straining for sounds. The cock filled her mouth completely, her tastebuds quivering as the slippery juice emerged from the mighty thing pressing into the back of her throat. Hands reached under her breasts, pinching the raised nipples. Other fingers felt between the inner lips hanging between her labia majora and fastened on her swollen clitoris, rolling and tormenting it. She was a piece of jetsam tossed by the waves, feeling the ocean lift and carry her to the crest of that surging sea as the tide of orgasm rose sharply, only to drop into a trough of disappointment as, suddenly, all stimulation was removed.

She slumped in her bonds, moaning, clitoris aching, breasts abandoned. Suddenly, without warning, something stung her buttocks. A light flick, but enough to make her strain upwards with shock. Then her yawning cleft was caressed again.

The lash flicked, harder this time, leaving a trail of fire that communicated with her bud. Hands were oiling her, massaging her, masturbating her, before being replaced by the next searing contact between whip and rump. Soon she could no longer differentiate between pain and pleasure.

Should she expect the lash or the clitoris rub that replaced it? The next unexpected sensation was a large object plunging into her vagina, then her rectum. Human or manufactured? She did not care, crying out piteously when it was withdrawn just as she was reaching a crazy climax.

'Very pretty.' murmured Ryder, close to her ear. 'Your bottom looks lovely, Lorna, patterned in red stripes. Later, I'll show you in the mirror. Do you want to come?'

'Yes ... yes ...' she sobbed, aware of tears running from her eyes, buttocks, clit and anus bathed in fire.

'How much?'

'Very much.'

'Is it bad?'

'Very bad.'

'All right. I'll let you come, but first you must receive six more strokes. Is that understood?'

'Yes.' Her heart was beating frantically as she rotated her hips in a vain attempt to put pressure on her pubis.

'Yes, master!' he said sternly.

'Yes, master,' she replied meekly, crafty now, willing to agree to anything if only he would bring her off.

Six times the whip rose and fell and at every stripe

Lorna's body was brought a little closer to crisis point. She counted the blows, each one a peak she was struggling to surmount in order to obtain nirvana. No cock now, just fingers sliding deep into her vagina and a thumb revolving on her clitoris.

She responded wildly, crying out, 'Give me more! Give it to me! Now ... now ... now!'

She came with a mindblowing violence, her arms and legs jerking, her blindfolded head twisting and turning. Then she hung lifeless in the yoke, convulsed with spasms.

Her eyes were freed and she kept them tight shut for a moment. She was lifted in powerful arms as if she weighed no more than thistledown. Sybil was lying on the bed and Lorna was placed beside her, embraced by warm arms and nestled close to a pair of perfect, satin-screened breasts.

Ryder pulled a black polo-neck sweater over his head and brushed back his hair, confining it once more. 'Serve tea in the drawing room, Marta,' he said blandly. 'We'll be down shortly.'

'Why are you avoiding me?' Chris asked, scowling at Lorna.

'I'm not,' she said, but he knew she was lying. He fought the urge to grab hold of her and kiss her till she came to her senses.

'Bollocks!' he growled abrasively. 'Whatever I've done or not done, you could at least have the decency to talk about it.'

The weather had cleared and, as the solstice approached, so the heatwave had returned. He had kept himself busy and there was much to sort out, not the least being the exacting demands of the historical preservation team. Nevertheless, he had been disappointed by Lorna's absence. Why hadn't she phoned and told him she was going away? Worse than this was the fact that her car had been parked up at the Priory for days now, and she had not put in an appearance till that morning.

Chris was angry, and annoyed with himself for being so. After several let-downs, he had succeeded in carving out a life where women took second place. Then he had met Lorna. He cared about her, not only in the rutting heat of bed, but at other times, too. A chink had developed in his armour and he had started to look forward to seeing her at the end of a day's work, daring to open up to her.

Her rejection was like a kick in the teeth.

Now she stood in front of him, irresistibly gamine in faded blue jeans, with her shapely legs and little rump and that cloud of hair framing her face. His cock stirred and his groin felt heavy as he looked at her breasts, the nipples erect, pushing darkly against the white T-shirt, betraying her lack of bra.

Perfume wafted from her skin, coupled with that sweet woman-scent which made his senses swim. It brought back memories of ensorcelled nights and the most satisfying sex he had ever experienced. He was aroused simply by being in the same space with her, his cock jutting in readiness, chafing against his jeans. This added to his irritation, making him more determined than ever to clear the air.

'I don't owe you any explanation,' she said, her chin lifted stubbornly. 'But if you must know, I went to see a friend.'

'Male?' He fired at her.

'Yes.'

'And before that? You've been acting strangely for days.'

She perched her bottom on a stool and hitched her feet up on the strut. Her face looked troubled, her eyes a stormy green. 'You've not been truthful with me,' she began.

'How so?' He took his cue from her, remaining cool and distant.

'Why didn't you tell me you're descended from the Erskines?'

'Is that all?' Relief swept through him. 'I didn't think it was important. It was generations ago. What's the matter? Afraid I might steal your precious property?'

'Well, mightn't you? Dudley Norcross told me about it as soon as he found out.'

'Bully for him!' he snapped, his sarcasm cutting through the sunny room.

'He was doing me a service.' She was on her feet again, so stiff and haughty that he almost turned on his heel and left her to her suspicions.

'And you decided to believe the worst possible scenario. Is that it? Well, Miss Erskine, you can think what you damn like. I'm here to do a job, nothing more. Unlike your bosom buddy, Ryder Tyrell.'

'Leave him out of this.' Her face was flushed under the tan, her eyes flashing. Even her hair seemed to spark.

'I see. So he's got to you, has he? You like kinky stuff, I presume, for that's all you'll get from him.'

'You know nothing about it.'

'Don't I? I told you, I had a friend who was involved. He let me in on what happens at the Club Dionysus.'

'And you condemn it. God, Chris, I never thought you had tunnel vision,' she mocked, laughing unpleasantly.

He was rapidly losing his temper, wanting to put her across his knee and spank some sense into her, then thinking ironically that, schooled by Tyrell, she would probably enjoy it.

'I'm not narrow-minded,' he grated, his fists clenched into white-knuckled balls.

'Good,' she said lightly. 'Then come to the Midsummer Ball at the vicarage.'

'No thanks!' he retorted.

Lorna rose and paced over to stand close to him. Her breasts touched his shirt-front. His cock jumped and it took every ounce of will-power to resist dragging her to him.

'What's the matter?' she asked languidly, her hip

brushing his groin. 'Are you afraid? Dudley's been invited, so have Cassie and Marc. You'd be surprised at the people who belong to the club.'

'I shouldn't,' he responded harshly.

'Don't be so sure. You might get to like it.' His skin crawled and his prick thickened as she walked her fingers provocatively up his chest. He felt a torrent of desire running through him, making him tremble.

He gripped her hand in one large fist. 'Stop it, Lorna. You're acting like Sybil.'

'How d'you know?' Her eyes were heavy lidded, the tip of her tongue shining pinkly between her parted lips. 'Have you screwed her?'

'That's none of your business,' he rapped out, thinking; two can play at this game.

She lifted her narrow shoulders in a shrug. 'Sybil is an amazing woman. I'm learning a lot from her.'

'Carry on then, but count me out,' Chris snapped, and swung towards the hall door. 'I'll need to see you later. There are some papers to sign.'

Chapter Twelve

'Greetings, Goddess, on this midsummer morn,' declaimed Cassandra in a richly dramatic voice.

She had decked the grotto with flowers, their pungent odour mingling with that of incense. Naked, as befitted a high priestess, she prostrated herself before the circles carved into the rockface.

Lorna lowered her gaze, the candlelight sparkling on the water trickling into the holy well. She could not help recalling the last time she had been there, and needed to confess to her friend.

'Ryder uses this place,' she said quietly. 'I should have told you before, but couldn't find the right moment.'

Cassandra's eyes cut to her, purple in the dimness. 'I'm not surprised. He's a pagan, too. Has to be to run a club named after the god of wine and revelry.'

'Ryder is special, too,' Lorna murmured, the little gold keeper inserted in her right labia majora a constant reminder of him.

But they had never yet had full intercourse. His tongue and lips had brought her to orgasm. He had watched her with Sybil, using a variety of dildoes. He had whipped her, entered her nether orifices, yet withdrawn before the union could be complete.

It bedevilled her, keeping her on a knife edge of

suspense. She was sure she would never feel complete until he had attained his zenith in the plushy warmth of her vagina.

'So I see,' Cassanura said acerbically, glancing at Lorna's pierced and shaven mons. 'I repeat my warning. He's a powerful man.'

'You're afraid of him?'

'Only of his influence on you.' Cassandra stood with her hands steepled together, murmuring, 'May the Goddess keep you safe.'

Lorna closed her eyes, and then felt a silky arm slipping around her waist, gently urging her to the floor. They rested on a carpet of petals, kneeling and facing each other, nude and flower-crowned. Race memories stirred in Lorna's psyche: spears of light danced over beautiful naked flesh, on breasts and mounds and long, sensitive fingers.

She shivered, the doorway to her senses opening. She became the heart of womankind: no longer Lorna Erskine, shrewd journalist: not even the pleasure seeker who melded her body with men. Now she was a priestess, devotee of the Great Mother.

Exaltation welled in her. Once again she was aware of an omnipotent presence. The cave walls seemed to crowd round her, each stone a vehicle for a spirit of earth, air or water. Her breasts were stippled with goosebumps, her nipples bunched like berries. The ring in her labia tightened as the pink flesh swelled.

She felt fingers on her teats, whisper-soft, then fondling firmly. Reaching out, she found Cassandra's breasts, returning the pleasure. Her palms skimmed over that curvaceous body, sinking into cavities and folds, exploring hollows and peaks.

Meanwhile Cassandra caressed her under the armpits, between her breasts and in her bottom crease. Lorna trembled and sighed, drowning in those amethyst eyes. They were huge, the pupils inky. Cassandra's coral lips were fuller and more lustrous. Lorna leant forward and took one of Cassandra's nipples into her mouth.

They lay down with their heads between each other's legs. Lorna moaned as Cassandra's tongue began a steady lapping rhythm, urging the clitoris from its hood. Without hesitation, Lorna feasted at the silkily enticing surface of Cassandra's moist sex. Fingers plucked at her nipples; the scent and taste of woman added to her excitement; passion gathered in great waves in her belly.

Slowly she sucked at Cassandra's hot nub, and with equal fervour her friend tongued her own engorged sliver of flesh. They moved against each other languorously, prolonging the moment, working inexorably towards their goal, that of mutual ecstasy.

Lorna had reached ethereal realms where she was almost out of her body yet intensely aware of it. Her clit throbbed with the white heat of desire, and the same heat radiated from Cassandra's epicentre. It roared like a forest fire. Sparks and flames, billowing red. Lorna was caught in it, spiralling upwards on the crimson smoke.

Ecstasy and anguish increased in pitch. Her womb contracted and the coil inside her relieved itself in a vast, annihilating spasm of intense and violent pleasure. In that instant, she heard her lover moaning, felt her thighs scissor about her head, while her mouth was flooded with the fresh, sweet potency of Cassandra's nectar.

They nestled close amidst the crushed flowers as the last waves of pleasure rippled through them. Finally Cassandra stirred and kissed her, a gentle, caring kiss that somehow reminded Lorna of Sean.

'We've pleased the gods, darling,' Cassandra whispered. 'There's nothing they like better than witnessing the simple act of loving.'

'Between women? I thought they were only interested in fertility,' Lorna reminded, sitting up and reaching for the loose flowing robe in which she had walked to the temple, barefoot through the dawn dew.

'Legend has it that in the beginning we were hermaphrodites, so there was no need to copulate for reproduction. But there must have been love and pleasure. You can't tell me those fabled inhabitants of Ancient Greece survived without these two emotions,' Cassandra said with a wise smile.

'I'm glad we're not like that any more,' Lorna answered as they climbed the steps into the sunlight.

'I guess it's more fun this way,' Cassandra agreed.

'Have you decided to come to the vicarage tonight?'

'I admit to being curious. Just what has Ryder Tyrell got that draws you like a magnet? Yes, I'll come, and find out for myself. I feel duty bound to protect both you and the spring. Marc's gone to Paris for an exhibition, so I'll be there on my own.'

Lorna felt immeasurably light-hearted. There was a party in the offing; her best friend would be with her; it was high summer and she was young, healthy and rich. What more could any woman want?

She refused to entertain the niggling worry concerning Chris. Whenever they met now, antagonism sizzled between them. Both Dudley and Hugo had assured her she was doing the right thing by snubbing him. She was not convinced, knowing them to be strangers to the truth. Ryder refused to talk about it, and she was so mesmerised when with him that sensible thought fled.

She bumped into Chris when she reached the Priory. He was accompanied by a sensibly dressed woman who Lorna recognised as Mrs Barnes, an expert from English Heritage who called frequently to monitor their progress. By a miracle the spring had escaped detection. Chris and the others had examined the temple, but no mention had been made of what lay beneath it.

Lorna put on her business head, talking earnestly to Mrs Barnes, but when they were alone, Chris cocked an eyebrow at the robe that was slipping off her shoulders and coming undone in the front and said, 'Been swimming?'

'No,' she answered tartly. 'I was attending morning prayers.'

'You? I find that hard to believe, or were you telling God how to run the universe?' he scoffed.

She stood with arms akimbo, wondering what there

was about him that provoked her into behaving badly. 'Even I have faith, you know. Faith in a higher power. Faith in fate.'

'Faith in Ryder Tyrell?' His eyes were black with anger and desire, his beautifully moulded lips in a tight line. He's invited me to the ball. Did you ask him to do that?'

'I certainly didn't.' She was shocked, unsure whether to be pleased or upset.

'I've a bloody good mind to accept,' he growled, glowering at her. You'll be there, I suppose.'

'Of course.'

Angry with him though she was, her wayward body responded to his swarthy good looks. She found it hard to keep her hands to herself. They drifted towards him of their own volition, wanting to touch. Her legs parted slightly, and even though Cassandra had just satisfied her, she could not help thinking of the serpent slumbering in Chris's crotch. Had he been sharing it with others? The idea hurt.

Afraid she might betray herself, she ran up the wide staircase and slammed into her bedroom. There she showered and prepared for the night. She had a new outfit, ordered from a mail-order firm who specialised in fetish gear.

It had been an impulse buy, something she would never have considered wearing had not Ryder released elements within her she had not dreamt she possessed. She had learned the strange dichotomy of pain/pleasure. He had spoken of the satisfaction to be gained by inflicting as well as receiving it. Lorna was ready to try. Whatever else he might have done, Ryder had strengthened and empowered her.

I'm a real midnight prowler now, she thought, as she pirouetted before the mirror. She felt irresponsible and wanton and entirely reckless. A whip had been included in the parcel. It cracked satisfyingly, and she imagined Dudley helpless under it or, better still, Hugo.

She looked taller, slimmer, naked beneath the purple leather two-piece. The bodice was laced down the front showing an expanse of cleavage, and her breasts were jacked up high. The sleeves were long and tight, laced at the wrists.

The leggings clung like a second skin, intersected by a thick metal zip that ran from waist to crotch and up the other side, parting her lower lips and caressing her clitoris, pressing into her crease and teasing the puckered rose of her anus. Her spangled heels were so high she tottered till used to them, her calves and buttocks exaggerated.

She swept her hair up and to one side. It cascaded in a tangle of curls. After applying vivid cosmetics, paying particular attention to mascara and lipstick, she fastened on a purple feather-crested mask, eyes glittering fiercely through the slits. She postured and paced, flourishing the whip. Now she was a creature who walked on the wild side, untamed and seductive.

Hugo turned the invitation card over in his broad hands. He had received it several days ago, and was still suspicious. Ryder Tyrell? Lorna's neighbour? He had gone into a huddle with Dudley, and Ian had supplied the answer.

Hugo, a bully at heart, enjoyed seeing the young man squirm. Intrigued, he had listened as Dudley got the truth out of him. The Club Dionysus. Ferreting back in his storehouse of items which might be used as blackmail, Hugo recalled hearing whispers of this cult where anything went.

'So, what do you do there?' Dudley asked, a cruel smile playing about his lips.

Ian shrank in his operator's chair, his face bright red. 'I'm a slave,' he whispered.

'A what? Speak up, man!' Dudley snapped.

'A slave. The mistress's slave.'

'Does she beat you?' Hugo bent forward eagerly, hands clasped between his legs, his cock beginning to swell.

'Yes,' Ian squeaked, embarrassed yet enjoying the burning shame.

'With a whip?' Dudley's body was betraying his interest. Hugo could see the bulge of a thick penis deforming the cut of his trousers.

'Yes.' Ian buried his face in his hands, but he was trembling and aroused.

'Who is this "mistress"?' Hugo questioned, wanting to find out more. He had never yet submitted to a dominatrix but the idea had a certain appeal.

'Sybil Esmond. Ryder Tyrell's partner. Oh, dear, I shouldn't be telling you this,' muttered Ian, writhing in his seat.

'Why not? We've been asked to their Midsummer Ball. They wouldn't have done that if they'd wanted to keep secrets,' Dudley opined sagely. 'Seems like you've been a mole, Ian, leaking information to them. That was bang out of order. I'd be within my rights to sack you.'

'I'm sorry,' whimpered Ian, wringing his hands together, then plunging them into his lap and clutching his cock. 'I didn't think it would do any harm and they were pleased with me. She lets me lick her shoes. She wears the most wonderful footwear. High spiked heels . . . so sharp and painful. They really hurt.'

'Good God! You get off on simply talking about them, don't you?' Hugo shouted, and the pressure in his balls was building. He needed to rub himself, or get someone to suck him off.

Actually, Ian has a neat little backside, Hugo thought. I haven't taken my pleasure from a male arse since public school, but there's no time like the present.

'Tell me more,' he insisted, and rose to lean on Ian's desk where the computer hummed, its green cursor blinking.

'She makes me wear chains, and I've had body piercing done,' Ian said, his eyes watery behind the thick lenses.

'Let's see,' Hugo ordered, and Dudley came to stand

beside him, the air quivering with the male need to find a hole – any hole – in which to thrust a hungry cock.

Ian staggered to his feet and undid his shirt, displaying his bony, sparsely furred chest. Rings shone in his nipples. Hugo licked his lips. 'Any more?' he asked in a husky voice.

Ian unzipped his trousers and showed the one in his navel then, hesitantly, lowered his Y-fronts. Dudley and Hugo craned forward and stared at his rapidly engorging dick with the ringed foreskin.

'You dirty bugger,' Hugo breathed unsteadily. 'Have you been beaten lately? Are there marks on your bum?'

He seized Ian in his big hands and twisted him round, then made him lean over. Next he pushed Ian's slacks and underpants down about his knees. A fork of desire stabbed through his gut as he saw the crimson weals on the young man's skinny rump.

He could feel Dudley's excitement, recognised that he would have been a head-boy's fag, performing forbidden acts in the dorm after lights-out. Without further ado, he unbuttoned his own trousers and freed his fully erect tool. Nothing mattered but the immediate relief of his balls. He rolled a lubricated condom over his stiff cock and rubbed the tip between Ian's crack.

Then, holding him steady, he eased his fiery cock-head into the receiver's fundament and, pressing firmly, succeeded in sinking in fully, till his wiry pubic hair brushed Ian's buttocks.

Ian opened himself wide, his cock throbbing, his mind filled with images of Sybil. 'She's beautiful,' he intoned in a sing-song voice. 'And her feet! She lets me come over her feet, then makes me lick it up, then tells me I'm a filthy beast and whips me.'

'Good. That's it. Talk away,' grunted Hugo, pumping furiously.

Dudley, his dick in one hand, was subjecting it to long, smooth strokes, massaging in the slippery juice escaping from its single eye and running down the stem.

'Come on, damn you! Come on!' he gasped. His

weapon was refusing to cooperate and he stormed round the desk and waggled it in Ian's face. 'Open your mouth, you little sod! Give it a severe sucking.'

Fire ran across the sky from the west, night clouds piling up and stars appearing. Cars were arriving at the vicarage, their lights sweeping across the Gothic façade. Music swelled from within, those dark, spine-chilling chords beloved of Ryder.

The guests had given full rein to their fantasies. Popes, cavaliers, emperors, pirates and dandified beaus escorted representations of whores down the ages; Nell Gwynnes, Madame de Pompadours, Renaissance courtesans, naughty nuns, Cleopatras and eastern houris. All were masked, velvet, feathers and sequins shrouding their features.

As she entered the reception hall with Cassandra, Lorna saw Alison and Gary. The redhead wore a full short taffeta skirt and wasp-waisted corset with her breasts bulging over the top. Her partner had on splendid livery, the front of the breeches pared away to show his penis.

'Business as usual,' Lorna murmured to her friend. 'The servants, it seems, go unmasked. Free for all to enjoy.'

'Is it always like this?' Cassandra was staring at Gary's bare genitals with prurient interest. 'I can't smell fire and brimstone yet.'

She had taken the opportunity to clothe herself in as little as possible. Her bacchante costume consisted of a transparent chiton, so brief that it barely hid her depilated pussy. It was girded with a silver cord that crossed and lifted her bare breasts. Vine leaves banded her hair.

'The night is young,' Lorna said. 'Just you wait.' She was conscious of a licentious undercurrent, even though the company was still controlled.

Buffet tables were spread with delectable food and, in honour of the occasion, the chef had prepared recipes from ancient Roman cookbooks. Much use had been made of fruit; wild strawberries reminiscent of aroused nipples; pineapples that brought spiked collars to mind; peaches with the bloom of a female pubis; luscious dark plums like juicy testicles. All were piled around the base of an immense gilded bronze centrepiece depicting fornicating homosexual lovers.

The plates were rimmed with gold, and the goblets inlaid with mother-of-pearl. There was an abundance of wines, their fire and aromas persuasive potions whose magical fumes fuddled the brain and released darkest desires.

The wineglasses were emptied and refilled. The voices grew steadily louder. Raucous laughter exploded like fireworks, drowning out the sound of a string quartet floating from the tall, thin stereo speakers.

Champagne corks popped and as Lorna accepted a glass, she saw Hugo and Dudley. They were not wearing fancy dress, but stood immaculate in dinner suits. They made for the bar, unaware she was watching them. She stalked across on her spiked heels, and tapped Hugo's bottom with the stock of her whip.

'Hello,' she said. 'Fancy meeting you.'

He peered at her closely. 'Do I know you?' Then he smirked, admiring her sleek contours under the clinging leather. 'If I don't, I soon will. What's your name?'

'Lorna Erskine,' she answered coldly. 'And this is Cassandra Ashley, the illustrator.'

He smiled ironically. 'I'm honoured, Miss Ashley, an admirer of your work. I didn't recognise you, Lorna. Are you handy with that whip?'

'I've been trained by experts.'

'Have you indeed?'

She knew by his tone that he wanted her to strike him. 'Would you like a private demonstration?' she asked, and sinful excitement gripped her loins as she imagined him chained to the whipping post.

'Maybe,' he answered with a return to his usual aplomb, then added, 'Where's Mr Tyrell? I want to meet him.'

Hugo left the bar, taking Dudley with him. Lorna was relieved to see them go, wondering if Chris would put in an appearance. Doors opened out from the main room, and different music swelled from them, different lights cast a glow, different scenes whetted the appetite and seduced the senses.

In one, petite oriental ladies performed a sensual dance of desire in the setting of a geisha house. Letting their exquisitely embroidered kimonos fall, they caressed each other's little breasts and dark wedges, taking up ben-wah balls and inserting them in rectums and vaginas. Their mewing sounds of pleasure mingled with the exotic notes of the *samisen*.

'How gorgeous,' Cassandra sighed, her hand pressed to her own damp triangle. 'Aren't they the sweetest things?'

In the next chamber, against a backdrop of luxurious drapes and to the strains of romantic classical music, dancers adopted almost unbelievable postures, a corps de ballet like no other.

Three naked men and three women, long-limbed and agile, their moves were superbly choreographed, sometimes joined at genitals or mouths. A girl lay on her back with a man poised at her entrance, his cock teasing the rosebud pink furls. Another was held above her partner as he slowly lowered her on to his thick, erect penis. A couple posed behind them, and the woman had her legs wrapped about the man's waist as she bent backwards while he supported her on his phallus.

'I always said ballet was erotic, but you wouldn't see anything like that at Covent Garden,' whispered Cassandra.

Lorna's love-juices were escaping from her vulva, wetting the labial ring, the champagne infusing her system with warmth and laxness. She was impatient for Ryder to come, lust running lava-like within her. Would this be the night when she derived pleasure from his phallus pounding to fulfilment inside her love-tunnel?

She wandered on, finding herself on the terrace where

strobe lights made a nonsense of reality. The music had changed to a throbbing beat, and people were gyrating to the rhythm. Restraint had gone, and everywhere she looked uninhibited sexual exchanges were taking place.

Rashid struck a gong, and Sybil stalked out from under a silken awning. The crowd exploded into cheers and rapturous applause.

She was like some bizarre bird, a phoenix in an elaborate scarlet headdress. Her body glittered, the naked nipples and mons gilded, a jewelled basque squeezing her into hourglass shape, a spread of plu-maged tail sweeping to the floor. Her legs were covered in stockings shot with red and gold, her feet encased in extravagantly lofty shoes. Ian caressed them, a bound and naked slave, his manacles and strappings a parody of hers.

At a nod from her, Rashid called in a cohort of gladiators. They were wearing breastplates and grieves and helmets, all stunningly well-developed, golden tanned and muscular. For a moment it was hard to tell which were women and which men, their bodies honed to perfection.

Handsome and full of bravado, they whipped up their short white kilts, displaying large appendages or high bare clefts. This was met with whistles, catcalls and yells of approval The leader strode over to Sybil, doffing his plumed headgear, his great arms banded with wide bracelets.

'Good evening, Sandor,' she said, bouncing his testicles in one hand and taking his cock in the other, rubbing it vigorously.

'Good evening, mistress. I'm at your service,' he said in a heavily accented voice. He had soulful black eyes and the face of a Botticelli angel.

Lorna stared as his dick grew larger under Sybil's artful fingers. She was fascinated by the sight of that massive penis rising between his powerful thighs. She trembled at the thought of sitting on it, thighs spread, its hugeness forcing its way into her.

His hands intrigued her, and she imagined those large fingers trailing over her labia and massaging her clitoris. Her vagina spasmed with hungry longing. Her bud thrummed as she looked at his wide mouth, and dreamed of him using that big, wet tongue to woo her into orgasm She moaned softly, and pressed her legs together, the ring chafing her clitoris.

The other gladiators stood in line, the men's large balls and outsized pricks exposed as they rubbed vigorously to make them even larger. The Amazons posed and preened, dipping their fingers into the shadowy areas of their clefts and smearing their juices on the faces of male guests.

'You fancy him, Lorna?' Sybil murmured, still toying with Sandor. His eyes glazed over and he started to jerk, spurting over her hand.

'Perhaps,' she whispered.

'Gladiators were in great demand among Roman ladies,' Sybil went on, wiping her fingers fastidiously on his tunic. 'I can understand why. So well-blessed, and so brave, ready to face death in the arena.' She speared Ian with her ice-blue eyes. 'You could take a leaf from his book.'

'Yes, mistress,' he babbled, looking up from where he was grinding himself against her foot.

Sybil called for Alison. 'Come here, slave. Let's see Sandor in action with you.'

'Oh, yes, mistress!' cried Alison, eyes riveted on his shaft that bobbed eagerly, already erect again. She lay down on the divan, legs gaping wide, her slit fiery between its darkly furred fringe. 'I want it right up there. Push it in as far as it will go,' she squealed, quite out of control.

Sandor lunged, feet nearly leaving the ground with the force as he buried his weapon in her. She bucked, gave a cry, tears of pain and pleasure running from her eyes. He thrust, pumped, then withdrew his phallus slightly, only to thrust it in again to the hilt. Alison lifted her legs high, moaning, sighing, transported in a frenzy of lust.

She strove to come, but it was not until he slipped a hand over her pubis and frigged her bud that she reached a climax. Sandor ejaculated, letting go in a convulsive frenzy.

The gong boomed again and a pair of wrestlers marched across the grass. They were even more magnificent specimens of manhood, fully six feet seven inches tall. Wearing nothing but loincloths that barely contained their weighty genitals, they flexed their muscles: rugged athletes with huge arms, broad chests and mighty thews.

The women howled like cats on heat, and several of the men, too. Rashid went round collecting bets; five, ten, twenty, fifty pound notes piled up on the salver he proffered. The strobes glinted on the wrestlers' oiled skin as they prowled round each other, then grappled.

Lust was palpable in the warm air, every eye fixed on the contenders. They were superb; one's skin was ebony, while the other was a Nordic blond. They heaved, grunted, sweated, clasped close as lovers, then breaking at the referee's command.

Fists were used, teeth and feet, too. The black man's right eye was closed to a slit; blood welled from the lips of the blond. The excitement was intense, the gamblers as aroused by money as they were by the sight of these impressive, sweating giants battering one another.

Finally the fair one went down with the crash of a falling oak. He did not rise again. The victor raised his arms triumphantly over his head and the crowd whooped as Sybil glided towards him holding out a laurel wreath. He swept her up, raising her aloft. Then he unwound his loincloth, laid her down and penetrated her with a single stroke of his ten-inch cock.

It was at that well-timed moment that a man strode on to the terrace. The crowd went wild. Lorna did a doubletake.

There stood her nocturnal paramour, in black from head to toe: black hair, black mask, pronounced black package between his thighs, long black gauntlets. He held up a hand in a regal gesture.

'The Midsummer Solstice is here, my friends,' he cried. 'A time of abandon, when Dionysus rules. At midnight we'll go to the holy spring and drink the invigorating magical water.'

He beckoned Lorna, and she went to him.

'It was you, Ryder,' she whispered, while his eyes devoured her through the slits of his mask. 'Why?'

'I wanted to frighten you, then discovered that you enjoyed it,' he said with a throaty chuckle. 'It amused me. I know what you need, better than you know yourself. Nothing has happened to you that wasn't a reflection of your own desires.'

'So we *have* had sex, and I didn't know. I never realised. You disguised yourself well. How did you get into my bedroom?'

'The Priory is honeycombed with secret passages, and these link with the vicarage, and the grotto. I've explored them all, and knew which one to use. I hoped to scare you into selling the house to me.'

'How unkind,' she said indignantly.

'Darling, you've no idea how unkind I can be, if I set my mind to it. But this isn't necessary now, is it? I've found another way.' He gripped the tag of her zip and slowly opened the front of her leather pants. His gloved finger tickled the top of her slit, where her clitoris sheltered beneath its cowl.

Lorna felt the responsive quiver of her flesh, her masked face staring into his. Only his eyes and lips were free. As she touched him, her fingers remembered those savage nights when he had plundered her, when her nails had ripped into the leather, feeling the delicious hardness of his buttocks as they clenched to give his phallus more power.

He drew her into the shadows, took off his mask and then hers, and kissed her strongly, his tongue taking possession of her mouth. Then he knelt in front of her, his hands running the zip open wide and parting her sex. It was his bare fingers she felt now, gliding along the ridge of her labia, pushing into her wetness. Her hips lifted towards him, and he slipped his tongue over her cleft, finding the stiff little bud. He flicked it, licked it, and subjected it to the magic of his mouth.

Lorna's hands fluttered and settled on his head. Her fingers gripped the long hair falling around his face. She stood with her eyes shut, holding him tightly, feeling the ripples of orgasm rising, ready to sweep her into the cosmos. But the release did not come. He left her on the brink, almost weeping with disappointment. He rose to his feet and kissed her again. She could taste her honey-dew on his lips.

'Why did you stop?' she moaned, tearing her mouth away.

'Discipline,' he said, but pushed his penis hard against her so she was tortured even more by the weight and heat of it.

'But, Ryder ... I want you.' She was trembling, her very core tensed and ready to spring.

'You shall have me,' he promised, 'as your bride-groom. We'll be married in the cave at twelve o'clock. It's all arranged.'

The heat of desire cooled, the mists of champagne dissipated and Lorna was suddenly stone cold sober. 'I haven't accepted you yet,' she reminded.

'You will, Lorna. You will.'

She was powerless to refuse him as, sinister and commanding, he led his acolytes to the stone-paved, arched dungeon. It was lit by flares stuck in sconces, the lurid light shining on damp walls and illuminating curious tableaux.

Women cried out in ecstasy as their bare bottoms were paddled by hefty gaolers, bright pink blotches staining their fleshy white rumps. A stout, middle-aged man writhed his hips in orgasmic joy, strapped to a bench while a large woman in a ruby-red satin corset and thigh-high boots applied a tawse to his chest, balls and cock, insulting him as she did so. A pale, slender young man stood beside them, his member in the older man's mouth, pumping madly till he released a stream of creamy semen.

Hatchet-faced Marta was whipping a lovely girl who was suspended from manacles fastened to a beam. Sandor upheld her, sucking her swollen clit between each blow, his square, sensual mouth glinting with silvery juices.

'Come, my children, stop your play!' Ryder ordered, hauling Lorna along by her wrists. 'Time to drink holy water and witness my marriage.'

He propelled her into a dark tunnel. Smoky torches sent up a wavering glow. Sybil led the way, a horde of awed, whispering, sexually stimulated club members following closely. The underground passage curved and dipped, then rose again till it reached a dead-end, blocked by a solid wall. Sybil leant to one side, pressed down on a lever, and the stone slid back noiselessly. Beyond lay the sacred cave, radiant in the misty glow of golden candlelight.

The air was perfumed and warm, and Lorna felt it to be a holy spot indeed. A little quiver of pride ran through her, angry though she was at Ryder's assumption. If she agreed, the cult would worship her. As his wife, she'd be even higher in rank than Sybil. It was a tempting prospect. And Ryder was so extraordinarily handsome. Lorna was ravenous for him, like a thing possessed. A natural-born leader, he had a quality which was sophisticated yet savage and unashamedly sexual.

He took a chalice from the granite slab that served as an altar and dipped it into the well. Lifting it to his lips, he drank deeply. Sybil followed suit. As did the others, coming up one by one.

He held out the cup to Lorna. 'Drink,' he said in those dark tones that shot straight down to her G-spot. 'The vicar is here, waiting to marry us.'

She shook her head, looking in vain for Cassandra who seemed to have vanished. Lorna felt dreadfully alone. This was no game. Ryder really did intend to go through with it. Was this how her independence was to end?

She wondered if it would be legal. There had been no notification to a registrar, no formal application. Or had he seen to all that? She suspected that he had, and arranged for the vicar to be present. He had taken up position near the altar and Sybil held a crimson velvet cushion on which gleamed two plain gold rings.

'Are you ready, vicar?' Ryder asked, gripping Lorna's icy fingers in his warm ones.

'I am,' he answered, prayerbook in hand.

'I'm not sure,' Lorna blurted out, trying to tug free. 'Can't we talk about this? It's too sudden.'

'That makes it all the more thrilling, don't you think?' Ryder purred, but there was a steely edge to his voice.

'Don't be in such a hurry, Tyrell,' Chris interrupted, materialising from the gloom at the top of the steps, backed by Cassandra and Marc. 'You can't force her to do anything.'

'It has nothing to do with you,' Ryder snarled. 'This is between Lorna and myself.'

Sensing trouble, Sybil clapped her hands, pasted on a smile and addressed their followers. 'Right. Have you all drunk from the spring? Fine. Then go back to the celebrations. We'll join you when this has been sorted. You, too. vicar. You'll be called when we're ready.'

Lorna could see Chris's eyes gleaming in the half-light. She was still reeling from his sudden arrival via the temple. He came closer, looming over her.

'Is this what you want?' he asked levelly. 'To make him part owner of the Priory?'

'No, it isn't. I wish you'd all leave me alone. It's my house and my land.' It was as if she was awakening from a dream, aware of Cassandra in her bacchante attire, and Marc's solid form at her side.

'Lorna. You don't mean that.' Ryder changed tack, protective and gentle. 'We're in love, aren't we?'

'Are we? I don't know. You've taught me so much,

and I'm grateful . . . but love and marriage? I'm just not ready.'

Away from the spell of his hands and lips, she could view the situation dispassionately, but let him touch her once and she would be lost again. She was in turmoil, her body throbbing with unsatisfied passion, her heart throbbing with the thought of betrayal, her mind totally confused.

Ryder could no longer contain his fury. 'Leave, Devlin, before I have you thrown out!' he roared. 'You too, Cassandra, you interfering bitch! I invited you here in good faith.'

'Hey, mind what you're saying to her, Tyrell. 'I'll not have her spoken to that way,' Marc said quietly, but Cassandra knew that when he was cool and quiet he was at his most deadly.

'You wanted to gloat. To prove your control. You're an unscrupulous bastard!' Chris shouted, equally large and menacing.

'You're angry because your plan didn't work. You wanted to take over the Priory and cheat Lorna of her inheritance,' Ryder retorted, a nerve jumping at the side of his mouth.

'OK, I'll admit it,' Chris said with a shrug. 'I did know I might have a faint chance of getting it, but it was unlikely. My great-great-grandfather was sired by an Erskine, but he was illegitimate. His father got a gypsy girl into trouble, apparently, and there was no way he could marry her. That's the story, anyhow. I'm not sure how much truth is in it.'

'Enough for you to try and make a case. Is that what you meant to do?' Lorna was torn between the two of them, not knowing who to believe.

'No, not seriously. I didn't have that kind of money. And after I'd met you, I forgot the idea,' Chris answered. 'I was happy to work on the place and make it into something you'd treasure.'

'How very noble,' Ryder sneered.

'Unlike your own motives,' Chris rapped out, rounding on him, his fists bunched. 'But I'm warning you to lay off. I know a lot about you. Made it my business to find out after Andy Richardson went bankrupt. You persuaded him to invest money in your schemes and then cheated him. He's never recovered.'

'You can't prove a damn thing.' Ryder's lips had thinned to a narrow line and his face was pale.

'He's not the only one who'd like to see you brought to justice,' Chris continued remorselessly. 'I've a list of people who'd give a lot to know where you're hiding. You could wind up in court facing fraud charges.'

'Try it!' Ryder hissed, his features distorted with fury.

'I will, if you don't leave Lorna alone.'

'Is that what you want, Lorna?' Ryder looked so demonic in his rage that she retreated to the edge of the pool.

'I don't want to marry you,' she said, testing herself. 'I don't want to sink the Priory into the vicarage and become a part of your organisation.'

'Right! I understand. Goodbye, Lorna,' Ryder spat out, and thundered off up the passage, Sybil in tow.

'Wait for me, mistress,' Ian cried, hopping along behind her, on a very short lead.

'Thanks for nothing, Chris,' Lorna snapped, but he grabbed her before she could move.

'Listen to me, woman! I've never meant to harm you, and Ryder's a scumbag. Surely you can see that by now?'

'How did you get here? Who told you about the temple entrance?' She was riding her rage, wanting to hate him.

'Chris came to see me this afternoon. He was concerned about you,' Cassandra put in, her eyes darting from one furious face to the other. 'I arranged to meet him there, certain Ryder was up to something devious.'

'I knew about the spring anyway,' he said.

'Then why didn't you tell your English Heritage buddies?'

He gave a quirky smile. 'I felt you deserved to have at least one secret. If this gets out they'll blacklist me. I'll probably never work for them again.'

'Seems he was acting in your interests all along the line,' added Marc, while Cassandra shot him a loving smile. 'Just as well I came home earlier than expected and was able to add a bit of muscle.'

'Do you think he's given up now?' Cassandra was not convinced.

'I guess,' Chris answered, then challenged Lorna. 'Have you?

'I don't want to talk about it. I'm going home. I need time to think.' She made for the stairs, wanting to put as much distance between them as possible.

'It's dark and late. Shall I come with you?'

'No.'

'Please yourself,' he said, and let her go.

But as she disappeared into the blackness above, Cassandra touched his arm. 'Go with her,' she advised. 'She's not as independent as she pretends.'

'What a party!' Hugo said to Dudley, his face flushed, eyes shining as he wondered what delight he should sample next. 'The Club Dionysus! I've a proposition to put to Tyrell. We could make a killing if I opened my leisure centre on his ground, and included sex therapy as an extra.'

'So you're dropping the idea of the Priory?' Dudley didn't want to talk business then. There was a lissom brunette eyeing him up, her long white hands with long green-painted fingernails playing with the knotted thongs of a whip. He had screwed himself silly, but could feel his prick rising again.

'Yes, of course, if Tyrell agrees. He's got no option really, as Lorna's turned him down. By all accounts the wedding was a fiasco and if he can't get his hands on more money soon he'll be up shit creek without a paddle.' Hugo slung an arm round Dudley's shoulders with tipsy bonhomie. 'That's where we come in, my boy. We're experts at shifting shit, aren't we?'

* * *

'That's it. then.' said Tara, hands on her hips as she surveyed the Great Hall. 'All ready for Christmas. Looks super, doesn't it?'

'It does indeed,' Lorna agreed.

The smell of resin seeped from burning logs. There were streamers, tinsel and holly festooning the beams, and a rafter-high fir tree dragged in earlier that day. She and Lorna had decorated it with fake snow, glittering frost, glass balls and fairy lights. Hinton Priory was fully restored now, a gracious home to be proud of.

'When are your friends landing?' Tara was her second-in-command, appointed as housekeeper.

'They'll be here on Boxing Day.'

'I can't wait to meet them. Gosh, just think, the staff of an American magazine coming here.' There was a naivety about Tara that Lorna found endearing.

Tara was the buffer between herself and the suspicious village people, so slow to make friends. Of course, Chris helped too, and Lorna had not given up her association with the vicarage. It was going from strength to strength after an injection of Hugo's money. Work on the complex was already under way and a grand opening planned for next summer. An influx of hunky labourers provided Tara with an endless source of delectation and delight.

Lorna found it impossible to resist visiting Ryder from time to time, needing his correction, that fascinating man with whom she could play out her basest, most shameful desires.

This infuriated Chris, but she refused to back down. No man was going to dictate to her. He was her lover and helpmate, but there dependency ended. She was mistress of Hinton Priory, and let no one forget it.

She had told him this in no uncertain terms when he had caught up with her as she fled home after the debacle in the grotto. She had been on an emotional high, anger fuelling her fires, making him irresistible. They had talked and talked, and ended up making love. He had wooed her into passion, forcing her to forget Ryder temporarily. Her body had throbbed and glowed as he brought her to pleasure in the baroque splendour of her bedroom.

'Rub your clit, and make yourself come,' he had panted urgently. 'We'll climax together on this solstice night, and it will bind us for ever.'

They had, reaching the wonderful little death simultaneously, and certainly the bond between them was strong, but she had learnt salutory lessons from Ryder, one of which was to keep her options open.

When Tara had gone, muffled to the nose against the cold, Lorna ran to the big bay window, looking out on the darkening landscape. Joy of ownership flooded her being, an even greater drive than sex. She was madly in love with Hinton Priory.

Nicole was coming. There were plans afoot for groups of authors to use the old house as a base whenever they toured England. But the excitement that warmed her belly and set her nipples tingling was the impending arrival of Sean.

Chris was in Italy on a course. She had given Tara time off and, after changing into a crushed velvet caftan with nothing underneath but a generous spray of expensive French perfume, she went into the library. Soon the evocative, sensual strains of Wagner's Prelude to *Tristran and Isolde* flooded the gracious room. A love theme like no other.

Lorna relaxed on the deep couch and let her hands stray beneath her robe. Eyes half-closed, fingers fondling her breasts, then slipping down to her cleft, she dreamed of waking on snowy mornings with him in her bed.

Her blood was heating, a slow fire at first, then rousing as she played with that tiny centre of power from which her life-force sprang. She was impatient for him to come, holding off from reaching climax, stemming the pleasure, reserving it for him.

She did not have long to wait. Within ten minutes the bell clanged. Pausing only to glance in the gilt-framed mirror and fluff up her hair, Lorna walked swiftly into the Great Hall.

He was there, waiting at the front door, frost on his lips as he swept her into his embrace. 'Lorna, Lorna!' he shouted on a laugh.

'Come in, Sean. Your first time in my house. Isn't it wonderful?'

She dragged him by the hand, wanting to show him everything, but he stopped her, pulling her into the heat of his body, letting her feel the pressure of his phallus rising in tribute.

Sean, winner of the Mr Image contest, shining new star of film and stage. A dashing swashbuckler, his tight jeans tucked into the tops of calf-length leather boots, his jacket slung over his shoulders like a cape, his hair longer, curlier, blue eyes sparkling wickedly.

'D'you want to eat?' she said breathlessly, as he inveigled a hand into her robe and stroked her damp maidenhair.

'Only you,' he whispered then, like a true hero, he lifted her in his arms and ran lightly up the stairs to the master bedchamber.

BLACK LACE NEW BOOKS

Published in June

JASMINE BLOSSOMS
Sylvie Ouellette

When Joanna is sent on a routine business trip to Japan, she does not expect that her sensuality will be put to the test. Enigmatic messages are followed by singular encounters with strangers who seem to know her every desire. She is constantly aroused but never entirely sated, and soon finds herself involved in a case of mistaken identity, erotic intrigue and mysterious seduction.

ISBN 0 352 33157 7

PANDORA'S BOX 2
An Anthology of Erotic Writing by Women
Edited by Kerri Sharp
£5.99

This is the second of the highly popular Pandora's Box anthologies of erotic writing by women, containing extracts from the best-selling titles of the Black Lace series, as well as four completely new stories. The diversity of the material is a testament to the unashamed nature of the female erotic imagination.

ISBN 0 352 33151 8

Published in July

COUNTRY MATTERS
Tesni Morgan

When Lorna inherits a country estate, she thinks she is set for a life of pastoral bliss and restfulness. She's wrong. Her closest neighbour, a ruthless businessman and a darkly handsome architect all have their own reasons for wanting to possess her, body and soul. When Lorna discovers that paganism is thriving in the village, the intrigue can only escalate.

ISBN 0 352 33174 7

GINGER ROOT
Robyn Russell

As the summer temperatures soar, art gallery director Eden finds it harder and harder to stick to her self-imposed celibacy. She starts to fantasise about the attractive young artists who visit the gallery, among them a rugged but sensitive sculptor who she sets out to seduce. It's going to be an exciting summer of surprises and steamy encounters.

ISBN 0 352 33152 6

To be published in August

A VOLCANIC AFFAIR
Xanthia Rhodes

Pompeii. AD79. Marcella and her rampantly virile lover Gaius begin a passionate affair as Vesuvius is about to erupt. In the ensuing chaos, they are separated and Marcella is forced to continue her quest for sybaritic pleasures elsewhere. Thrown into the orgiastic decadence of Rome, she is soon taking part in some very bizarre sport. But circumstances are due to take a dramatic turn and she is embroiled in a plot of blackmail and revenge.

ISBN 0 352 33184 4

DANGEROUS CONSEQUENCES
Pamela Rochford

After an erotically-charged conflict with an influential man at the university, Rachel is under threat of redundancy. To cheer her up, her friend Luke takes her to a house in the country where she discovers new sensual possibilities. Upon her return to London, however, she finds that Luke has gone and she has been accused of theft. As she tries to clear her name, she discovers that her actions have dangerous – and very erotic – consequences.

ISBN 0 352 33174 7

THE NAME OF AN ANGEL
Laura Thornton

Clarissa Cornwall is a respectable university lecturer who has little time for romance until she meets the insolently young and sexy Nicholas St. James. Soon, her position and the age gap between them no longer seems to matter as she finds herself taking more and more risks in expanding her erotic horizons with the charismatic student. This is the 100th book in the Black Lace series, and is published in a larger format.

ISBN 0 352 33205 0

If you would like a complete list of plot summaries of Black Lace titles, please fill out the questionnaire overleaf or send a stamped addressed envelope to:-

Black Lace, 332 Ladbroke Grove, London W10 5AH

BLACK LACE BACKLIST

All books are priced £4.99 unless another price is given.

-------✂------------------------

Please send me the books I have ticked above.

Name   ....

Address   ....

              ....

              ....

          .... Post Code   ....

Send to: **Cash Sales, Black Lace Books, 332 Ladbroke Grove, London W10 5AH.**

Please enclose a cheque or postal order, made payable to **Virgin Publishing Ltd**, to the value of the books you have ordered plus postage and packing costs as follows:

UK and BFPO – £1.00 for the first book, 50p for each subsequent book.

Overseas (including Republic of Ireland) – £2.00 for the first book, £1.00 each subsequent book.

If you would prefer to pay by VISA or ACCESS/MASTERCARD, please write your card number and expiry date here:

....

Please allow up to 28 days for delivery.

Signature   ....

-------✂------------------------

BLACK
lace

WE NEED YOUR HELP . . .
to plan the future of women's erotic fiction –

– and no stamp required!

Yours are the only opinions that matter.

Black Lace is the first series of books devoted to erotic fiction by women for women.

We intend to keep providing the best-written, sexiest books you can buy. And we'd appreciate your help and valued opinion of the books so far. Tell us what you want to read.

THE BLACK LACE QUESTIONNAIRE

SECTION ONE: ABOUT YOU

1.1 Sex *(we presume you are female, but so as not to discriminate)*
Are you?
Male ☐
Female ☐

1.2 Age
under 21 ☐   21–30 ☐
31–40 ☐   41–50 ☐
51–60 ☐   over 60 ☐

1.3 At what age did you leave full-time education?
still in education ☐   16 or younger ☐
17–19 ☐   20 or older ☐

1.4 Occupation _____

1.5 Annual household income
    under £10,000   ☐   £10–£20,000   ☐
    £20–£30,000   ☐   £30–£40,000   ☐
    over £40,000   ☐

1.6 We are perfectly happy for you to remain anonymous;
but if you would like to receive information on other
publications available, please insert your name and
address

_____

_____

_____

_____

SECTION TWO: ABOUT BUYING BLACK LACE BOOKS

2.1 How did you acquire this copy of *Country Matters*?
    I bought it myself   ☐   My partner bought it   ☐
    I borrowed/found it   ☐

2.2 How did you find out about Black Lace books?
    I saw them in a shop   ☐
    I saw them advertised in a magazine   ☐
    I saw the London Underground posters   ☐
    I read about them in _____
    Other _____

2.3 Please tick the following statements you agree with:
    I would be less embarrassed about buying Black
    Lace books if the cover pictures were less explicit   ☐
    I think that in general the pictures on Black
    Lace books are about right   ☐
    I think Black Lace cover pictures should be as
    explicit as possible   ☐

2.4 Would you read a Black Lace book in a public place – on
a train for instance?
    Yes   ☐   No   ☐

SECTION THREE: ABOUT THIS BLACK LACE BOOK

3.1 Do you think the sex content in this book is:
   Too much ☐   About right ☐
   Not enough ☐

3.2 Do you think the writing style in this book is:
   Too unreal/escapist ☐   About right ☐
   Too down to earth ☐

3.3 Do you think the story in this book is:
   Too complicated ☐   About right ☐
   Too boring/simple ☐

3.4 Do you think the cover of this book is:
   Too explicit ☐   About right ☐
   Not explicit enough ☐

Here's a space for any other comments:

SECTION FOUR: ABOUT OTHER BLACK LACE BOOKS

4.1 How many Black Lace books have you read? ☐

4.2 If more than one, which one did you prefer?

4.3 Why?

SECTION FIVE: ABOUT YOUR IDEAL EROTIC NOVEL

We want to publish the books you want to read – so this is your chance to tell us exactly what your ideal erotic novel would be like.

5.1 Using a scale of 1 to 5 (1 = no interest at all, 5 = your ideal), please rate the following possible settings for an erotic novel:

Medieval/barbarian/sword 'n' sorcery ☐
Renaissance/Elizabethan/Restoration ☐
Victorian/Edwardian ☐
1920s & 1930s – the Jazz Age ☐
Present day ☐
Future/Science Fiction ☐

5.2 Using the same scale of 1 to 5, please rate the following themes you may find in an erotic novel:

Submissive male/dominant female ☐
Submissive female/dominant male ☐
Lesbianism ☐
Bondage/fetishism ☐
Romantic love ☐
Experimental sex e.g. anal/watersports/sex toys ☐
Gay male sex ☐
Group sex ☐

Using the same scale of 1 to 5, please rate the following styles in which an erotic novel could be written:

Realistic, down to earth, set in real life ☐
Escapist fantasy, but just about believable ☐
Completely unreal, impressionistic, dreamlike ☐

5.3 Would you prefer your ideal erotic novel to be written from the viewpoint of the main male characters or the main female characters?

Male ☐   Female ☐
Both ☐

5.4 What would your ideal Black Lace heroine be like? Tick as many as you like:

Dominant	☐	Glamorous	☐
Extroverted	☐	Contemporary	☐
Independent	☐	Bisexual	☐
Adventurous	☐	Naïve	☐
Intellectual	☐	Introverted	☐
Professional	☐	Kinky	☐
Submissive	☐	Anything else?	☐
Ordinary	☐	_____	

5.5 What would your ideal male lead character be like? Again, tick as many as you like:

Rugged	☐		
Athletic	☐	Caring	☐
Sophisticated	☐	Cruel	☐
Retiring	☐	Debonair	☐
Outdoor-type	☐	Naïve	☐
Executive-type	☐	Intellectual	☐
Ordinary	☐	Professional	☐
Kinky	☐	Romantic	☐
Hunky	☐		
Sexually dominant	☐	Anything else?	☐
Sexually submissive	☐	_____	

5.6 Is there one particular setting or subject matter that your ideal erotic novel would contain?

_____

SECTION SIX: LAST WORDS

6.1 What do you like best about Black Lace books?

_____

6.2 What do you most dislike about Black Lace books?

_____

6.3 In what way, if any, would you like to change Black Lace covers?

_____

6.4   Here's a space for any other comments:

_____

_____

_____

_____

*Thank you for completing this questionnaire. Now tear it out of the
book – carefully! – put it in an envelope and send it to:*

> **Black Lace**
> **FREEPOST**
> **London**
> **W10 5BR**

No stamp is required if you are resident in the U.K.

December 7th, 1993

Toni Morrison

LECTURE AND

SPEECH OF ACCEPTANCE,

UPON THE AWARD OF THE

NOBEL PRIZE FOR LITERATURE,

DELIVERED IN STOCKHOLM ON

THE SEVENTH OF DECEMBER,

NINETEEN HUNDRED AND

NINETY-THREE

Alfred A. Knopf · New York · 1994

Toni Morrison
"who, in novels characterized by visionary
force and poetic import, gives life to an
essential aspect of American reality"

—SWEDISH ACADEMY

Narrative has never been merely entertainment for me. It is, I believe, one of the principal ways in which we absorb knowledge. I hope you will understand, then, why I begin these remarks with the opening phrase of what must be the oldest sentence in the world, and the earliest one we remember from childhood: "Once upon a time . . . "

"Once upon a time there was an old woman. Blind but wise." Or was it an old man? A guru, perhaps. Or a *griot* soothing restless children. I have heard this story, or one exactly like it, in the lore of several cultures.

"Once upon a time there was an old woman. Blind. Wise."

In the version I know the woman is the daughter of slaves, black, American, and lives alone in a small house outside of town. Her reputation for wisdom is without peer and without question.

Among her people she is both the law and its transgression. The honor she is paid and the awe in which she is held reach beyond her neighborhood to places far away; to the city where the intelligence of rural prophets is the source of much amusement.

One day the woman is visited by some young people who seem to be bent on disproving her clairvoyance and showing her up for the fraud they believe she is. Their plan is simple: they enter her house and ask the one question the answer to which rides solely on her difference from them, a difference they regard as a profound disability: her blindness. They stand before her, and one of them says,

"Old woman, I hold in my hand a bird. Tell me whether it is living or dead."

She does not answer, and the question is repeated. "Is the bird I am holding living or dead?"

Still she does not answer. She is blind and cannot see her visitors, let alone what is in their hands. She does not know their color, gender or homeland. She only knows their motive.

The old woman's silence is so long, the young people have trouble holding their laughter.

Finally she speaks, and her voice is soft but stern. "I don't know," she says. "I don't know whether the bird you are holding is dead or alive, but what I do know is that it is in your hands. It is in your hands."

Her answer can be taken to mean: if it is dead, you have either found it that way or you have killed it. If it is alive, you can still kill it. Whether it is to stay alive is your decision. Whatever the case, it is your responsibility.

For parading their power and her helplessness, the young visitors are reprimanded, told they are responsible not only for the act of mockery but also for the small bundle of life sacrificed to achieve its aims. The blind woman shifts attention away from assertions of power to the instrument through which that power is exercised.

Speculation on what (other than its own frail body) that bird in the hand might signify has always been attractive to me, but especially so now, thinking as I have been about the work I do that has brought me to this company. So I choose to read the bird as language and the woman as a practiced writer.

She is worried about how the language she dreams in, given to her at birth, is handled, put into service, even withheld from her for certain nefarious purposes. Being a writer, she thinks of language partly as a system, partly as a living thing over which one has control, but mostly as agency—as an act with consequences. So the question the children put to her, "Is it living or dead?," is not unreal, because she thinks of language as susceptible to death, erasure; certainly imperiled and salvageable only by an effort of the will. She believes that if the bird in the hands of her visitors is dead, the custodians are responsible for the corpse. For her a dead language is not only one no longer spoken or written, it is unyielding language content to admire its own paralysis. Like statist language, censored and censoring. Ruthless in its policing duties, it has no desire or purpose other than to maintain the free range of its own narcotic narcissism, its own exclusivity and dominance. However, moribund, it is not without effect, for it actively thwarts the intellect, stalls conscience, suppresses human potential. Unreceptive to interrogation, it cannot form or tolerate new ideas, shape other thoughts, tell another story, fill baffling silences. Official language smitheried to sanction ignorance and preserve privilege is a suit of armor, polished to shocking glitter, a husk from which the knight departed long ago. Yet there it is; dumb, predatory, sentimental. Exciting reverence in schoolchildren, providing shelter for despots, summoning false memories of stability, harmony among the public.

She is convinced that when language dies, out of carelessness, disuse, indifference, and absence of esteem, or killed by fiat, not only she herself but all users and makers are accountable for its demise. In her country children have bitten their tongues off and use bullets instead to iterate the void of speech-lessness, of disabled and disabling language, of language adults have abandoned altogether as a device for grappling with meaning, providing guidance, or expressing love. But she knows tongue-suicide is not only the choice of children. It is common among the infantile heads of state and power merchants whose evacuated language leaves them with no access to what is left of their human instincts, for they speak only to those who obey, or in order to force obedience.

The systematic looting of language can be recognized by the tendency of its users to forgo its nuanced, complex, mid-wifery properties, replacing them with menace and subjugation. Oppressive language does more than represent violence; it is violence; does more than represent the limits of knowledge; it limits knowledge. Whether it is obscuring state language or the faux language of mindless media; whether it is the proud but calcified language of the academy or the commodity-driven language of science; whether it is the malign language of law-without-ethics, or language designed for the estrangement of minorities, hiding its racist plunder in its literary cheek—it must be rejected, altered and exposed. It is the language that drinks blood, laps vulnerabilities, tucks its fascist boots under crinolines of respectability and patriotism as it moves relentlessly toward the bottom line and the bottomed-out mind. Sexist language, racist language, theistic language—all are typical of the policing languages of mastery, and cannot, do not, permit new knowledge or encourage the mutual exchange of ideas.

The old woman is keenly aware that no intellectual mercenary or insatiable dictator, no paid-for politician or demagogue, no counterfeit journalist would be persuaded by her thoughts. There is and will be rousing language to keep citizens armed and arming; slaughtered and slaughtering in the malls, courthouses, post offices, playgrounds, bedrooms and boulevards; stirring, memorializing language to mask the pity and waste of needless death. There will be more diplomatic language to countenance rape, torture, assassination. There is and will be more seductive, mutant language designed to throttle women, to pack their throats like pâté-producing geese with their own unsayable, transgressive words;

there will be more of the language of surveillance disguised as research; of politics and history calculated to render the suffering of millions mute; language glamorized to thrill the dissatisfied and bereft into assaulting their neighbors; arrogant pseudo-empirical language crafted to lock creative people into cages of inferiority and hopelessness.

Underneath the eloquence, the glamour, the scholarly associations, however stirring or seductive, the heart of such language is languishing, or perhaps not beating at all—if the bird is already dead.

She has thought about what could have been the intellectual history of any discipline if it had not insisted upon, or been forced into, the waste of time and life that rationalizations for and representations of dominance required—lethal discourses of exclusion blocking access to cognition for both the excluder and the excluded.

The conventional wisdom of the Tower of Babel story is that the collapse was a misfortune. That it was the distraction or the weight of many languages that precipitated the tower's failed architecture. That one monolithic language would have expedited the building, and heaven would have been reached. Whose heaven, she wonders? And what kind? Perhaps the achievement of Paradise was premature, a little hasty if no one could take the time to understand other languages, other views, other narratives. Had they, the heaven they imagined might have been found at their feet. Complicated, demanding, yes, but a view of heaven as life; not heaven as post-life.

She would not want to leave her young visitors with the impression that language should be forced to stay alive merely to be. The vitality of language lies in its ability to limn the actual, imagined and possible lives of its speakers, readers, writers. Although its poise is sometimes in displacing experience, it is not a substitute for it. It arcs toward the place where meaning may lie. When a President of the United States thought about the graveyard his country had become, and said, "The world will little note nor long remember what we say here. But it will never forget what they did here," his simple words were exhilarating in their life-sustaining properties because they refused to encapsulate the reality of 600,000 dead men in a cataclysmic race war. Refusing to monumentalize, disdaining the "final word," the precise "summing up," acknowledging their "poor power to add or detract," his words signal deference to the uncapturability of the life it mourns. It is the deference that moves her, that recognition that language can never live up to life once and for all. Nor should it. Language can never "pin down" slavery, genocide, war. Nor should it yearn for the arrogance to be able to do so. Its force, its felicity, is in its reach toward the ineffable.

Be it grand or slender, burrowing, blasting or refusing to sanctify; whether it laughs out loud or is a cry without an alphabet, the choice word or the chosen silence, unmolested language surges toward knowledge, not its destruction. But who does not know of literature banned because it is interrogative; discredited because it is critical; erased because alternate? And how many are outraged by the thought of a self-ravaged tongue?

Word-work is sublime, she thinks, because it is generative; it makes meaning that secures our difference, our human difference—the way in which we are like no other life.

We die. That may be the meaning of life. But we *do* language. That may be the measure of our lives.

"Once upon a time . . ." Visitors ask an old woman a question. Who are they, these children? What did they make of that encounter? What did they hear in those final words: "The bird is in your hands"? A sentence that gestures toward possibility, or one that drops a latch? Perhaps what the children heard was, "It is not my problem. I am old, female, black, blind. What wisdom I have now is in knowing I cannot help you. The future of language is yours."

They stand there. Suppose nothing was in their hands. Suppose the visit was only a ruse, a trick to get to be spoken to, taken seriously as they have not been before. A chance to interrupt, to violate the adult world, its miasma of discourse about them. Urgent questions are at stake, including the one they have asked: "Is the bird we hold living or dead?" Perhaps the question meant: "Could someone tell us what is life? What is death?" No trick at all; no silliness. A straightforward question worthy of the attention of a wise one. An old one. And if the old and wise who have lived life and faced death cannot describe either, who can?

But she does not; she keeps her secret, her good opinion of herself, her gnomic pronouncements, her art without commitment. She keeps her distance, enforces it and retreats into the singularity of isolation, in sophisticated, privileged space.

Nothing, no word follows her declaration of transfer. That silence is deep, deeper than the meaning available in the words she has spoken. It shivers, this silence, and the children, annoyed, fill it with language invented on the spot.

"Is there no speech," they ask her, "no words you can give us that help us break through your dossier of failures? through the education you have just given us that is no education at all because we are paying close attention to what you have done as well as to what you have said? to the barrier you have erected between generosity and wisdom?

"We have no bird in our hands, living or dead. We have only you and our important question. Is the nothing in our hands something you could not bear to contemplate, to even guess? Don't you remember being young, when language was magic without meaning? When what you could say, could not mean? When the invisible was what imagination strove to see? When questions and demands for answers burned so brightly you trembled with fury at not knowing?

"Do we have to begin consciousness with a battle heroes and heroines like you have already fought and lost, leaving us with nothing in our hands except what you have imagined is there? Your answer is artful, but its artfulness embarrasses us and ought to embarrass you. Your answer is indecent in its self-congratulation. A made-for-television script that makes no sense if there is nothing in our hands.

"Why didn't you reach out, touch us with your soft fingers, delay the sound bite, the lesson, until you knew who we were? Did you so despise our trick, our modus operandi, that you could not see that we were baffled about how to get your attention? We are young. Unripe. We have heard all our short lives that we have to be responsible. What could that possibly mean in the catastrophe this world has become; where, as a poet said, "nothing needs to be exposed since it is already barefaced"? Our inheritance is an affront. You want us to have your old, blank eyes and see only cruelty and mediocrity. Do you think

we are stupid enough to perjure ourselves again and again with the fiction
of nationhood? How dare you talk to us
of duty when we stand waist deep in the
toxin of your past?

"You trivialize us and trivialize the bird
that is not in our hands. Is there no
context for our lives? No song, no literature, no poem full of vitamins, no history connected to experience that you
can pass along to help us start strong?
You are an adult. The old one, the wise
one. Stop thinking about saving your
face. Think of our lives and tell us your
particularized world. Make up a story.
Narrative is radical, creating us at the
very moment it is being created. We
will not blame you if your reach exceeds
your grasp; if love so ignites your
words that they go down in flames and
nothing is left but their scald. Or if,
with the reticence of a surgeon's hands,

your words suture only the places where blood might flow. We know you can never do it properly—once and for all. Passion is never enough; neither is skill. But try. For our sake and yours forget your name in the street; tell us what the world has been to you in the dark places and in the light. Don't tell us what to believe, what to fear. Show us belief's wide skirt and the stitch that unravels fear's caul. You, old woman, blessed with blindness, can speak the language that tells us what only language can: how to see without pictures. Language alone protects us from the scariness of things with no names. Language alone is meditation.

"Tell us what it is to be a woman so that we may know what it is to be a man. What moves at the margin. What it is to have no home in this place. To be set adrift from the one you knew. What it is to live at the edge of towns that cannot bear your company.

"Tell us about ships turned away from shorelines at Easter, placenta in a field. Tell us about a wagonload of slaves, how they sang so softly their breath was indistinguishable from the falling snow. How they knew from the hunch of the nearest shoulder that the next stop would be their last. How, with hands prayered in their sex, they thought of heat, then sun. Lifting their faces as though it was there for the taking. Turning as though there for the taking. They stop at an inn. The driver and his mate go in with the lamp, leaving them humming in the dark. The horse's void steams into the snow beneath its hooves and the hiss and melt are the envy of the freezing slaves.

"The inn door opens: a girl and a boy step away from its light. They climb into the wagon bed. The boy will have a gun in three years, but now he carries a lamp and a jug of warm cider. They pass it from mouth to mouth. The girl offers bread, pieces of meat and something more: a glance into the eyes of the one she serves. One helping for each man, two for each woman. And a look. They look back. The next stop will be their last. But not this one. This one is warmed."

It's quiet again when the children finish speaking, until the woman breaks into the silence.

"Finally," she says. "I trust you now. I trust you with the bird that is not in your hands because you have truly caught it. Look. How lovely it is, this thing we have done—together."

The Acceptance Speech

I entered this hall pleasantly haunted by those who have entered it before me. That company of laureates is both daunting and welcoming, for among its lists are names of persons whose work has made whole worlds available to me. The sweep and specificity of their art have sometimes broken my heart with the courage and clarity of its vision. The astonishing brilliance with which they practiced their craft has chal-

lenged and nurtured my own. My debt
to them rivals the profound one I owe
to the Swedish Academy for having selected me to join that distinguished
alumni.

Early in October an artist friend left a
message which I kept on the answering
service for weeks and played back every
once in a while just to hear the trembling pleasure in her voice and the faith
in her words. "My dear sister," she said,
"the prize that is yours is also ours and
could not have been placed in better
hands." The spirit of her message with
its earned optimism and sublime trust
marks this day for me.

I will leave this hall, however, with a
new and much more delightful haunt-
ing than the one I felt upon entering:
that is the company of the laureates yet
to come. Those who, even as I speak,

are mining, sifting and polishing languages for illuminations none of us has dreamed of. But whether or not any one of them secures a place in this pantheon, the gathering of these writers is unmistakable and mounting. Their voices bespeak civilizations gone and yet to be; the precipice from which their imaginations gaze will rivet us; they do not blink or turn away.

It is, therefore, mindful of the gifts of my predecessors, the blessing of my sisters, in joyful anticipation of writers to come that I accept the honor the Swedish Academy has done me, and ask you to share what is for me a moment of grace.

— TONI MORRISON,
December, 1993

The Works of
Toni Morrison

THE BLUEST EYE (1970)

SULA (1974)

SONG OF SOLOMON (1977)

TAR BABY (1981)

BELOVED (1987)

JAZZ (1992)

PLAYING IN THE DARK (1992)

(Editor) RACE-ING JUSTICE,
EN-GENDERING POWER (1992)

A Short Biography

Toni Morrison was born in Ohio and is a graduate of Howard University and Cornell University. She has worked in publishing and taught at various colleges and universities, among which are Yale, Rutgers, and SUNY Albany as the Schweitzer Chair. She is currently Robert F. Goheen Professor at Princeton.

The text of this book was set in
Monotype Bell, and it was printed by Lake
Book Manufacturing, Melrose Park, Illinois.
It was designed by Peter A. Andersen,
Carol Devine Carson, and
Archie Ferguson.